IRONBARK

IRONBARK

WAYNE RUSSELL

26 Infinity Publishing

26 Letters Infinite Worlds

Ironbark
© 2025 Wayne Russell

Published by
26 Infinity Publishing

ISBN (Paperback): 9780628645481
ISBN (eBook): 9780648645498

Cover design by Dan

For information, contact:
waynerussellbooks.com

Printed by independent print partners worldwide

First Edition: 2025

26 Infinity Publishing

For Dad, Jason, and Travis—
and for anyone who hasn't
cracked the spine on a book in a while.

"It isn't safe to cut a bloke who comes from Ironbark."
— Banjo Paterson, The Man from Ironbark

"The whirlwind is in the thorn tree.
It's hard for thee to kick against the pricks."
— Acts 26:14 / Johnny Cash, When the Man Comes
Around

CHAPTER 1

The smell hit McBride halfway down the corridor, a gut- punch of rot and something worse. Not just filth. Not just sweat. Something deeper. The kind of stink that clung to the back of your throat and wouldn't let go.

Ironbark Block always had its own stench. Damp concrete, stale breath, too many bodies crammed into tight quarters, but this was different. Sharper. Fresher. Like someone had smeared shit across the walls and left it to bake. Summer in the guts of inland New South Wales did that. Heat soaked through stone and skin and stayed there.

Beneath it all, something metallic and old. Rust. Blood. Sun-warmed death.

He slowed outside Cell 42.

The other inmates. Murderers, rapists, monsters in sweat-stained greens , were unusually quiet. Not out of respect. Out of something else. A hush that settled heavy in the air, like even they knew something was wrong. Like the block itself was holding its breath.

McBride narrowed his eyes and tightened his grip on the baton at his side. His knuckles stood out white against the smooth wood.

The door creaked open. Metal hinges gave their own muffled scream.

Inside, the smell surged. A wall of shit and death that hit like a wet slap. The beige concrete walls were smeared in broad, angry arcs of human excrement and something darker, half-hidden in the shadows. A jagged smear of blood, or what he hoped was blood, ran across the floor.

McBride stepped inside, slow and cautious, his boots scraping against something sticky. The bile rose in his throat. He swallowed hard.

The body was curled near the far wall. Pale. Still. Eyes wide open. Watching.

He looked again at the walls. What had first seemed like chaos was starting to show shape. Lines. Loops. Symbols.

Then he saw it.

A smiley face.

Drawn in blood.

Crude and uneven. Two dots and a curved mouth, smeared into the filth. But it felt fresh. Deliberate. Like it had been done last. Like whoever made it had time to think about it.

His skin crawled.

His radio crackled.

"Control to Ironbark Three. Report."

He tore his eyes away from the wall and clicked the mic. "Ironbark Three. I think we've got a dead inmate in Cell 42. It's Henry Redmond. Request immediate backup and medical."

He paused, gagged, and turned to the sink just in time to vomit. The retching echoed off the tiles. He wiped his mouth with the back of his hand, took a deep breath. Regretted it instantly, and keyed the radio again.

"You're going to want to send a cleaner, too."

Silence.

McBride was about to repeat the message when the radio spat back to life, the voice sharp, urgent.

"Ironbark Three… McBride. Warden wants you out of there. Medical will retrieve the body. In the meantime, you touch nothing. Do you understand? We need confirmation. Touch nothing. Nothing."

McBride blinked. Hesitated. The corner of his mouth twisted slightly, not confusion, not fear exactly, but something caught between the two.

He lifted the mic again. "Yeah. Understood."

He clipped the radio back onto his belt, covered his mouth and nose with one hand, and stepped back into the corridor.

As the door swung shut behind him, he muttered under his breath.

"What the actual fuck."

CHAPTER 2

Dave Callahan rolled into the prison parking lot, his battered old Holden wheezing like an asthmatic. Weekend detention was not supposed to be fun, but he'd never imagined it would come with this kind of humiliation. His usual spot, right near the entrance, beneath the gnarled old eucalypt, was taken by a gleaming government-issued car parked diagonally across two spaces.

He sighed, pulling into a spot farther back and slamming the door shut. "Real nice, asshat." He grumbled, louder than he had thought. Loud enough to carry across the parking lot.

The driver of the offending car stepped out as Dave passed. The man was tall, sharp-featured, with a cheap suit stretched taut across his shoulders. Something about him screamed trouble or worse, authority.

"You want to watch your mouth, son?" the man said, his voice low but laced with menace.

Dave stopped, squaring up despite the knot forming in his stomach. "Just saying, mate, there's plenty of room. No need to park like a tool."

For a moment, the man just stared, his lips curling into a faint sneer. "Morons everywhere, and I don't got time for this bullshit today." He glared at Dave, then his car, like he was committing it to memory before turning away.

Dave shook his head and walked on, the exchange leaving a sour taste in his mouth. Inside, the prison was as grim as ever. Harsh fluorescent lights buzzed overhead, casting an unnatural glow over the cracked tiles. The smell of bleach failed to mask the underlying stench of sweat and despair.

At the check-in desk, Dave caught the tail end of an argument.

"I don't care about your cleaning schedule," the man from the car park — Senior Detective Sergeant Adrian Blake, Dave now learned, was telling the warden. "That cell stays untouched until I say otherwise, and the body damn well better still be here." Dave closed his eyes, bit his lip, and cursed himself silently for picking the wrong person to goad.

The warden's face was stone, but there was a flicker of annoyance in his eyes. "Fair enough. But don't expect me to clean it for you."

"I don't think that's going to be a problem. Your weekend guest there is going to do it for us." Blake nodded toward Dave as he whispered to the warden.

Minutes later, Dave was called to follow Blake to the cell. He trailed behind the detective carrying a large plastic tub, the air growing heavier with each step. Cell Block Ironbark he discovered, had a unique stink. Sweat, stale air, a metallic tang and something much worse.

"Jesus Christ," Dave muttered as they reached the door. "Smells like shit."

Blake shot him a sly glance. "You'll get used to it."

Inside, the cell was a nightmare. Blood and filth streaked the walls in jagged smears, mingling with a darker, more nauseating foulness that clung to the air. The bed, eerily still made, was a grotesque tableau. The blanket stiff with drying blood and filth, forming a sickening crust of human fluids. The room was devoid of life, save for the faint, macabre traces of the man's final, desperate moments.

Blake worked with clinical precision, methodically checking and passing Redmond's sparse belongings to Dave, who placed them into the tub: a few dog-eared novels, several photographs of a woman who might have been a sister, judging by the resemblance, a box of crayons, a tattered Bible, and a handful of yellowed letters. Dave's eyes took it all in, every last detail.

From his jacket pocket, Blake pulled a pair of gloves, snapping them on with practiced ease before ripping the blanket and sheets off the mattress and shaking them sharply. He flipped the mattress, his eyes tracing the seams, then repeated the process with the pillow before dropping them back onto the bare bedframe.

As he turned, a single sheet of paper fluttered loose, drifting toward the grime-covered floor. With a quick motion, Blake snatched it from the air, his eyes scanning its contents for the briefest moment before tucking it into the box with the rest of Redmond's life.

Dave watched in silence as Blake took the box from his grip, snapped the lid shut and turned to him.

"That's everything," Blake said, his voice flat, almost bored. Then, with a faint smirk tugging at the corners of his mouth, he gestured to the walls and cleaning gear, that now sat beside the doorway. "And now, you can literally clean this shit up."

Dave stared at him, his brows furrowing. "You're serious?"

Blake didn't bother to reply. He hefted the box, the smirk still lingering, and strode out without another word, leaving Dave standing alone in the stench and filth.

CHAPTER 3

The cell was a crypt.

Dave Callahan had felt it the moment he stepped inside, the air thick and suffocating, as if the prison itself was bearing down on him. Bloodstains streaked the walls, dark and clotted, baked into the concrete by the relentless summer heat. The metallic tang of iron lingered, mingling with the faint, artificial sting of cleaning chemicals that failed to mask the underlying decay.

Behind him, Officer McBride leaned casually against the doorway, arms crossed. "Get on with it, Callahan. I don't have all day. I had to cart this cleaning shit up here, so you better do a damn good job with it."

Dave glanced back at the guard, biting down on a retort. He wasn't here to argue, just to endure. With a resigned sigh, he dipped the mop into the bucket, the soapy water darkening as soon as it touched the stained floor.

"Red's cell," McBride said, almost to himself. "Never thought I'd see the day it was empty."

Dave said nothing, but the silence only seemed to encourage McBride. He shifted his weight in the doorway, his gaze steady, as if waiting for a reaction.

"Do you even know who he was, Callahan? That old man you're cleaning up after?"

"Nope," Dave replied, scrubbing at a particularly dark streak near the cot.

"Henry Redmond. Red," McBride said, letting the name hang in the air with a note of grim satisfaction. "The guy behind that opal heist back in '79. Made off with a fortune and shot a cop in the process. Never told a soul where he hid the loot. Took it to his grave."

Dave paused mid-swipe, the mop still in his hand. "Shot a cop?"

"Constable Parker," McBride confirmed, straightening slightly as though the memory lent him authority. "Partnered with Detective Blake back in the day. Blake's been after him ever since."

Dave frowned, pressing the mop harder against the floor. He hadn't known the details of Red's crime, but something about the way McBride said it felt… off.

He moved to the wall, where blood smears and hardened filth seemed to tell a story of their own. The largest stain was centred on the concrete, marking where Red had collapsed and bled out. But higher up, streaks and swipes told a different tale. The man's final moments spent standing, reaching, and smearing the wall with his own gore.

Curiosity stirred, and Dave grabbed a sponge, scrubbing at the dried blood. As the crimson layers thinned, faint lines began to surface. Straight, deliberate, and anything but random.

He scrubbed faster, his breath hitching as the lines sharpened.

"What the hell are you doing?" McBride barked from the doorway.

"Cleaning," Dave shot back, not bothering to look around.

The guard grunted, unimpressed, but didn't intervene. Dave took that as permission and continued. The lines gradually coalesced into a rough shape. Crude and uneven, but unmistakable.

A map?

Dave froze, the sponge still in his hand. The outline was rudimentary, sketched in bold, colourful strokes that had resisted the cleaning solution. Crayon. He leaned closer, eyes tracing jagged peaks, winding trails, and scattered marks that might have been trees or buildings. Words, seemingly randomly strewn throughout it all. In the lower corner, half-obscured by a smear of blood, Red had scrawled something else. Numbers. A date? A time?

"What's the holdup, Callahan?" McBride's voice cut sharply through his thoughts.

Dave instinctively shifted, angling his body to block the wall. "Nothing," he said quickly, his voice steady despite the hammering in his chest.

McBride pushed off the doorframe, his boots clomping against the concrete as he stepped inside. "Move," he ordered.

Dave hesitated, his eyes darting to the map one last time before stepping aside.

McBride froze, his eyes narrowing as he took in the crayon-drawn lines and symbols on the wall. His expression darkened, a flicker of something unreadable passing across his face. "What the hell is this?" he muttered, his tone low and edged with menace.

Dave swallowed hard, his grip tightening on the sponge. "I don't know," he said, keeping his voice steady. "It was under the blood."

McBride's jaw clenched, his hand instinctively moving to the radio on his hip. His fingers lingered there for a moment before curling into a fist. "Stay here," he snapped, stepping back toward the door, his gaze not leaving the wall until he turned and stepped into the hall.

**

In the stark, sterile confines of the prison morgue, Detective Blake stood over Red's lifeless body. The old man seemed impossibly frail now, his deeply weathered skin waxy and pale under the unforgiving glare of fluorescent lights.

The attending officer cleared his throat, his voice breaking the silence. "Cause of death is self-inflicted. Bit into his wrists and tore through an artery. Messy job. Never seen anything like it."

Blake's jaw tightened; his eyes fixed on Red's face. "He bled out?"

"Yeah," the officer confirmed. "Must've taken hours. Didn't make a sound, though. Nothing anyone reported anyway. Found him like that in the morning."

Blake didn't respond. His gaze dropped to Red's hands, taking in the faint smudges of blood beneath his nails, the way his fingers curled inward, as if still gripping some unseen secret.

The box of personal effects sat nearby; items Blake had pulled from Red's cell. Blake's attention shifted to a small box of crayons, the waxy tips dulled and worn.

"Crayons?" he said, turning the box over in his hand.

The officer shrugged. "Guess he was passing the time."

Blake set the box down, his thoughts churning. He'd spent decades chasing Red. Pressuring him, interrogating him, waiting for him to break and give up the stash. And now, even in death, the old man seemed to be taunting him, leaving behind one final riddle.

His phone buzzed in his pocket, yanking him from his thoughts. He pulled it out, frowning at the screen. A message from the warden:

Get back to the cell. Now.

Blake's grip tightened around the device, his knuckles whitening. He glanced down at Red's lifeless body, his gaze lingering on the frail form that seemed to mock him even in death. A grim smile tugged at his lips.

"What the fuck have you done now?" he muttered, his voice low, the words barely audible in the sterile silence of the morgue.

CHAPTER 4

Dave had done exactly what he'd been told. "Stay here." McBride's last words echoed in his ears, half an order, half a dismissal, and somehow, a permission he hadn't been seeking. Now, alone in the dim, musty cell, Dave stood frozen, his eyes glued to the map scrawled beneath the streaks of blood and grime.

He didn't just see the map; he absorbed it. Every line, every curve of the crayon markings burned into his mind as if it had been drawn there. His memory, sharp as a scalpel, carved out every detail. It was both a gift and a curse. One that had brought him here in the first place.

"You'll never forget anything." His mother had said it like a blessing. It wasn't.

Memory trapped everything. Every slight, every mistake, every betrayal. He could recall them all, step by step, like they were still happening. That's what had landed him here in the first place.

And now this. This crude drawing, so childlike, yet layered with a riddle he didn't yet understand, felt like something out of a storybook, except there was nothing whimsical about it.

He crouched closer, his pulse quickening as he traced a faint mark with his finger, smudging the edge. Placing his palm against the wall, he closed his eyes and ran it over the image, feeling every imperfection. The cracked paint, the dried blood, the slight bulge beneath the surface, like an old screw or nail buried in the wall. His stomach knotted as his mind raced, piecing together the fragments and making connections.

"Why here? Why now?" he muttered under his breath.

The crayon markings glinted faintly in the light. They almost seemed alive, pulsing with a strange energy. In his mind they were alive, telling their story, Red's story. Dave knew he shouldn't be here any longer than necessary, but he couldn't stop himself. He wanted to look away, to walk out like McBride expected. Instead, he stayed, committing every last detail of the map to memory. It wasn't just a habit, it was instinct.

Because somewhere in the recesses of his mind, Dave already knew: this map was going to change everything.

McBride stepped into the corridor, his radio already in hand. "Get the warden," he barked, pacing as he waited for a response.

When the static cleared and the warden's voice came through, McBride wasted no time. "There's a map. On the wall. Covered in three different kinds of shit, but it's a map."

A brief pause crackled over the line before the warden responded, his tone clipped. "I'm almost there. Entering the block now."

Moments later, the far hallway door swung open, and the warden strode in, his movements brisk and purposeful. He stopped in front of McBride, his expression stern. "Show me."

Together, they stepped into the cell. The warden's eyes immediately landed on Callahan, crouched at the wall, his hands hovering near the blood-streaked surface.

"Get him out of here," the warden ordered, his tone sharp.

McBride stepped forward without hesitation. "Callahan. Out. Now."

Dave's eyes lingered on the crayon markings, his fingers brushing the wall one last time under the guise of steadying himself as he rose. The touch felt almost instinctive, as though the wall itself held him in its grip. Standing, he blinked, shaking off the haze that seemed to cloud his thoughts.

"Sorry, what was that?" he muttered, his voice distant.

McBride's voice cut through the room like a blade, sharp and menacing. "Get... the fuck... out. Wait in the hall."

The threatening edge in McBride's words jolted Dave back to reality. He swallowed hard, forcing himself to step between the two men and out the door, his pulse hammering as the tension lingered behind him.

The warden stood motionless before the wall, his eyes darting erratically over the crude markings. His gaze never wavered as he reached for his radio.

"Ironbark Control, this is the warden. Is Detective Blake still in the building?"

"In medical, sir," came the reply.

Lowering the radio, the warden clipped it back onto his belt and fished his mobile phone from his pocket. His fingers fumbled as he punched in Blake's number, his focus split between the screen and the symbols on the wall. Abandoning the call, he hastily typed a text:

Get back to the cell. Now.

Blake rarely, if ever, ran. Today, he did. Though hardly more than a jog, it left him winded by the time he reached the cell. Leaning against the doorframe, he sneered at Callahan, who stood patiently in the hall.

"You a fucking guard now?" Blake spat.

Dave shrugged, unfazed. Blake drew a ragged breath and stepped inside.

In the cell, McBride stood back while the warden was snapping photos of the wall with his phone. Blake's glare sharpened as he took in the scene.

"What the hell are you doing? Why'd you make me run four corridors and a flight of stairs for this?"

The warden stepped back beside McBride, and in unison, they gestured toward the wall. Blake pushed his glasses up his nose as he stepped closer. His eyes scanned the markings. Lines, crude drawings, numbers, and scattered words, all scrawled across the surface. In the bottom right corner, a barely legible sentence caught his attention.

He snorted. "So this was your plan, Red? Some weird pirate map shit?"

He turned to the warden, irritation crackling in his voice. "And you're taking photos? This isn't some damn amusement park. It's an active fucking investigation. Send those photos to me… and delete the fucking things."

The warden fumbled with his phone, trembling as his fingers jabbed at the screen, missing every target.

"For fuck's sake." Blake's patience snapped. "Send them to me, delete them, and make it quick."

The warden's hands trembled worse, and finally, he handed the phone to McBride.

"McBride, send the photos to Detective Blake. He's in my contacts. Then delete them, like he said."

McBride took the phone and tapped confidently on the screen, hesitating momentarily before continuing, unfazed by Blake's growing anger. After a few moments, he handed it back to the warden.

"Done."

"And delete the message to me," Blake growled.

"Already did it," McBride replied coolly, snatching the phone back from the warden and passing it to Blake. "Cleared the recently deleted folder too."

Blake studied the screen briefly, nodded, and handed it back. "Good. Now go find me something to scrape this shit off the wall."

McBride moved for the door, eyeing Blake as he went.

"Both of you."

The warden hesitated, but after a moment, shuffled out. Outside Dave trailed behind them without a word. Blake was left alone in the cell, his eyes fixed on the wall, studying the map intently, a smug smile creeping across his face.

**

On the other side of the detention complex, in a dimly lit staff room, CSO McBride's phone buzzed within the confines of his locker. A new message appeared on the screen.

Sending the photos to Blake wasn't the only thing McBride had done with the warden's phone. Now he had his own copies.

CHAPTER 5

Sunday afternoon. Five p.m.

Dave was done. Another weekend detention ticked off the calendar.

Ironbark Correctional Centre shrank in his rearview mirror, but it never really left him. A place like that clung to you, seeped into your bones. Dave shifted in his seat, flexing his grip on the wheel, but the tension stayed.

The road stretched ahead, long and empty. Normally, this drive was his reset. A way to clear his head before he got home. But today, his father's voice cut through the silence, rough and certain, like it always had been.

"Always do the right thing, even when it's hard — sometimes even when it's wrong."

Dave's hands tightened on the wheel. That lesson had stuck with him. Maybe too well.

Because that's exactly how he'd ended up here.

Twelve months of weekend detention. Not because he'd stolen. Not because he'd dealt. Not because he'd hurt anyone.

Because he saw something he wasn't meant to see. Because he couldn't forget it. And because, when no one else gave a shit, he did something about it.

It had been late, near midnight when he'd seen the coal baron stumble out of a private club, his expensive suit rumpled, tie loose around his neck. He was drunk, barely standing. The woman with him? Not so lucky.

The escort hit the pavement hard, her cheek striking the curb with a sickening crack.

Dave had been across the street, working late at a garage, closing up. He'd looked up at the exact moment the man's ringed hand had left the woman's face.

She hadn't screamed. Just curled in on herself, one arm cradling her ribs.

The minders were on him in an instant. Not to help the woman, but to bundle their boss into a black car.

No one looked at her. No one helped. The car peeled away, and she was left there, a crumpled heap on the pavement.

Dave's memory wouldn't let it go. The way the bastards gold signet ring had caught the streetlight. The exact make and model of the car. The time on the club's neon sign. Every detail was burned into him like a brand.

He did the right thing first. He called the cops.

They took their time arriving. Too much time. By the time the flashing lights pulled up, the woman was gone. No complaint. No crime. No case.

"You sure you saw what you saw?" the officer asked, barely looking at him.

It was the way he said it. Like it was a warning, not a question.

Dave had pushed back, rattling off the details. The car, the ring, the time. The cop had barely blinked.

"Bad idea getting involved in things that aren't your business, mate."

That should've been the end of it. But Dave couldn't let it go.

So, he broke into the club's security office. No weapons, no plans. Just his memory and his gut. He found the CCTV footage, ripped it onto a USB, and leaked it to the press.

It should've blown up. It should've mattered.

But the woman never came forward. Maybe she was paid off. Maybe she was threatened. Maybe she just wanted to forget.

The prick had walked free.

And Dave? He got twelve months ICO for unlawful entry and theft of private data.

The cops didn't waste time charging him. Someone had wanted this buried, and fast.

The judge had called him reckless. A fool trying to play hero.

Maybe he was.

Dave let out a slow breath, forcing his grip to loosen on the wheel. He'd spent too long regretting that night. But the truth was, if he had to do it over?

He'd do the exact same thing.

And now, here he was. A house with no family, a past he couldn't shake, and a future tied to a dead man's map.

The heat hadn't relented by the time his car shuddered into the cracked concrete driveway, a jagged, weed-choked scar in the street. Home was a two-bedroom fibro house. Once a housing commission property, but even they had given up on it.

Inside, the air was stifling, a suffocating wall of heat that clung to him like a second skin. The house was still, save for the fridge humming its tired, monotonous tune. At least it was working, for now. He appreciated that small mercy.

His wife and daughter weren't here. They hadn't been for weeks. She'd taken their daughter and gone to her parents' place on the Central Coast. He couldn't blame her. The house was an oven in summer, a freezer in winter, and barely liveable in between. It was temporary. They both said that, but there were things to work through. Things that had happened. Things that were still happening.

But maybe, after today he could find a way to shortcut their path back.

And for now, this sweltering, empty shell was all his.

Dave moved through the house, throwing open the windows and muttering a quick prayer for a southerly breeze to break the day's relentless heat. He sat at the kitchen table, the surface cluttered but familiar. A stack of his daughter's art paper and one of her many pencil cases sat before him, borrowed without hesitation.

Time to recreate the map.

The map was still vivid in his mind, every seemingly random marking coming together with purpose. He picked up a black pencil, the tip hovering over the paper, ready to bring it to life. He drew in the one thing that he had recognised instantly. The Mudgee clock tower.

Then the phone rang.

It was not unexpected, in fact…ten past seven…it was overdue.

"Hey babe. Sorry I'm a bit late. Huge storm just swept through here. Cooled things down but it was pretty wild there for a while."

"Hope it rolls through here soon. The house is like a Turkish bathhouse."

"Really." Dave could almost hear his wife's eyebrows arching. "Lots of fat half-naked men there?"

"Yeah babe, that's exactly what I mean."

"How was the day?"

Dave gave his wife, Sally, the sanitised version. The one without the blood, the grimy cell, and, for now, without mention of the map.

They traded stories about their past few days, filling the silence between them with easy, familiar chatter before wrapping up the call.

"Love you, babe."

Dave closed his eyes. Loving each other wasn't the problem. "Yeah, love you too."

"Cassie wants to say goodnight," Sally said, and Dave could hear the phone fumbling its way into smaller hands.

"Dad! Guess what? Grandma bought me school shoes! They've got straps. I don't do laces yet, but I can learn. You can teach me, or Mum, or Grandad!"

Her voice brimmed with excitement and pride, and Dave felt it too. Tinged with shame. New shoes. Something so simple, something he should be doing.

"That's awesome, baby girl. What is it now…two weeks till school starts? Or three?"

"Two! You have to come see me on my first day."

"Try and stop me."

"Okay. Love you. Goodnight. Don't let the bed bugs bite!"

"Love you too, baby."

Dave ended the call and set the phone down on the table. The shame still lingered, but beneath it was a spark of something else. Resolve.

More than ever, he was sure of one thing: he was going to change the direction of their lives.

For better this time.

CHAPTER 6

McBride sank into the couch, the rattling air conditioner above him fighting a losing battle against the summer heat. It hung awkwardly through the side window of his modest brick-and-tile house. His house, he thought with a smirk, though maybe one day, if he played his cards right, he'd actually win it from the bank.

The mortgage, the interest rates… a complete shit show.

Even the weekly boost he got for keeping tabs on Red barely made a dent. Fifteen years of loyalty, two hundred dollars, every week. Like clockwork. Right into his account.

Pity most of it went on the horses.

The ice in his drink had melted, leaving the whisky diluted, but he knocked it back anyway. He stared at the mobile phone on the coffee table, calculating. He was expecting a few hundred for the photos, maybe two grand at most. This was likely his last payday from the client, after all.

He'd never met the guy, only spoken to him once. For all he knew, he wasn't even talking to the one footing the bill. Just some lackey. But it didn't matter. Money was money.

Decision made, he picked up the phone and typed out a message to a number long since embedded in his memory.

Subject deceased. Self-inflicted.

The reply came in less than a minute.

Any further information acquired?

McBride hesitated, fingers hovering. He could push for more.

Yes. Payment required for photo.

A pause. Then he added, **He left a map on a wall.**

The waiting made him restless. He stretched his legs, scratching at his ankle where a heat rash had started flaring up. He was about to take another sip when the phone buzzed.

$10,000 transferred. Send photos.

McBride choked, spraying whisky into his lap, the burn searing his throat. His coughs echoed through the house, drawing attention only from the pale-yellow lap dog curled up in the corner. It lifted its head, eyeing him with apparent disdain before settling back down to sleep.

Ten grand.

This was big. Bigger than he had thought. The photos of the map meant something to someone, and ten grand meant something to McBride.

He wiped his mouth with the back of his hand, staring at the phone. He fumbled into the banking app. The digits were there, clear as day, sitting in his account. Immediate transfer. No hesitation.

That wasn't just a payoff. That was a payout.

His heart pounded as he fumbled the phone, nearly dropping it between the couch cushions. He swiped through his gallery, found the photos, and attached them to a message. A final breath, then he hit send.

It was done.

McBride sat back, exhaling hard. "Damn. You should neck yourself more often, Red."

He drummed his fingers against the armrest, staring at the ceiling fan as it made its slow, rhythmic rotations. A thought settled in. If those photos were worth ten grand, what the hell was the real thing worth?

The idea wormed its way into his brain, taking root. Maybe he should figure out what the map meant. If there was a fortune in opals, why shouldn't it be his?

But then, how would it look if the prison officer who'd worked Red's block for fifteen years just happened to stumble across it? There'd be questions. People digging into his affairs. Affairs best kept quiet.

No, hunting for Red's hidden loot wasn't for him.

But selling the map? That was different.

He wasn't expecting a windfall. Just a bit of extra cash to throw on the horses. Enough for a weekend flutter and maybe a bottle to go with it.

There were others who'd likely pay a pretty price for the photos. Contacts he'd made on the job. The kind of men who had resources.

His fingers hovered over his contacts.

Tombs.

The name fit. A guy with a presence as heavy and imposing as a headstone. He wasn't the boss of anything big, but he was well-connected. Careful. Unlike some of the others in his crew, he'd never spent a night behind Ironbark's walls. That took discipline.

McBride hit call.

Nothing. Straight to voicemail.

He smirked. Routine. Tombs liked to vet his calls. Let them ring out, then call back when it suited him. A way of letting people know where they stood.

McBride tossed his phone onto the table and reached for the whisky bottle. He wasn't worried. Tombs would call.

Tombs and his crew weren't the biggest operators. Just small-time criminals playing at being big league. But they were careful. Caution had kept Tombs out of Ironbark. So far.

Other members of The Ragged Sons hadn't been so lucky. Those were the ones McBride dealt with most. Smuggling contraband, passing information. All the little things that made prison life a touch easier.

Tombs, though? Tombs used McBride for one thing. Watching for snitches.

The favours McBride got in return would've made his wife's blood boil if she ever found out. A few free drinks, a few whispered tips on the next big race, and, on occasion, the kind of company a married man shouldn't be keeping.

He swirled the whisky in his glass, watching the liquid catch the dim glow of the lamp. This was good money. Easy money. And easy money was what made the world go round.

The callback came half an hour later.

"What do you need now, McBride?"

McBride felt a flicker of irritation. Tombs knew damn well he never called unless he wanted something.

"Nah. It's what I've got for you. For the right price. Could be a big earner."

A pause.

"Keep talkin'."

McBride laid it out. Red, the heist, the missing loot, and most importantly, the map.

Another silence. This one stretched longer.

Tombs was weighing angles. Calculating.

Finally. "And what do you want for yourself?"

McBride licked his lips.

"Five hundred. Cash… and a girl. Next weekend. And if it works out, if you find something. I want a percentage."

More silence.

Then, finally.

"Meet me at the tavern car park in an hour. Near the drain that runs into the gully. This better be worth it, McBride."

McBride grinned, rolling his shoulders. "Trust me. If it pays out, you'll never have to pull another job in your life."

A beat.

Then, "One hour."

The line went dead.

McBride sat forward, rolling his glass between his palms. His heart was still hammering. Ten grand, just like that. No hesitation. That was what stuck with him. Whoever was on the other end of that deal hadn't even bargained.

That kind of money meant something bigger was at play. Bigger than just a dead man's secret.

The air conditioner rattled, spitting out a stream of half-warm air.

McBride took another drink, ice clinking against the glass.

This was more than opals.

This was the opportunity of a lifetime.

And if he played it right, he'd never have to take another shitty bribe again.

CHAPTER 7

Blake slid the glass panel door open and stepped onto the balcony, whiskey in one hand, phone in the other. The storm was climbing up the coast, moving slow but deliberate, its dark mass rolling over the ocean like a living thing. The wind had shifted. Cooler now, carrying the scent of rain and salt.

It suited his mood.

He set the whiskey down on the balcony railing, fingers tightening around the rim as he stared at the images on his phone. The photos of the map were crude, almost childish in some places, but he recognised enough.

Red hadn't just marked a route to his hidden stash. He'd left a goddamn confession. A reckoning.

Blake's gaze locked onto the numbers, the strange five-by-five grid scrawled among the landmarks. His gut twisted. Red had always been a vindictive bastard, and now, even in death, he was playing his last card.

The truth was buried in those markings, hidden beneath layers of misdirection. The opals? They were bait, meant for the desperate. The real prize. The real threat was something else.

Blake steadied his breathing. Controlled it. Controlled everything.

He'd kept this secret for nearly fifty years.

And if Red thought he could claw his way back from the grave and ruin him, he had another thing coming.

He swiped through the photos again, zooming in on different sections, his pulse steady but his mind racing.

A crude sketch of a clock tower. Mudgee. Without a doubt. Beneath it, the words:

Be here after 9 PM.

A meeting place? A dead drop? Or just another one of Red's tricks?

Then there was the second message. The one that made Blake's jaw tighten.

"140 NM opposite."

Opposite what? Opposite who?

Blake had spent decades ensuring that no one could find the truth. He'd buried those secrets as deep as Red had buried his fortune.

If Red had left behind evidence, real, undeniable evidence, then Blake had no choice.

He had to get there first.

Blake downed the rest of his whiskey in a single swallow and turned back inside. The air in the house was cool, still, untouched by the storm. The contrast felt unnatural, a reminder of how far he'd come from the days when he used to worry about things like the heat.

No. He didn't worry anymore.

He placed the empty glass down on the kitchen counter, next to a folder. Not the official police folder. His own.

Inside were summaries of Red's last movements.

• Every visitor he'd had.

• Every book he'd borrowed from the prison library.

• Summaries of all his mail, incoming and outgoing.

Blake flipped the folder open, running his fingers down the list. The bastard had been careful.

Atlases. Dictionaries. Crime novels.

But then, near the end —

Something new.

Books about codes and ciphers.

Blake's fingers curled into a fist.

Red had been planning this for a long time.

He closed the folder, his mind already moving to the next step.

The rain started, tapping against the balcony railing, the wind carrying it in sheets against the glass doors. Blake didn't move, didn't even look outside.

His eyes stayed on the map.

He hated that it existed.

He hated that Red had left something behind, something that still had power.

Blake was good at removing problems. He'd done it before.

But Red had known that.

And yet, he'd drawn this anyway.

Lightning cracked, illuminating the room for a split second. The shadows seemed deeper when it faded.

Blake's jaw clenched.

This wasn't about opals.

This was survival.

28

CHAPTER 8

Tombs pulled at the ring on his middle finger, spun it, and pushed it back above his knuckle. He did it again and again.

"Where the fuck is he?"

His enforcer, Lynch, sat in the driver's seat of the Hilux, hands resting lightly on the wheel. He didn't answer. He didn't need to. The slight grunt that rumbled from his throat was enough.

McBride was late.

Tombs had expected that. The little prick was probably half-drunk already, full of his own self-importance. McBride had always thought he was smarter than he was. Thought that knowing a few secrets made him powerful.

What McBride didn't know, not fully, was that Tombs owned him.

Headlights washed across the potholed car park, bouncing off rusted utes and dented sedans. Tombs recognised the car instantly.

The headlights, the way one dipped slightly to the left from years of negligence.

McBride's vehicle crawled through the lot, weaving between parked cars, engine growling in protest. He pulled into a space near the drain. Killed the ignition.

For a moment, he just sat there.

Tombs watched as McBride hesitated. Muttered something to himself. Turned back and fumbled with the handle before finally switching off the headlights.

"Let him know we're here."

Lynch tapped the Hilux's high beams twice.

McBride lifted a lazy hand in greeting and started toward them, his steps slow, unsteady, either from booze or nerves. Maybe both.

Tombs let the moment stretch, enjoying it.

"In the back."

Lynch's voice was sharp, gruff. Always a surprise to Tombs, even after all these years.

To McBride, it was a slap in the whisky-addled face. He stepped back from the window without thinking.

He knew Lynch too well. Knew he was a man who didn't say things twice. Sometimes not even once.

McBride climbed into the back seat of the twin-cab and drew in a long breath, held it for a count of ten, then let it go.

It didn't make him any more sober, but it gave him a moment of clarity. A moment of courage.

He straightened his shirt, wiped his mouth with the back of his hand, and leaned forward like he had something valuable to offer.

"Alright, let's talk business."

Lynch didn't turn around. Didn't even acknowledge him.

Tombs did.

A slow glance in the rearview mirror, the kind that made McBride's stomach lurch.

"Did I say you could fucking speak?"

McBride's jaw hung open like he was waiting for permission. Eyes wide. A faint trail of spit creeping down his chin.

Tombs grinned.

"Ha. Just fucking with you. You should see your face."

Lynch let out a rare laugh. A low, rough sound.

McBride shut his mouth, shut his eyes, and let the warmth of the whisky take hold again.

When he spoke, his words were slow, deliberate. Letting the alcohol do what it did best.

"So…we can deal. Do a deal. I said five hundred… but I'll do four."

Tombs didn't blink.

"Show me the photos first. Then we'll talk money."

McBride leaned back hard against the seat, straightened his leg, and shoved a hand into his pocket. He fished out his phone, found the pictures, and held it out.

Tombs pulled a pair of glasses from his vest pocket and slid them on. Scrolled. Zoomed. Tilted the phone.

"This was in Red's cell? And he's dead?"

McBride nodded. "Yeah, he necked himself… and yeah, it was in his cell. On the wall when we found him. Covered in blood and shit."

Tombs kept his eyes on the screen.

"And who else knows about it?"

McBride hesitated. A fraction of a second too long.

"Hardly anyone. Me, the warden, a copper from the city, and the guy that was doing the cleaning."

Tombs caught the lie. The way McBride's fingers twitched when he left someone out. Didn't push it. Not yet.

Instead, he handed the phone back.

"Alright. Four hundred. But this could turn out to be a load of bullshit. He was an mad old bastard."

Tombs knew about Red. Anyone with ties to Ironbark did.

He gave McBride the impression of disinterest, but inside, he was already thinking — already plotting.

This could set him up with the big boys. This was a shot at the big time.

"Send me the photos."

A moment later, his phone chimed.

He flicked his hand toward the door.

"Now get the fuck out of my car."

McBride stumbled back to his vehicle, barely keeping his balance. They watched as he pulled away, his headlights flickering over the wet asphalt.

Tombs opened the photos again, zooming in on the one detail that mattered.

A tiny, hand-drawn symbol.

It was barely noticeable. But he knew it.

"Tomorrow," he said, slipping his phone into his pocket.

"You, me, and maybe a few of the boys are going on a road trip."

Lynch finally turned his head, a smirk tugging at his scarred mouth.

"You ever been to Mudgee before?"

CHAPTER 9

The city sprawled beneath him, a sea of neon and glass stretching to the horizon. From the penthouse balcony, Liu Jianhong watched the traffic below move in choreographed chaos, a thousand tiny decisions flowing like blood through the arteries of Hong Kong.

He sipped his tea. Proper tea, not the Western filth businessmen served in boardrooms. It was brewed the way his grandfather had taught him, steeped in a porcelain pot older than the skyline itself.

The past never truly fades. It lingers, waiting for its moment.

A discreet knock at the door. Liu set his cup down.

"Enter."

The man who stepped inside bowed his head before speaking.

"Our operative in Australia has been contacted by the informant at Ironbark. Redmond is deceased. We've received and verified the details of a map he left behind before taking his own life."

Liu didn't react, only lifted his cup again, letting the steam curl into the humid air.

The man continued, more careful now.

"Our operative has begun analysing it, but for now, they have little to go on. Only a location and a time. A place called Mudgee."

The word felt unnatural in the man's mouth, a foreign syllable clashing against his carefully measured Mandarin.

Liu blinked once, slow and deliberate.

The words faded beneath the rush of something he had not allowed himself to feel in years.

Not quite relief. Not quite anger. Something deeper, something nameless.

The map.

For nearly fifty years, there had been nothing.

No leads. No whispers. No hope.

The sword had been stolen from him. From his family. As if they had no right to it.

As if he had no right to reclaim what was already his.

Liu reached for the jade pendant at his throat, tracing its smooth edges.

The sword had been more than a weapon. It had been a gift of favour, a seal of honour.

Three hundred years ago, Emperor Kangxi had placed it into his ancestor's hands.

A Jian sword, forged from the purest steel, its blade folded a hundred times over.

A blade that had cut down rebels. A blade that had protected a dynasty.

A blade that had given his family status, wealth, power.

Until history stole everything.

During the Taiping Rebellion, his ancestor had fled to Australia, seeking to rebuild the fortune that war had stolen.

Yet even in exile, fate had been cruel.

The sword, his family's legacy, had been taken from him, lost to time like so many others who had left China in search of gold.

And without the sword, status was meaningless. His family had been forced to claw at the sheer face of the world to find their place. Methods that left rivals destroyed in their wake. Power had become theirs through years, decades of hardship.

Yet still, without the sword, his family was nothing.

For years, Liu had traced its path, following dead ends, losing its trail entirely at times.

Until finally, he found it again.

Not in a palace. Not in the home of a collector.

But in a nothing-town.

A small, dusty museum in Tingha.

Behind smudged glass, surrounded by two-headed snakes and rusting war relics, reduced to a curiosity.

He had wanted to kill the old fool behind the counter.

Instead, he had offered more money than the man had ever dreamed of.

And just like that, the sword was his family's once more.

But honour could not be bought.

Liu had defended it this time. He had ensured it would not be lost again.

But fate had taken its chance anyway.

Because days later, it was stolen.

Liu's grip tightened around the pendant.

"Does anyone else have this information?" His voice was steady, but his jaw was locked.

"Unclear. A detective, possibly. Others have seen the map, but access has been limited. Only the warden and a cleaner. They may suspect the opals, but they don't know what they're truly chasing."

Liu gave a quiet breath, unreadable as ever

They thought this was about opals. About fortune.

Greedy men scrambling for wealth they could measure.

Fools.

This was never about the opals.

This was about honour.

This was about the sword.

The servant hesitated. "Should we be concerned about the detective?"

Liu said nothing for a long moment. The question unanswered.

Liu lifted his tea and drank the last sip, the bitterness grounding him.

"Send our people," he said quietly. "I want them in Mudgee by tomorrow night."

The man bowed deeply and left.

Liu remained on the balcony, the city stretching out below him, glittering and vast.

He should have felt powerful.

Instead, he felt hollow.

His mind drifted, back to that final night that the sword had still been his.

The sting of betrayal. The rage of loss.

The sword had simply disappeared.

And now, decades later, the first clue had surfaced in a dead man's cell in a prison across the sea.

Soon, the past would be set right.

He would not be wronged again.

CHAPTER 10

Dave Callahan hesitated before handing over the two fifty-dollar notes. The little change he'd get back would have to last four more days until payday. But with a full tank of petrol, Mudgee would no longer be just a scrawl on Red's map. By afternoon, it would be real.

The rain had set in. Not the storm front that had rolled through earlier, but a steady drizzle, enough to wash out any chance of work. Such was the life of a brickie's labourer. Today, though, it suited him just fine.

There was one stop he needed to make before heading to Mudgee. He needed information on Red, and the only place he could think to look was the library. He hadn't set foot in one since he was seventeen. No idea what to expect.

Hopefully, internet.

The servo attendant took the notes without a word, sliding back a few notes in change. Twenty-five dollars. Dave pocketed it without looking. Wouldn't do him much good anyway. A feed on the road somewhere. He stepped out into the rain, the damp air thick with petrol fumes and wet asphalt.

His car sat at pump four, the battered old Holden that had seen better days but still got the job done. He wrenched wthe nozzle free, shoved it back into place, and climbed in.

Mudgee.

He traced the word in his mind like it was a place he'd always meant to visit but never had a reason to. Now, thanks to Red, it was more than just a town on a map. It was the first real lead in a hunt he hadn't even meant to join.

But first, the library.

He wasn't sure what he expected to find there. Old newspaper clippings, maybe. Prison records, if he was lucky. Red's name wasn't one you heard often, not news of the day, not anymore. But there had to be something. Some thread to pull at.

Dave started the engine, the wipers sweeping away the rain. He pulled out onto the slick road, heading for the one place he'd never thought he'd return to.

Seventeen years ago, the library had been a place to kill time, warm up in winter, or pretend he was looking for work when the dole office started asking questions. Now, it held something else.

Answers.

Maybe.

The library car park was nearly empty. It had just gone ten a.m., and the rain had picked up, hammering against the windscreen and filling the potholes like a makeshift obstacle course. The suspension groaned as he rolled over them. One more thing to ignore until payday.

Inside wasn't how he remembered libraries. Sure, there were books, but it wasn't quiet. A group of young mums wrangling toddlers had taken over a side room, their voices carrying over the occasional squeal. A few old blokes sat near the newspapers, swapping footy opinions between sips of coffee.

Near the counter, a woman with glasses that clung to her face like barnacles spotted him hovering and made a beeline. "Need some help?"

A few minutes later, Dave had a computer, a cup of coffee, and a search bar blinking at him. He cracked his knuckles and typed the name.

Henry Redmond.

The first headline hit him like a punch to the ribs.

OPAL HEIST ENDS IN BLOODSHED: CONSTABLE KILLED IN 1976 ROBBERY

A week after the daring Lightning Ridge opal heist that stunned authorities, Constable Michael Parker was shot and killed during a confrontation near Baradine. The suspect, Henry 'Red' Redmond, a former pilot and alleged mastermind of the robbery, remains at large.

Sources say Parker and his partner, Constable Adrian Blake, were responding to a reported sighting of Redmond on a remote property west of Baradine when the incident occurred. Details remain scarce, but police confirmed that Parker was fatally shot at close range. His partner, Blake, survived the encounter but has yet to release a public statement.

Redmond, a skilled pilot with a history of smuggling, was hired to transport an unidentified Chinese national and a shipment of opals from Lightning Ridge to Brisbane. However, he allegedly double-crossed his associates, taking off alone and vanishing without a trace. Authorities believe he landed somewhere in the vast interior, offloading the stolen goods before abandoning the aircraft.

Despite an extensive manhunt, neither the opals nor Redmond have been found. Police are urging anyone with information on his whereabouts to come forward.

Constable Parker, 28, was described by colleagues as a dedicated officer with a bright future. He is survived by his wife and young daughter. His funeral will be held in Mudgee later this week.

Dave made notes as he read, his checklist growing with each new detail. He had started with the basics. Things he thought might be relevant to the map.

Where was Red born?

Where did he live?

What was his profession?

Did he have family still alive?

One by one, he ticked off answers. But with every fact uncovered, more questions surfaced.

Further down the search results, he spotted something unexpected. A Wikipedia page. Someone had thought Red important enough to dedicate an entry to him. Dave clicked the link, skimming through the text, filling in the blanks.

Henry 'Red' Redmond.

Full name: Henry Lawson Redmond.

Born: 17th January 1946, Narrabri.

Family: Eldest of two children. Parents — Andrew Henry Redmond and Helen Eliza Redmond (née Lyneham), both deceased. One sister, Martha Iris Redmond (Carter), still living.

Education: Attended school in Narrabri, but the family moved frequently.

Father's occupation: Drover and station hand.

Mother's occupation: Seamstress.

Dave tapped his pen against his notebook. Martha Redmond. A name to remember.

By the end of his allotted internet time, Dave had covered considerable ground.

Red had grown up moving between towns across northwest New South Wales. He'd left school early and found work in Broken Hill with a mining survey company. That was where he'd learned to fly. As the company expanded, so did Red's skills. Until the crash.

An engine failure at altitude brought Red's plane down. No one was badly hurt, but the investigation uncovered company neglect. The fallout forced the business into administration, and it folded soon after.

Red was out of a job.

So he went freelance. Made smart decisions. Not always legal, and bought his own plane. The money was good… but it was even better for the jobs that didn't exist on paper.

He flew survey teams, ferried cargo, even ran tourists out to remote airstrips. But there were whispers too. Stories about quiet deals, about flights taken with no questions asked. Nothing proven. Nothing that stuck.

Then came the opal job.

It should have been simple. A pickup in Lightning Ridge, a flight to Brisbane. Red was hired to transport Liu Jianhong and his opals, but the moment the cargo was loaded, he took off, leaving his passengers stranded on the tarmac. By the time anyone realised what had happened, Red and the plane had vanished.

A week later, he was spotted near Baradine. That's when the chase began.

For days, the police tracked him across the scrub. Then, near an old stock route, shots were fired. When it was over, Constable Parker was dead, and Red was in cuffs.

The loot was never found. The plane was never recovered.

For decades, Red had lived behind bars, his silence absolute. Whatever secrets he'd taken with him, they were buried deep.

Until now.

Dave kept running every bit of information through his head, trying to force a connection between Red's history and the cryptic scrawl on the map. Nothing clicked. If there was a pattern, he couldn't see it. Maybe Mudgee would change that. Maybe it'd be just another dead end.

Rain hammered the windscreen, wipers smearing it into a murky blur as the miles and hours passed away. The car's suspension groaned as he hit another pothole, the check engine light flickering like a warning he didn't have time for.

He shifted in his seat, cracking his neck to shake off the stiffness.

Then, finally, Mudgee. A faded sign on the roadside, a handful of low buildings huddled against the wet, marking the outskirts of the growing regional centre. Not much to look at yet, but deeper in, past the petrol stations and motels, into the heart of the town, maybe there were answers.

Or at least the next question.

It was late afternoon when Dave pulled up near the clock tower, choosing a spot where he could watch without drawing attention. From the relative comfort of his car, he scanned the street — eyes on the tower, the people drifting past, the steady flow of cars. He had time to kill. Time to watch. Time to think.

But first, he needed a slash and a feed wouldn't hurt either.

He found what he needed. Public toilets and a bakery, then took his pie to a bench in the park, eating while the town moved around him. When he was done, he walked the main street slow, taking everything in. The shopfronts, the passing faces, the rhythm of the place.

When he reached the clock tower, he stopped, letting his eyes trace the names etched into the war memorial. Some were worn down by time, others still sharp. Generations of dead, frozen in stone. He read them all, his mind turning over the clues on Red's map.

It gave him nothing. Just names and silence.

Dave climbed back into his car, shifted the seat back, and closed his eyes. The rain had settled into a steady rhythm, tapping against the roof like a slow, tired heartbeat. He let it lull him, but sleep came in fits. Snatches of rest cut through with the nagging feeling that he was missing something.

Dave woke to the sound of rain tapping softly against the car roof. The air was damp, the windows fogged at the edges. He checked the clock.

8:45 PM.

The streets were quieter now, just the odd car rolling past, the glow of shopfront signs flickering on the wet pavement. But something felt... off.

He sat up, rubbed the stiffness from his neck, and took another look at the cenotaph.

People were hanging around.

Not tourists. Not locals having a chat. They stood apart, watching the memorial like it might do something. Waiting. Was he imagining it?

A pair of bikers, leather jackets dark with rain, helmets tucked under their arms. One of them had his phone out, snapping photos. Too careful, too deliberate.

Further off, two blokes in bikers vests, standing by a Hilux. One built like a gorilla, the other, restless, shifting his weight. They weren't talking much. Just observing.

Then, parked illegally across from the memorial, a sleek black luxury car. Tinted windows, one rolled halfway down, with the low purr of an engine still running. Inside, two men. Asian, sharp suits, unreadable expressions. They weren't talking either. Just watching.

And then, off to the side, leaning against a post like he had all the time in the world. Blake.

Dave's pulse kicked up a notch. The detective wasn't just loitering. He was scanning the area, eyes sharp, looking for something.

Or someone.

Dave drummed his fingers against the wheel, trying to settle the rush building in his chest. He hadn't even considered that anyone else might be trying to decipher the map. So where the hell had all these assholes come from?

How had they heard about it?

His face burned. How could he have been so stupid?

But he was here now, and he had to get closer.

Sitting in the car wasn't an option. If anyone clocked him watching, he'd stand out.

He needed to move.

And he had an idea.

Joggers didn't get a second glance.

He pulled his hoodie up, climbed out, and started running. Not fast. Not slow. Just a steady, even pace, like he'd done it a hundred times before. The footpath was slick underfoot, puddles dotting the road.

He passed the bikers first. Gave them a nod. One glanced up, barely acknowledging him.

Then the pair by the Hilux. The restless one flicked him a glance, then went back to shifting impatiently.

The men in the luxury car didn't react. Just sat there, waiting.

Blake didn't even look his way.

Good.

Dave kept moving, rounding the block, looping back to his car. He waited. One hour. Then two.

One by one, the groups gave up. The bikers got back on their rides, the suits climbed into their car, and the black luxury car pulled away, silent as a ghost.

Blake. Blake stood there a little longer. Thinking. Calculating.

Then he began a purposeful stride back toward his own car.

Dave let out a breath and slid back into the driver's seat. He turned the key.

The engine coughed, then cracked like a whip, the sound tearing through the damp night air.

A backfire loud enough to wake the dead.

Across the street, Blake stopped mid-step. His head snapped toward the noise, eyes locking onto Dave's car.

And Dave knew, in that instant, he'd just been made.

He didn't panic. Didn't gun it. Just shifted into gear and pulled out smooth and steady, like he hadn't just handed Blake a flashing neon sign.

But in the rear-view mirror, he saw it.

Blake, standing still, watching him go.

And Dave knew damn well the detective hadn't forgotten that car. Detectives remember shit like that.

CHAPTER 11

Dave rolled into his driveway just before midnight, killed the engine, and sat there, fingers clenched around the wheel. The night pressed in around him, thick with the scent of damp earth and rust. The rain had passed hours ago, but water still dripped from the tin awning of the carport, a slow, rhythmic tap that felt too much like a countdown.

His heart hadn't settled since Mudgee.

Blake had seen his car. That much he knew. How much that mattered. How much trouble it meant, was the question clawing at the back of his mind. Maybe Blake had just logged it away, another oddity to pick apart later. Or maybe, right now, he was already making calls, digging into who owned the rusted-out wreck that had coughed its way out of town. Maybe he already knew.

Dave ran a hand through his hair, jaw tightening. No point chasing ghosts.

Inside, the house was a goddamn sauna, the walls still sweating after the storm. The old carpet had soaked up the damp, thickening the air with that mildew stench that never really left. He flipped on the kitchen light, its hum filling the silence, and dropped into the chair at the table.

Red's notes were still spread out where he'd left them, the map staring back at him like it had a secret it refused to share.

He traced the markings again. Born. Job. Home. And that damn time. 9PM.

Everyone thought it meant Mudgee. That's why they were all at the cenotaph, watching, waiting, hoping for some revelation at the stroke of nine. But nothing had happened. No magic. No sudden answers. Just another wasted lead.

He flipped through the notes, searching for something. Anything that made sense. Red had spent time in Mudgee, sure, but he wasn't from there. Narrabri. Broken Hill. Baradine. A dozen towns, all linked, all meaning nothing.

But that still didn't explain 9PM.

Too late for sunset. Too early for midnight deals. Kids are asleep. Damn that reminded him of Cassie and just how much he missed her. Missed them. How he used to read to her when she went to bed.

Then it hit him. Bed

Bedtime.

Prison.

9PM was lights out.

The pieces snapped together like a lock turning. Every last one of them. The bikers, the Asians, Blake. They'd all been looking in the wrong place.

The answer wasn't where. It was when.

Be there at 9PM. Be in Red's cell.

Dave's stomach turned. A trip to Mudgee was one thing. Breaking into a prison? That was a whole different level of stupid, even with half a reason to be there.

He leaned back, trying to slow his breathing. The picture was coming together. But with Blake sniffing around, time was running out. Fast.

CHAPTER 12

By Tuesday, the idea had settled into Dave's gut like a bad meal. It was reckless, sure, but not stupid. Stupid was breaking into a prison. This? This was just bending the rules in his favour.

He waited until lunch to make the call, slipping away from the site while the crew sat around eating sandwiches and arguing about sport. The air was thick with the stink of wet mortar and sweat, but away from the chatter, behind the stack of pallets, it was just him, the distant drone of a cement mixer, and his phone ringing in his ear.

"Ironbark Correctional." A woman this time. Bored. Probably shuffling papers with one hand, scrolling her phone with the other. "What do you need?"

Dave kept his tone easy. "Hey, it's Dave Callahan. I'm on weekend detention. Normally do Sundays, but I was wondering if I could swap to Saturday this week?"

A pause. He could hear her clicking around on a keyboard. "Why's that?"

"Boss lined up some extra work Sunday. Can't really knock it back." That part wasn't even a lie. Work was work.

More clicking. "You're already rostered for cleaning."

"Yeah, I know. Just thought I could knock out two jobs. I heard Red's old cell still stinks. Figured while I'm there, I could paint it. Make it usable again." He let out a half-laugh, casual but not too casual. "Unless you lot enjoy the smell of dead bloke and whatever else was on those walls."

A beat of silence. Then: "Hang on."

Muffled voices in the background. The chair creaking as she leaned back, talking to someone off-mic. Then the voice returned, brisk now, a little more interested. "Warden says there's paint in the storeroom. You'll get access after lock-in, so you're not underfoot. Be here at 8PM."

Dave nodded to himself, voice even. It would be a damn long night, but the opportunity couldn't have presented itself better. "Sounds good. Cheers."

"Yeah, yeah. Just don't half-arse it." The line went dead.

Dave tucked the phone back into his pocket, the tension still coiled in his muscles.

That was the easy part.

Now came the waiting

Four days. Four long days.

He made his way back to the group, dropped onto an upturned bucket, and unwrapped the greasy pie he'd picked up that morning. Across from him, one of the brickies, big, red-faced, always sweating, was mid-rant about how some dickhead ref had cost his team the match.

Dave half-listened, nodding where it fit, but his mind was already elsewhere. Already in that cell. Already standing beneath those flickering lights, watching the paint dry, waiting for 9PM.

Wondering just how badly this could go.

**

Blake didn't believe in coincidences. Not after thirty years on the job.

He sat in his office, the overhead light flickering, casting shadows along the nicotine-stained walls. His fingers tapped against the desk, a slow, deliberate rhythm as he stared at the screen in front of him. The prison logs. The CCTV feeds. The registration check on that rust-bucket of a car.

David Callahan.

Blake had seen the name before, back when Red's cell had been cleaned out. Some weekend detention bloke. ICO. At first glance, just another pisshead working off a DUI.

But he'd dug deeper. Pulled his file.

Callahan wasn't inside for drink-driving. He'd tried to bring down a local coal magnate. Snuck evidence out through a back door, tried to blow the whole thing open. Assaulted a woman according to Callahan.

And for what?

The sleazy prick had gone down months later. His own undoing. A press conference, a scandal, the whole bloody circus. Prostitution, drugs and worse.

But Callahan?

All he got was a judge's name ringing in his ears and wasted Sundays scrubbing walls for a system that didn't give a damn.

Blake sneered at the screen.

A try-hard hero. The worst kind.

Yeah. He'd seen that car before. Once outside the prison, once on that rainy Mudgee road when it backfired and caught his ear. It had stuck with him ever since.

Blake ran a hand down his face. The first time, he'd brushed it off. A shitbox like that stood out in the staff car park, but not enough to raise alarms. Some poor bastard doing his hours, nothing more. But now?

Blake flicked open another window. The traffic cam still showed it in crisp black and white: 8:37 PM. That rusted-out piece of shit creeping through Mudgee, headlights cutting through the drizzle, pulling up just down from the cenotaph.

Dave Callahan had been there.

Blake leaned back, eyes narrowing. That changed things.

He thought back to the cenotaph. The faces in the crowd. Two bikies playing it tough in their cuts, standing in front while another two, leaner, meaner, watched from near a Hilux. A couple of Asians in a luxury car, parked illegally like they owned the place. None of them looked at each other, but Blake knew they'd all come for the same reason.

And so had Callahan.

He rolled his chair closer, pulling up the prison logs again. Who had been in that cell before all this started? Who had actually touched Red's things?

Blake's jaw tightened. Three names.

McBride. The bastard had sniffed through Red's gear, looking smug as always. But McBride was a vulture. He only showed up when he smelled something worth picking at.

The Warden. Too spineless to be in on anything. The man barely wiped his own arse without checking policy first.

And then there was Dave Callahan.

Blake drummed his fingers against the desk again, slow and steady. He knew the way criminals thought. He knew how men lied.

Dave had found something. Maybe he didn't even realise what.

Blake reached for his notebook and flipped to a fresh page, scrawling a single line:

Callahan – Question Sunday.

He'd catch him after his shift. Pull him aside, press him a little. No need for a formal sit-down. Just two blokes having a chat. And if Callahan had half a brain, he'd be smart enough to play along.

If not?

Well, Blake had broken tougher bastards than him.

He closed the file, stood up, spine straightening like a man ready for war. Sunday, then.

What he didn't know. What he wouldn't realise until it was too late. Was that Callahan wasn't coming in on Sunday.

And that was Blake's first mistake.

CHAPTER 13

Tombs' knuckles whitened around the wheel as the Hilux chewed up the highway, the glow of the dashboard the only light in the cab. The wipers flicked once, smearing bird shit across the glass. His jaw ached from being clenched too long, but he barely noticed. His mind was still in Mudgee, standing in the rain, staring at that useless bloody cenotaph.

It hadn't made sense. None of it. Red's map had pointed them there, the 9PM clue had lined up. So why had it all felt like a goddamn waste of time?

The frustration gnawed at him. He flexed his fingers, trying to shake it off, but his grip stayed tight, the tension locked in his muscles. Instead of sitting down to dinner with his wife like a normal bloke, he was out here, burning through fuel, trying to cool the slow burn of anger in his gut.

But it wasn't just about the wasted trip.

It was who else had been there.

His mind ran through it all again, picking apart the scene in his head like he was still standing in the rain, watching. Looking for what he'd missed.

Mudgee, Monday Night

The cenotaph had loomed in the drizzle, slick with rain, the names carved into stone blurring in the dim streetlights. The air was thick with that sharp, clean scent that only comes after a storm.

Tombs had stood in the shadows, hands in his pockets, eyes scanning the small groups lingering nearby. His boys were spread out, pretending not to be together, but they weren't the only ones.

He'd noticed the suits first. Asian. Standing by that black luxury car, tinted windows rolled halfway down, like they were waiting for someone to come to them.

Then there was the lone bloke in the hoodie.

He hadn't looked important at first. Just another ghost drifting through the wet night. But something about him was off. Too casual. Too steady. And when he ran past, Tombs had caught the way his eyes flicked toward them all. Just a quick glance, but enough.

And then there was Blake.

Tombs hadn't needed an introduction to know who that bastard was. Everyone in the game knew the name. Detective Adrian Blake. Not some local plod. Big city. Hard bastard.

Blake had just stood there, watching. He hadn't made a move, hadn't flashed a badge, but he saw everything. And that meant something.

Tombs had left that night with nothing but questions.

The memory left a sour taste in his mouth.

Blake showing up wasn't a coincidence. The suits, even that jogger-looking prick. They weren't there by chance.

So who else was chasing Red's secret?

Tombs needed answers. And McBride owed him some.

He reached for his phone, thumbed through to McBride's number, and hit call. It rang twice before the prison officer picked up, his voice half-muffled like he was chewing. The prick was probably still in the staff canteen, shovelling down his free lunch.

"Yeah?"

Tombs didn't waste time. "That was bullshit."

A pause. "Tombs?"

"No, the fuckin' Pope," he snapped. "Yeah, it's me. And yeah, I'm pissed."

McBride swallowed, and Tombs could hear chairs scraping in the background. He was moving. Getting away from listening ears. Good.

"I told you what I knew," McBride said carefully. "Red marked that cenotaph for a reason."

"Then why was it a whole lot of nothing?" Tombs growled. "No sign. No clue. Just rain and wasted time."

A longer pause. McBride was stalling.

Tombs let the silence stretch, tapping his thumb against the wheel. "We got photos," he said. "Clock tower. Cenotaph. Whatever the fuck else looked important. Maybe you'll see something in 'em that we don't."

McBride didn't answer straight away. "Tombs, mate —"

"That wasn't a question."

McBride went quiet again, weighing his options.

Tombs made the decision for him. "Sunday. Morning. You're meeting me."

McBride hesitated. "Tombs —"

"You're meeting me." His voice was flat. Final. "And if I think you've been holding out on me, we're gonna have a different conversation."

There was a beat of dead air. Then: "Yeah. Alright."

Tombs hung up.

He stared at the road ahead, the Hilux humming beneath him, the night stretching on into nothing. His gut still churned. Something wasn't right.

He pulled the glovebox open, fingers curling around the cold grip of the pistol inside. Just sat there for a moment, feeling the weight of it.

He needed to get ahead of this.

Mudgee had been a bust. But there were too many players in the game now.

And Tombs didn't like playing blind.

He let out a slow breath, flexing his fingers against the wheel.

There was more to dig up.

Or more bodies to bury.

Either way, he'd be ready.

CHAPTER 14

The tea had gone cold.

Liu Jianhong sat motionless, staring at the delicate porcelain cup in front of him as if it had personally insulted him. His fingers rested lightly on the polished wood of the desk, his breathing slow and even.

Not a single muscle twitched.

But the air in the room had shifted. Thick, suffocating.

A kind of pressure that made a man's pulse slow, skin prickle, like something unseen was about to strike.

Across the desk, Zhao stood rigid, his back straight, his face impassive.

But inside?

His stomach coiled tight.

Zhao had delivered bad news before. But never to this man.

Liu said nothing at first. Just sat there, perfectly still, as if whatever he might release with a breath would be too dangerous to name. His gaze didn't lift.

"Say it again."

Zhao swallowed, throat dry. He hadn't been made to repeat himself since he was a child.

Not until now.

"The cenotaph was nothing," Zhao said. Even his own voice sounded thin. "There was no sign, no clue. Our men waited. Watched. Nothing happened."

Liu finally looked up. The weight of that gaze hit Zhao like a hammer to the chest.

The man's eyes were impossible to read. Dark, endless, holding no anger, no warmth, no humanity.

For the first time in his life, Zhao felt what it was like to be prey.

"And the others?" Liu asked, his voice barely above a whisper.

Zhao hated that his pulse jumped at the question. He forced his hands to stay loose at his sides.

"Some bikers were there," he said carefully. "So was the detective."

A pause.

The moment stretched.

"And others," Zhao admitted. "We don't know who they were."

Liu's fingers drummed once against the desk.

Just once.

Zhao's heartbeat mirrored the sound.

"And did they find anything?" Liu asked.

"No."

The silence that followed was absolute.

Zhao's skin felt tight over his bones.

Somewhere in the distance, he could hear the faint ticking of a clock.

The murmur of Hong Kong traffic beyond the floor-to-ceiling windows.

The sound of his own breath, too shallow.

Liu reached for the cup.

Lifted it.

Turned it slowly in his fingers, studying it like something fragile, something he might consider preserving.

Then, with no change in his expression, he shattered it against the desk.

CRACK.

The sharp sound ripped through the silence.

Porcelain shards scattered across the polished wood, tea spilling in dark ribbons that dripped to the floor.

Zhao did not move.

His heart pounded, but his body knew better than to react.

To flinch now was to show weakness.

And weakness did not survive in Liu's presence.

Liu sat back, his fingers flexing once, as if shaking off an inconvenience.

"Then someone," he murmured, "lied."

Zhao forced himself to breathe.

"The information came from McBride," he managed, voice steady but dry.

Liu tilted his head slightly, considering. "McBride."

The name sat on his tongue like something bitter.

Zhao nodded once. "He worked closely with Red. If anyone knew something, it was him."

Liu's face remained unreadable. A mask carved from stone.

"And yet," he said softly, "nothing."

Zhao did not answer.

The room held stillness like a blade to the throat.

Then, Liu let out a quiet breath, his fingers trailing lightly over the broken porcelain.

A small, casual movement.

Like a man sifting through bones.

"Perhaps McBride was mistaken," he murmured.

Zhao felt his mouth go dry.

"Or," Liu continued, his voice smooth as silk, "perhaps he was not."

A single droplet of tea slid off the desk's edge, darkening the polished floor.

Liu stood.

The movement was slow. Unhurried.

He walked around the desk, steps silent against the hardwood.

Zhao forced himself to stay still, even as his stomach coiled tighter.

Liu stopped beside him.

Not facing him.

Just close enough that Zhao could feel the weight of his presence.

Like standing next to a coiled viper.

"Find him," Liu said softly. "I want you there."

Zhao didn't dare nod. Didn't move.

"Have a conversation," Liu continued, as if discussing a business deal. "A real one."

His voice dropped lower, barely more than breath.

"Make sure he understands how costly lies can be."

Zhao gave the smallest nod. "Yes."

Liu's fingers drifted lightly across the back of the chair.

"And Zhao?"

Zhao forced himself to meet his gaze.

"If he was lying…"

Liu smiled.
A slow, cold thing.
Something that never reached his eyes.
Zhao felt his stomach sink.
Liu didn't need to finish the sentence.
But as Zhao turned to leave, something flickered in his expression.
Something gone in an instant.
Not defiance. Not fear.
Something colder. Calculating.
A thought he would never speak aloud.
Then the door clicked shut behind him, and he was gone.

CHAPTER 15

By Wednesday, Dave felt like a runner stuck at the starting line, muscles coiled, waiting for the gun.

The days blurred into a haze of brick dust and sweat, his hands raw from hauling stacks of blocks, his back a knot of pain. Work was good, honest, steady, but it wasn't enough. Not with what was coming. Not with Red's secret sitting in his gut like a loaded gun.

The heat at the worksite pressed down thick and heavy, mixing with the acrid tang of wet mortar and dust. Cement coated his forearms, sticking to the sweat, drying in rough patches that cracked when he moved. The crew sat around during smoko, perched on esky lids, shovelling pies and sausage rolls, arguing about cricket. Someone was cursing the umpires, another was calling bullshit, their voices rising and falling in the humid air.

Dave leaned against the ute, pretending to check messages while his mind worked ahead. Saturday. The prison. The painting job.

It had to hold. No last-minute changes. No admin screw-ups.

He scrolled through his contacts, found the number, and pressed call.

Three rings.

"Corrections Admin." A woman this time. Bored. Probably scrolling her own phone with one hand, flicking through paperwork with the other.

Dave kept his tone easy. No reason to sound too interested.

"Hey, it's Dave Callahan," he said. "Just checking in about the painting job in Red's old cell. Still all good for Saturday?"

A pause. Papers shuffled. Keys clacked on a keyboard. Then —

"Yeah, you're still on the list. You'll need to bring your own gear, though. No spare rollers here."

Good.

"Got it," Dave said. "And the smell? Still bad?"

A snort. "Christ, yes. You'd be doing us a favour."

He let out a short, easy chuckle, not too keen, not too rehearsed. "Alright. See you then."

The call ended. No issues. No last-minute changes.

His fingers flexed against the phone.

It was set.

But his gut still churned. The job was locked in. But everything else? That was still a gamble.

By the time the workday wrapped up, his body was screaming for rest, but his mind wouldn't slow down.

Payday came and went, same as always. Just enough to keep things moving, never enough to get ahead.

$1200 in. $1020 out.

Rent. Bills. A grocery run that barely made the fridge look full. He stared at the numbers in his account, jaw tight, the back of his neck burning.

He needed this.

Needed a win.

That night, he called Sally.

She answered on the first ring, her voice warm, familiar.

"Hey, babe."

Some of the tension in his chest unwound. Didn't disappear. Just loosened its grip.

"Hey, love. Just checking in."

"Mm, good timing," she said. "Cassie wanted to call you earlier, but I told her to wait till the weekend."

Dave smiled, but it felt tight. "She been good?"

"She's been great. Misses you, though." A pause. "We both do."

Something in him tightened, then loosened again. He closed his eyes for a second.

"I know. I miss you too."

For a while, neither of them spoke. Just listening. Breathing.

It was the kind of silence that only came when you knew someone inside out.

"You alright?" she asked eventually.

Dave ran a hand down his face, fingers dragging over stubble.

"Long week."

"You sure that's all?"

A beat too long before he answered.

"Just work stuff. You know how it is."

She didn't push. Just sighed softly.

"Alright. Just don't go running yourself into the ground, yeah?"

He wouldn't.

Another lie.

One that sat between them, unchallenged.

And then, because he hadn't planned to say it, but the thought had been lingering, he cleared his throat and asked —

"Hey… we still got that old sleeping bag?"

A pause. "The blue one? Yeah, it's in the top of the wardrobe, I think. Why?"

Shit. He should've thought that through.

"Just wondering," he said, voice light. "Might be good for the site if I do any long shifts."

"You never stay over for work."

He forced a chuckle. "Nah, just thinking ahead."

Another pause, just long enough for him to feel the weight of it.

"…Alright."

And just like that, the moment passed.

When the call ended, Dave sat staring at the phone, the quiet of the house pressing in. The hum of the fridge. The faint creak of the old fibro walls cooling under the night air.

He got up, grabbed his duffel, and started packing.

By the time Saturday rolled around, the plan was locked in.

The car was fuelled up. Parked down the road in the only damn shade on this sun torched street. Toolbox in the boot. Paint rollers in the back.

Just another weekend job. Just another favour for admin.

But the weight in his chest told him the truth.

This wasn't just another job.

This was the point of no return.

CHAPTER 16

The road to the prison felt different this time.

Dave had driven it before, weekend after weekend, working off his time, counting down the hours until he could be free again. But tonight, the air was thick, the night too quiet, his grip too tight on the wheel. The rain from earlier had dried, leaving the highway slick with mist, the white lines blurring under his headlights. The drone of the tyres against the bitumen filled the cabin, but it wasn't enough to quiet the static in his head.

This was it. The moment where everything either came together or fell apart.

He pulled into the staff car park just as the last of the evening shift was heading out. Their figures moved through the moth-cluttered glow of the overhead lights, shoulders hunched, tired faces set in grim lines. Just another shift in a place that ground people down.

McBride was among them, peeling off his uniform shirt as he walked, sweat-darkened undershirt clinging to his back. He moved with a strange energy. Quick but not rushed. Like he didn't want to linger, but didn't want to be seen leaving too fast either.

Dave climbed out of his car, ignoring the sideways glances from a few of the officers passing by. Even on weekend detention, there was a divide. An unspoken wall between them and him. It wasn't hostility, not outright. Just that quiet reminder that he didn't belong.

McBride barely looked at him.

"You're a day early aren't you. You're not due till the morning."

Dave didn't bother with small talk. "Painting Red's cell. Warden wanted it done after hours. Out of everyone's way."

McBride grunted, scratching the back of his neck. "Yeah, well, make it quick. The sooner that cell stops smelling like a fucking dead bloke, the better."

Dave nodded. No banter. No casual conversation. Just the bare minimum.

McBride held his stare for a second longer, then turned away, heading for his car.

Dave walked inside.

The stink in Red's old cell hit him the second the door opened.

Damp concrete. Sweat. Rot.

The kind of filth that soaked into walls, into plaster, into the bones of a place. Even after they'd stripped the wall back, the air still carried the memory of it.

The map was gone, wiped out by brute force, but Dave stepped closer, fingers ghosting over the plaster. If you didn't know, if you hadn't stood here before, you wouldn't see anything.

But Dave knew.

His hand brushed over a small, uneven bump. A nail, maybe a screw. Not part of the map. Not part of Red's message. But it had been there before. A fixed point, something his memory had latched onto without realising.

A reference.

His fingers hovered over it, mind ticking over. If the nail was here, then…

He turned, aligning himself with the wall, eyes tracking the empty space where Red's markings had once been.

The clock on the far side of the corridor read 8:58 PM.

He set up the rollers, the tray, the tin of off-white paint. All for show. It needed to look like he'd been here for a reason.

Then he leaned against the opposite wall, arms crossed, waiting.

At exactly 9 PM, the fluorescent lights in the hall flicked off with a low electric hum.

The corridor fell into darkness.

Dave tensed, eyes locked on the wall.

Nothing.

The silence stretched, thick and suffocating. His heart pounded harder than it should.

Nothing.

He swallowed, licked his lips. Maybe he'd gotten it wrong. Maybe Red's clue, the time, the angle, the whole goddamn thing, meant nothing.

A slow, cold slither of doubt worked its way into his gut.

Then, almost on impulse, he reached over and flicked off the cell light.

Darkness swallowed the room.

For a second, nothing changed.

Then —

Thin shafts of light seeped through the high windows, fractured through the cracked cover of the security light in the hall. Thin silver blades, slicing through the gloom.

They hit specific points on the wall.

Dave's breath caught.

He moved closer, slow and careful, eyes tracking the light. The beams landed on three, maybe four spots along the stripped-back plaster.

At first, they seemed random.

Then his mind clicked into gear.

The map. The layout. The memory burned into his skull.

The nail.

He placed his fingers on it again, using it to ground himself — to align the spots of light with the places he knew Red's markings had once been.

It lined up.

Not perfectly. Not obviously.

But it was there.

His fingers hovered over the faintest outlines. Nothing visible, nothing left behind, but his memory filled in the gaps.

A real location. A real goddamn clue.

A slow thrill crawled up his spine.

But he shoved it down.

No time for that now.

He memorized the positions, burning them into his brain, fixing them in relation to the nail and the scars of the old map.

Then he turned, half-ready to leave —

And his stomach clenched.

The job.

The painting.

If he left now. If he walked out without doing what he was supposed to, someone would notice.

A guard. The admin staff. The warden.

Someone would ask questions.

So, with one last glance at the wall, at the spots marked by light, Dave picked up the roller and started painting.

Thick, even strokes. Slow and methodical.

The cell walls drank the paint like they were starving for it, each pass of the roller barely enough to cover the memories trapped beneath. Sweat trickled down his back, his muscles aching from the strain of keeping steady. He forced himself through it, one coat, then another, until the last shadow of what had been, was buried under government-issue off-white.

By the time he was done, the prison was silent. Even the guards had settled into their night routine, footsteps fewer, voices distant.

Dave cleaned up, locked the paint away, and signed himself out.

It was past three in the morning when he finally rolled out of the car park. The highway stretched in front of him, long and empty, the glow of the dashboard the only thing keeping him anchored to the present. His eyes burned, his body running on fumes. At some point, his grip on the wheel loosened. The world blurred.

Then he was home.

He had no memory of the drive. No recollection of pulling into the driveway, shutting off the engine. Just the feeling of his feet dragging across the floorboards, the dim glow of the kitchen light, the map calling to him from the table.

But he couldn't.

Not now. Not like this.

His body had nothing left to give.

He made it as far as the bedroom, collapsing onto the mattress, still half-dressed. His last thought before sleep took him was the spots of light on the wall, the puzzle waiting to be solved.

Then everything went dark.

CHAPTER 17

McBride felt the sweat pooling under his collar before he even stepped out of the ute. The morning sun was barely up, but the heat was already pressing down like a thick, suffocating hand. The kind of heat that turned everything sluggish, except his nerves, which were running hot and fast beneath his skin. He should have been having a Sunday morning sleep in.

Across the car park, Tombs leaned against his Hilux, arms crossed, unreadable. No golf clubs, no smokes, no bullshit pretence. Just standing there in the open like he had nothing to hide.

That wasn't a good sign.

McBride killed the engine and sat for a second, swallowing down the sour taste creeping up his throat.

He already knew that this wasn't going to be a friendly chat.

Tombs barely moved as he approached.

"This some kind of joke?" McBride muttered, wiping the sweat from his forehead.

Tombs didn't smile. "You look like a bloke who could use some fresh air."

"Yeah? And you look like a bloke who's about to waste my fuckin' time."

Tombs pushed off the ute. "Let's walk."

McBride sighed but followed. They cut along a gravel path skirting the course, the smell of cut grass and sunscreen thick in the air. A few golfers in the distance, too far to hear anything. That's why Tombs had picked this place. Privacy, but not isolation. A place where bodies didn't go missing, but messages could still be sent.

"Mudgee was a waste," Tombs said flatly.

McBride kept his face neutral. "Yeah, well. That's not on me."

Tombs stopped walking and turned. The look in his eyes made McBride's stomach tighten.

"I paid you for good intel," Tombs said. "Instead, I got a history tour and a soaking."

McBride forced himself to keep breathing evenly. "I told you what I knew. Red never mentioned that cenotaph to me, but the map —"

"The map was fuck-all use."

McBride shifted his stance. "Then maybe we missed something."

Tombs pulled his phone from his pocket, swiped through a few screens, then held it up.

"Maybe you did."

The first image was the cenotaph, empty and rain-slicked under the streetlights. The second. Same scene, but now with figures in the background.

McBride squinted.

Then he saw him.

Blake.

That wiry bastard, standing just at the edge of the light, watching.

A weight settled in McBride's gut.

"Shit."

Tombs tilted his head. "That all you got to say?"

McBride scratched his jaw, mind working fast. "Blake was in Red's cell the day he died. Whatever he found in there, it was enough to get him out in the rain, same as you."

Tombs nodded like he'd already figured that much out. He swiped to the next photo.

McBride's stomach clenched for a different reason this time.

The black European car, sleek and silent, parked illegally across from the cenotaph.

Inside, two men in suits.

They hadn't stepped out. They hadn't even moved much. Just sat there, watching. Waiting.

McBride kept his expression neutral. If he acknowledged them, that opened a whole other can of worms.

But then —

He froze.

A jogger. Hood up. Mid-stride, moving past like he didn't belong in the scene.

Something itched in McBride's brain. He'd seen that bloke before. Not just in passing. Recently.

"Hey." He zoomed in. "Hang on. I know that prick."

Tombs didn't react, just waited.

McBride's mind ticked over. Then it clicked.

"Callahan."

A shift. Small. But it was there. The interest sharpening behind Tombs' eyes.

"Where's he live?"

McBride hesitated a fraction too long.

Tombs didn't ask again.

McBride licked his lips, the heat suddenly heavier. "Muswellbrook. Works as a brickie's labourer. Does odd jobs. Picks up weekend detention shifts at the prison."

Tombs' eyebrows lifted slightly. Not much, but enough.

McBride pushed forward. "He was on cleaning duty in Red's cell when we found the body. Saw the map before anyone wiped it out."

That got Tombs' full attention.

"He saw the map?"

McBride nodded, feeling the trap snap shut. "And he was back in that cell last night. Painting."

Silence.

Then a slow, knowing smile crept across Tombs' face.

"That's a bit weird, isn't it?"

McBride forced himself to keep breathing evenly.

Tombs studied him for a long moment, then nodded. "You'd better hope your info's better this time."

He slid the phone back into his pocket and turned, heading toward his ute.

McBride watched him go, stomach twisted into knots. He'd just put a target on Callahan's back.

That should've made him feel safer.

It didn't.

Twenty Minutes Later

McBride pulled into his driveway, rubbing a hand down his face. His shirt was damp with sweat, his head pounding. He wanted a beer, a chair in front of the aircon, and an hour where no one needed a damn thing from him.

Then the car pulled up.

Black. Expensive.

McBride's gut went ice cold.

The back door opened, and a man stepped out. Slim. Sharp suit, the kind that didn't come off a rack. His face smooth, unreadable, but his eyes had weight.

McBride stayed where he was.

The man, Zhao — tilted his head slightly. "Mr. McBride."

His voice was calm. Almost pleasant.

"Get in."

McBride's jaw tightened. "Who the fuck are you?"

Zhao took a measured step forward, his expression unmoving. "We have paid handsomely for your assistance." A pause. "You will get in."

McBride's throat went dry.

He glanced at his watch. His shift at the prison was in a few hours.

Not that it mattered.

Zhao didn't give a shit about schedules. Zhao wasn't here for a quick chat.

This was different.

This was a real talk.

McBride hesitated.

Zhao didn't.

"You work at the prison," Zhao said, as if discussing the weather. "You have been useful." A pause. "Let's discuss how much longer that will be the case."

McBride swallowed. The air felt too thick.

"Get in," Zhao repeated.

He hesitated, just for a second.

Then he opened the car door and climbed inside.

Everything was turning to shit.

CHAPTER 18

Detective Sergeant Adrian Blake pulled into the prison lot and rolled to a stop beneath the shadow of the admin block. He killed the engine but didn't move. The heat outside was climbing fast, the asphalt shimmering under the midday sun, but inside the car, the air was still cool. The hum of the aircon was the only sound.

Something felt off.

Blake had been in this game too long to ignore a gut feeling.

He ran his tongue over his teeth, then pushed the door open. The heat hit like a fist.

It was the kind of day that made tempers short and patience shorter.

He slammed the door harder than necessary and stalked toward the entrance.

The prison always had a feel to it. Something stale, something heavy. The scent of sweat, dust, and overcooked cafeteria slop mixed with the distant stink of hot asphalt baking in the sun. The place didn't just house criminals. It held things. Bad decisions, bad luck, bad men. And sometimes, the ghosts of the ones who never made it out.

Inside, the duty officer was leaning back in his chair, scrolling his phone, giving off the lazy confidence of a bloke who never expected trouble. The kind of officer who did his hours, collected his pay, and never stuck his nose too deep into anything that might make his life difficult.

Blake didn't bother with pleasantries.

"Where's McBride?"

The officer startled, nearly dropping his phone onto the desk. He fumbled to pocket it, straightening. "Uh… he hasn't signed in."

Blake narrowed his eyes. "You mean he's late?"

"No," the officer said, frowning now. "He hasn't come in at all."

Blake exhaled slowly, fingers tapping against the counter. The faintest flicker of something sharp and ugly curled in his gut.

McBride was a lot of things, lazy, greedy, a pain in the arse, but he wasn't stupid. He knew how to cover himself. Just not showing up? That wasn't his style.

"Call him," Blake ordered.

The officer hesitated, then reached for the landline. He dialled, waited. After a few rings, he shook his head. "Nothing."

Blake's jaw ticked.

"Try his mobile."

A nod. The officer switched to his own phone, dialled, and put it on speaker. The line rang. And rang. And rang. Then —

"This is McBride. Leave a message."

Blake's stomach knotted. McBride's voice had that usual lazy drawl, but there was something else. Something he couldn't quite put his finger on.

The duty officer hung up. "Voicemail."

Blake ignored him, replaying McBride's voice in his head. It wasn't recent. That wasn't a bloke who just missed a call. That was a bloke who was done answering.

He clenched his jaw, forcing himself to focus.

"Who covered his shift?"

The officer scrolled through the log. "No one. He was on afternoons yesterday. Left when his shift was done, but didn't show up this morning."

Blake's fingers drummed against the desk.

That was worse. McBride hadn't called in sick. He hadn't swapped shifts. He'd just… vanished.

Blake looked up, his gut already telling him the next name to ask for. "Where's Callahan?"

The officer hesitated. "Callahan?"

Blake's eyes narrowed. He knew that hesitation.

"Yeah. Dave Callahan. Weekend detention guy. Supposed to be here."

The officer checked the log again, then frowned. "He was here last night. Came in to paint a cell."

Blake's pulse kicked.

"What cell?"

The officer sighed, rubbing his forehead like he already knew where this was going. "Red's old cell."

Blake went still.

For a moment, the entire prison faded around him. The fluorescent buzz, the distant clang of a gate locking, the murmur of guards in the hallway. All of it disappeared under the weight of that sentence.

Red's cell.

The last place the old bastard had breathed. The last place he'd bled. The last place he'd left something behind.

Blake turned and strode away, boots striking hard against the tile.

"Hey, uh —" the officer started, but Blake didn't stop.

McBride was missing.

Callahan had worked Red's cell, alone.

Blake wasn't leaving this to chance.

The hallway smelled of stale sweat and cheap industrial cleaner. The kind of scent that never quite left, no matter how many times it was scrubbed down. Blake pushed through the door to the wing, nodding once to the guard on duty.

"I need to see Redmond's old cell."

The guard gave him a look. "Bit late for that, isn't it?"

Blake didn't answer. Just waited.

The guard sighed, gestured him through. "Still smells like hell."

The second the door opened, the stench slammed into Blake. Not just the sweat and damp concrete. Something else. Something clinging beneath the surface. It had been cleaned, repainted, scrubbed down, but death never really left a place. It stayed.

He stepped inside, let his eyes adjust. The walls were fresh, covered in a layer of government-issue off-white, but something about them felt wrong. Too new. Too deliberate.

Blake's eyes flicked over the room. The position of the vent. The way the light from the corridor slanted in. The scuff marks near the door, half-covered by fresh paint.

Callahan had been in here.

Painting. Fixing things up. Doing a job.

Blake turned slowly, taking it in.

Something didn't sit right.

He walked to the wall, ran his hand along it. The paint was dry. No fresh streaks. But something about the texture. Something off, nagged at him. His fingers found a small raised bump, barely noticeable, beneath the layers of fresh paint.

He pressed against it, feeling the resistance.

He stood still for a moment. Red wasn't a fool.

Maybe something had been here. Maybe something had been covered.

Blake pulled back, stepped away.

If Callahan had found something, he'd taken it with him.

Blake squared up and straightened his coat.

He'd find Callahan.

Because if McBride had disappeared and Red's secrets had resurfaced, then Callahan was standing on a very thin patch of ice.

And Blake was going to be there when it cracked.

CHAPTER 19

Dave sat at the old kitchen table, its laminate surface scratched and stained, a ghost of past meals and forgotten mornings clinging to it. He stared at his sketches like they might rearrange themselves if he looked hard enough.

His hands were clenched on either side of the paper, knuckles pale, tendons standing out like cables under his skin. He'd been here for hours. Same chair. Same page. Same fucking dead ends.

It wasn't working.

The angles. The security light. The way it had slashed across the wall in Red's cell. It had all felt so goddamn obvious at the time. Like something sacred being revealed. Like a message lit just for him.

But now?

Now he was just a man hunched over half-sketched lines and second guesses.

His leg bounced under the table, the tremor running through him like a fault line about to give.

He turned the page sideways.

Then upside down.

Still nothing. Just smudged pencil and frustration.

He swore, low and bitter, pressing his palms hard into his face. The skin was hot beneath his hands.

The real map was gone. Scraped back to concrete. Painted over in a shade of institutional beige that might as well have been a burial shroud.

Lost forever.

He would've given a kidney to see it again. Even for a minute. Just long enough to fit the pieces together the way Red had meant them to be seen. Not this half-formed memory, warped and slipping.

But the wall was blank now. Like it had never held meaning. Like the map had never been real at all.

That was what kept cutting through him.

He'd never see it again.

And now, no matter how hard he tried to recall the streaks of light how they'd arced across the wall, where they'd landed, what they might have pointed to, it was fading. Slipping through him like smoke through cupped hands.

He shoved back from the table, the chair legs scraping loud against the lino, and paced to the sink. Gripped the edge of the benchtop with both hands until his fingernails ached.

The kitchen was still. Too still. No music, no TV. Just the quiet tick of the wall clock and the rustle of heat through the old flyscreen.

His eyes flicked up.

Just past noon.

He was running out of time. Tomorrow it all started again. The grind, the silence, the endless loop of work, sleep, work. The mask he wore at the job. The one he barely held together on the drive home.

He didn't want another week like that.

Didn't want to keep waking up at 3 a.m. wondering if he'd missed something. Wondering if Red had left a message he wasn't smart enough to read.

His mind reeled, looping through angles and guesses, trying to force something to click.

The light had hit three points.

Three exact spots.

One had landed just above where the map had been centred. He was sure of that.

The second, lower, near the rusted screw in the wall. His only real anchor.

But the third?

It wouldn't come.

It was right there, buried in his skull like a splinter he couldn't reach.

He slammed a hand against the counter. The sound cracked through the silence like a shot. His jaw clenched tight. This was driving him insane.

The coffee in his mug was stone cold now, a skin forming across the surface.

The room was still.

Too still.

No birds outside. No neighbours yelling through fences. Not even the hum of the fridge. Just the steady tick of the wall clock, and the sound of his own blood pushing through his ears.

Every second that passed, the memory slipped further away.

He turned back to the table and snatched up the pen, circling the known points again, pressing harder this time. Like pressure might force the answer loose.

Nothing.

His knee bounced, wild now, jittering the table.

His fingers clenched around the pen until the plastic creaked.

Where the hell was he going wrong? He just needed to see it one more time. One clean look at that wall. He was sure it would all fall into place.

Then —

The knock at the door.

Hard. Sharp. Final.

His head snapped up.

Pulse kicked in his throat.

Another knock. Louder. Heavier. Like they weren't asking anymore.

Dave set the pen down with care. Like it might go off.

His hand hovered there for a second, fingers twitching. A cold weight settled behind his ribs.

His gut was already screaming.

This wasn't good.

He pushed back from the table and moved toward the door, each step thudding louder than it should have. His boots felt like they were echoing through the walls.

At the window, he lifted the blind just enough to peer through the slats.

Two men stood on the porch.

Not cops. Not debt collectors.

But not good.

One was massive. Arms folded across his chest, built like a slab of concrete with eyes.

The other was leaner, colder, still. His sunglasses reflected the sky, but there was no warmth in his posture. Just stillness. Control.

Dave's jaw tightened.

He didn't know them. Not by name. Not by face.

But he knew what they were.

They knocked again.

He had two choices. Open the door or wait for them to do it the hard way.

His hand moved to the lock. Slow. Measured.

He twisted it.

And let them in.

The lean one stepped across the threshold first, moving like a man used to taking up space. No hesitation. No glance for permission.

Dave stayed where he was, arms folded, feet planted. Forcing them to come to him.

The big one followed, ducking slightly through the doorway. He pulled the screen shut behind him with a careless jerk. The rattle of the frame hit Dave like a warning shot.

"You Callahan?" the lean one asked.

Dave didn't answer.

The big one's eyes moved across the room. Took in the peeling paint, the cluttered table, the mess of sketches.

Then his gaze stopped. Locked onto the drawings.

And that was it.

That was the moment Dave knew.

They weren't here by chance.

The lean one sighed like the whole thing bored him already. "We should talk."

Dave's hands balled into fists at his sides.

"Don't think I know you."

A pause.

A flicker of something behind the sunglasses. Just a twitch, like the barest signal passing between wolves.

Then — fast — the lean one stepped deeper into the room.

Dave moved on instinct. He reached for the kitchen door, tried to push it shut, but the big bastard caught it mid-swing with one heavy hand.

A slow, creeping grin spread across the man's face. Then without a word he shoved the door open hard.

It crashed against the wall, slamming into Dave's shoulder and nearly throwing him off balance.

That was it.

That was the line crossed.

This wasn't a social call.

Not a warning. Not some debt collector bluff.

This was something else entirely.

The lean one's gaze swept the room again. His head barely moved, but his eyes scanned with purpose, until they landed on the table.

The sketches.

He stepped closer, casual as anything, and plucked one off the surface. Turned it sideways. Studied it.

"What's this?"

Dave forced his voice to stay steady. "Nothing."

The lean one let out a quiet breath through his nose, like he'd expected better. "That's a shame."

Then without warning, he flipped the table.

The whole thing went up with a violent crash. Papers, pens, and cold coffee scattered like shrapnel. The mug hit the tiles and exploded in a burst of ceramic.

Dave didn't flinch.

But his jaw locked tight.

The big one chuckled under his breath. A low, ugly sound that curled in the back of the throat.

The lean one stepped in closer now, close enough that Dave could smell the faint tang of cologne and sweat.

His voice dropped, smooth and deliberate.

"You were in Mudgee."

Dave held still.

"You were at the cenotaph. Hanging around. Watching. Fucking jogging."

No response.

Just the faint creak of Dave's teeth grinding together behind a clenched jaw.

Nothing.

The lean one clicked his tongue, like he was waiting for something that wasn't coming.

Then his tone shifted. Dropped, just enough to change the air in the room.

"We know you were in Red's cell."

A slow, crawling feeling crept into Dave's gut. Cold. Heavy.

"That's right," the lean one said with a small nod. "Cleaning. Painting. Seeing things. Remembering things."

Dave didn't move, but his jaw flexed. "And?"

"And," the lean one echoed, voice still maddeningly calm, "you're coming with us."

It wasn't a suggestion.

Dave's shoulders drew tight. "Why the fuck would I do that?"

The big one moved first.

A sudden, jarring shove, hard enough to send Dave slamming into the wall. Not a knockout blow. Just a warning. A message.

Dave gritted his teeth.

"Because we said so," the big one muttered.

His breath hitched, sharpened, body coiled like a spring. Ready to fight. Ready to run.

Then the lean one tilted his head.

A silent command.

The big bastard grabbed Dave by the shirt, spun him, and slammed him forward.

His chest hit the wall with a sickening thud.

Pain flared across his ribs. Sharp and hot.

Before he could react, his arms were wrenched behind his back, twisted up until his shoulders screamed.

He bit down on a groan, jaw clenched tight enough to crack a tooth.

The big one leaned in close, voice low and casual, like this was just another job.

"You don't wanna make this hard, mate."

Dave sucked in a sharp breath through his nose, shoulders still tense, eyes burning.

The lean one sighed and rubbed at his temple, like all this was giving him a headache.

"Let's go."

The big one didn't wait.

He yanked Dave back hard, dragging him toward the door like a misbehaving dog.

Dave fought, twisted, shoved, tried to plant his feet, but the bastard was a wall of muscle. Unmovable.

The screen door banged open, rattling against the frame.

Then they were outside.

The heat slammed into him like a wave. Dry. Brutal.

The whole street was quiet. Still. Not a single car. Not a neighbour peeking through the curtains.

No one to see.

No one to help.

Dave's boots scuffed against the concrete as they forced him across the yard, his body half-lifted, half-dragged.

Straight toward the Hilux.

The passenger door was already open, waiting like a mouth.

He dug his heels in. Useless.

The lean one slid into the driver's seat, one arm draped lazily over the wheel like this was just another trip to the shops.

Dave's head snapped toward him. "Where the fuck are we going?"

A pause.

Then the smallest flicker of a smile.

"To get some answers."

Then —

Lynch shoved him.

Hard.

Dave hit the seat awkwardly. The door slammed shut behind him.

The locks clicked.

The engine came to life with a low, satisfied growl.

And just like that, Dave Callahan disappeared.

CHAPTER 20

McBride groaned, spitting blood onto the cold concrete floor. His ribs screamed with every breath, his wrists raw where the ropes cut deep into his skin. The chair beneath him wobbled, one uneven leg scraping against the floor with every movement. The whole place stank of dust, oil, and the metallic tang of his own blood.

A warehouse, judging by the exposed beams above. Bare bulbs hummed against corrugated iron walls, their weak glow barely touching the corners of the room. The space before him was barren except for the table in front of him and the three men surrounding it. Nothing soft, nothing warm, nothing forgiving.

One of Zhao's men flexed his hand, shaking out his knuckles. His expression was blank, almost bored, like McBride's face had been nothing more than a punching bag for the last ten minutes. The other one stood by the door, arms crossed, unmoving. A presence more than a person. A threat held in reserve.

Zhao sat across from McBride, still as stone. A cigarette rolled lazily between his fingers, its tip burning low. His suit remained crisp, unruffled, like none of this mattered. Like the blood dripping from McBride's lip was just another minor inconvenience.

"You're lying," Zhao said. Soft. Measured.

Not a question. A statement.

McBride's throat was thick with blood and bile. "I told you what I know," he rasped. "Red's dead. The map's gone. That's it."

Zhao said nothing. Just flicked his fingers.

The fist came from nowhere. Driven into McBride's stomach like a hammer, folding him over. His breath tore out in a strangled wheeze, his vision flaring white. Bile surged up, thick and burning. He choked it back, blinking hard, his body trembling against the ropes.

Zhao's voice remained calm, patient. "Try again."

McBride coughed, dragging in a breath that felt like knives. His body sagged against the chair, but he forced himself upright. His voice came out hoarse. "I swear —"

The man behind him grabbed a fistful of his hair, wrenching his head back.

"There are others," Zhao murmured. "I want names."

McBride clenched his jaw.

He could hold out.

Another nod from Zhao.

The next punch shattered something. A wet, splintering crack inside his ribs, sharp enough to rip a sound from his throat that barely sounded human.

McBride let out a shuddering breath. His world was spinning now. The pain was real, a living, breathing thing inside him. His body screamed at him to fold, to give them something, anything, just to stop the fists, the fire in his ribs.

His mouth opened before he could stop it.

"Tombs," he wheezed. "Biker. Tough bastard. He's been looking for Red's stash, same as you."

Zhao didn't move. Didn't blink.

"Go on."

McBride squeezed his eyes shut. His whole body was trembling now.

The silence stretched.

Zhao's fingers twitched.

Another punch, a hammer against his side. The chair rocked. His whole world turned white.

McBride let out a weak, rattling breath. "Callahan."

That got Zhao's attention.

He leaned forward slightly, exhaling a thin stream of smoke.

McBride coughed, chest heaving. "Dave Callahan. Weekend detention guy. He was in Red's cell after he died."

A pause.

Zhao rolled the cigarette between his fingers. "Go on."

McBride licked the blood from his teeth. "He's on weekend detention at the prison. Does cleaning and stuff. He had access to Red's map. If anyone figured something out… it's him."

The cigarette stopped moving.

Zhao considered this. His face unreadable.

"Where is he?"

"Muswellbrook," McBride croaked. "Lives there. Works as a brickie." He swallowed hard, barely able to get the next part out. "He was in Red's cell again last night. Painting."

The cigarette rolled again between Zhao's fingers.

He said nothing, but his gaze had already moved on, ten steps ahead.

McBride knew he should stop talking. But fear had its claws in deep.

"There's one more," he croaked. His voice was weak, but the name carried weight.

"Blake."

Zhao's fingers stilled.

The air in the room shifted.

"Detective Sergeant Adrian Blake," McBride continued, spitting blood. "Dirty cop. He's been hunting Red's secret for years."

Silence.

Zhao didn't react, not at first. But something in his posture changed. Just a fraction.

Then, without warning, he lifted the glass ashtray from the table and smashed it against the wall.

Shards rained down like jagged ice.

McBride flinched. The guard behind him didn't.

Zhao stood. Adjusted his jacket with slow, practiced ease. Smoothed out the lapels like nothing had happened.

He looked down at McBride, his expression blank.

"That wasn't so difficult, was it?"

McBride's breathing was ragged. He knew better than to answer.

Zhao turned to his men and gave a small, almost imperceptible nod.

Then, without another word he walked out.

The door clicked shut.

McBride's stomach twisted.

He'd given them what they wanted.

But they weren't finished with him.

The big man flexed his fingers.

McBride barely had time to brace before the next blow landed.

Then everything went black.

Outside, Zhao moved through the warehouse, his steps slow, unhurried. He exhaled the last of his cigarette, flicking the smouldering stub away. Then, as he approached the waiting car, he spoke, voice low, deliberate.

A string of quiet Cantonese, sharp and efficient.

His driver nodded once, then reached for his phone.

Zhao slid into the back seat, closing the door with a soft click.

The warehouse behind him fell silent.

Somewhere in Muswellbrook, Dave Callahan had no idea that the hell he was in was about to escalate to a whole new level.

CHAPTER 21

Blake pulled up outside Callahan's house, the government-issued sedan rolling to a stop with a low hum. He didn't move immediately. Just sat there, fingers flexing against the wheel, scanning the place with a cop's eye.

Something was wrong.

It wasn't obvious, not the kind of thing that would make a neighbour stop and stare, but it was there. The bin near the porch had been knocked over, lid half-open, a few scraps of rubbish caught in the breeze. The curtain inside the front window hung slightly askew, as if someone had pulled it back too fast. The front door — shut, but not quite right.

Blake shifted in his seat, trying to ease the tightness that had settled in since dawn. His ribs ached, sleep had been scarce, and he trusted himself even less without it.

Still, the feeling in his gut was undeniable.

Something had happened here.

The afternoon sun was brutal, hammering the cracked pavement, making the air shimmer above the tin roofs. The kind of heat that made people slow, made them stay inside, made them avoid looking too closely at things that weren't their business.

Blake stepped out, adjusting his jacket, boots crunching over loose gravel as he moved toward the door. He tested the handle.

Unlocked.

His gut tightened.

He pushed it open slowly, the hinges groaning against the frame. Heat from inside rushed out to meet him, thick and stale, carrying the scent of dust, sweat, and something faintly metallic. Blood.

Blake's hand hovered near his weapon as he stepped inside, eyes scanning the room.

The mess hit him immediately.

The kitchen table had been knocked over, its legs tangled in the scattered chairs. Papers were everywhere — maps, scrawled notes, half-finished sketches. Some of the pages were crumpled, others torn at the edges, as if they'd been grabbed in a hurry.

Blake crouched, fingers brushing over one of the drawings. A crude, hand-drawn map. The roads of Mudgee. The cenotaph.

Fucking Callahan.

Blake flipped through the other sketches, each page rough and incomplete. Just fragments. But they meant something. A puzzle half-finished. A trail of thought, interrupted.

Then his fingers stopped.

A footprint. Smudged across one of the pages. Someone had stepped on it mid-struggle.

And just beside the overturned chair, streaked across the linoleum — a dark smear.

Blake pressed his lips together. Blood.

It wasn't a lot, but it was there.

His gaze lifted, tracing the scene, putting it together in his head. This wasn't a break-in for cash, or some junkie looking for something to sell. This was targeted. Someone had come here for a reason. Someone had been looking for something. Or someone.

A movement outside caught his attention.

Blake turned sharply, flicking his jacket back just enough to rest his hand on his gun.

Beyond the low front fence, a woman stood near her driveway, watching. Sixties, maybe older. Wiry, sharp-eyed. The kind of woman who saw everything that happened in her street. The kind who remembered.

She hesitated when he looked at her, like she was debating whether to say something.

Blake stepped outside, his movement slow and controlled. "You see anything?"

She licked her lips, glancing at the house. "Maybe."

He just waited. Didn't push. Didn't need to.

She caved fast.

"There were two of them," she said. "One was a big bloke. Rough-looking. Had one of those —" she motioned vaguely at her chest, "— biker patches."

Blake's pulse ticked up. Bikers. That narrowed things down.

"You see what it said?"

She shook her head. "Didn't get a good look."

"And the other?"

"Didn't see him too well. He kept back."

Blake stayed quiet, letting her talk.

"They had a ute — a Hilux, I think. Dark blue or black. Took the man from here. Didn't look friendly."

Blake already knew who they'd taken.

"You get the plate?"

The woman hesitated, then nodded. "Yeah. Wrote it down."

She reached into the pocket of her cardigan and pulled out a small notepad. An old habit, maybe. Maybe just the kind of person who noticed things. She read out the numbers.

Blake memorized them instantly.

"You call the cops?" he asked, already knowing the answer.

She stiffened. "Thought about it. But… bikers."

Didn't need to explain.

Blake just nodded, tucking the information away. He turned back toward his car, his mind already running.

Someone had Callahan.

Which meant Callahan had something worth taking.

He slid into the driver's seat, hands tightening around the wheel.

This wasn't just a beating.

This was a question.

And Blake needed the answer before Callahan talked.

CHAPTER 22

The ride was rough.

Dave's wrists burned, the zip ties biting deep every time the ute jolted over a pothole. Lynch sat beside him, his bulk pressing in, the bastard's beer-and-sweat stink clogging the air.

Tombs drove in silence. One hand on the wheel, the other drumming against his thigh. Steady. Measured. A man in control.

They turned off the highway onto a dirt track, winding through dry scrub. The place they stopped at looked like it had been abandoned decades ago. An old service station, windows boarded up, fuel pumps rusted to shit.

Ragged Sons territory.

Lynch yanked him from the ute and shoved him forward.

Inside, the air was thick and stale. Oil. Sweat. The tang of old cigarettes, edged with the sourness of weed. A pool table stood in the middle, its felt ripped, cigarette burns marking its edges. No other bikers. Just Tombs and Lynch.

This wasn't a gang clubhouse. This was a butcher's shop.

And Dave was the meat.

Tombs pulled out a knife.

"Relax," he said. "Just making things comfortable."

The blade flashed, slicing through the zip ties. Blood rushed back into Dave's fingers, pins and needles crawling up his arms.

Didn't last long.

Lynch's heavy hand clamped down on his shoulder, shoving him into a chair.

Tombs sat across from him, elbows on his knees, casual as a man having a smoke on his front porch. "You thirsty? Beer? Something stronger?"

Dave stared at him, saying nothing.

Tombs sighed. "Look, I don't wanna do this the hard way. You've got something we want. Let's talk."

Dave smirked, wiping blood from his split lip. "Yeah? And what's your definition of 'hard'?"

Lynch chuckled. "You'll find out."

Tombs gave a patient nod. "Where's the map lead?"

Dave didn't answer.

Tombs rubbed his jaw. "Alright then." He reached into his pocket and pulled out his phone.

"Let me show you something."

He swiped through a set of photos. First, the cenotaph in Mudgee. Empty. Rain-slicked.

Next — Blake. That wiry bastard standing in the shadows, watching.

Then — the suits. The Asian blokes in the luxury car.

Tombs held up the next photo, and Dave's stomach went cold.

A jogger. Hood up. Mid-stride.

Him.

Tombs smirked. "See, I wasn't sure at first. Just some random jogger, right? But then…" He swiped to the last photos.

The map.

Red's wall. The scrawled markings. The crayon. The numbers.

Dave's throat dried. He kept his face blank.

Tombs watched him. "I know you saw it. And I know you worked it out. So, let's try again. Where's it lead?"

Dave clenched his jaw.

Tombs rubbed his jaw. "Alright then." He glanced at Lynch.

Lynch cracked his knuckles and reached for him.

Dave moved fast. Braced his feet. Swung hard.

His fist connected clean, snapping Lynch's head sideways. A solid hit.

Lynch turned back, smiled.

And threw a punch that detonated inside Dave's skull.

The second blow caved into his ribs, a deep, sickening crunch that stole his breath. He doubled over, gasping. Lynch hauled him back up like a rag doll.

Then came the rope. Arms yanked behind his back, tied tight. No more quick moves. No more smart-ass grins.

Just pain.

Measured. Precise. Designed to hurt.

Fists slammed into his stomach, his ribs, his face. The chair rocked with the force of it. Dave's head snapped back, stars exploding behind his eyes. His body screamed for air, for relief.

Tombs leaned in. "Let's try again. Where's it lead?"

Dave spat blood onto the floor.

Tombs sighed. "Alright. Guess we do this properly."

Lynch stepped away, returning with something in his hand. A knife? Pliers? A blowtorch? Dave's vision blurred too much to tell.

Then —

BANG.

A loud, heavy pounding at the door.

Not a knock. A demand.

The room went still.

Lynch frowned and moved to check, cracking the door open.

A man stepped inside.

Dark suit. Unshaken. Unhurried. His gaze swept the room like he already owned it.

Zhao.

But Tombs didn't know that name.

And he sure as hell didn't like the attitude. "Who the fuck are you?"

Zhao didn't answer. Didn't even look at him. Didn't tell him that McBride had told them everything. His eyes landed on Dave — tied up, bleeding. Then flicked back to Lynch.

"Who is this?" Zhao asked, voice smooth as glass.

Lynch smirked. "No one you need to worry about."

Zhao's expression didn't change. "I asked a question."

Lynch's smirk flickered.

Tombs leaned back, jaw tight. "Look, mate — this is club business. Whatever you're after, you're in the wrong fucking room."

Zhao finally looked at him. A slow, measured glance. Then, just as casually —

"Untie him."

Lynch folded his arms. "Nah."

A heartbeat of silence.

Then Zhao moved.

The gun was in his hand so fast it barely seemed real.

Barrel pressed against Tombs' forehead.

Tombs froze.

"Untie him," Zhao repeated.

Lynch hesitated. Just for a second.

Too long.

Zhao's breath left him quiet and cold. Then he turned the gun to Lynch. A sharp, precision movement —

BLAM.

The gunshot shattered the silence.

Lynch's head snapped back, red mist bursting from his skull. His body hit the floor with a wet thud.

No one spoke.

Tombs' hands twitched toward his waistband — stupid, instinctive. Zhao was already ahead of him.

The gun whipped back — not to fire, but to strike. CRACK — the barrel slammed against Tombs' temple. He dropped hard, out cold before he hit the ground.

Zhao turned back to Dave.

The ropes came loose. Blood rushed back into his arms. His body screamed with every movement, but relief swelled through him.

For half a second.

Then Zhao leaned in, voice quiet. Too quiet.

"You are coming with me."

Dave swallowed hard.

His eyes flicked to the floor.

Tombs' phone lay face-up, the screen dark.

Dave reached for it, slow and deliberate, like it was his own. "I need my phone."

Zhao watched him, unreadable. Then, almost amused, he gave the smallest nod. Silent approval.

Dave palmed the device, but before slipping it away, his gaze shifted to Tombs' slumped body. His expression hardened, lips pressing into a thin line.

"This one dead?" His voice was hoarse, thick with blood and exhaustion.

Zhao didn't answer immediately. His gaze flicked toward the door, a slight frown creasing his forehead.

A noise outside.

Soft. Faint.

A dog barking in the distance.

Zhao barely reacted, but his head tilted slightly, attention shifting for just a second.

Dave used it.

He crouched, pretending to check Tombs for a pulse.

His fingers brushed the man's jaw, tilting his face just enough — just for a second. He could feel Tombs breath against his palm, hot and shallow, like a man clinging on from somewhere far away.

The phone vibrated softly in his grip.

Unlocked. Facial Recognition.

Dave didn't linger. He let Tombs' head drop back, wiped his bloody hand on his jeans, and pushed himself upright.

Zhao's eyes were back on him now, the moment gone.

"Move."

Dave slid the phone into his pocket. His ribs screamed. His head throbbed. But he had it. The map was in Tombs' phone.

Didn't mean he was safe. Didn't mean he hadn't just been involved in some twisted prisoner exchange program.

Just meant he had a chance.

For now.

CHAPTER 23

Detective Sergeant Adrian Blake turned off the highway, the tyres kicking up a trail of fine dust as the sedan rolled onto the dirt track. The road was rough, uneven, riddled with potholes that jostled the car with every dip. The sun was dropping lower, stretching the shadows of the scrub, twisting them into long, jagged fingers. It was dry out here. The kind of dry that made the air taste like rust, that made everything brittle — land, trees, even the people who called this place home.

Ragged Sons territory.

Blake had never had a reason to come out here before. The local uniforms turned a blind eye to these blokes, letting them play tough in the sticks while the real criminals operated elsewhere. Petty shit. Fights. Stand-over work. Nothing that made headlines. But now? Now someone had made a mistake.

The old service station loomed ahead, slouched and forgotten, boarded-up windows staring out like blind eyes. The rusted fuel pumps stood leaning, their faded price displays frozen in time. The building itself was barely standing, its roof sagging like an old man's shoulders.

But it wasn't abandoned.

Two bikes were parked out front. Harleys. Not just passing through, then.

Blake killed the engine, but didn't move right away. His gut told him to take a second. He scanned the scene, noting the fresh tyre tracks in the dust, the way the weeds near the porch had been recently trampled. Someone had been here. Someone had left in a hurry.

He stepped out, boots crunching on gravel. The heat was thick, pressing down on him, the kind that made everything feel slower, heavier. The scent of dust and oil clung to the air, but beneath it, something else. Something sour.

Blood.

His fingers hovered near his holster as he approached the warped wooden steps. They groaned under his weight. He pushed open the door.

Inside, the air was thick. Stale. The remains of cigarette smoke clung to the walls, mixing with sweat and old beer. The pool table in the centre of the room was a wreck — its felt torn, the edges scarred with burns. The overhead light cast weak yellow circles across the floor.

Two bikers stood near the bar.

Scar-Eye. Built like a fridge, a scar splitting through his left eyebrow. The other was younger, wiry, fingers twitching. A rag in one hand. A mop bucket near his feet.

Cleaning.

Blake's stomach turned.

"What's the rush?" His voice was casual, but sharp enough to cut.

Scar-Eye gave a thin smile. "Just keeping the place tidy."

Blake stepped further inside, his eyes moving over the scene like a camera lens, taking in the details. The scratches on the wooden floor. The faint drag marks near the pool table. Then —

The stain.

Dark. Wet. Seeping into the cracks.

Not oil. Not beer.

Blood.

He followed the trail around the table. His jaw tightened.

A body.

Sprawled on the floor, arms limp, eyes open but vacant. A bullet hole dead centre in his forehead. Close range. No hesitation.

Blake crouched, pressing two fingers to the neck, more out of habit than anything. Nothing. Cold, but not long dead. The metallic scent filled his nostrils. He straightened slowly.

"Who's the stiff?"

Scar-Eye didn't blink. "No one that concerns you."

Blake tilted his head, eyes narrowing. "You see a badge on me?"

Scar-Eye hesitated. The younger biker swallowed.

Blake looked back at the mop bucket. "You always this eager to scrub your floors?"

Scar-Eye's lips twitched, but he didn't answer.

Blake let the silence stretch before speaking again. "Tombs called, didn't he? Told you to clean this up."

Scar-Eye gave a slight nod. "Yeah."

Blake folded his arms. "Why?"

Another pause. Then, finally —

"Someone walked in. Shot him like it was nothing. Took the bloke Tombs and Lynch had grabbed."

Blake's pulse ticked up. Callahan. It had to be.

He turned to the younger biker. "Who?"

The kid hesitated. Wrong move.

Blake grabbed his vest and slammed him against the bar.

The kid yelped, struggling. "I — I wasn't here!"

Blake's grip tightened. "Then why the fuck are you cleaning up?"

The kid swallowed hard. "I just got called in! I didn't see it happen!"

Blake released him, stepping back. His jaw clenched. Too many gaps. Too many missing pieces. But one thing was clear — Tombs wasn't in control anymore.

He turned back to Scar-Eye. "Where's Tombs?"

Scar-Eye smirked. "Like we'd tell you."

Blake didn't blink. Didn't speak. Just stared. The kind of stare that made people second-guess their next words.

Scar-Eye's smirk cracked. "Tombs is keeping his head down. He's all busted up. That's all I got."

Blake scanned the room again. The blood. The body. The bikers trying to wipe away a murder like it was spilt beer. He pulled his phone from his pocket. Snapped a photo.

Scar-Eye's whole posture stiffened.

"You calling that in?" His voice was forced.

Blake slipped the phone back into his jacket. "Not yet."

The younger biker swallowed.

Scar-Eye shifted his weight. "That a threat?"

Blake tilted his head slightly. "That's a timer."

Scar-Eye muttered something under his breath.

Blake turned for the door, pausing at the threshold.

"If I were you," he said, voice calm, quiet, dangerous, "I'd tell your boss that if he doesn't find me first —"

His hand hovered near his holster.

"I'll find him."

Then he stepped outside.

The sun was setting.

Time was running out.

And for the first time in a long time — Blake wasn't sure if he was chasing ghosts or being followed by them.

CHAPTER 24

Dave's world was darkness.

The bag over his head stank of sweat and old canvas, the thick, suffocating scent pressing in on him. It triggered something deep in his memory — the smell of his footy kit after a wet game, the damp fabric clinging to his skin. And worse, it reminded him of the grand final. The knockout hit. The flash of white. Waking up in the sheds, missing the rest of the game, missing the win. That same helplessness crawled through his chest now, only this time, there was no waking up to teammates celebrating.

They'd dragged him out of the Ragged Sons' clubhouse, thrown him into a car, and driven him... somewhere. No sirens. No talking. Just the hum of an engine, the occasional crunch of gravel beneath the tyres.

Now he was here.

Wherever here was.

A chair beneath him. A cold floor. His wrists were pulled back — bound, but not with zip ties. Something thinner. Tighter. Cord, wound with discipline. His fingers tingled, circulation already fading. They hadn't done that for fun. That was precision. That was intent.

A voice. Calm. Unhurried. "You have my attention, Mr. Callahan."

The bag was ripped from his head.

Blinding light. A flood of white-hot agony seared through his skull as his vision swam, spots bursting across his eyes. His stomach lurched. The air smelled of concrete, sweat, and blood — so much blood.

The room was bare. Windowless. A cell, not an office.

Zhao stood before him, hands folded neatly behind his back. The same man who had walked into the Ragged Sons' clubhouse, executed Lynch in cold blood, and taken Dave like he was collecting a debt.

Back then, Dave had thought he was being saved.

Now, blinking in the harsh overhead light, he wasn't so sure.

Two black-clad men flanked Zhao. Silent. Still. Efficient.

And then there was the fifth man.

Dave hadn't noticed him at first. A second chair sat beside him, positioned at an angle. A figure slumped forward in it, hooded, unmoving.

Still.

Breathing. Possibly.

But for how much longer?

Zhao studied Dave for a moment, then spoke.

"Let's talk, Mr. Callahan."

Dave swallowed. His throat was raw and dry — probably from screaming.

He clenched his jaw, trying to steady the thump in his chest.

"Funny way of asking."

Zhao's lips twitched slightly. "You intrigue me."

He took a step closer. "Why were you at the cenotaph in Mudgee?"

Dave's pulse spiked.

They knew.

He hesitated.

A nod from Zhao.

One of the men moved fast. A sharp, precise punch — measured, controlled.

A rib shot.

Pain tore through Dave's side. He gritted his teeth, breathing through it.

Zhao waited.

Dave let out a short breath, rough with pain. "I was curious."

Zhao's expression didn't change. "Curious?"

"Curious," Dave rasped. "About who else showed up."

Another nod.

Another gut punch.

Dave convulsed, stomach threatening to empty, breath coming in short gasps. The restraints kept him upright when he would've doubled over.

Zhao crouched slightly, tilting his head. "This will continue until I am satisfied."

Dave forced a weak smirk. "You want me to talk? Why not ask McBride? He was there."

Silence.

Zhao's expression barely changed. A flicker of something unreadable.

"Yes," he murmured. "Let's ask him."

A gesture.

The man behind Dave yanked the bag off the other prisoner's head.

Then kicked Dave's chair sideways.

His vision spun as he was turned toward the other chair —

And his breath stopped.

McBride.

Or what was left of him.

His head lolled unnaturally, jaw slack, mouth slightly open like he'd tried to get the last word in. One eye was gone — a bullet hole punched clean through the socket, dark and sunken. Blood had trickled down his cheek, now dried into a gruesome streak. The wound wasn't fresh, but the pool of black-red beneath his chair said it hadn't been long.

A sour, coppery smell clogged Dave's throat.

His body jerked before he could stop it — a reflexive recoil. His wrists pulled at the bindings, his breathing turning sharp, uneven.

No. No, no, no —

Zhao adjusted his sleeve, voice light. Almost amused.

"So, Mr. McBride," he said, turning to the corpse. "What can you tell us?"

Dave's stomach twisted.

He wasn't being interrogated.

He was being shown what came next.

CHAPTER 25

B lake pulled off the main road onto the winding track toward Lake Glenbawn, the sedan's tyres crunching over dry gravel. Dust rolled up in thick plumes behind him, catching in the stagnant summer air. The lake stretched out ahead, shimmering under the punishing afternoon sun, its surface so bright it hurt to look at directly.

The water was low — too many dry seasons bleeding it out — but still deep enough to glisten like glass where the sun caught it. Gums leaned lazily over the shoreline, their bark stripped pale by the elements. Further along, campers had set up by the water's edge — families, kids splashing, tinny radios buzzing with sport, raucous music and lazy laughter.

But Blake wasn't here for a weekend away.

The tip from Tombs' wife hadn't come easy. At first, she'd clammed up, arms folded, chin lifted in defiance. But then Blake had laid it out — the way Lynch had been found, a bullet in the skull. The way Tombs might end up if he wasn't careful.

That had cracked her.

"We've got a caravan at Lake Glenbawn."

And here it was.

Blake slowed as he reached the clearing, his grip flexing on the wheel. The caravan sat in the shade of a leaning gum tree, paint sun-bleached, but otherwise well-kept. Not some hovel in the scrub. This was a proper setup

— a getaway. Somewhere a bloke brought his family when he wanted to escape everything else.

A Harley sat beside it, partially covered with a canvas sheet, the shape unmistakable.

Got you.

Blake rolled to a stop, killed the engine, and barely had time to register movement before the caravan door flew open.

Tombs bolted.

Blake didn't hesitate.

"Stop, you bastard!"

Tombs didn't.

He tore through the scrub, boots crunching over dead leaves, shoulders hunched low as he ran. He was fast — fast enough to make it to the tree line. But he was panicked. And panic made men sloppy. He glanced back, misstepped on a root, stumbled.

Blake lunged.

Grabbed the back of his shirt.

And slammed him into a tree.

Tombs hit hard, the breath leaving his body in a choked grunt. He twisted, throwing an elbow — caught Blake in the ribs.

Bad move.

Blake bared his teeth, swung hard, and drove a fist deep into his gut.

Tombs doubled over, wheezing.

Blake didn't wait.

He wrenched his arms back and snapped the cuffs on. "You're under arrest, you piece of shit."

Tombs spat into the dirt. "For what?"

Blake yanked him toward the car. "Resisting, for starters. And we'll work our way up from there."

The drive back was long. Too quiet.

Tombs slouched in the back seat, wrists twisted awkwardly in the cuffs. He shifted constantly, muscles flexing and twitching against the restraint. The leather of the backseat was scorching against his skin, and the lack of movement made the discomfort worse. Blake could feel his agitation filling the space between them.

"You know," Blake muttered, adjusting the rear-view mirror, "you might be the only bloke dumb enough to try running in a place with one road in and one road out."

Tombs didn't rise to it. He was thinking. Calculating.

Blake let the silence stretch before he spoke again. "Let's talk about Callahan."

Tombs scoffed. "Who?"

Blake's jaw tightened.

He flicked the wheel, sending the car swerving onto the gravel shoulder.

Tombs' body lurched sideways, the cuffs biting deeper into his wrists. "Jesus —"

Blake straightened. "You think I'm your biggest problem? That means you know exactly who is."

Tombs stayed quiet, staring out the window, jaw tight.

Blake's lip curled. "Fine. Let's talk about your wife instead."

That got a reaction.

Tombs' head snapped up.

"Nice woman," Blake continued. "Still trying to protect you, even now." He glanced in the mirror. "But you think whoever took Callahan is gonna stop at you?"

Tombs' shoulders tensed.

Blake let it hang. Let him picture it. Not himself. The real people looking for him.

"If they came for her," Blake pressed, "you think she'd get off as easy as Lynch did?"

That broke through.

Tombs' breath left him in a harsh grunt. "They fucking killed Lynch," he muttered. "Put a bullet in his head. Took Callahan."

Blake kept his eyes on the road. "Who?"

Tombs hesitated. "I don't know his name. Asian guy. Suit. Dead-eyed. Walked in, took over."

Blake processed that. Someone outside the usual gangs. Not a street thug. Someone clean. Connected.

This was worse than he thought.

Tombs shifted. "They took my phone."

Blake glanced at him. "Who?"

Tombs shook his head. "I don't know. The Asian guy, probably. Maybe Callahan. Someone has it."

Blake sat with that for a second. Then flipped open his own phone. "Call it."

Tombs hesitated.

Blake turned in his seat, voice cold. "Call. It."

Tombs licked his lips. "We should track it instead."

Blake's eyes flickered. He exhaled, considering.

He pulled the car to the side of the road, opened the rear door and eyed Tombs.

"Don't make me regret this."

He removed the cuffs, then he handed Tombs the phone.

Tombs shook his uncuffed hands awkwardly, and began tapping in the details.

A location popped up.

Blake stared at the screen. Then snapped the phone shut.

He shifted into gear.

"Buckle up."

CHAPTER 26

Dave's world had shrunk to pain, sweat, and the weight of Zhao's stare. His wrists throbbed, raw from the bindings. His ribs ached with every shallow breath. But none of that mattered. He was still alive. And as long as he was breathing, he had options. He just had to wait for the right one.

Zhao's eyes stayed on him, unreadable. Behind him, two of his men loomed near the door, silent, waiting. The air was thick, humid with sweat, fear, and something darker.

Then Zhao spoke. "Let's talk about what you know. About the map. Tell us everything."

Dave swallowed against the dryness in his throat, keeping his expression flat. "I don't remember shit like that," he muttered. "That's why I write stuff down."

The moment the words left his mouth, he felt the mistake. Zhao tilted his head slightly. "So perhaps you've written it down. At home. Drawn it, maybe?"

Dave fumbled. "I mean… maybe. I might've sketched something."

Zhao barely reacted. "I don't enjoy wasting time, Mr. Callahan." He flicked two fingers toward his men. "We'll confirm that for ourselves."

One of the guards nodded and moved toward the door. Zhao turned to follow.

Dave's stomach lurched.

If Zhao got his hands on those sketches, it was over. They didn't have to be perfect — just enough to keep Zhao interested. Enough to put Dave on the radar of men who never let things go.

He needed to shift the game. Fast.

"Wait." His voice cracked, rough from exhaustion. "I —" He hesitated, looking like he was struggling to hold onto something. "I remember something."

Zhao paused. Turned slightly. Watching.

Dave blinked like he was trying to hold onto a thought. "It's coming back, but… if I don't write it down, I'll lose it." He forced a weak chuckle. "You'd be pissed if I forgot something important, right?"

Zhao's silence stretched. Then, finally, a small nod. "Write it down."

The remaining guard hesitated, looking toward Zhao.

"Untie him. Give him something," Zhao ordered, already halfway to the door. "If he tries anything, break his hands."

Then he was gone. The door clicked shut behind him, and the heavy bolt slid into place.

Dave's pulse kicked up.

One guard.

The man moved to a rusted metal cabinet, pulling out a battered notepad and a cheap ballpoint pen. He tossed them onto the table beside Dave.

The guard was younger than the others. A thickset guy with a shaved head, his expression flat but wary. Dave knew the type. Hired muscle, not a killer. And judging by the way he hesitated before stepping back, he wasn't used to giving orders — only following them.

Dave flexed his fingers. His hands were stiff, blood barely flowing back into them. He reached for the pen, held it between shaking fingers, let the tip hover over the page.

Then, in a single motion, he snapped it.

Ink spurted across his fingers, across the table.

The guard frowned. "No break." His English was broken, thickly accented. He stepped forward, brow furrowed.

Dave moved.

He lunged, driving the jagged pen shaft into the man's neck — just below the jaw. Not deep, but sharp enough to draw blood.

The guard yelled, flinched back, hand flying up. Dave didn't stop. He grabbed the chair, kicked it aside, then drove the guard backwards — slammed him face-first into the edge of the table.

Bone met hardwood with a sickening thud.

The guard collapsed sideways, groaning once before going limp.

Dave stood there, chest heaving, ink and blood dripping from his fingers.

Nothing. The guy wasn't getting up.

Dave didn't waste time. He patted down the body — no phone, no weapon.

His fingers went to his pocket.

Tombs' phone.

He pulled it out, thumbed the screen.

Locked.

"Shit."

His eyes flicked to McBride's body.

He didn't know if McBride had a phone. But if he did…

Dave swallowed against the rising bile as he stepped closer.

McBride's head lolled unnaturally, jaw slack, blood pooling beneath the chair. His hand — or what was left of it — hung limp, fingers missing. The wounds were dark and clotted.

Dave's gut twisted.

His gaze shifted to the small table nearby. A second phone lay there.

He grabbed it. Pressed the power button.

Locked.

His pulse pounded.

His eyes moved back to McBride's hands.

Or what was left of them.

His throat tightened.

No other choice.

He crouched, forcing himself to pick up the severed thumb. It was cold. Too light in his hand. His stomach churned, but he pressed it to the phone.

The screen unlocked.

Dave wiped his bloody hands on his jeans, jaw clenched.

He moved fast, fingers flying through the gallery.

There.

The photos. The map. Red's scribbled scrawl. The numbers. The landmarks.

He didn't hesitate.

Tapped the share function. Scanned options.

An idea hit.

One shot. One play.

He searched the phone for an website he hadn't used in years. The one place where nobody asked questions about digital orders. They just printed them and most of the time, damn quick.

Photo Lab.

He attached a vague note. Print ASAP. Will collect.

Sent.

A noise outside.

A door.

Dave's head snapped up. Footsteps. Heavy. Close.

He bolted.

Through a rusted side door, into a storage shed thick with dust and forgotten junk. Metal shelves, discarded tyres, old oil drums.

He didn't stop — because if they caught him again, they wouldn't bother leaving a body.

CHAPTER 27

The alley stank of piss and rotting food, the air thick with decay, but Dave didn't slow down. His legs burned, his ribs screamed, and his pulse thundered in his ears. He wasn't even sure if Zhao's men were behind him. His body just kept moving, pure animal instinct, the desperate drive to survive overriding everything else.

The world was narrowed to shadows, the uneven pavement slick beneath his boots. A bin rattled as he brushed too close. A cat bolted past, sending a beer bottle skittering. He flinched hard, half expecting hands to grab him, to drag him back into the dark.

Then —

Headlights.

Blinding, burning, cutting through the night.

Dave staggered, blinking against the sudden glare. His chest heaved, his vision swimming. The alley opened into a street, empty but for the idling sedan parked at the curb.

A cop car.

Blake.

And in the back seat — Tombs.

Shit.

For half a second, every part of him screamed to keep running. Didn't matter that he was battered, exhausted. Running had kept him alive this long. But where? There was nowhere left to go.

He lunged for the passenger door, yanked it open, and threw himself inside.

"Drive. For fuck's sake, drive."

Blake didn't move. Didn't even flinch. He turned his head slowly, his expression unreadable, taking in the sweat, the blood, the wild-eyed panic rolling off Dave like heat off the road.

"This ain't a fuckin' Uber, mate."

Dave twisted in his seat, scanning the alley, waiting for figures to step out of the dark, for headlights to creep toward them. His whole body braced for it. But the street was empty. No movement. No sound beyond his own ragged breathing.

That was worse.

Blake must've caught something in his face — the sheer animal desperation — because without another word, he put the car into gear and pulled away.

Not fast. Not peeling out. Smooth. Controlled.

Like a man who didn't rattle easy.

In the back seat, Tombs let out a low whistle. "Jesus. You look like shit."

Dave gave a rough grunt. "Feel like it, too."

His ribs ached with every breath. His hands were numb. His jaw throbbed where Lynch had landed that first hit. He was bleeding somewhere — he could taste it in his mouth, feel it slick in the creases of his knuckles.

But he was alive.

Blake drove in silence for a moment, his fingers tapping the wheel. "You wanna tell me what the hell you were running from?"

Dave pressed a hand against his side. Every word felt like a knife in his ribs. "McBride's dead."

Silence.

Tombs stopped moving. Just sat there, stiff and still.

Blake's eyes flicked up to the rearview. "You sure?"

Dave reached into his pocket.

Not the one with Tombs' phone.

The other one.

He hesitated for half a second.

Then he pulled it out.

McBride's thumb.

Shrivelled, crusted with dried blood. Stiff with rigor. He held it up, let the streetlights flash over it as the car rumbled along.

"Still don't believe me?"

Then — he dropped it into Blake's lap.

The car swerved.

"FUCKING HELL!" Blake barked, jerking the wheel to straighten them out.

Tombs made a low noise, half a snort, half something else. "Well," he muttered, voice tight, "that's one way to give the cops the finger."

Blake didn't speak.

His knuckles were white on the wheel, jaw clenched so hard Dave thought his teeth might crack. He grabbed a napkin from the console and pinched the thumb between its edges, his nostrils flaring as he shoved it into the glovebox like a rotten sandwich.

"Jesus Christ." His voice was hoarse. "That's gonna stink up the car."

"Yeah, well, McBride's gonna stink up that shed a lot worse," Dave muttered. "That's if they don't torch it to get rid of the evidence."

Blake stiffened. "They?"

Dave ran a hand over his face. "No clue who they are. But they're professional. Asian and deadly as all fuck. They don't fuck around."

Blake's eyes sharpened. "What did you tell them?"

Dave hesitated. "That my notes were at my place."

Blake swore under his breath.

"That's where they are now," Dave added. "Him and his mate. Probably ripping my house apart."

Blake tapped his fingers against the wheel. "Then I guess we know where we're going."

Tombs scoffed. "You think you can take on these guys? Jesus, Blake. You heard what they did to McBride. You saw his fucking thumb."

Blake turned, meeting his eyes in the rearview mirror. "You saying you don't want payback?"

Tombs clenched his jaw. Didn't answer.

Blake smirked. "Didn't think so."

A silence settled over them. Heavy. Charged.

Dave shifted, his back pressing into the worn seat, the smell of leather and old coffee wrapping around him. He still felt rattled, still jumped at every noise outside, but for the first time since this whole nightmare had started, the car felt safe.

Or at least, safer than anywhere else.

Blake turned onto the highway, the engine humming beneath them, the road stretching ahead.

For a long moment, nobody spoke.

The tyres hummed. The dashboard lights glowed softly.

Blake flexed his hands on the wheel, loosening the grip.

"Let's go ruin someone's fucking day."

CHAPTER 28

Blake's car rumbled through the darkened streets, headlights cutting through the night. The air inside was thick, the kind of quiet that came before a storm.

Dave sat in the passenger seat, knee bouncing, his head spinning with second thoughts.

I should bail.

This was madness.

McBride was dead, butchered like an animal. Zhao had nearly done the same to him. And now, instead of getting as far away from this as possible, he was riding shotgun with a possibly dirty cop and a biker — heading straight for the one man who wanted him dead the most.

Blake, though? Blake was in his element.

"We go in fast. We go in hard. Zhao's not expecting us — he thinks you're still tied to a chair, Callahan. That's our edge."

Tombs, now uncuffed, rubbed his still sore wrists in the backseat. "You sound like you've done this before."

Blake smirked. "I have."

Dave shifted in his seat. "This a good idea?"

"No," Blake admitted. "But it's the only play we've got."

That answer sat like lead in Dave's gut.

"If this is so solid," he asked, "why aren't we calling backup?"

Blake didn't even hesitate. "Because I don't want other cops in on this."

That sounded shady as hell.

Before Dave could press him, Blake reached under his seat and pulled out two pistols. He kept one for himself, weighing the other in his palm like he was picking a winning horse.

Tombs leaned forward. "If you're handing that out, I'll take it."

Blake hesitated — then flipped the pistol, grip first, toward the biker. "Don't make me regret that."

Tombs checked the mag, racked the slide — smooth, practiced. If he'd been rattled earlier, he wasn't anymore.

Blake didn't even look at Dave.

"You're not giving me one?" Dave asked.

Blake shot him a glance. "Mate, you just got out of a torture session. You're shaking like a shithouse in a cyclone."

Dave wanted to argue, but… yeah. He was.

His hands were trembling. His ribs ached. His whole body was running on fumes.

The car rolled to a stop outside Dave's house.

The front light was on.

The door… slightly ajar.

They were inside.

Blake stared for a moment, then nodded once. "Alright. Let's go."

Inside was a disaster.

Drawers yanked out, contents scattered across the floor. Shelves ripped from the walls, cushions slashed open, stuffing floating like ash.

And standing in the middle of it all?

Zhao.

Calm. Focused. Methodically sorting through papers.

A brick wall of a man stood by the kitchen — Zhao's muscle. A human wrecking ball just waiting for an excuse.

For a second, nobody moved.

Then Blake raised his gun.

The goon was fast.

He lunged — knocking Blake's pistol from his hand, sending it skidding under the couch.

Then all hell broke loose.

Tombs snapped up his pistol, fired twice at Zhao. The bullets shattered a lamp, punched into the wall — but Zhao was already moving.

He dived behind the kitchen counter.

Dave scrambled to cut him off, keeping low.

Blake and the goon?

They were going to war.

Fists flew — bone cracking against bone. The goon grabbed Blake, slammed him into the fridge hard enough to knock the magnets off.

Blake grunted, drove a knee into the bastard's ribs, then unleashed a flurry of punches into his gut.

The goon just grinned.

Spit blood.

Then grabbed Blake by the throat, hurled him across the now upright kitchen table — splitting it in half.

Blake hit the floor, gasping. The goon came after him.

Blake grabbed a broken chair leg, swung it full force into the bastard's skull.

The wood splintered.

The goon barely flinched.

Blake scrambled for his gun.

The goon grabbed a knife off the counter, raised it —

Two bullets punched through his forehead.

Blake had recovered his pistol and fired without hesitation.

The man staggered.

Like he hadn't realized he was dead yet.

Then collapsed.

At the same time, Zhao made his move.

He popped up from cover, trading shots with Tombs, forcing the biker back.

Dave dove low, trying to cut Zhao off.

Zhao saw him.

Saw the fight turning against him.

He needed an exit.

His eyes flicked across the room — searching.

And then —

He made his decision.

He reached into his coat, pulled out a metal flask. Unscrewed it smoothly, without panic.

Dave barely had time to react before Zhao hurled the liquid across the cushions, the curtains, the ripped stuffing.

A sharp, acrid smell filled the air.

Petrol.

Zhao pulled a lighter from his pocket, flipped it open with a click.

Held it just long enough for them to see it.

Then dropped it.

Flames exploded to life.

They raced up the walls, swallowed the furniture, turned the carpet into an inferno.

Dave stumbled back, heat licking at his skin.

Blake swore. "Son of a bitch set the place up!"

Tombs fired at Zhao — but Zhao was already gone.

Blake turned, eyes darting to the fire already reaching the ceiling. "We need to go. Now."

Dave clenched his jaw. His home was going up in flames, and all he could do was watch it burn.

As they moved toward the door, Blake glanced at the goon's body — flames licking at his boots, creeping up his legs. His mind worked fast, weighing the risk.

A corpse burned beyond recognition? No prints. No ID. No trail back to them.

He didn't hesitate. "Leave him."

Tombs frowned. "What?"

Blake didn't look back. "Fire's doing us a favour. He's just a body in a torched house now."

Tombs grunted but didn't argue.

They stepped outside. The night air was thick with smoke and heat.

And that's when Blake saw it.

The curtain. The movement.

Across the street, a shadow shifted behind the glass — barely visible through the smoke-hazed glow of the streetlights.

Blake's jaw clenched. "We're done. We need to go. Now."

Tombs hesitated. "What —"

Blake shoved him toward the car. "Nosy neighbour. Probably already reaching for the phone."

Dave barely glanced back at his house — his life going up in flames. But he didn't argue.

Tombs was already at the kerb, gun up, scanning for Zhao.

Blake and Dave ran after him.

Zhao had a car.

A black sedan, engine already running, sitting at the end of the street.

Blake shoved Dave and Tombs toward his car. "Get in! We're going after him!"

Dave barely had time to yank his door shut before Blake threw it into reverse —

And something hit them. Fast.

Metal crunched. Glass exploded. The airbag detonated into Dave's face, stunning him, shoving him back into his seat.

Zhao's car had T-boned them, hard — then reversed away, smooth as ever, vanishing into the night.

Blake roared, yanking at the wheel. The entire car screamed — metal grinding against metal. It was still driveable, but only just.

They weren't chasing anyone.

Through the cracked windshield, Dave saw Zhao's taillights disappear into the dark.

Tombs, dazed, coughed out a breath. "Well, that went to shit."

Blake, seething, slammed a fist against the wheel.

Dave just stared at the flames consuming what was left of his life.

Zhao was still out there.

CHAPTER 29

Zhao rolled the burner phone between his fingers, the smooth plastic cool against his skin. The farmhouse was silent except for the faint hum of air conditioning, a controlled, artificial coolness that stood in stark contrast to the oppressive summer heat outside. The place was pristine — polished hardwood floors, minimalist furniture, not a single thing out of place. Liu Jianhong did not tolerate disorder, not in his environment, and certainly not in his people.

A single security camera blinked in the corner. A silent, mechanical observer. A reminder.

Zhao shifted in his seat, exhaling slowly. He had been here before, but never under these circumstances. This wasn't a place for guests. It was a place for problems. And right now, he was the problem.

His ribs ached, bruised from Blake's ambush, but it was the weight pressing on his shoulders that burned deeper. He knew what this call meant. There was no stalling. No spinning it to sound like anything other than what it was.

Failure.

He pressed the call button.

The line clicked open. Silence.

Then Liu's voice — calm, even, expectant. "Report."

Zhao let the silence stretch, then spoke, calm and precise. "McBride is dead. The opals, the sword. All are still missing."

Silence stretched across the line, thick and suffocating. No shift in breath. No reaction. Just absence, stretching long enough for Zhao to feel it coil around his throat.

Liu never raised his voice. He never needed to.

"How?"

"Callahan escaped." Zhao kept his tone neutral, controlled. "He had help. A police officer — Detective Sergeant Blake. A biker, Tombs. They killed Shen and the others."

Still, Liu said nothing.

Somewhere on his end of the line, a soft click. Ceramic against glass. Tea being set down.

A small, controlled sound.

A reminder that while Zhao was bleeding, Liu was untouched.

Zhao swallowed. "We underestimated them. That won't happen again."

The silence dragged on. Zhao resisted the urge to shift in his chair, to fill the void with anything other than waiting.

Then Liu spoke.

"And what do you have to show for this failure?"

The words were gentle. Measured.

Zhao's jaw clenched. "Intel," he said quickly. "I know who's involved. I know what they're chasing. I will correct this."

Another long pause. Another soft clink of porcelain.

Then Liu said, "You don't have time."

Zhao straightened slightly. "I won't need much. We underestimated them. That won't happen again. They are still men."

His voice cooled, sharpening. "And all men have weaknesses."

Liu let that settle. Then, finally —

"Say it again."

Zhao hesitated. The request was so simple, yet it sent a fresh spike of unease through him. Why?

Liu didn't repeat himself. He didn't have to.

Zhao's lips parted slightly. "All men have weaknesses."

Another beat of silence. Then Liu spoke, his voice as weightless as falling silk.

"Find their weakness. Exploit it."

The call cut out.

Zhao lowered the phone. Pulse steady. But something colder curled in his chest.

He had been given one last chance. And he knew exactly what that meant.

Last.

No more mistakes. No more underestimating.

Callahan had run. That meant he had something worth running for.

Zhao reached into his pocket, pulling out the crumpled page of information garnered from McBride. Scraps of intelligence, scribbled notes, messy but useful. His gaze skimmed down the page, eyes catching on a single line.

Callahan, David. Married. One child.

A wife. A daughter.

Zhao's fingers traced the words, the ink slightly smudged. He murmured them softly, committing them to memory.

He drew a long breath through his nose, then let it go — silent, final. Not a smile. Not triumph.

Something colder.

A weakness he could exploit. Liu's resources were considerable, and his contacts, he knew with their help he could find a feather in a typhoon. Finding a woman and child would hardly be an effort. And then there was the man that he had utilised before. A man that would hunt down the bird from which the feather had been plucked. Callahan and his family stood no chance.

Finally, he had his leverage.

CHAPTER 30

Dave had nowhere to go. No place that felt safe.

So he drove.

His car still sat where he had left it earlier. Beneath a huge gum at the end of the street. Covered in bird shit, but on a sun blasted day it was worth every last spatter.

The highway stretched ahead in a never-ending black ribbon, his headlights carving through the darkness. The hum of the engine was the only thing tethering him to reality. His grip on the steering wheel was too tight, his knuckles bone white, his hands slick with sweat and dried blood. He was shaking, but he wasn't sure if it was from exhaustion, pain, or the sheer fucking insanity of the last twenty-four hours.

His home was gone. His life was gone. Zhao was still out there. Watching. Hunting.

Every flicker of headlights in his rearview sent adrenaline slamming through his system. He half-expected to see Zhao's car appear, creeping up behind him, closing in. Or worse — Blake's. He had no illusions about the detective's loyalty. Blake played whatever side suited him. Right now, that side might include Dave. But that could change in an instant.

He turned off the highway onto a dirt track, the tyres crunching over gravel. The river stretched ahead, dark as oil under the moonlight. He let the car idle, the low rumble vibrating through his bones. For the first time, the weight of everything settled onto his chest, pressing him into the seat.

McBride was dead. Murdered. Tortured first.

And in his pocket — proof.

Dave swallowed hard and reached in, fingers brushing against the rough fabric of a napkin. He pulled it out, unwrapped it with slow, deliberate movements. His breath caught.

McBride's thumb.

Blake had stuffed it in his pocket before they split. Like some kind of sick, twisted joke. Or a test. You found it. You get rid of it. It's a fucking liability.

Dave's stomach turned. He wanted to throw it into the river, watch it disappear beneath the black surface, let it sink into oblivion. But something stopped him.

Maybe it was just morbid curiosity. Maybe it was the knowledge that, as fucked as this was, it was still useful. A piece of evidence. A bargaining chip.

Or maybe, deep down, he knew he was past saving.

That a severed thumb in his pocket wasn't the thing that made him a monster.

He barely looked at it as he shoved it back into his jacket, reaching for McBride's phone instead.

It was locked, the screen mocking him.

Then a thought hit. His pulse skipped.

His gaze dropped to the napkin-wrapped bundle in his palm.

He pressed the dead flesh against the fingerprint scanner.

A soft click.

The screen unlocked.

A humourless laugh tore from his throat. "That's a new level of fucked up."

He scrolled fast, ignoring the texts, the emails, the endless clutter of a dead man's digital life. Then he found it.

A Notes file. Personal.

He opened it.

Bank logins. Passwords. Transactions.

His eyes locked onto the account balance.

$10,271.32.

Deposits from a Hong Kong account.

Dave let out a breath — half a laugh, half something else. McBride had been a corrupt, lazy bastard. He wouldn't be needing this money anymore.

The thumb did the rest.

With a few taps, he booked a motel room under McBride's name. Then ordered food.

"Guess I just got a severance package."

The motel was the kind of place that had seen too many sad stories, and Dave was just another one. The fluorescent sign buzzed outside, flickering, struggling to stay alive.

Inside, the air smelled of industrial cleaner and old cigarette smoke. The bed was too soft, the walls too thin. The food tasted like cardboard. Everything felt wrong.

He switched on the TV. The news was already running footage of his house.

Suspicious Blaze Destroys Family Home. No Reported Injuries.

Dave turned it off. His own life was now just a headline.

His hand hovered over the motel phone before he finally dialled.

Sally picked up on the first ring. "Oh, thank god." Relief, raw in her voice. "I saw the news. Are you okay?"

"Yeah," he rasped. "I wasn't home."

"The house —"

"It's gone."

Silence.

Then a slow, measured sigh. "I always said that place was a firetrap."

She didn't know the truth. Didn't know men had torn through it looking for answers. That he'd stood over a dead body last night. That he still had a severed thumb in his pocket.

"We'll figure it out," she said softly. "Things can be replaced."

Not everything.

The main street Photo Lab was too bright, too crowded. He hated every second of it.

He grabbed the photos, shoving them under his arm before the cashier could make small talk. Someone looked at him a little too long, and for a brief, terrifying moment, he thought they knew. That they saw him for what he was.

He got out fast.

Back at the motel, he spread the prints across the table. His pulse pounded. The images stared back at him.

Red's map.

He traced the markings, the numbers. The dead-end cenotaph.

His mind flicked back to the prison cell. The light streaming through the cracked fixture, fixing on a few points.

Now, with the photos, Dave could see it — one word and three numbers that stood out.

JOB.

He frowned. Job? A worksite? A bank job?

Then —

The motel drawer. The Bible.

His hands moved before his brain fully caught up. He flipped through the pages, scanning the combinations.

Job 6:19.

His breath caught.

"The caravans of Tema look for water, the traveling merchants of Sheba hope to find it."

His pulse thundered in his ears.

Tema. Sheba.

His brain rifled through memories at breakneck speed.

Mudgee. The drive.

He punched the names into McBride's phone.

Sheba Station Farm Stays. 45 minutes from Mudgee. Tema Road. Coxs Creek.

A crossroads. The intersection of Tema and Sheba roads.

His gut screamed at him.

This was real.

This was it.

Dave sat back, breath heavy.

Outside, another truck rumbled past, its headlights sweeping across the motel wall.

He watched the light fade.

Then he stood.

He knew where he was going next.

And he wasn't going alone.

CHAPTER 31

Dave sat in his car, fingers drumming against the wheel, watching the blank screen of his burner phone. The number rang twice before Blake picked up.

"Jesus, Callahan, you ever sleep?" Blake's voice was half-annoyed, half-curious.

"Need to meet. Got a location."

Silence. Then, "That right?"

"Yeah," Dave said, glancing out at the empty motel car park. "Need you to bring Tombs, too."

That got Blake's attention. "Why?"

Dave wasn't even sure how to answer that. Blake was useful, but something about him didn't sit right. He had cop instincts, but not the kind that always followed the law. Dave needed a second set of eyes on him — someone who didn't give a shit about police procedures. Someone who'd call him out if things got weird.

Tombs fit the bill.

"Just bring him," Dave said.

Another pause. Then Blake sighed. "Fine. Where we heading?"

Dave checked his notes. "Tema and Sheba roads. East of Mudgee."

"Middle of fuckin' nowhere," Blake muttered. "Be there in an hour."

Blake's replacement vehicle — a rented SUV — rattled over the dirt roads, dust billowing behind them. Every bump in the track jolted through the cab like an aftershock.

Tombs groaned. "Jesus, mate, this thing's got worse suspension than a shopping trolley."

Blake smirked. "Sorry, princess. Should've brought your fuckin' limo."

Tombs shifted in his seat. "You drive like a pensioner. You know that?"

Blake didn't even glance at him. "You wanna get out and walk?"

Tombs leaned back with a smug grin. "Might be quicker."

Dave just listened, arms folded, tuning them out. The way they sniped at each other was almost entertaining, like two old blokes arguing over who made the best pub schnitzel.

The sky stretched wide and empty. The land was vast, swallowing them in rolling hills, scattered gums, and dry creek beds long since drained by the heat. The smell of sunbaked dirt seeped through the vents — eucalyptus, dry grass, something wild.

Dave stared out the window. The further they drove, the more isolated it felt. No streetlights, no traffic noise. Just the hum of the engine and the occasional chirp of cicadas.

It was out here. Proper out here.

Tombs cracked his knuckles. "So, Callahan — what's at this place?"

"Dunno," Dave muttered. "It's a crossroad. That's all I got."

Tombs scoffed. "Great. We're chasing ghosts now."

Blake flicked his eyes to the rearview. "You don't have to be here, mate."

Tombs leaned back, grinning. "And miss out on whatever dumb shit you two get into next? No chance."

Blake ignored him. Dave just let them go at it.

The road narrowed as they turned onto another rutted track, winding through scrubland. Rugged sandstone formations loomed ahead — jagged rock faces, weathered by time, standing like forgotten sentinels in the dusk.

Dave checked the GPS. They were close.

Blake slowed the ute to a crawl as they reached the intersection of Tema and Sheba roads.

And that was it.

Just dirt. Just bush. And then they were there.

The three of them climbed out, boots crunching on dry earth. The air was cool but carried the scent of dust and eucalyptus, sharp and clean.

The crossroad itself was nothing special. Just a rough intersection where two tracks met, cutting through a sparse clearing before disappearing into the trees. A dried-up creek bed ran parallel to Sheba Road, its banks crumbling from years of neglect. To the north, sandstone cliffs rose from the land, sheer and hulking, their edges softened by scrub.

Tombs stretched, cracking his back. "Well. This is fuckin' underwhelming."

Blake ignored him. He stood still, scanning the area, seeing things the way cops did — like the land itself had something to confess.

Dave wasn't sure what he was looking for. So far, it was just dirt and rocks. He sighed, ran a hand through his hair. "Well, I'm taking a piss."

Tombs threw up his hands. "Christ, Callahan, we just got here!"

Dave ignored him, heading for the nearest tree.

He took his time. Let the night air settle around him. Listened to the silence. A few cicadas, the rustle of wind through dry leaves. No road noise, no distant hum of traffic.

He zipped up, heading back. Ten minutes passed. Still nothing.

Tombs was pacing near the creek bed, kicking at loose stones, wandering further and further. Blake stood with his hands on his hips, scanning the land.

Then —

"Oi!"

Tombs' voice cut through the quiet.

Dave and Blake turned.

Tombs was crouched near a half-buried rock. "Check this out."

They gathered around. It wasn't just some random chunk of bush stone — it looked deliberate. Worn, rounded edges. Maybe placed there. Maybe important.

Dave's pulse ticked up.

Could this be it?

Tombs hooked his fingers under it, straining. "It's stuck. Gimme a hand."

Blake grabbed the other side. "On three."

Dave watched, anticipation building as they heaved — muscles straining, dirt shifting.

And then —

Dave smirked. "Yeah… about that."

Tombs frowned. "What?"

Dave shrugged. "I just pissed on it."

Tombs recoiled so fast he lost his balance, landing flat on his ass. "Oh, you're a dead man, Callahan!"

Blake just shook his head. "You two are idiots."

They searched for another thirty minutes. Checked the creek bed. The rock. Even climbed partway up the escarpment.

Nothing.

Tombs wiped sweat from his face. "I'm callin' it. Either this is bullshit, or we're missing something."

Blake dusted off his hands. "I'll check topographic maps back at the station. See if anything matches the area."

Dave stared at the road, uneasy.

Something felt right about this place.

But also wrong.

They weren't seeing it.

Yet.

Blake clapped his hands. "We're done here."

Tombs sighed. "All this way for nothing."

"Not nothing," Dave muttered. Just not enough.

Tombs paused, eyeing the dirt crossroads. "Didn't it say something about opposite. Maybe one of these roads."

Blake huffed as he opened the car door. "That's a lot of fucking ground to cover. Like I said, I'll check some maps."

"Yeah…and I can just see you ringing us when you do find something."

"You're lucky you got this far. Now get it the damn car."

They loaded up, heading back toward the highway.

The road hummed beneath them. The cab was quiet, just the occasional grumble from Tombs about Blake's shitty driving.

Dave sat in the back, phone in his lap, waiting for reception.

Finally — signal.

He pulled up Google Earth and zoomed into the coordinates. Tema and Sheba.

Still dirt. Still nothing obvious.

He scrolled. Zoomed out.

And then he saw it.

To the north, the escarpment cut across the land — massive, weathered sandstone, stretching like a scar.

It wasn't just terrain.

From above, it was unmistakable.

An arrow. Easily 500 metres long and pointing almost dead south.

Dave's breath hitched. Red was a pilot — of course he'd seen it from the sky.

And that clue?

Opposite.

Not where the arrow pointed.

The other way.

His gut twisted — this was it.

It was real. The kind of real you didn't say out loud.

He stared at the screen a moment longer, heart thudding behind a blank face.

Didn't say a word.

Not yet.

This one, he was keeping to himself.

CHAPTER 32

Dave kicked the motel door shut behind him, the weight of the maps, supplies, and the week-long 4WD rental settling into his arms like a commitment he wasn't sure he could walk away from. He dropped everything onto the bed, the mattress springs groaning beneath the weight.

The room looked bare, the ceiling stained in yellow patches. The smell crawled into your head and stayed there. It was like a chain-smoking monk had been the last guest. The bedside lamp cast a dull yellow glow, highlighting the creases in the maps spread across the bedspread. He cracked open a bottle of water, took a long pull, and got to work.

The sandstone arrow had been the key. From the air, it was clear as day — nature's signpost carved into the land over millennia. From the ground? Just another escarpment, a formation lost among the trees.

Red was a pilot. Everything about his clues had to be seen through that lens.

Dave traced his fingers over the map, finding the exact latitude and longitude of the arrow's tip. That was his starting point. The 140 reference had been nagging at him since he'd first seen it, but now it made sense.

Not kilometres.

Not miles.

Nautical miles.

140 NM was about 260 kilometres. Almost exactly due north.

Dave grabbed McBride's phone and plugged in the coordinates, shifting the point 140 NM up the same longitude. The screen refreshed. His heart kicked.

A stretch of old farmland. No town, no markers. Just a name that barely registered — nothing but dry land, scattered trees, and whatever was left of a forgotten past.

This was it.

No hesitation. He started packing.

He dialled his boss, already knowing how this would go.

"Hey Ted, it's Dave. I need the week off. I don't know if you heard about that house fire."

"You light it?"

"No, I didn't fucking light it. It was my house. Everything is gone."

"Shit. That's fucked up."

"So… I need to take some time."

Silence. Then a scoff. "The fuck you do. I can't afford this shit. I already pay you off the books."

Dave gritted his teeth. "It's not a request."

A heavy exhale. "Jesus, Callahan, you're barely holding on to this job as it is. You pull this shit again, don't bother coming back."

Dave felt a flicker of something. Not anger. Not regret. Just… nothing.

"Right. Well, I guess this is me not coming back."

"You serious?"

Click.

Fuck 'em.

He stared at the phone for a moment before tossing it onto the bed. Another bridge burnt. Another piece of his life gone.

Rock bottom.

He cracked open a beer from the motel fridge, let the cold settle in his palm. He never really liked the taste, but it was something to mark the moment. One last toast to the life that wasn't worth holding onto.

Then he drained it, tossed the empty, and walked out the door.

The rental 4WD was nothing special — just a dusty, second-hand thing that screamed "weekend warrior." But it had goodtyres, a full tank, and no attachment to his real life. That was all he needed.

The road stretched out ahead, dark and empty, the kind of drive where your thoughts ran wild. He threw on some music, something old-school with a steady rhythm, and let the miles slip past.

He wasn't running anymore. He was chasing.

Every few towns, he stopped to refuel, even though the tank had barely reached half. Grabbed snacks — chips, beef jerky, a couple of drinks. It almost felt like a road trip, something casual, something normal.

For a while, life was good.

At a fuel stop near the last stretch of nowhere, he filled up the 4WD, stretching his legs while the pump ticked over. Inside the servo, a couple of bikers leaned against the counter, shooting the shit with the attendant. One of them, a wiry bloke with a faded tat creeping up his neck, gave Dave a passing glance.

Just a bloke in a rental.

Nothing worth remembering.

Dave's eyes caught the bikes and scanned the station. The last thing he wanted was one of Tombs' boys spotting him. Time to move on.

The road turned from bitumen to dirt, then to something worse — ruts and dry creek beds, the kind of track that hadn't seen maintenance in decades. The 4WD bounced and groaned,tyres spitting gravel as Dave pushed through.

The coordinates led him to a broken-down gate, barely hanging onto its hinges. Beyond it, the land stretched out in brittle grass and scattered trees, leading to a weathered old shed that stood like a relic of another time.

Dave killed the engine.

Silence.

The place was dead. Long abandoned.

He climbed out, the air thick with the scent of dry earth and rust. The shed loomed ahead, its corrugated iron walls bleached by the sun, riddled with bullet holes and time-worn scars.

He tried the door. Bolted shut.

Figures. Whatever was inside had been locked up for a reason.

Dave walked the perimeter, boots crunching on dry dirt, running his fingers over the warped metal panels. Then he found it — a loose sheet, rattling in the wind.

He grabbed the edge, braced his foot against the wall, and yanked.

The panel came free with a teeth-grinding screech, sending rust flakes scattering. Behind it, darkness. Thick with dust. Cobwebs stretched like old scars.

He ducked inside, brushing strands of silk from his face. The air was stale. Dead. Like no one had breathed it in years.

His boots kicked up dust as he moved deeper, letting his eyes adjust.

Then he saw it.

What was left of Red's plane. It had to be Red's plane.

The fuselage had been stripped, the wings long removed, but the shape was unmistakable. The bones of a machine that once tore through the sky.

It had been sitting here for decades. The metal dull, eaten away by time and weather.

But it wasn't just the plane that caught his attention.

The boxes.

Stacked in the corner, covered in dust so thick that it buried the rat shit.

Old. And a shitload of them.

Dave's pulse ticked up. He moved to one, pulling at the lid. Forced it open.

Empty.

Lined with old newspapers.

He grabbed a handful of pages, the yellowed sheets crumbling in his hands. He scanned the date before it flaked apart.

The year of the heist.

Dave turned back to the plane, stepping closer. Inside, it had been gutted. Just an empty shell. As empty as the boxes stacked in front of it.

Except for one thing.

Planted on the floor of the cabin. A small box. Metal. Hardly bigger than a loaf of bread.

And holding the lid down — a combination lock.

Dave stared at it, pulse quickening.

This was different. This wasn't trash. Someone had left this here for a reason.

His fingers hovered over the lock, heartbeat loud in his ears.

Before he could touch it —

A noise behind him.

A boot crunching against dirt.

The sharp, unmistakable scrape of a shotgun being racked.

Then cold steel pressed against the back of his skull.

A voice. Low. Rough. Controlled.

"You got about ten seconds to explain what the fuck you're doing on my property."

CHAPTER 33

Dave didn't move.

The shotgun barrel stayed planted against the back of his skull—hard, unblinking, and steady as death.

The locked box sat barely a metre away, taunting him with its silence. Dust motes swirled in the dim light filtering through the gaps in the rusted shed walls, the air thick with the smell of oil, old metal, and time.

"Ten seconds," the voice behind him said, rough as gravel. "Start talking."

Dave licked his dry lips. No point in lying. Not when he'd come this far. "Red sent me."

A long pause. Then a quiet, bitter chuckle. "Bullshit. Red's dead."

Dave closed his eyes briefly. "Yeah. He is."

Silence stretched between them. The man shifted behind him, the shotgun's barrel nudging against his scalp as he adjusted his stance.

"Red said someone might come one day," the man muttered. "Said if it was the right someone, they'd be able to open that box. If not…"

Dave didn't need him to finish that sentence.

There was a pause. Subtle, but enough. A shift in weight. A breath held. "Turn around. Slow."

Dave did as he was told, keeping his hands up.

The man in front of him was older than he'd expected — sixty, maybe more, face lined from years in the sun, eyes sharp despite the grey at his temples. He held the shotgun steady, like a man who'd spent a lifetime using it.

"You got a name?"

"Dave Callahan."

The name didn't register any recognition. That was good.

The old man studied him, then nodded toward the crate. "Let's see if Red was right about you."

Dave swallowed. He had no idea what the code was. The combination lock looked old but solid, three metal dials waiting for the right numbers. He crouched, fingers hovering over them, brain scrambling.

Red's clues had led him here. The sandstone arrow. The Bible verse. The numbers carved into the wall of his cell.

Six. One. Nine.

Dave's heart pounded as he turned the dials. The numbers clicked into place. He held his breath and pulled the latch.

The lock snapped open.

A sharp inhale from behind him. The shotgun lowered an inch.

"Well, I'll be damned," the old man murmured.

Dave opened the box.

Inside, nestled in the dust-lined interior, was a single photograph. Old, edges curled with time. He recognised it immediately.

The one from Red's cell.

A young boy and a girl, standing in front of a towering eucalyptus tree. The boy — Red, no doubt — held a small metal toy plane. The girl, slightly younger, clutched a spinning top, the old-fashioned kind with a push-down centre to make it spin.

Dave turned the photo over.

Henry and Martha Redmond. 8 years and 7 years.

Martha. The sister.

His fingers traced the names. He'd seen this before. Back in Red's cell. The photo he had placed into the box with Red's other things. And now another copy here.

Next to the photo, sitting in the box like a relic of another time, was the same spinning top from the picture. A faded tag dangled from a frayed piece of twine.

If found, return to Martha Redmond.

Dave stared at the ground, the weight of it all sinking in.

This wasn't just about the opals. It never had been.

Red had left something more than a trail of clues.

He'd left a legacy.

The old man leaned in, staring at the contents of the box, his lips tightening.

"He really is dead, then?" he asked quietly.

Dave nodded. "Yeah."

The old man sighed, his grip finally relaxing on the shotgun. "Bastard always had a plan. Even for his own ghost."

Dave ran a hand over his face, exhaustion pressing in on him. "How did you know him?"

The old man pulled up a rusted chair and sank into it. "He leased this shed from me. Paid up front. Ninety-nine years."

Dave's eyebrows lifted. "That's a hell of a lease."

The man smirked. "Red had money. Even before the job that got him locked up. Always had something going. He was smart. Sly. Taught himself to fly, you know? Bought that plane for dirt cheap when his company folded. Stashed it here before anyone even knew he was up to something."

Dave looked back at the stripped-down fuselage. "And you never asked questions?"

The man shrugged. "Didn't need to. Part of the deal was simple — I keep it locked, no one touches it unless Red says otherwise."

Dave hesitated. "And if someone showed up?"

The man patted the shotgun resting against his leg. "Then I was supposed to do what needed doing."

A long silence. The weight of what could have happened sat between them.

Finally, the old man sighed, rubbing a hand over his weathered face. "Guess it's a damn good thing you knew the code."

Dave reached back into the box, shifting aside the spinning top. There was one more thing tucked at the bottom.

A sealed envelope.

Thick. Yellowed with age.

Six words scrawled on the front in Red's sharp, deliberate handwriting.

Blake's Eyes Only. Do Not Remove.

Dave felt his stomach turn.

Blake.

What the hell was Red keeping for him?

The old man noticed his hesitation. "Something wrong?"

Dave tucked the envelope back into the box. No reason to tempt fate. He masked the unease curling through him. "Nothing," he said. "Just more questions."

The man smirked. "Welcome to Red's world."

Outside, the wind whispered through the trees, rustling the dry leaves against the tin walls. Somewhere in the distance, a crow called out into the empty sky.

Dave had found his next step.

But for the first time since this started, he wasn't sure if he wanted to take it.

But he had a delivery to make.

CHAPTER 34

The police station in Muswellbrook was chaos. Phones rang off the hook. Boots stomped across tile. Voices clashed — cops shouting over each other, arguing, demanding answers no one had. The walls vibrated with the weight of it all.

Blake barely noticed. He sat in a borrowed office, hunched over maps spread across a scratched-up desk, the dim glow of a flickering fluorescent light making everything look washed-out and grim. It wasn't his space — his real office was back in Sydney — but right now, this was where he needed to be. He'd labelled this an official investigation, and the badge outside the door let him have it.

Everything outside this room? A goddamn nightmare.

McBride was missing. The Ragged Sons' clubhouse had turned into a slaughterhouse. Callahan's house had burned to the ground. A neighbour had reported hearing gunshots before the fire. And a turf war was brewing in the wake of the massacre at the clubhouse.

Blake wasn't officially touching any of it. Not yet. Not until he had to.

Instead, he focused on what mattered.

The maps.

They were creased and marked-up, satellite images showing the bushland east of Mudgee. The dirt crossroads where he, Tombs, and Callahan had stood just over a day ago. They had stood there expecting something big.

They had found jack-shit.

But Red had left clues. Blake had seen enough riddles, hidden messages, and cryptic codes in his career to know this wasn't over.

140 nautical miles. Opposite.

That number had stuck with him. It wasn't random. It was a distance, a measurement. But opposite to what?

He ran the maths. 140 nautical miles — around 260 kilometres. It gave him a radius. A big fucking radius. More than 212,000 square kilometres. That was damn near the size of Victoria.

Blake traced his finger across the map, narrowing the possibilities. The region covered farmland, bushland, abandoned properties, and enough rugged terrain to hide a thousand secrets. He couldn't just pick a direction at random.

He needed something else. A reference point. A clue.

He zoomed in on the satellite image of the crossroads, studying it. Dirt roads. Scrub. A dried-up creek bed. A few scattered sheds.

Nothing.

Then, on instinct, he zoomed out.

And saw it.

A massive sandstone formation, just north of the crossroads. The shape was unmistakable.

A giant arrow.

Blake straightened. His breath slowed.

Red was a pilot. Nautical miles. Aerial navigation. He would've seen that arrow from the sky.

And Red's clue?

Opposite.

Not where the arrow pointed — the other way.

Blake exhaled sharply, running a hand through his hair. That's it.

He grabbed a notepad, started working through the numbers. 140 nautical miles, almost due north. He followed the line up the map —

And stopped.

Farmland. Dry country. A name that meant nothing. No towns, no landmarks, just another forgotten stretch of bush.

Blake tapped the pen against the desk.

He didn't know that Callahan was already a day ahead of him.

He wouldn't have liked that.

Wouldn't have liked it at all.

The office door swung open without a knock.

Detective Senior Sergeant Perry filled the doorway, arms crossed, looking like he hadn't slept in twenty-four hours. His eyes were bloodshot, his mouth a hard line of frustration. "Blake, what the fuck are you actually doing here?"

Blake didn't look up from the map. "Working."

"That so?" Perry's voice was tight. "Because outside this room, we've got a corrections officer missing. McBride. A neighbour reported gunshots before that house fire. A house owned by one David Callahan, another fucking link to the prison. And the Ragged Sons' clubhouse? Looks like a goddamn war zone. You wouldn't happen to know anything about any of that, would you?"

Blake finally looked up. "Not a thing."

Perry's jaw flexed. "Right."

Blake went back to his notes.

Perry stepped inside, lowering his voice. "You're pushing your luck, mate. If I find out you're in the middle of any of this —"

Blake gave him a slow, measured look. "You won't."

They stared at each other. A long, heavy silence.

Perry sighed, rubbing a hand down his face. "You think I'm fucking stupid?"

Blake's smirk was slight. "No, Perry. I think you're exhausted."

Perry muttered a curse, turned, and walked out.

Blake waited until the door shut. Then he grabbed a fresh notepad, scribbled Tema-Sheba Arrow. 140 NM Opposite.

And then he turned to Zhao situation.

Blake pulled up another file — this one separate from his maps.

Zhao.

Before last night, he hadn't even known the guy's name. But now, he had enough to start digging.

He ran the name through internal databases, cross-referencing known criminal associates, import-export businesses, financial records.

It didn't take long to hit something real.

Zhao Wei.

A name tied to Hong Kong. To Chinese syndicates operating in Australia.

More digging. Blake's eyes scanned the screen, absorbing the details. Zhao had been careful. No obvious heat, no known Australian address. But a lot of offshore money. Connections to a Hong Kong-based outfit that dabbled in everything — diamonds, money laundering, high-end corporate fraud. And all backed by a legitimate business. A big fucking business. A billionaire who apparently had little regard for laws or borders.

Liu Jianhong.

And opals.

Liu Jianhong was the one Red had stolen the opals from in the first place.

What a fucking web this was turning out to be.

Blake's grip on the mouse tightened.

Zhao wasn't just muscle. He wasn't just some hired gun.

He was something else. Something worse.

Blake shifted his weight, eyes narrowing.

Callahan had no fucking clue what he was up against.

And then there was Tombs.

Blake smirked. The dumb bastard had no idea he was being kept on a leash just to be a scapegoat. When the shit hit the fan, Tombs would be the one holding the power cord.

But Blake had bigger problems.

This all started with Red.

Red had spent a long time inside. And every single time his parole hearings came up? They'd been shot down.

Blake knew why.

Because he was the one who made sure they never succeeded.

He hadn't faked evidence, hadn't done anything technically illegal. But he'd pulled strings. Found people who could influence decisions. Made sure Red stayed locked up.

Because if Red got out? He'd lead people straight to whatever he was hiding. The opals for sure, but there was something else.

Something that Red had said would destroy Blake.

Blake tapped his pen against the map, staring at the sandstone arrow.

Red had known this was coming.

He was leading them somewhere.

Even from the grave.

Blake closed the files, folded up the maps, and reached for his keys.

He had a long drive ahead of him.

And he wasn't going to be the one left behind.

CHAPTER 35

Tombs sat in the back corner. Alone. Quiet. Watching. The overhead fan wheezed as it spun, doing little more than shifting the stale cigarette smoke around from one side of the pub to the other. A jukebox in the corner was stuck on some country song that felt like it had been playing for the last forty minutes, or maybe forty years.

He nursed a bourbon, rolling the glass between his fingers, his gaze flicking toward the door every few minutes. The place was quiet, but that didn't mean it was safe. Not for him. Not with everything circling the drain.

Tombs had gone to ground. He hadn't had a choice. Lynch got his head ventilated, Callahan had been grabbed, and that Chinese bastard Zhao was still out there, making moves. He wasn't some grunt who could pretend nothing was happening — he'd been in the game too long to be that stupid. The way he saw it, there were only two kinds of men in situations like this: the ones who made things happen and the ones who got buried.

Right now, Tombs wasn't sure which category he fell into.

His phone sat face-up on the sticky wooden table, silent. He'd put the word out discreetly, casting lines to the people who mattered. The kind of men who operated on favours and debts, where trust was measured in scars. Loose alliances between clubs weren't uncommon — survival depended on knowing who had a reason to keep you alive. And Tombs? He needed reasons. He needed leverage.

Two objectives: find Blake and find out whether Callahan was still breathing.

Blake had gone radio silent, buried himself in his cop bullshit. That wasn't good. If there was one thing worse than a dirty cop, it was a dirty cop with too much time to think. And Callahan? That idiot had walked straight into something bigger than any of them. If he was still kicking, that meant he had a head start on the next move.

A shadow moved past the window. Tombs straightened, fingers curling around the handle of the knife tucked against his belt. A figure entered, his bulk filling the doorway, eyes scanning the room before making a beeline straight for him.

Shit.

Tombs recognised the leather cut, the patched insignia. Gravediggers. Northern border club. No friends of his, but not outright enemies either. A wary truce, the kind built on convenience rather than loyalty.

The man pulled out a chair, dropping into it like he owned the place. He was thick-set, the kind of bloke whose knuckles told more stories than his mouth ever would. A broken nose that had never been set right. Scarred hands, the tattoos faded from time and too many fights.

Tombs took a slow sip of whiskey. "Well, this is either good news or real bad news."

The biker didn't smile. He reached into his jacket, pulled out a battered phone, and flicked to a picture. Turned the screen around.

Tombs' stomach knotted.

Callahan.

Grainy servo cameras. Timestamped earlier that day.

Still scruffy. Beaten up. Looking like he'd been dragged backwards through hell, but alive. He stood at a fuel pump, hands in his pockets, scanning the area like he knew someone might be watching. A rental 4WD behind him.

Tombs leaned in. "Where?"

"Up north. Some backwater servo just past Gunnedah."

Tombs swore under his breath. That was miles from where they'd last seen him. The bastard was moving. Fast. Why?

The biker pocketed the phone. "Figured you'd want to know."

Tombs nodded, his mind already racing. Callahan was onto something. If he was still breathing, then maybe, just maybe, the story wasn't over yet.

He reached into his own jacket, pulled out a thick wad of cash, and slid it across the table. "You see anything else, you call me first."

The man took the money, tucking it away without a word. He didn't linger. Just stood, adjusted his cut, and disappeared back into the night.

Tombs sat there, the weight of it all pressing down.

The smart move was to leave it alone. Let Callahan do whatever dumb shit he was doing and stay the hell out of it.

But that wasn't how this worked.

Callahan wasn't some lucky idiot. He had a direction. A purpose. He was chasing something big. And Tombs had never been the type to sit back while someone else found the goldmine first.

He downed the rest of his bourbon, the burn trailing down his throat, and pushed back from the table. The old wood groaned under his weight. He tossed a few crumpled notes onto the bar, barely acknowledging the bartender's nod.

As he stepped outside, the air was thick with the scent of rain on hot asphalt. A storm was brewing somewhere on the horizon.

Fitting.

Tombs pulled out his phone, thumb hovering over the screen. He thought about calling Blake. About giving the cop a heads-up.

Then he snorted, shaking his head.

Fuck that.

This was his play now.

He slid the phone back into his pocket, stepped toward his bike, and swung a leg over.

He had a long ride ahead of him.

And Callahan? That bastard better hope he found what he was looking for before Tombs did.

CHAPTER 36

Zhao sat in the outdoor seating of a beachfront café in Terrigal, sipping black coffee as the ocean rolled in, its foamy whitecaps crashing against the shore. The late-morning was crisp, the air carrying the salt-heavy tang of the sea. Families strolled along the esplanade, children licking melting ice creams, retirees taking slow, deliberate steps along the footpath. Zhao paid them no mind.

His eyes were fixed on one family in particular.

Sally Callahan. Cassie Callahan.

Sally sat at a shaded table outside a café, stirring sugar into her coffee, eyes on her daughter. Cassie was running along the sand, giggling as she chased the waves back and forth. The child was small, full of energy. Carefree.

A stark contrast to her father.

Zhao snapped a photograph. The shutter sound was barely audible, but he quickly muted his phone anyway. He wasn't careless. He had watched them all morning, tracking their movements, their routines. They were too relaxed. Too unaware.

That would change soon.

He leaned back in his chair, fingers tapping against the phone screen as he flicked through the images. He didn't need them for reference. He had already memorised everything. The way Sally's gaze constantly flicked toward her daughter, protective but distant. The way she never quite settled in her seat. The tiredness in her eyes. She was holding it together, but barely.

Zhao smirked. She wasn't worried enough yet.

It had taken time, but tracking McBride's phone had been worth the effort. Callahan was using it. The fool probably thought he was being smart—burner phones, keeping off the grid—but McBride's phone had been compromised long before his death.

They had triangulated the signal, traced patterns, followed digital breadcrumbs. Callahan was moving. Heading north.

He sent a message. Simple. Direct.

"We need to talk."

"Who the fuck is this?"

"You can call me Zhao. Do not pretend you do not know who I am."

The response came minutes later.

"What the fuck do you want now."

Zhao chuckled. He liked that Callahan still had some fight in him.

He sent the photos. Sally. Cassie.

"We need to talk. Face to face."

The next reply came faster.

"You touch them and you won't ever talk again."

There it was. The shift.

Fear. Rage. Desperation.

Zhao took his time before responding. Let Callahan stew in the uncertainty. Then he typed:

"We need to talk."

There was a long pause. Callahan would know this wasn't an empty threat.

Finally, the next message arrived.

"Where."

Zhao smiled.

He typed the location carefully. Somewhere isolated but open. Public enough that Callahan wouldn't try anything stupid, but empty enough that Zhao would still hold all the power.

An abandoned timber yard outside Coonabarabran. Midnight.

No cops. No backup. Just you.

He hit send.

Then, Zhao pocketed his phone, downed the rest of his coffee, and stood.

He had a long drive ahead of him.
And Callahan? Callahan had something to lose.

CHAPTER 37

Dave's hands locked around the wheel, tendons tight, fingers aching from the grip.

His head felt like it was filled with static, a radio refusing to hit the station, a dull hum of pressure building behind his eyes.

Zhao had his family.

Not physically. Not yet.

But he had them under his gaze, under his control.

The photos said it all. Sally and Cassie, caught in time — walking along the beach, getting ice cream, smiling like they didn't have a fucking clue their lives had just become a bargaining chip.

Dave clenched his jaw, forcing the bile back down his throat.

He needed leverage of his own.

The spinning top sat on the passenger seat, its worn surface catching the faint glow of the dashboard light. It was the only thing he had, the only clue that might give him something — anything — to push back with.

Martha Redmond. Red's sister.

The old bloke at the shed — who still hadn't given his name, just a gruff "Don't get yourself killed" — had given Dave her address.

He'd also given him a warning.

"She's tough as nails, mate. Won't like you sniffing around. Best you know that before you go pissing her off."

Dave didn't give a shit if she liked it or not. He wasn't looking for friendship. He needed answers.

He tapped his fingers on the wheel, checking the time. The midnight meet with Zhao was still half a day away. The meet place was a two-hour drive. From Martha's even less.

He had time.

Dave drove deeper into the bush, past dry creek beds and brittle paddocks where cows stood like statues, ribs sharp beneath their hides, too heat-drunk to move. The land out here was starving, gasping for rain that never came.

And then came the Pilliga.

The road through the Pilliga stretched ahead, a thin, cracked ribbon of bitumen swallowed by endless scrub. Eucalyptus and cypress pines crowded the edges, their gnarled limbs twisting toward the sky, casting broken shadows across the dirt. The land here felt old — older than the roads, older than the towns that dotted its edges, older than any man who thought he could claim it.

The air was thick with the scent of dust and hot gum leaves, and the sun sat low, bleeding gold through the branches. Kangaroos watched from the roadside, motionless but ready, their eyes glinting in the patchy light. Every now and then, one would bolt, a blur of muscle and instinct, crossing the road just far enough ahead to make your gut clench.

No signs, no towns. Just the bush. Deep, endless, indifferent.

The road dipped and climbed, winding past dry creek beds and abandoned timber yards, their skeletons of rusting machinery left to rot. Birds cut across the sky, sharp cries carrying through the trees, but otherwise, it was quiet. Not silent — never silent — but the kind of quiet that made you feel like you didn't belong.

Out here, if something went wrong, it stayed wrong. A busted radiator, a wrong turn, the sun dipping too fast — it all added up. The Pilliga didn't care if you made it through. It had swallowed plenty before.

And then, like a mirage, he found it.

A house.

Not just any house — a colonial-style farmhouse with a wraparound veranda and a deep green roof, standing defiant against the wasteland that stretched out around it.

And the garden.

Lush, thriving — a burst of colour and life where nothing else should be. Vines crawled up trellises, vegetable patches brimming with green, sunflowers standing tall like soldiers.

The house didn't belong out here.

It wasn't part of the landscape—just something the land tolerated, like a splinter buried deep in the palm of a hand.

Too small to dig out. Too deep to forget.

This place shouldn't exist out here.

And yet, it did.

Dave pulled into the gravel driveway, dust swirling in his rearview. The house felt like a fortress — not in size, but in presence. Whoever lived here wasn't just surviving.

They were winning.

The first thing Dave noticed was the music.

Old-school country — Patsy Cline, maybe Johnny Cash — playing from somewhere inside the house. Scratchy vinyl.

The second thing he noticed was her.

A woman, standing at the edge of a vegetable patch, hose in one hand, cigarette in the other.

She looked late sixties, maybe early seventies, skin toughened by decades under the sun, her grey hair pulled back in a loose bun. She wore faded jeans, a checked shirt rolled to the elbows, and boots that had seen more years than he had.

She didn't look up. Didn't even acknowledge his existence.

Dave stepped out of the car. His boots crunched on gravel.

Nothing.

She kept watering the plants, dragging deeply on her cigarette. The smoke curled into the afternoon air.

Finally, she spoke. Didn't even turn around.

"If you're selling Jesus, I already told the last lot to get fucked."

Dave kept his voice steady. "Not here to sell anything."

She gave a slow nod. "Right. Debt collector then?"

"No."

"Council?"

"Nope."

She turned her head slightly, just enough to glance at him. Sharp green eyes. Cold. Measuring.

She took another drag on her cigarette.

"Bikie?"

Dave shook his head.

She blew smoke out of her nose. "Good. Hate the pricks."

"You got a name?"

"Dave. Dave Callahan."

She turned off the hose and finally faced him fully, hands on her hips. Sizing him up like she was deciding whether or not to shoot him.

"You look like shit, Dave Callahan."

Dave barely cracked a smirk. "Long week."

"Don't care. What do you want?"

Dave reached into his jacket and pulled out the spinning top.

Martha Redmond stilled.

A slow inhale. The only sign that something had shifted inside her.

Dave held it out. "It was in a box. Locked up with Red's plane."

A beat.

Then — her voice came, low and rough.

"So he's dead then."

It wasn't a question.

Dave swallowed. "Yeah."

Martha looked away, taking a long drag on her cigarette, staring at nothing.

When she turned back, her expression had hardened.

"And someone finally figured it out."

She took the spinning top from his hand. Turned it over.

Her thumb traced the old tag tied to it.

"If found, return to Martha Redmond."

She exhaled, shaking her head. "Thought I'd never see that again."

Silence stretched between them.

Then, her dogs arrived.

Three of them. Two big bastards — solid, broad-shouldered mutts that looked like they'd happily chew through a car door — and one little scrappy thing, a yappy terrier with the confidence of a wolf.

Dave tensed.

The big ones sat beside Martha, eyes locked on him. The little one stood in front, growling like it was personally offended by his presence.

Martha gestured with her cigarette. "Don't move too quick. Bruce there" — she nodded to the biggest dog — "he don't like strangers."

Bruce let out a low, threatening growl.

Dave swallowed. "Noted."

Martha crossed her arms, studying him.

"So," she said finally. "Henry left you a trail. And you actually followed it."

Henry.

The name hit different when she said it.

Not Red. Not a legend, not some ghost of a convict from a decades-old heist.

Henry.

A brother.

Dave met her eyes. "I need answers."

Martha took another slow drag on her cigarette.

Then she turned. "Come inside."

She walked toward the house, boots crunching on the gravel.

The big dogs followed. The little one — the bastard still growling — stayed put, right in the path, staring at Dave like he was on borrowed time.

Dave sighed. "You gonna move, or do I have to fight you?"

The dog barked once. A warning.

Martha's voice came from the veranda. "Stop talking to the damn dog and get inside."

Dave shook his head, shoving his hands in his pockets.

This was going to be interesting.

And he had a feeling Martha Redmond wasn't just holding onto memories.

She was holding onto secrets.

CHAPTER 38

Dave stepped into the house, feeling the temperature drop instantly. It was cooler inside, the thick stone walls holding back the worst of the afternoon heat. The place smelled clean but lived-in — wood polish, old books, fresh-baked bread.

Martha walked ahead of him, moving like she owned the world. No hesitation, no wasted effort. Dave followed, taking in the high ceilings, dark wooden furniture, the old photographs in dusty frames.

Everything meant something here.

The kitchen was the heart of it all. A massive wooden table took up most of the space, the surface scarred from years of use. Shelves stacked high with preserves, spices, old tins, a record player crackling softly from the counter.

Martha grabbed a jug of water, poured it into a thick glass, and shoved it toward him. "Drink. Then sit."

Dave took the glass and drained it in seconds. His throat burned from the dryness of the road, the stress, the whole fucking mess of it all. He set the empty glass down.

Martha just raised an eyebrow.

"You really do look like shit."

Dave half-smirked. "It's been a rough couple of days."

Martha pulled out a chair and sat across from him.

The three dogs trailed in behind them, padding across the wooden floor, settling near her feet. The two big bastards flopped down, their heavy breathing filling the space. The small one hopped onto a seat, staring at Dave like he owed him money.

Martha folded her arms, eyes still sharp, still watching.

"Tell me why you're here."

Dave gestured to the spinning top now sat on the table. Let it speak first.

Martha didn't reach for it. Didn't even blink.

"So, he's really dead then."

Dave nodded. "Yeah."

A silence.

She reached for her cigarette case, lit one with steady hands, and took a long drag.

"Took you lot long enough to come knocking."

Dave ran a hand over his face. "You expected someone?"

Martha tapped ash into a heavy tin dish. "Eventually. Red always said if the right person came looking, they'd find their way here. If they weren't the right person…"

She eyed the shotgun leaning against the doorway.

"Well. You get the idea."

Dave swallowed.

She gestured toward him with the cigarette. "And what makes you the right person?"

Dave leaned back, let out a slow breath.

Then, he told her.

Everything.

The prison cell. The scratched-up map. The cenotaph. The Ragged Sons. The bloodshed. The burned-down house. Zhao.

When he mentioned Zhao, Martha's expression didn't change. But something in her eyes shifted.

Dave felt it as much as he saw it.

She let him talk. No interruptions. No questions. Just let it spill out like a confession at the altar.

When he finished, the room was silent except for the distant whine of a cicada outside.

Martha took another drag, exhaled slowly.

Then, she stood.

"You're bleeding."

Dave blinked. "What?"

She pointed at his arm. "That's gonna turn septic if you don't clean it properly."

Dave looked down. The gash near his elbow had been there since McBride's shed. It had dried into a crusty mess.

Martha grabbed a tin from the counter, set it down. "Roll up your sleeve."

Dave hesitated. "It's fine."

Martha's look could have turned a man to stone.

"I said roll up your fucking sleeve, Callahan."

Dave rolled it up.

Martha grabbed a cloth, doused it with antiseptic, and pressed it against the wound.

Dave gritted his teeth.

Martha smirked. "That's the look of a man who ain't used to being taken care of."

Dave let out a breath. "Yeah, well, it's been a long time."

Martha finished, tossed the used cloth into the bin, and sat back down. "Alright. Now tell me the part you were holding back."

Dave paused.

Martha didn't. "It's in your face. You're carrying something heavier than all this treasure hunt bullshit."

Dave stared at her.

Then, he told her the rest.

Sally. Cassie. The photos Zhao sent. The meeting tonight.

By the time he finished, Martha was gripping her cigarette so tight, the filter had flattened.

She stubbed it out violently, stood up, and paced to the window.

"You tell her? Your wife?"

Dave shook his head. "No."

Martha scoffed. "Fucking idiot."

Dave didn't argue.

Martha thought for a moment. Then she reached for the phone.

Dave frowned. "What are you doing?"

Martha dialled. "Fixing it." She pushed a notebook and pen toward him, like she had been holding them the whole time. "Names and address. Quick."

Dave eyed her, the notepad. Then wrote.

The call rang twice. Then someone picked up. Martha spoke fast, low, sharp. Dave couldn't catch the words.

By the time she hung up, she turned back to him.

"Handled."

Dave stared.

Martha sat back down, picked up her cigarette case again.

"Callahan, you don't live as long as I have without knowing how to make people disappear."

Dave swallowed. "Disappear?"

Martha smirked. "Sally and Cassie will be off the grid before nightfall."

Dave felt something shift in his chest.

Relief.

The kind that made his eyes burn.

Martha lit another cigarette. "Now tell me about this meet."

Dave explained. The midnight rendezvous. Zhao's warning not to bring anyone.

Martha listened. When he finished, she reached down, scratching behind Bruce's ears.

"Alright, then." She took another drag. "Bruce is going with you. He's not an anyone."

Dave frowned. "Bruce?"

Martha smirked. "Yeah. He'll be hungry by then."

Bruce licked his chops.

"You make sure you bring him back."

Dave's mouth twitched, just a little. "I'll do my best."

He wasn't sure if she was joking.

"I wasn't talking to you."

Martha grinned.

"Tell me, Callahan… you ever seen what a hungry dog this size can do to a man?"

CHAPTER 39

Dave's headlights carved through the thick, black air, pushing back the shadows on the road to Coonabarabran. Bruce sat beside him, a mountain of muscle, fur, and barely controlled menace. His massive head rested against the half-open window, nostrils flaring as he took in the night's scents. The dog's calm, rhythmic breathing was oddly reassuring.

Outside, the night was clear and sharp, stars like broken glass scattered across a moonless sky. The land itself felt like an endless void, stretching out dark and vast, indifferent to the tiny dramas of the men who crawled across its skin. Dave's forearms were locked, muscles tight with pressure that had nowhere to go. His gut was a twisted knot, coiled with anxiety and anger. Zhao had crossed a line, threatening Sally and Cassie. Dave was walking a tightrope — one misstep, one wrong word, and everything he cared about would vanish.

As he drove, his thoughts ran through every scenario, every possibility of what Zhao might say or do. Zhao was calculating, cunning, dangerous. He was the kind of man who measured each breath, each heartbeat, for maximum advantage.

The meeting place was an abandoned timber yard outside Coonabarabran, tucked off an unmarked dirt road that had long since forgotten the taste of tar. When Dave arrived, it loomed from the darkness like the skeleton of some dead beast, logs piled high in rotten stacks, rusted machinery crouched like sleeping predators in the gloom.

Dave parked in the shadows, killed the lights and engine, and waited. The silence was thick and oppressive. After a moment, Bruce let out a low, rumbling growl, sensing something unseen. Dave opened the door, and the dog dropped effortlessly to the ground, powerful shoulders rolling as he padded silently forward. Dave followed, scanning the landscape. Escape routes, ambush points, hiding places — he noted them all.

Exactly at midnight, headlights appeared, slicing harsh beams across the dilapidated buildings. Zhao's black sedan rolled smoothly into the yard, stopping a careful distance away. Zhao stepped out, calm, impeccably dressed, as if he were attending a board meeting rather than a clandestine rendezvous. He took in the surroundings, his gaze finally settling on Dave, then Bruce.

Zhao's eyes narrowed slightly. "You brought company."

Dave shrugged, deliberately casual. "Didn't think he'd bother you. Bruce is my companion dog."

Zhao studied Bruce, clearly unimpressed. "Let's hope, for his sake, you're right."

Dave said nothing, letting the silence hang heavily between them.

Zhao stepped closer, stopping just out of the dog's reach. "Let's get straight to it, Mr. Callahan. You've had time. What have you found?"

Dave's voice was cold, measured. "Enough."

Zhao's lips curled slightly, a flicker of amusement. "I need details, Callahan. Not vagaries."

"I've followed Red's trail exactly where he wanted me to. To a crossroads, a sandstone arrow, and a shed with nothing but ghosts and dust," Dave replied, careful to keep key details to himself.

Zhao's gaze hardened. "I warned you not to hold anything back. You have more. You know more. Tell me."

Dave forced himself to remain steady, though his pulse hammered against his ribs. "That's it. That's all there was."

Zhao sighed softly, reaching beneath his coat. Bruce growled louder, fur standing rigid along his spine. Zhao slowly drew a pistol — not aiming, just making a clear statement of dominance. "You're a poor liar, Callahan."

Dave didn't move, didn't blink, didn't flinch. "You asked. I told you."

The silence stretched between them, brittle as glass. Then Zhao's phone buzzed sharply. He hesitated, annoyed, then glanced at the screen. Whatever he saw made his jaw clench, his fingers tightening around the weapon. For a moment, Zhao's perfect composure cracked, revealing something raw beneath.

"Trouble in paradise?" Dave asked, seizing the brief opportunity.

Zhao recovered instantly, his expression smoothing out. He holstered his pistol slowly, deliberately. "One day, Callahan. You have one day to bring me something useful — or your family suffers the consequences. Remember, you are never beyond my reach."

Dave nodded tightly, barely containing the rage boiling inside him. Zhao turned on his heel, returning swiftly to his car. He cast one final glance at Bruce, wary this time, before disappearing inside.

The sedan spun out, wheels biting into the gravel, leaving behind a cloud of dust as it vanished into the darkness. Only when the silence had fully returned did Dave let his shoulders relax, exhaling heavily into the cool night air.

Bruce stood at Dave's side, massive head tilted, ears still alert, eyes fixed on the spot Zhao's car had occupied moments before. Dave reached down, burying his fingers into the thick fur around the dog's neck. "Good job, mate. You scared him good."

But Bruce didn't relax. He growled again, deeper this time, a primal, rumbling threat directed into the empty darkness. Dave felt a chill run down his spine.

Bruce sensed something Dave hadn't yet grasped. Zhao hadn't left out of fear.

He'd left because whatever message he'd received had changed his priorities.

Zhao wasn't running away.

He was getting ready to strike.

CHAPTER 40

The night was deep, the kind of black that swallowed the land whole. Out here, there were no streetlights, no distant glow of a town. Just stars, sharp as shattered glass, burning cold in the sky.

Martha sat on the veranda, her rifle resting against her knee, the warmth of a fresh cup of tea curling steam into the air. The air was crisp, dry, carrying the scent of dust and eucalyptus. Somewhere beyond the fence line, something rustled through the brush.

She listened.

Another rustle. A grunt. Pigs.

Martha sighed, lifted the rifle, and rested it against her shoulder. Wild pigs were a menace out here. They tore through gardens, rooted up crops, wrecked fences. A good shot behind the ear was the only solution.

She lined up, exhaled slow —

A crunch of gravel.

She didn't lower the gun, just tilted her head slightly, listening. A car. Not a stranger. Strangers hesitated, uncertain, rolled in slow like they knew they shouldn't be here.

This one came steady, sure.

She smiled to herself.

Callahan.

The pigs could wait.

She squeezed the trigger one last time. The shot cracked through the night, rolling over the hills like a thunderclap. The biggest of the pigs squealed once, staggered, then dropped into the dirt.

Martha stood and worked the bolt.

By the time Dave pulled up, she was waiting.

The vehicle's engine cut out, leaving only the tick of cooling metal and the rustling of the night. Bruce jumped down first, shaking off the night's tension, trotting up the veranda steps like he belonged there. Martha gave him a once-over, nodded.

"Good lad. You keep Callahan in one piece?"

Bruce let out a huff, sniffed the air, then padded inside like his job was done.

Dave stepped out slower. He looked worse than when he'd left. Like the night had put something heavier on his back.

Martha didn't say anything right away. Just looked at him, then took a long sip of her tea.

"You want to tell me why you're back at my door at this hour, Callahan?"

Dave rubbed a hand down his face, exhaustion catching up now that the adrenaline had bled away. "Figured you'd still be up."

Martha snorted. "Damn right I'm up. Pigs don't shoot themselves."

Dave glanced past her at the limp shape in the dirt beyond the fence. "Nice shot."

She smirked. "Yeah, well, I was about to go for another when I heard you coming."

Dave gave a tired nod, but he wasn't really there, his thoughts somewhere else.

Martha saw it. She set her tea down and crossed her arms. "So. You alive?"

Dave blinked.

It took him a second to process the question.

Then he nodded. "Yeah."

"You kill the bastard?"

"No."

Martha clicked her tongue. "Shame."

Silence stretched. Only the constant hum of cicadas.

Then Martha sighed. "Well, don't just stand there lookin' like a lost dog. Sit your arse down."

Dave lowered himself onto the top step, resting his elbows on his knees. His whole body ached.

Martha disappeared inside for a moment, then came back with a bottle and two glasses. She poured him a measure of brandy, slid it over.

"Drink. You look like you need it."

Dave took the glass, swallowed a mouthful. It burned, but it helped.

Martha sat beside him. "So tell me."

Dave didn't answer right away. Just ran a hand through his hair, then rested his forehead against his palm.

Martha watched him. Her voice softened, just a fraction.

"I heard back."

Dave lifted his head.

She nodded. "They're safe."

For a second, nothing happened.

Then Dave closed his eyes.

His shoulders slumped. His breath came out sharp, ragged.

He didn't make a sound, but Martha saw it. The way his jaw clenched. The way his hands curled into fists, like he was holding it in, forcing it down.

She let it sit.

She didn't offer comfort, didn't pat his back or tell him it was alright. That wasn't her way.

Instead, she poured him another drink.

"Go on, then," she said. "Get it out."

Dave wiped his eyes, swallowed hard. "They're safe."

Martha nodded.

He let out a breath, shaking his head. "Jesus. When can I call them?"

"They'll call us. Tomorrow. That's just how it works."

"That fucker had me rattled. I was ready to bow down and do anything he asked. Thank you."

Martha took another sip of her brandy. "Didn't think I'd let some slick prick like Zhao get the drop on me, did you?"

Dave gave a small, breathless laugh. "No. Guess not."

Martha smirked, but there was something else in her eyes. Something softer.

Bruce nudged Dave's leg, then flopped down beside him.

Martha watched them both.

"You did good, Callahan," she said quietly.

Dave leaned forward, elbows on his knees.

"Yeah," he muttered. "Let's see if I can keep it up."

Martha just took another slow sip of her drink.

No promises. No reassurances.

Just a shared brandy, the night, and the quiet understanding of two people who knew the world didn't give a damn if you lived or died.

But for now, just for this moment, the fight could wait.

CHAPTER 41

The road stretched ahead, a vein of black asphalt cutting through the empty land. No streetlights, no markers — just an unbroken void swallowing the night. Zhao's headlights barely pushed back the darkness, illuminating little more than the next ten metres. Beyond that, the world did not exist.

Inside the car, silence reigned. The low hum of the engine was the only sound, steady and relentless. Zhao's thumb tapped a slow, deliberate rhythm on the steering column—controlled. Measured. Like a man counting down.

The meeting with Callahan had gone as expected. Almost.

The man hadn't caved. That was a problem.

But Zhao had expected resistance. Had planned for it.

Because Callahan was predictable.

He could be pushed. Bent. Broken.

Leverage was the key.

And Zhao had leverage.

Or at least, he had.

His phone had vibrated mid-meeting. A single message had flashed across the screen.

Urgent. Call. Situation changed.

Zhao let out a slow breath through his nose. Without looking away from the road, he pressed the button on the console.

The call connected after one ring. A voice answered — tight, hesitant.

"Sir."

Zhao's fingers tightened around the wheel. "Talk."

A pause. Too long. The kind of silence that preceded bad news. Then —

"The Callahan woman and the child… They're gone."

Zhao did not blink. Did not react. He let the words settle.

"Define gone."

His voice was calm. Too calm.

The hesitation stretched.

"No sign of them. No struggle. No forced entry. They just — vanished."

Zhao felt it before he heard it. A ripple of something uncalculated.

The man on the other end cleared his throat. "We moved in as planned, at the same time you were meeting Callahan. The house was empty. Like they were never there."

Zhao's grip on the wheel tightened slightly.

"Surveillance?"

"Nothing. No vehicles in or out for six hours. We had eyes on the residence all night. No movement. Then —"

"Then they disappeared."

"Yes, sir."

Zhao kept his eyes on the road, fingers drumming once against the wheel. His mind was already working.

This wasn't Callahan.

The man had been too rattled, too desperate. He hadn't even known they were being watched until Zhao had shown him the photos. He'd barely kept himself together.

No.

This was someone else.

A new player.

Zhao pulled a cigarette from the packet beside him, flicked his lighter. The flame flared against the windshield, carving shadows across his face. He inhaled deeply, let the smoke curl around his exhale.

"Check airports, train stations, bus depots. If they've left town, I want to know how."

The man on the line hesitated.

Zhao noticed. His fingers tapped once against the wheel. "Problem?"

"Sir… I don't think they left town."

Zhao narrowed his eyes. "Why not?"

The hesitation again. This time, the man spoke quickly, like he needed to get it out before he lost his nerve.

"Because it's too clean."

Zhao said nothing.

The man continued, voice lower now. "If it was Callahan — if he had panicked and tried to run them out — there would be a trail. A purchase, a ticket, a car rental. Something. But this?" A breath. "It is like they were plucked out of thin air. No trace. No footprint."

Zhao's fingers stopped tapping.

A professional job.

Someone who knew how to disappear.

Someone he hadn't accounted for.

He flicked ash from his cigarette, his thoughts turning over like gears clicking into place.

Had someone been watching him while he was watching Callahan?

That meant he wasn't just hunting.

Someone else was hunting too.

Zhao took another drag, exhaled slowly.

"Find them." His voice was ice. "Every resource we have. Find them."

A beat.

"Yes, sir."

The call ended.

The night swallowed the silence whole.

Zhao kept driving. The stars above were cold, distant, a scatter of dead light across the void.

This was not how it was supposed to go.

He had calculated for Callahan's resistance. Had prepared for it.

But not this.

Not a ghost move.

Zhao flicked the cigarette out the window. His expression did not change. His eyes stayed fixed on the road.

His phone sat silent.

For now.

But it wouldn't stay that way.

No one disappeared without leaving a shadow.

And he would find it.

CHAPTER 42

The morning light stretched long and golden over the verandah, spilling across the worn wooden boards and casting soft shadows over the scrubland. The air was crisp, dry, carrying the scent of dust, eucalyptus, and the lingering smoke from Martha Redmond's cigarette. She sat in her usual chair, one boot propped up on the railing, her rifle balanced across her lap. A half-drunk cup of tea rested beside her, long since cold, but she wasn't the type to fuss over things like that.

She heard Dave before she saw him. The crunch of gravel under boots. The slow, heavy steps of a man running on fumes. A man that had just spent the night sleeping in his car.

Martha didn't look up. Just lined up another shot and squeezed the trigger. A feral rabbit flipped sideways in the distance, kicking up dust before going still. The dogs — Bruce among them now, back from his midnight adventure — perked up at the sound but didn't move from their spots at her feet. The world kept moving, even after the kill.

"Don't mind me," Dave muttered, stepping onto the verandah, voice rough with exhaustion.

"Wouldn't dream of it," Martha said, setting her rifle down. She glanced at Bruce, who thumped his tail against the boards, his big head swivelling toward Dave. "At least you brought my dog back in one piece."

Dave ran a hand over his face. "Think this only comes in one piece."

Martha studied him for a long moment. Then she pushed herself up and disappeared inside.

When she returned, she had two mugs in her hands. She shoved one into his.

"Drink."

Dave took a sip. Coffee. Strong, black, thick enough to chew. It hit like a punch to the gut, burning all the way down. He wasn't sure if it was helping or making things worse.

Martha sat back down, stretching out her legs. "Your girls are safe."

Dave's fingers clenched around the mug. He'd known it the moment he walked onto the verandah, but hearing it still hit like a fist to the ribs. He stared into his coffee, blinking hard, forcing down the lump in his throat.

Martha pretended not to notice.

"They're with good people," she said. "People who don't take kindly to men who think they own women and kids."

Dave finally looked at her. "How?"

Martha tapped ash off her cigarette. "Got a few friends in places most people don't know exist. We help women disappear. Women who need it. Men like Zhao, the ones who think they can just take what they want? They don't get to have their way. Not with my people."

Dave let out a slow breath. "Thank you."

Martha shrugged. "Don't thank me. Thank The Bush Widows."

Dave frowned. "Who?"

Martha took another drag of her cigarette. "It's what we call ourselves. Started years back, just a handful of women who'd had enough of men doing as they pleased. Now? We're bigger than you'd think. We've got places all over. Farms, properties, safe houses. No one finds them unless we want them to be found."

She smiled, dry and slow. "Sort of like the CWA. Less scones and morning teas, more shotguns and silence."

Dave stared into his coffee. "And you just took them? Moved them?"

Martha's eyes sharpened. "They weren't yours to lose, Callahan. They were theirs to take back."

Dave swallowed hard. A knot tightened in his throat. He had spent so much time thinking of them as his — his family, his responsibility, his failure to protect. But Martha was right. Sally had never belonged to him. And Cassie? She was her own person, growing, learning. They had taken back their freedom, not waited for him to hand it to them.

Martha didn't soften, but she let out a slow breath. "The Bush Widows don't just protect women, Callahan. We bury the men who deserve it."

Dave finally let out a breath he hadn't realised he'd been holding. For the first time since Zhao sent those photos, he felt something close to relief.

Martha watched him for a moment before reaching under her chair and pulling out a small, battered tin box. She placed it on the table between them and unlatched the clip.

"Henry left something for you."

Dave eyed the box. "For me?"

Martha gave him a dry look and lifted the item out. "Not you specifically, but whoever made it this far. Which, for now, is you."

Dave knew it instantly. The toy plane from the photo in Red's cell. The picture locked in the plane's hidden compartment. The one with two kids — Henry as a boy, gripping this very toy.

Martha picked it up, turning it over in her hands.

Not Red.

Henry.

Dave watched as she traced her fingers over the worn metal, the places where time and childhood had left their marks. Then she handed it to him.

"Turn it over," she said.

Dave did.

Etched into the underside of the wing were a series of numbers.

Coordinates. Faded, worn down by time.

His breath caught. He looked up at her.

Martha gave a knowing smirk. "Henry always was a sneaky little shit."

She sat down again, stretching out her legs. "You know, I always thought I'd be the one to go looking for it one day."

Dave sat down across from her, still holding the plane. "For what?"

Martha nodded once. "For the truth."

She met his gaze, her expression unreadable.

"You want to know the real Henry Redmond?" she asked.

Dave nodded.

Martha leaned back, folding her arms. "Henry was smart. Smarter than most. Didn't matter if it was books, machines, people — he figured them out. Fast. Didn't have a father worth a damn, so he learned how to be his own man quick. Knew how to talk, how to charm. Learnt to fly a plane when most kids were learning to drive. And he had big ideas. Always looking at the angles."

She paused, shaking her head. "But life doesn't give a shit about brains or charm. Our mother died young. Left us with nothing but a drunk old bastard who barely remembered we existed. Henry took care of me, made sure I had what I needed. And when he got old enough, he got the hell out."

Her fingers drummed against the table. "But he never forgot me. Even when he got mixed up in the wrong shit. Even when the stories started coming out about the opal job, the murder, the arrest."

She went quiet for a moment, letting the weight of it all settle.

Martha took a final drag of her cigarette, then crushed it out.

She didn't speak for a moment. Just stared at the tabletop like it held more than dust and memories.

"He came here once," she said finally. "After the job. After Parker was killed."

Dave looked up, watching her closely.

"Dropped in just before dawn. Like a ghost. Hadn't seen him in months." She gave a soft, dry laugh. "Didn't even knock. Just sat on the veranda with a mug of tea like nothing had changed."

She leaned back, eyes narrowing with the memory.

"Handed me a wad of cash. Fresh notes. Fifties and hundreds, thick enough to choke on. Told me to use it for the place. To make things right if he didn't come back."

Dave stayed silent.

"Said he'd dropped an envelope on the front step of a copper's house, too. Parker's widow, I reckon. Wouldn't say what was in it. Just said it was 'what was owed.'"

Her voice didn't shake, but her knuckles whitened around her cigarette case.

"He wasn't proud of what he'd done. But he didn't run from it either. He made his choices. Paid for them his way."

She paused, then nodded toward the toy plane.

"And now he's asking someone else to carry the last piece."

Dave exhaled sharply. Coordinates.

Martha took a final drag of her cigarette, then crushed it out. "That's where Henry wanted you to go."

Dave closed his fist around the plane. "What's there?"

Martha leaned back, eyes sharp. "Only one way to find out."

Dave stared at the numbers, his pulse ticking up. The next step was clear. Even if the numbers were almost illegible.

"You want to come see, don't you?"

"Other than a funeral and a headstone, this might be the last time Henry plays any part in my life. So yeah, I do."

Dave gave a small nod.

"Then let's find out what he was hiding."

CHAPTER 43

The road out to the property was worse than Blake expected. Corrugated dirt, potholes big enough to swallow a small car, and no sign of life except for the occasional wedge-tailed eagle picking apart some roadkill. Dust clouded in his rearview, rolling like smoke.

Every jolt of the suspension shook something loose — metal, bone, and memory.

And that's when it came back. Uninvited. Unwelcome.

The first time he met Red.

Christ, the land out here looked the same as it did fifty-five years ago.

Same brittle paddocks. Same rusted fence lines leaning like old men. Same stink of heat and dry grass.

Back then, Blake had been fresh off training — Constable Adrian Blake. Posted out west, like they all were. Earn your stripes where no one's watching. Where a blind eye could be bought with a beer and a nod.

He took the beer. Took the counter meal. Took the folded cash with a smile.

Didn't take long before word got around — Blake was easy. You didn't need to twist his arm, just grease it.

And that's when he met Red.

Coonamble, 1960s

Coonamble hadn't changed much either. Back then, it was all beer guts, sunburnt brickwork, and the slow churn of rumour.

Blake walked into the pub like he owned the place. Uniform. Rolled sleeves. A swagger that came with knowing the rules, and knowing exactly when to ignore them.

He saw Red at the back — long hair, boots on the rung of the chair, a quiet smirk that said he didn't give a shit who walked in.

Whispers had been circling Red for months. Nothing proven. Nothing clean. Just enough to catch Blake's ear.

Blake ordered a beer, wandered over, and leaned on Red's table like they were old mates.

"Name's Blake," he said. "Senior Constable. I know things. You want to keep things running smooth... might be worth knowing me too."

Red didn't say much that first time. But his eyes never left Blake's face.

Blake leaned in closer. Quiet. Controlled.

"Funny thing, that property outside Baradine. Not in your name, but you visit it more than your own mum's grave. You're good at hiding, Red. But not good enough."

That's when it started.

At first, Blake fed him scraps — info on patrol schedules, who was sniffing around what. And in return? Red kept things civil. Kicked up a bit of cash. A bottle here. A nod there.

But it changed. Blake changed.

The threats got heavier. The demands more pointed. He started mentioning Red's sister.

"Martha," Blake had said once, slow and deliberate. "Pretty girl. Real quiet. Be a shame if someone thought she was mixed up in something."

That was the line. Crossed and buried.

Red didn't forget.

And neither did Blake.

Then one day, Blake heard something. Quiet. Too quiet to be public yet. A whisper out of Lightning Ridge.

A Chinese billionaire. Wanted a plane. No records. No names. Just a runway, a quiet pilot, and a promise to stay invisible.

Cargo?

Blake never got the full story.

Only that it was worth everything.

And Red was the one they picked to fly it.

The memory bled out as the landscape grew sharper again — real, immediate.

The shed came into view, wavering through the heat shimmer and dust. A squat, weather-beaten structure hunched low against the horizon, like it was trying to hide.

Blake gripped the wheel tighter. His knuckles ached.

"All these years, Red…" he muttered, voice dry as the windscreen dust. "All that sneaking around. You thought you got away with it."

He killed the engine a hundred metres out, letting the silence swallow him whole.

The dust hung like breath over the land. Nothing moved.

But Blake knew better.

Something always moved.

Blake had done his homework before making the trip. The property was leased — 99 years, paid upfront. No paper trail led back to Redmond directly, but it didn't take much to figure out who had been using the place. The real owner was some old bastard named Frank Tolliver. Lived alone. Kept to himself. The kind of guy who didn't ask questions as long as the cheque cleared.

The place looked like a relic from another time. The land was brittle and cracked, a sea of dead grass stretching to the horizon. A rusted-out tractor sat half-buried in the dirt, long since abandoned.

And then there was the shed.

The structure itself was a mess of corrugated iron and old timber beams. The roof sagged in places, eaten away by rust. But the door — the door was solid. Proper heavy-duty steel, locked up tight with a thick padlock. Someone had made damn sure that whatever was inside stayed inside.

Blake stepped out of the car, the heat hitting him like a wall. The air smelled like dry earth and sunbaked metal. He rolled his shoulders, stretched, then reached into his jacket, pulling out his handgun.

No point pissing around.

Blake raised the pistol, took a step closer, and fired.

The shot cracked through the silence, shattering the stillness of the bush. The lock exploded in a spray of metal fragments. The door groaned open an inch under its own weight.

Blake stepped forward —

And heard the shotgun rack behind him.

"That was a dumb fucking move."

Blake froze. Frank Tolliver. The voice was old but firm, carrying the weight of a man who wasn't about to be intimidated.

Blake turned slowly.

The old man stood about ten metres away, double-barrelled shotgun raised, the stock planted firm against his shoulder. His hair was white, his skin weathered leather, and his eyes — his eyes didn't blink.

Blake sighed. "Frank Tolliver, I presume."

Frank didn't lower the gun. "You wanna tell me why the fuck you're shooting at my shed?"

Blake gave a slow, easy shrug. "Door was locked."

Frank's jaw twitched. "That's usually the point."

Blake kept his hands loose, non-threatening. "Relax, old man. I'm police." He reached into his jacket, pulled his badge, and held it up.

Frank didn't even glance at it. "You shooting the door a part of official police work?"

Blake smirked. "Creative policing."

Frank finally lowered the shotgun. "Don't see many city cops out this way."

Blake nodded toward the shed. "That because most of them don't know what's in there?"

Frank huffed a humourless laugh. "You mean the plane?"

Blake's eyes narrowed. "So you do know what's inside."

Frank gave a slow nod. "Knew it the moment Red showed up with it. Paid for the lease up front, told me to keep the place locked up tight until he came back." He spat onto the dirt. "But you already knew that, didn't you?"

Blake said nothing.

Frank slung the shotgun under one arm and walked past Blake toward the shed. He grabbed the edge of the heavy steel door and yanked it open the rest of the way.

Dust and darkness.

The interior was thick with cobwebs, the air stale, untouched for decades.

Blake stepped inside.

And there it was.

The plane.

What was left of it, anyway.

The Piper Navajo. Stripped, gutted, its wings removed. A skeleton of metal and lost time.

Blake ran a hand over the fuselage. "When's the last time you saw Red?"

Frank sighed. "A long time ago."

"Did he leave anything behind?"

Frank's eyes flicked to the small metal box sitting near the plane's cockpit.

Blake followed the look.

Walked toward it.

Kneeled.

The box was old but solid, sealed with a combination lock.

And then he saw it.

A letter wedged beneath the box.

A folded envelope, yellowed with age, the ink faded but still clear enough to read.

Blakes Eyes Only. Do Not Remove.

Blake's stomach knotted.

Frank crossed his arms. "That one's been waiting a long time."

Blake swallowed, ripping the envelope free.

Tore it open.

His eyes scanned the page.

And his blood went cold.

Time to pay your dues, Blake. He had a Logbook and taped very fucking word. You dumb bastard.

Blake clenched his jaw.

He folded the letter, slipping it into his pocket. His hand hovered over the locked box.

Frank watched him carefully. "Whatever's in there — you ready for it?"

Blake didn't answer.

He just reached for the lock.

Blake crouched down, running his fingers over the combination lock. The numbers were dulled with age, the dial stiff from years of dust and disuse.

He tapped the metal once with a knuckle.

Yeah, fuck this.

Without hesitation, he stood, drew his pistol, and lined up the sights.

Frank, still leaning in the doorway, let out an unimpressed grunt. "That's one way to do it."

Blake pulled the trigger.

BANG.

The lock exploded, fragments pinging off the walls. Dust swirled from the rafters. The shot echoed in the tin shed like a thunderclap.

Frank didn't even flinch. Just let out a slow, tired sigh. "You impatient prick. What if it had something fragile inside?"

Blake ignored him. He holstered the gun, kicked away the broken lock, and wrenched the box open.

Empty.

Blake froze, his pulse hammering against his ribs.

No notes. No opals. No evidence.

Just a hollow, rust-streaked interior.

His jaw clenched so tight his teeth ached.

Red played me.

He'd been sure — fucking sure — that this was it. Red's final move. And now? Nothing.

Blake slammed the lid shut so hard the hinges squealed. "Fucking hell!"

Frank snorted. "Yeah, that'll fix it."

Blake turned on him, eyes dark. "Did you open it?"

Frank let out a humourless chuckle. "If I'd opened it, don't you reckon I'd know what was inside?" He nodded at the empty box. "Someone else got here first, mate. And unless you think the bloody tooth fairy cracked the lock, you already know who it was."

Blake clenched his jaw, already pulling out his phone.

The call connected after two rings.

Tombs' voice came through, thick with amusement. "Well, well. The prodigal cop calls."

Blake cut straight to it. "Where's Callahan?"

A pause. Then, smirking, "Why? Lose something?"

Blake's grip tightened around the phone. "Don't fuck with me, mate. Where is he?"

Tombs chuckled, slow and knowing. "Relax. Last I heard, he was heading west. Somewhere near Gunnedah. Pretty keen on chasing ghosts, that one."

Blake didn't respond. Just ended the call.

His eyes flicked back to the box. Then to the letter, and he read it again.

Blake —

Time to pay your dues. He had a Logbook and taped every fucking word. You dumb bastard.

No signature. It didn't need one.

Blake's fingers tightened around the paper, his nails digging into the parchment.

Red had something or was it all bluff. Something he had tried to hold over Blake for nearly fifty years. And this was all spiralling to hell.

And if Callahan had something. Something real.

Then he had to take him down.

Blake shoved the letter into his pocket, jaw tight. His mind was already shifting gears.

Frank crossed his arms. "So, what now? You gonna shoot something else and hope it gives you a different answer?"

Blake turned to him, his patience gone. "Who else knew about this place?"

Frank snorted. "Like I'm gonna tell you shit."

Blake took a step closer. "Listen, old man —"

Frank pushed off the doorway, stepping in close, eyes burning with something fierce. "No, you listen, you smug prick. I don't owe you a goddamn thing. You barge in here, waving your badge like it means something, shooting shit up like a cowboy, and now you wanna act like you're in charge? Mate, I don't give a single fuck who you are."

Blake's nostrils flared. He wasn't used to being spoken to like that. Especially not by some bush relic.

Frank jabbed a finger into his chest. "Red paid me upfront, ninety-nine years to keep this place locked up. You think I was about to let some dickhead in a badge just waltz in and take what he wanted? Nah. But guess what? Someone figured it out before you did. And that means you're a day late and a dollar short, Detective."

Blake stared him down, but Frank didn't back off.

Finally, Blake let out a slow breath, stepping back.

"Fine." His voice was tight. Controlled. "Then I guess I'm done here."

Frank smirked. "Yeah? Well, don't let the door hit you on the arse on the way out."

Blake walked past him without another word, climbing into his car, his mind already working through the next move.

As the engine roared to life, he fired off a single text. To the only other person he could half trust.

Tombs, but maybe trust was the wrong word. Use.

"Find Callahan. Now."

Then he gunned the engine, sending gravel flying as he tore out of there.

If Callahan thought he had the upper hand, he was dead fucking wrong.

CHAPTER 44

Zhao sat in the dimly lit motel room, the glow from his laptop screen casting sharp angles across his face. The room smelled of stale air conditioning and cheap aftershave, but he barely noticed. His mind was elsewhere.

Sally and Cassie Callahan had vanished.

He steadied his breathing. His contact in Hong Kong had already sent a dozen frantic messages.

Liu was waiting.

Zhao reached for his Bluetooth earpiece and tapped the line open. It rang once.

Then Liu's voice cut through, cool and detached.

"Report."

Zhao glanced at the encrypted files on his screen. He could lie. He could twist the truth just enough to keep Liu satisfied.

But Liu Jianhong didn't tolerate uncertainty.

"Callahan's family. They're gone."

A pause.

"When?"

Zhao kept his voice even. "Sometime last night. We moved in during the meet with Callahan. The house was empty. No signs of struggle, no sign of them leaving in a hurry. They were removed."

Silence. Then —

"Who took them?"

"Unknown." Zhao scrolled through the surveillance images. "Whoever it was, they were professionals. Left nothing behind. No tyre tracks. No digital footprint. No calls or messages. It was a ghost move."

Liu was quiet. Then, a slow exhale.

"Unacceptable."

Zhao's jaw tightened. His fingers curled into a fist beneath the desk.

Liu's voice stayed even, almost soft. "The wife and child were your leverage. Now you have none. And yet, Callahan is still breathing. Explain."

Zhao gritted his teeth. Not yet. Callahan couldn't die yet.

"We still need him," Zhao said. "He's following the trail. I'm letting him do the hard work for us. When he finds what Red left behind, then we take him."

Liu didn't speak right away. Zhao forced himself not to fidget. He adjusted his cuff instead, smoothing out a wrinkle that wasn't there.

Then —

"Your mistakes are stacking, Zhao." Liu's voice was quiet, but the weight behind it was suffocating. "And I don't let other people's mistakes become mine."

A small bead of sweat trickled down Zhao's temple. "I understand."

Liu's voice dropped further, something worse than anger. "Then don't make another one."

The line went dead.

Zhao sat still for a moment, heart steady but too loud in his own ears.

Then he reached for his phone.

He scrolled through his contacts, stopping at a name few people in this country knew.

Declan Holt.

Ex-military. Discharged with honours, but too dangerous for peacetime. A man with no moral compass, no loyalty — except to money and the hunt. The kind of operator you didn't hire unless you were ready to burn everything down.

Zhao tapped out a message.

Got a job. Tracking. Need you watching a man named Callahan. A Detective Blake assisting him. Payment as usual.

Minutes passed.

Then a reply.

Understood. Send details.

No questions. No hesitation. Holt was already moving.

Zhao set the phone down. Took a breath. Then, finally, he pulled up another contact.

This one, even more dangerous.

Not Liu.

Someone else.

Zhao's lips curled into the faintest smirk as he typed the message.

"It's time. Start moving the pieces."

A moment later, the message was marked as read. No reply.

He didn't need one.

Zhao leaned back in his chair, tapping a single finger against the armrest.

Let Liu think he was scrambling.

Let Callahan think he had a chance.

Let them all keep chasing ghosts.

Because in the end?

They wouldn't even see him coming.

CHAPTER 45

Declan sat in the dim glow of his laptop, fingers moving with the kind of steady precision that came from years of practice. Hunting wasn't just about instinct. It was about data. Information. The right trail.

And Declan was very, very good at following trails.

He leaned back in the shitty motel chair, the cheap wood creaking under his weight. Outside, the neon flicker of a half-dead 'Vacancy' sign hummed against the night.

The call from Zhao had been short. Efficient.

"Callahan's a ghost. But not completely. He has a dog."

"Dog?"

"Large breed. Callahan called him Bruce."

"Bruce," Declan repeated, rolling the name over in his mouth.

Zhao had given him the rest of the puzzle pieces. A rough description of Callahan. The plate from the small 4WD. The places he'd been seen. The fact that he wasn't alone anymore. Someone was helping him.

Declan wasn't just a gun-for-hire. He wasn't some ex-military burnout, or a thug who solved problems with fists and bullets. He was a tracker. The kind of man who found people who thought they couldn't be found.

And now, he had a name. Bruce.

Declan cracked his knuckles, then got to work.

Hacking wasn't his primary skill, but he knew enough. More than enough.

The plate went nowhere. Rented to some prison officer. McBride. Declan didn't know the name or how it fit into this. He mentally filed that away for later. No GPS or tracking available on the vehicle.

Time to try a different angle.

He dug into vet databases. Not directly — too much security. Instead, he ran through third-party scheduling apps, old appointment records, automated reminders.

In a five-hundred-kilometre radius, there were forty-seven large dogs registered under the name Bruce.

Too many.

He narrowed it. Owners with rural addresses. That cut the list down.

Then he ran a cross-check with other data Zhao had fed him. Callahan had gone west. Deep country. No major towns. The name Redmond had come up.

Declan adjusted the search.

A match.

Martha Redmond. Rural property. Middle of nowhere. Perfect place to hide.

Declan smirked. Gotcha.

The drive was long. But Declan was used to waiting.

He stopped at a petrol station along the way, buying a sausage roll that tasted like disappointment and a black coffee that barely deserved the name. He sat in his car, eating slowly, watching.

No sign of Callahan yet. But that was fine.

He was ahead of the bastard now. Already in position before the prey even knew he was being hunted.

He reached into the glovebox, pulling out a pair of binoculars. The land stretched ahead, dusty and bare, brittle grass swaying in the lazy heat. A property sat in the distance. A house. A garden — too green for this wasteland. Someone here knew how to survive.

And there, at the edge of the verandah, lay Bruce.

Big. Heavy. Muscled. A dog built to fight.

Declan smiled.

He lifted his phone, sent a quick message to Zhao.

"I have them."

Then, he settled in.

Watching.

Waiting.

Because Callahan had no idea he was already dead.

Declan adjusted the dial on his receiver, fine-tuning the signal. The eavesdropping device was simple — a directional microphone. It wouldn't pick up everything, but it didn't need to. He just needed enough.

The frequency crackled. Then —

"Dave?"

A woman's voice.

Declan leaned in, listening.

"Sally," Callahan's voice came through, rough, quiet.

A pause.

"Are you safe?"

Another pause.

Then Sally exhaled. Her voice distant, barely audible. "We're safe. I just needed to hear your voice."

Declan could hear the weight behind it. The fear.

She didn't know who he was. But he knew her.

He'd seen the photos Zhao had sent. Watched them on the beach, ice creams in hand, oblivious.

He could use this.

For now, he let them talk.

Nothing valuable. Just emotion. People clinging to things that wouldn't save them.

Then — a shift.

"Dave. What the fuck is going on? People turn up in the middle of the night and say we have to go. We're not safe and that you arranged it."

"I am sorry babe. But you need to trust these people. I'll sort this out. Things will be better soon."

"Are you safe?" It was a question Dave didn't know the answer too.

"Yeah, but I have to go," Callahan said. "Stay put. Don't call me again unless you have to."

"I love you."

Callahan didn't say it back before hanging up.

Declan smiled. Cold. Detached. That was good. Men like that were easier to break.

Declan refocused on the house.

Martha Redmond stepped onto the verandah, her stance solid, like she owned the dirt beneath her boots. Which, in a way, she did.

She gestured toward Callahan, then toward his car.

Declan frowned.

This wasn't random. She had something in mind.

Then Callahan grabbed his keys.

They were leaving.

Declan watched as they climbed into the car. Martha in the passenger seat, Bruce hopping in behind.

Declan didn't follow immediately. He waited. Let them put some distance between them.

Then he started his car and eased onto the road, trailing far enough back to be a ghost. Following the cloud of dust that led him on for the next forty-five minutes.

Declan parked on a ridge, switching to his binoculars.

The shed sat low in the dust, its corrugated iron walls dulled by years of neglect. Callahan and the old woman got out.

That's when Declan noticed the other man.

Declan tensed.

Not just some old bush bastard. His posture was wrong. Not slouched, not slow. Disciplined. The kind of man who had muscle memory that never left. And carrying a rifle.

The way he watched Callahan. The way he stood.

Declan knew that stance.

This wasn't just some hermit.

He was military. Declan needed intelligence. This time he rang. He gave his location and a few commands. Property owner. Military history.

Declan lowered the binoculars slightly.

The only sound a keyboard clacking on the other end of the call.

Vietnam. Covert ops. Highly decorated. A ghost in the jungle. Tolliver, Frank. Sniper.

This wasn't ideal. He didn't need another variable.

He let out a slow breath, recalculating.

The trio had all gone inside the shed. After a minute Tolliver had come back outside. His rifle gone from his hand.

Callahan wasn't alone anymore.

And that changed things.

Declan steadied the rifle, adjusting his scope with care.

He wasn't one for mistakes.

One shot. One clean kill.

And yet — something wasn't right.

His crosshairs settled on Frank Tolliver, the old bastard standing outside the shed, leaning against the fence post like he had all the time in the world.

Declan knew enough about the man now. Frank Tolliver.

Vietnam. Covert ops. Highly decorated.

That part didn't bother him. Hell, he respected it.

But old soldiers were still just that — old.

Slower. Weaker.

That's what he told himself, anyway.

Declan exhaled, squeezed the trigger —

And at the last second, Frank moved.

The bullet punched into his shoulder instead of his skull, a red mist kicking up as Frank spun back, dropping hard to the dirt.

"Shit."

Declan immediately shifted position. Something was off.

He watched through the scope, expecting panic. Confusion.

Instead?

Frank was already rolling behind cover, his good hand yanking a pistol free from beneath his shirt.

Declan gritted his teeth.

The old fucker knew.

**

Dave jerked his head up as the rifle shot cracked through the air. Martha was inside the old plane, lifting panels. Studying every inch.

When the shot came, Martha was already moving.

"What the fuck —" Dave started, but she was already shoving him toward the far wall.

Frank's shouted curse came from outside, followed by a heavy thud. He was hit.

Martha's eyes sharpened. "That wasn't some random shot."

She grabbed Frank's rifle from beside the door.

Bruce growled, his ears back, pacing near the door.

Dave pressed himself against the inside of the shed, heart hammering.

Another shot didn't come.

Whoever was out there was watching. Waiting.

Dave's eyes darted to Martha. "Frank —"

"He's breathing," she muttered, glancing toward the crack in the shed door. Her jaw was tight. "And he's got a gun, which means the bastard who shot him is gonna have a bad fuckin' day."

She tilted her head slightly. Listening.

Nothing.

Whoever had fired that shot wasn't making a move.

Not yet.

But that didn't mean they wouldn't.

Martha shifted to the side of the door, grip tight on the shotgun. "Dave, get ready to move."

Dave didn't argue.

Bruce whined, then crouched low. The dog had sensed it too.

Whoever had taken the shot?

They weren't done

******

Declan adjusted the scope.

Frank was alive. But that didn't mean much. A clean shoulder shot would slow him down, but not stop him.

And now the other two were alert.

The element of surprise? Gone. The situation was compromised. And now adrenaline was fuelling his body. Not something that made for good decisions.

This wasn't the time for a full engagement.

Declan packed up smoothly, no wasted movement. Within thirty seconds, his position was cold.

As he slid into his vehicle, he flicked open his phone.

Sent a message.

Lost visual. Target not neutralized. Adjusting strategy.

No name. No context. Just information.

He wasn't done.

He drove for five minutes. Putting some space between predator and prey. He moved to the rear of the vehicle, opened the boot and pulled out a small box.

The drone took to the air almost immediately, quickly climbing above the scrubby terrain and making its way back toward the shed.

This wasn't over yet.
Not by a long shot.

CHAPTER 46

The shed smelled of dust, old oil, and time gone still.

Cobwebs stitched it together while rust worked to tear it apart. And in the centre of it all sat the plane.

Dave ran a hand along the stripped fuselage of the Piper Navajo, its metal cold and pitted under his fingers. The place was a tomb, locked up tight for decades, waiting for someone to crack it open.

Martha stood beside him, arms folded, eyes scanning every inch of the plane. Her face was still, unreadable — but Dave had learned that meant she was working through something, thinking ten steps ahead.

Frank was propped against a workbench near the entrance, his shoulder wrapped in a makeshift bandage, blood seeping through the fabric. The bullet had only grazed him, but it had rattled him enough that he was keeping a tight grip on his revolver.

Outside, the three dogs lingered at the doorway, ears twitching, eyes locked on the scrubby bush in the distance.

Bruce sat beside Martha, his deep chest rising and falling in slow, measured breaths — alert, waiting. The second dog — a lean, wiry kelpie mix with a dark coat and sharp amber eyes — paced near Frank. Tilly. All work, no nonsense.

Then there was Banjo. A scrappy little terrier with the attitude of a junkyard brawler, standing near the open doorway, hackles raised, eyes locked on something unseen.

The air felt… different. Charged.

Banjo yapped sharply, the sound cutting through the shed like a warning shot. His little body was tense, vibrating with something the others hadn't caught yet.

Martha exhaled, resting a hand on Bruce's head. "Place feels different now."

Dave turned to her. "How so?"

She didn't answer right away, just stared at the plane, at the open doors, at the shadows beyond. Then —

"It's been locked up tight for decades, but now it's open." She rubbed a thumb along the side of Bruce's ear, gaze distant. "And Henry always knew that when this shed got cracked, things would start moving real fast."

Dave pulled the toy plane from his pocket, rolling it in his palm.

The coordinates etched underneath were barely legible. The years had worn them down, the middle numbers all but lost.

"Good luck and this thing got me this far," he muttered. "But I need the rest."

Martha nodded toward the real plane. "Then we better find it."

Dave moved to the cockpit, shining his flashlight over the gutted interior. Stripped controls. Empty panels. Someone had taken their time pulling it apart, making sure nothing useful was left.

But Red had left something. He had to.

Martha leaned in, running her fingers along the metal near the pilot's seat. "Henry wouldn't just leave things in the open."

Frank grunted from the doorway, still watching the bush. "Man was too bloody smart for that."

Dave crouched, sweeping his light lower.

The floor of the plane was a mess of dirt and debris, but something caught his eye. A scratched-up metal panel near the base of the seat. The screws were old, rusted. Except for one.

Newer.

His pulse kicked up.

Dave reached for his knife, jamming it into the groove, twisting.

The screw resisted. Then popped loose.

He pried up the panel, heart hammering as he reached inside.

Nothing.

A sharp exhale.

His fingers ran along the panel's edge, checking for anything else, any hidden compartment. But it was just empty space.

Frustration burned low in his gut.

Dave straightened, shining his light over the plane's undercarriage. And then —

He saw it.

Etched into the metal, in the exact same place as on the toy plane.

Coordinates.

Dave ran his fingers over the engraving, the numbers standing out despite the years of dust and decay.

The full set.

Martha leaned over his shoulder, her breath hitching.

"That's it."

Dave traced the numbers, comparing them to the half-worn etching on the toy plane. They matched. The missing digits filled the gaps perfectly.

He let out a slow breath.

This was it. The next step.

Frank, you seeing this?" Dave turned toward the old man.

Frank wasn't looking.

He was watching the doorway.

Eyes narrowed. Gun resting in his lap.

"I see it." His voice was lower now, gritted. "I also see that our shooter ain't coming back right now. Means he wasn't looking to finish the job."

Martha's jaw tightened.

"He was watching."

She turned toward the open door, scanning the tree line, the movement of the wind through the leaves.

Measuring.

Dave ran a hand over the seat, over the faded fabric where Red had once sat, once flown. His mind spun through everything. Zhao, Blake, the opals, the past that had somehow dragged him right into its depths.

This wasn't just about opals anymore.

Martha let out a long breath, staring at the plane like it had whispered a secret she wasn't sure she wanted to hear.

"Henry was good at hiding things." Her voice was quiet. "But he was even better at making sure the right people found them."

Dave looked at her. "And the wrong people?"

Martha's mouth twitched into something that wasn't quite a smile.

"They usually didn't live long enough to find anything."

Outside, Tilly let out a low, rolling growl.

A sound of warning.

Frank tensed, sitting forward.

Banjo's ears flattened, his little frame stiffening.

The smallest dog was the only one that saw it.

Something moved. Small, fast, gliding just above the trees.

An engine. Faint. Almost nothing.

Banjo barked twice — sharp, insistent.

Then it was gone.

Dave felt it. A ripple in the air.

His muscles tightened.

 He gave the shed a final look and turned to Martha.

"We should go. You think Frank should come?"

Martha shifted her stare to Frank.

The old man shook his head.

"I ain't going nowhere." He rolled his shoulder, winced slightly. "You two go. I'll be fine."

Martha's school-teacher death stare locked onto him.

"Okay, tough boy. But if you need us…"

Frank nodded once.

Dave and Martha moved to the car.

As he slid into the driver's seat, Dave felt it again.

The weight of eyes. The sense of something out there, waiting.

Whoever had fired that shot wasn't done watching.

And neither was he.

CHAPTER 47

The pub was stale, smoky, and half-dead. Tombs wasn't sure which half he was looking at.

He sat in a corner booth, back to the wall, boots planted firm against the scuffed wooden floor. The place was the kind of shithole that hadn't seen fresh paint since the seventies. The walls were yellowed from years of cigarette smoke, sweaty bodies, and mould no one had bothered to clean.

The air was thick with the scent of spilled beer and sweat.

A jukebox in the corner wheezed out an old Cold Chisel track, the same five songs it had been playing on a loop since they walked in.

The bartender — a wiry old bastard in a faded blue singlet — stood behind the counter, arms crossed, watching them like they were about to start a war.

Maybe they were.

Tombs sipped his beer, barely tasting it. Warm. Flat. Shit. He pushed the glass aside and ran his tongue over his teeth. His boys were spread out across the room, talking in low voices. They were waiting. And waiting didn't sit right with him.

Blake had gone quiet. Too fucking quiet.

Tombs wasn't stupid — he knew Blake had used him. That was fine. It was the way things worked. But lately, things felt different. Off. Like Blake was keeping too much to himself.

That didn't sit right, either.

He was only willing to play the game if he knew the rules — and Blake wasn't sharing the fucking rules anymore.

The bartender cleared his throat. "You lot planning to sit there all night?"

Tombs flicked his eyes up. "You got a problem?"

The bartender hesitated. He had the look of a man who'd been punched in the face a few times in his life, but not enough to get used to it. "Just saying. If you're drinking, drink. Otherwise, move on."

One of Tombs' boys, Barrow, smirked, tipping his chair back. "Relax, old man. We're just waiting on a mate."

Tombs rolled his neck. He wasn't interested in bar fights. Not tonight. He pulled out his phone, checked the screen. Still nothing from Blake.

Then — his burner buzzed. A single text. Intel finally in.

He opened it, scanned the message.

Callahan spotted. Heading toward a rural property west of Gunnedah. Not alone.

An address followed.

Tombs sat back, jaw tightening.

"Alright, boys," he said, pushing off the table. "We've got movement."

They were on their feet in seconds. They'd been waiting too long.

The bikes roared to life in the car park, engines coughing black smoke into the night air. The locals in the pub watched from the doorway, squinting into the glare of the headlights.

Tombs pulled his gloves on, flexing his fingers. The moment the engine rumbled beneath him, he felt better.

This was what made sense.

This was how things should be.

He gunned the throttle, leading the pack out of town.

The night air was warm, dry, thick with the scent of dust and cattle. The road stretched ahead, black and empty, lined by endless paddocks and brittle scrub.

Tombs' thoughts churned as the kilometres burned away beneath them.

Callahan had a head start. If the bastard had gone to ground, this was his best chance at pulling him out.

And Blake?

Tombs' jaw clenched. Blake was starting to look like a loose end.

Blake knew more than he let on. He always had. And if he'd been feeding Tombs bullshit just to keep him moving like a puppet on a string, then that was a problem that needed fixing.

Tombs wasn't the kind of bloke who sat back and waited for things to play out. If something stank, he cut it off at the source.

And right now?

Blake stank.

They pulled up just off the road, engines growling low as the dust settled around them. The property was ahead — dim porch lights glowing against the dark, the faint outline of an old farmhouse standing against the night.

Tombs cut the engine, the others following suit.

He sat there for a moment, listening. Watching.

A dog barked in the distance. The sound carried across the empty land.

This wasn't just some random property Callahan had passed through.

He was staying here. Had to be.

Tombs swung off the bike, adjusting his jacket. His boys followed, moving in silence. This wasn't an ambush. Not yet.

This was a conversation.

But if Callahan didn't like it?

Well. That was up to him.

Tombs gestured to Barrow. "Flank right. Check the side of the house. If he bolts, I want eyes on where he goes."

Barrow nodded, slipping off into the shadows.

Tombs took the lead, walking up the gravel path toward the front of the house.

The place was quiet. Still.

Then — movement.

A figure stepped onto the verandah.

A woman.

Not Callahan. Not who he expected.

She stood with one boot propped against the railing, a rifle in her hands, the barrel resting easy against her arm like it belonged there.

Even in the low light, Tombs could tell she was older, but tough. The kind of tough you didn't earn from lifting weights but from a life that didn't leave much room for softness.

She didn't say a word. Just took a long drag of her cigarette, watching them like she was deciding whether or not they were worth the bullets.

Tombs stopped at the bottom step. "Looking for Callahan."

Martha Redmond exhaled smoke through her nose. "That right?"

Tombs tilted his head. "He inside?"

Martha took another drag. Flicked the cigarette away. "Maybe. Maybe not. So, you and your boys want a coffee, biscuits."

Tombs' eyebrows raised. He turned a looked at the men behind him. "You know what. I reckon that would go down well."

Martha didn't move a muscle, but a glint of light seemed to catch the barrel of the rifle.

"Good. There's a truck stop about a half hour back the way you came from. Now get the fuck off my property."

Silence.

The wind shifted.

Tombs smiled, slow. "You wanna let him know he's got visitors?"

Martha finally moved. Just a small shift of weight, her fingers tapping against the wood of the rifle. Not nervous. Just measuring.

She sniffed. "You lot don't take a hint. Do you?"

Tombs' smile tightened. "Something like that."

Martha's eyes narrowed. "Huh. I'm guessing someone's pulling your strings. Too fucking dumb to make decisions yourself. That cop maybe." She glanced toward the dark paddocks. "Where is he, then? Thought he'd be the type to turn up himself."

Tombs' jaw flexed.

That was the thing, wasn't it?

Blake should be here.

Instead, he was off doing fuck-knows-what, keeping Tombs on a leash.

Tombs' gut twisted.

Martha saw it. Read it. Smirked.

"Guess that means he ain't telling you everything, huh?"

Tombs held her gaze. "Callahan. Get him out here. Now."

Martha didn't move. "Or what?"

Silence.

Tombs heard the sound before he saw it.

A click.

Not from Martha.

From inside the house.

Dave Callahan stepped into the doorway, a shotgun aimed square at Tombs' chest.

Tombs didn't flinch. Just let out a low chuckle.

"Well, well." He met Callahan's eyes. "Didn't think you had it in you."

Dave's finger flexed near the trigger. "A lot's changed."

Tombs nodded slow. "That so?"

Martha smiled, just slightly. "I'd listen, son. He's got a bit more bite these days."

Tombs flicked his eyes between them.

Martha. Callahan. The rifle. The shotgun.

This wasn't what he expected.

But maybe it was exactly what he needed.

Blake had been keeping secrets.

Callahan had answers.

And now?

Now, it was just about making sure he got them first.

Tombs opened his mouth to speak, then stopped.

A whirring noise cut through the night air. Not the wind. Not a bird. Something else.

Martha's gaze flicked upward. Dave followed.

A drone. Small, fast, barely visible against the dark sky.

Tombs' gut went cold. That wasn't some farm kid's toy.

It hovered for a beat. Then shot off, disappearing into the night.

Silence.

Martha raised an eyebrow. "Guess you're not the only ones looking for answers."

Dave's grip on the shotgun tightened.

Because whoever was behind that drone?

They already had more than they should.

CHAPTER 48

The silence held.

Tombs, Martha, and Dave remained locked in place, every muscle strung tight as razor wire. No one moved. Not yet. The night stretched around them, thick and heavy, carrying the weight of something unseen, something waiting.

Bruce let out a low, uneasy growl, his massive frame tense beside Martha. Banjo yapped once, tail stiff, his eyes locked on the darkness beyond the treeline. Tilly paced, sharp and alert. The dogs had sensed it before the humans. They always did.

Then —

THWIP.

A whisper through the night.

Barrow jerked. His body stiffened, fingers twitching toward the wound blooming red across his chest. He staggered back, eyes wide, breath shallow, hands clutching at the blood seeping between his fingers. He exhaled shakily, a stunned, "The fuck...?" before his knees buckled and he hit the dirt, gasping.

Tombs turned sharply, rage flaring hot. This wasn't Callahan. Wasn't the old woman. He knew that much. But anger had its own momentum, its own burning logic. His shotgun swung toward the house. "Who the fuck —?"

The dogs bristled. Bruce's growl deepened. Tilly's pacing turned frantic. Banjo's yapping escalated, sharp and furious. A warning. A call to arms.

Martha moved first.

Her rifle snapped up. BOOM.

The gunshot ripped through the night, a deafening crack that echoed off the trees and sent a fresh wave of unease rolling through the clearing. The bikes rattled. The moment shattered like glass.

"Enough," Martha snapped, voice steel-hard, her eyes locked onto Tombs. She wasn't just talking to him — whoever was out there had been put on notice.

Tombs clenched his jaw, fingers white around the shotgun grip. He was breathing through his nose, steady but tight. This wasn't a fight he controlled anymore. And Tombs didn't fight blind. His men shifted uneasily, the weight of something bigger than all of them settling over the clearing.

He turned without a word, grabbed Barrow by the vest, and hauled him upright. Blood dripped onto the dirt in thick, sluggish drops, the metallic scent cutting through the dust. "Back on the bikes. Now."

No hesitation. His men moved fast, dragging Barrow onto the back of a bike, his head slumping against the handlebars, breath rattling in his chest. Engines roared to life, splitting the night open. Tombs swung into his saddle, boots digging in, gaze still locked onto Callahan. This wasn't over. Not even close.

Then they tore out of there, headlights cutting sharp through the dark, dust swirling in their wake. A single bike remained behind, forgotten in the scramble.

**

From the ridge, in the darkened cab of his 4WD, Declan barely blinked. His rifle was still warm. Scope trained. Finger loose on the trigger. He exhaled, watching. Letting them run. A calculated move. He hadn't needed a second shot. One was enough to fracture the moment. Now? Now, he let the chaos unfold the way he wanted.

Lowering his rifle, he leaned forward, the cab bathed in the soft blue glow of his rig's custom surveillance setup. Monitors flickered — heat signatures, movement, distance, all feeding into his system in real time. A satellite uplink mapped the roads ahead, showing topographic changes, shifts in terrain, possible bottlenecks. A police scanner ran on a separate channel, sifting through static and chatter.

Noise. Patterns. People. All of it funnelling into him.

One of the screens blinked, shifting to a mapped overlay of local roads. The dust kicked up by the bikers left an imprint on the land, a temporary scar, one Declan could trace like a thread pulling him toward the next move. He smirked. Tombs didn't even know he was already being followed.

The 4WD hummed to life, engine purring low. No headlights. No need. His dashboard bathed the cab in an infrared glow, mapping the terrain ahead, feeding him everything he needed to see. The bikers were moving fast, but Declan didn't have to keep up. He already knew where they were going.

He clicked his earpiece, the encrypted line connecting. A voice crackled through. No greetings. No names. Just business.

"Tracking now. Target bled out?"

A pause. Then — "Not yet."

Declan didn't blink. It didn't matter.

If Barrow lived, he'd be a liability.

If he died, he'd be a message.

Either way, it worked.

"Keep monitoring. Tell me when they stop."

A short pause. "Copy that."

The line went dead.

Declan tapped the wheel with slow, measured movements, eyes flicking between screens. A live heat map showed a small glowing cluster of bodies. Callahan, the old woman, the dogs. They were staying put. For now.

This was going to plan.

But something felt wrong.

Tombs was reacting like a man who didn't have the full picture. That meant someone was keeping him in the dark. Someone was playing him. Declan needed to know who.

He tapped his phone again, this time using a different line. No encryption. A number only a few people had.

He didn't get a chance to hit dial, instead an incoming call.

It rang twice before Declan answered.

Then —

A voice, smooth, measured, with an edge of control. Dangerous. Unfamiliar

"Declan."

Declan shifted slightly, watching the dust trail where Tombs' taillights had disappeared into the night. He let the silence stretch just long enough to make a point. Then the voice. Calm and just a hint of menace broke the quiet.

"I think we've got a problem. I don't like problems. I don't like being shot in the fucking shoulder."

Panic. "How did you get this line." Then the line cut out.

Declan didn't know the voice, but he could guess.

Frank Tolliver had just introduced himself.

CHAPTER 49

The highway stretched out in an endless ribbon of blacktop, the night pressing in on either side. Declan drove in silence, fingers loose on the wheel, eyes flicking between the road and the digital readouts on his dashboard. The 4WD was custom-fitted with infrared cameras, motion sensors, a reinforced chassis. A hunter's vehicle, built for pursuit. Built for control.

And yet, something felt off.

And that something was Tolliver.

He had been tracking Tombs' crew from a safe distance, letting them lead him toward whatever hell Callahan had stumbled into. They were reckless, loud, predictable. But the deeper they pushed into the bush, the less predictable the night became.

The first sign came as a flicker on his security display — a disturbance near the rear of the vehicle. Too quick to be an animal, too quiet to be a man stumbling in the dark.

Declan's grip tightened.

He tapped a command on the touchscreen, flipping through the different feeds. The thermal scanner showed nothing but the distant heat signatures of the bikers ahead.

Then —

A click.

Faint. Subtle.

Declan barely heard it over the hum of the engine, but his instincts screamed.

He slammed the brakes.

The 4WD skidded to a stop, dust swirling around the beams of his headlights. Silence settled in, thick and unnatural.

He let out a slow breath and reached for his rifle. This wasn't right.

Declan killed the lights. Opened the door. Slipped into the night.

The air smelled of eucalyptus and dry earth, the stillness too perfect, too precise. He moved with controlled steps, circling around his vehicle. The motion sensor beeped again.

Something was out there.

And then, the shot came.

Close. Too close.

The bullet punched into the dirt near his boot, a sharp crack splitting the night.

Not a kill shot.

A warning.

Declan ducked low, rolling behind cover, rifle pressed against his shoulder, scanning the dark. Nothing.

His radio crackled.

A voice. Low. Calm. Amused.

"You ain't as good as you think you are."

Declan's blood ran cold.

He shifted his position, moving fast, silent. What the fuck was this guy?

His earpiece stayed quiet, but the sensation that someone was watching him grew stronger. This wasn't just a random shooter. This was someone who knew exactly what they were doing.

Declan had spent years hunting men in war zones, in jungles, in city sprawls. He knew the difference between an amateur with a rifle and a professional. And whoever this was —

They weren't an amateur.

He climbed back into the car and reached for his tactical tablet, pulling up the area scan. The drone was still overhead, its infrared picking up the residual heat signatures from the bikers down the road.

But nothing behind him. Nothing on the scanner.

Another voice crackled through the radio. The same voice. Measured. Unshaken.

"If I wanted you dead, you'd already be in the dirt."

Declan's jaw tightened. He had the training to stay calm under pressure, but something about this was wrong.

He stayed crouched, rifle raised, eyes darting between the ridgeline and the scattered scrub around him. His mind worked through the angles. Sniper. Maybe suppressed. Maybe hidden in the trees.

But no second shot came.

Because the son of a bitch was toying with him.

The realisation settled in his gut like a lead weight.

Another voice crackled through. A different voice.

One of his contacts.

"Declan… you there?"

He pressed the receiver. "Here."

A pause. Then —

"We've got a problem."

Declan said nothing.

"Info on the new player is behind a wall thicker than Kevlar on a General's arse."

"I pay you to breach those walls."

"Thought you'd say that. So, I went the extra mile. You need to be careful."

Declan's eyes flicked back to the ridgeline, scanning every inch of darkness. He knew what the problem was before his contact even said it.

The shooter wasn't just anyone.

It was Frank Tolliver.

Vietnam. Covert ops. Sniper. Ghost.

Declan exhaled slowly, a bead of sweat tracing the back of his neck. Tolliver wasn't just good — he was a relic from another era, a soldier trained in the art of war long before Declan had picked up his first rifle.

This wasn't some bush hermit with an old hunting rifle.

This was a man who had once hunted other hunters. And he was better than Declan.

The radio crackled again. Frank's voice this time, lazy, like he was enjoying himself.

"I suggest you start running."

Declan stayed still, heart hammering. Running wasn't his style.

But this time… he might not have a choice.

CHAPTER 50

The road stretched ahead, dark and empty, the last traces of moonlight barely cutting through the thick bush. Declan's 4WD hummed quietly beneath him, engine smooth, a machine built for silence and survival. His hands were steady on the wheel, his breath slow and controlled. But deep inside, a feeling he hadn't known in years was growing.

Something was wrong.

He wasn't used to this.

The hunter. Becoming the hunted.

It had started the moment he pulled back from the failed shot on Tolliver. It should've been clean. A single bullet, straight through the skull, over before the old bastard even knew what was happening.

Instead, Tolliver moved.

Declan didn't believe in luck. The old man knew. He'd sensed it. And now, Declan wasn't just dealing with Callahan and some washed-up ex-cop playing outlaw.

Now he had a real threat to deal with.

The landscape blurred past, endless black trees cutting jagged shapes against the sky. The road was narrow, nothing but loose gravel and dirt. He was deep in nowhere. And that was the problem.

Because someone else was here too.

Somewhere behind him, in front of him, maybe even above him.

Tolliver.

Declan adjusted his grip, forcing himself to slow his breathing. His instincts told him to get off the road, ditch the 4WD, move on foot. But that would mean admitting that he'd lost control.

And Declan never lost control.

He just needed to reset.

First thing. Ditch the tracker. If Tolliver had managed to lock onto him somehow, that was his opening move. Declan reached beneath the dashboard, feeling for the GPS unit he'd installed himself. He ripped it free, yanked the battery out, and tossed the device out the window.

Problem solved.

He pressed the accelerator.

Then — a flicker.

Just in the edge of his vision. A shape.

Not ahead. In the rearview.

Declan's fingers flexed on the wheel. He forced himself not to react. He just watched.

A second pair of headlights.

Faint. Distant.

Matching his speed.

Declan's mouth twitched. So, the old bastard had eyes.

Alright.

Game on.

Declan didn't speed up. That's what they'd expect. Instead, he slowed just enough. Letting whoever was behind him think he hadn't noticed. Letting them move in.

He flicked off his main lights, rolling into the darkness. The dash-mounted night vision took over, turning the black road into a world of eerie green shapes.

The headlights behind him stayed on.

Arrogant.

Declan smirked.

He veered right, taking a side road that cut deeper into the trees, winding through dry creek beds and old cattle tracks. His 4WD barely made a sound as he adjusted the suspension, letting the terrain absorb the movement.

The headlights followed.

Tolliver was good.

But Declan was better.

He took another turn. Then another. A route that looped back on itself.

A trap.

His heartbeat slowed. This was it. He reached under his seat, pulling the suppressed pistol from its holster.

One target.

One shot.

His eyes scanned ahead and flicked to the rearview. Empty.

No lights.

Declan frowned.

He eased off the gas, rolling the vehicle to a silent stop.

Nothing.

No dust trail. No sound.

Just silence.

He checked the map in his head. That car should somewhere in front of him. Declan's manoeuvre should have brought him up right behind the old bastards car. It should be right in front of him.

It wasn't. His grip on the pistol tightened.

Where the fuck are you, Tolliver?

A breeze shifted the trees, making the leaves hiss against one another. The bush had a sound. Even at night. The chirr of insects, the occasional rustle of something small moving through the undergrowth.

But this?

This was too quiet.

Declan's instincts roared.

He reached for the gear shift — too late.

A shadow moved outside the driver's window.

A shape.

A man.

Right there.

Declan turned, gun coming up, but the barrel of a rifle was already pressed against his temple.

A voice. Low, calm, edged with something colder than steel.

"Miss me, son?"

Frank Tolliver stood beside the open window, his rifle steady. His left shoulder was bandaged, the wound from earlier clearly still bleeding, but his stance was loose, confident. The way a man stands when he knows he's already won.

Declan's brain moved fast. Options.

Gun in his hand, but wrong angle.

Knife under the dash, but too slow.

Could try to floor it, but not without taking a bullet to the skull.

Tolliver gave a low chuckle, watching the thoughts run behind Declan's eyes.

"You boys think you're ghosts. But I've been killing ghosts since before you learned how to hold a gun."

Declan didn't move. Didn't blink.

"First time being on this side of the hunt, huh?" Tolliver mused.

Declan clenched his jaw. "You don't know who I am."

Tolliver's smirk didn't waver. "That's where you're wrong, mate. I know exactly who you are. Ex-army. Tracker. Cleaner. You work quiet, efficient, never leave a trail."

He leaned in slightly.

"But you made a mistake."

Declan's finger twitched against the trigger. "And what's that?"

Tolliver's smile faded.

"You hunted the wrong bloke."

Silence. Thick. Heavy.

Declan's heartbeat slowed. Calculating. Waiting.

Then — Tolliver stepped back.

Just a single step.

The barrel of the rifle lowered.

"Drive," Tolliver said.

Declan's eyes narrowed.

Tolliver jerked his head toward the road. "You've got five seconds before I change my mind."

Declan hesitated.

Then he tucked the gun back under his seat and pressed the accelerator.

The 4WD moved, slow at first, then faster, dust kicking up in the headlights.

Declan didn't look back. Didn't need to.

He could still feel Tolliver's eyes on him.

Declan pulled off the main road five minutes later, stopping just long enough to breathe.

His hands weren't shaking. He wouldn't let them.

But Tolliver had done something no one had done in a long time.

He'd let him go without a fight.

That wasn't mercy.

That was a message.

Declan grabbed his phone. Dialled a number he rarely used.

It rang twice before a voice answered.

"You're calling late."

Declan exhaled. "Change of plans. The job's compromised."

A pause.

"Compromised how?"

Declan's fingers tightened around the wheel. "We've got a problem. Frank Tolliver. A new player. A good one...Too fucking good."

The voice on the other end didn't react at first. Then — "Fix it. I'll find out what i can."

The line went dead.

Declan tapped the phone once against his thigh, a slow rhythm, like counting down to something no one could stop.

Tolliver wasn't just a loose end.

He was the start of a much bigger problem

And now, Declan had two choices.

Either disappear.

Or start hunting back.

CHAPTER 51

Blake sat in the motel room, staring at the water-stained ceiling. The hum of the air conditioner rattled in the background, struggling against the heat. His beer sat untouched on the table beside him, the condensation running in slow trails over the battered wood.

His phone buzzed. A single text lit up the screen.

Callahan has become a fucking problem. With fucking problem friends. Friends that don't play nice. I'm out.

Tombs. Running scared and in the wind. And now Callahan had protection.

Blake's grip found the beer and tightened. Of course he had fucking protection.

It was slipping — everything.

For decades, he'd held the line. He'd buried Parker. He'd buried Red. He'd buried every goddamn loose end that could ever point back to him.

And now with Callahan digging at these clues everything was coming to the surface.

Blake rubbed at the back of his neck, fingers brushing over the old scar at his hairline. A relic from another life.

The motel room smelled like burnt toast, but something about it — maybe the stale, heavy air, the flickering fluorescent light — dragged him back.

Back to a different night.

Back to the bush.

Back to the moment everything turned to shit.

1979

The scrub was thick, the dry heat settling into his collar, sweat pooling at the base of his spine. They'd been tracking Red for days — running leads, hitting dead ends, retracing steps.

Parker was getting frustrated.

"This is it, Blake. No more fuck-ups." Parker wiped a hand down his face, looking around. "No more losing him."

Blake barely reacted. He kept his hands in his pockets, fingers brushing over the cool weight of his pistol.

Parker started toward the ridge, scanning for any sign of movement.

Then he hesitated.

Blake could feel the shift in the air.

"You know, it's funny," Parker said, turning back. "Every single lead we've had. Dead end."

Blake tilted his head slightly. "That's how it goes."

"No," Parker muttered. "That's not how it goes."

His voice hardened.

"Every single lead, Blake. Every time we get close, something goes wrong. And it's always when you're around."

Blake felt his pulse slow.

Measured. Controlled.

He knew this moment would come eventually.

Parker wasn't stupid.

The younger cop took a step closer, eyes narrowed. "You've been feeding Red. Haven't you?"

Blake didn't blink. Didn't speak.

Parker knew.

He remembered things now. The phone calls Blake took alone. The tips that led nowhere. The way every single trail went cold when Blake was nearby.

Parker's hand hovered near his belt. Near his gun.

"Jesus Christ." Parker's voice was barely a breath. "You set this whole thing up. The opals. The smuggling gig. Liu Jianhong. You —"

His hand started to move.

"It didn't have to come to this. For fucks sake."

Blake pulled first. Not his service revolver. This was one he kept just in case.

The gun barked once, a sharp crack that echoed through the trees.

Parker staggered, his breath catching.

Shock filled his eyes before his legs gave out beneath him, his knees hitting the dust hard. He gasped, a wet, shuddering sound, fingers grasping at his chest where the bullet had torn through.

Blake crouched next to him, watching.

Parker's lips trembled. He tried to speak, but blood bubbled at the corner of his mouth.

Blake leaned in, his voice low, cold, steady as a metronome.

"Should've left it alone, mate."

Parker shuddered, his body stilling beneath the weight of death.

Blake took a slow, measured breath. Then got to work.

He wiped his prints. Took Parker's gun and fired it into the dirt. A struggle. A botched arrest. That was the story now.

This was all Red.

Red would take the fall.

Blake stood up, dusted himself off.

He didn't see Red watching. Would never know what Red did next.

The moment Blake's car disappeared down the track, Red moved.

He sprinted to Parker's body, his heart hammering. He'd been hiding just beyond the ridge, close enough to hear everything — close enough to watch his entire life go up in flames.

He crouched beside Parker, hands shaking. The younger cop's face was frozen in shock, eyes wide, unseeing. Red reached for a pulse — nothing. But then — his fingers brushed something. A wire. A microphone in Parker's collar.

Bile rose in his throat. This wasn't part of the plan. Robbing a billionaire was supposed to be clean. No casualties.

And now Blake had pinned this on him.

Which meant Blake couldn't be caught. Not yet.

Red needed proof.

His gaze snapped to Parker's car. He sprinted for it, yanking open the glovebox.

There it was.

A leather-bound logbook.

His breath hitched as he flipped through the pages. Parker had been documenting everything — his doubts about Blake, the holes in their case.

And then —

A tape recorder.

Red grabbed it, thumb trembling as he hit play.

Parker's voice crackled through the tiny speaker.

"Jesus Christ, Blake. You think I don't see it? You've been feeding Red for years. You planned this whole thing, didn't you? The opals… Liu Jianhong. The smuggling gig. You set this all up, didn't you?"

[Pause.]

"…You're gonna tell me I'm wrong? Say something, Blake."

[Silence.]

"…Blake?"

[Gunshot. Tape cuts out.]

Red's stomach twisted.

Blake was going to get away with it.

Unless…

Red swallowed, forcing himself to move.

He grabbed the logbook, the recorder, and whatever else he could.

Then he ran.

Now

Blake stood in the motel bathroom, gripping the edge of the sink.

His own reflection stared back.

Decades later, and the past still had its claws in him.

He needed help. And he knew who.

The line rang twice. A voice answered — calm, smooth, dangerous.

Declan.

Blake's fingers tightened.

"I need a problem handled."

A beat of silence on the other end.

"Let me guess. Callahan?"

Blake smirked. "How the fuck? You're already on him, aren't you?"

A low chuckle. "You could say that."

Blake steadied his grip on the phone.

"Then let's stop playing games. Find him. End this."

Declan paused. Then —

"You're gonna owe me for this."

Blake smiled darkly.

"I don't owe anyone."

The call ended.

Blake pocketed his phone, fingers flexing like they wanted to break something.

Red was dead. Parker was long gone.

And Callahan?

He wouldn't make it to the truth.

Not if Blake got to him first.

**

Declan had put enough distance between himself and Tolliver to feel safe. Blake's call had been unexpected. He knew the cop was unorthodox. Rogue, bordering on criminal, but this? This was something bigger.

An alignment of these bastards. Blake, Zhao, Tombs, even Tolliver, meant a payday bigger than anything he'd been offered so far.

What the fuck was Callahan into?

Maybe it was worth playing out. Watching from the sidelines until the time was right. He could play the long game — take payment from Zhao and Blake, then swoop in for whatever prize was really waiting at the end.

Fuck the lot of them.

234

CHAPTER 52

The farmhouse kitchen was quiet, the heavy weight of the night settling in around them. The only sounds were the slow tick of the wall clock and the occasional creak of the old wooden floorboards as Martha moved about, pulling out a collection of old maps from a battered tin box.

Frank sat at the kitchen table, his arm stiff but no longer bleeding, a cup of black coffee steaming in front of him. Dave leaned over a spread of modern maps and satellite images on the table, frowning as he traced his finger along the faded lines of forgotten roads and watercourses.

Martha dropped a stack of folded maps next to him.

"You trust that GPS bullshit too much," she muttered, unfolding one of her old survey maps. "These'll tell you what the land used to be."

Dave ran a finger along the edge of the map, eyes narrowing as he studied the coordinates again.

"Alright," he muttered. "Let's see where Henry was sending us."

He tapped the numbers into his phone, pulling up the satellite image. The screen refreshed, revealing nothing but a vast stretch of dense bushland — deep in the heart of the Pilliga.

Martha peered over his shoulder, then looked down at her own map. She ran a calloused finger over the faded ink, her expression unreadable. "Well, I'll be damned," she murmured. "That's deep country."

Frank leaned forward, squinting at the location. "That's near the old forestry runs," he muttered. "Way back, the timber mob used to push tracks through there. But fifty years ago? There were still old stations, stock routes, and —" He tapped a spot on the map, just southeast of the coordinates. "— a landing strip."

Dave straightened. "An airstrip?"

Frank nodded. "Yeah. Small, rough as guts, but it was there. Used for forestry surveys, cattle mustering, and if the stories were right, a bit of off-the-books business. But it's been gone for decades. Last I heard, the scrub took it back. Probably just ghost trails now."

Martha sat back in her chair, arms crossed. "Henry knew how to fly. If he wanted to disappear something big…or small, an old strip out there would've been perfect."

Dave looked at the satellite image again, but there was nothing left — just thick, untouched wilderness. Whatever was there had long since been swallowed by the land.

Frank ran a hand over his stubbled jaw. "Getting in won't be easy," he said. "Fifty years ago, you could've driven a ute through half those tracks. Now? Bush has reclaimed most of it. Any old logging roads are either buried under scrub or washed out by years of rain and fire."

Dave muttered a curse under his breath. "So we're looking at what? Hiking in?"

Frank shook his head. "Maybe. Some fire trails might still be open, but they don't always go where you need them to." He gestured at the map. "That whole section is dead land. No towns, no people, no help. You break down out there? You're on your own."

Martha exhaled sharply. "And we're not the only ones looking."

Dave nodded, gripping the edge of the table. His gut twisted. He knew what that meant. If they'd put the pieces together, the others wouldn't be far behind. They were heading into the unknown, but they wouldn't be alone for long. Blake, Tombs, Zhao — they'd all be closing in soon enough.

Martha finally spoke, her voice quieter. "Henry didn't just hide the opals. He built a goddamn test." She flicked her eyes to Dave. "He made sure only the right person would find them."

Dave looked down at the map, his pulse steady but heavy. A test. He wasn't sure if Henry would have thought him worthy. Hell, he wasn't even sure if he deserved to find what Red had left behind. But it didn't matter now. If they didn't get there first, it wouldn't matter at all.

"Then we better be the right people."

Martha gave him a slow nod. "We leave at first light."

Frank drained his coffee, then stood with a grunt, joints clicking like old timber. "I'll get the gear sorted. You two get some sleep."

Dave barely heard him. His fingers traced the edge of the map, following the faded lines leading into nothingness. His mind wouldn't settle. The Pilliga. People went in and didn't come out. The kind of land that swallowed mistakes whole.

Frank had said it outright — if something went wrong out there, no one was coming.

Outside, in the thick of the night, something moved beyond the tree-line. A shadow between the trees. No sound. Just stillness. Watching. Waiting.

CHAPTER 53

The tap in the bathroom dripped — slow, steady, like a countdown. Somewhere behind the wall, a fridge hummed with a dying motor, the rhythm just off enough to unsettle.

From the next room came the muffled thump of a headboard, a breathless giggle, the low rhythm of something private being made public. Romantic noises, personal ones — too intimate for how thin the walls were. Too human.

Zhao sat at the desk, unmoving.

The air carried the faint tang of someone's meal, curry perhaps, sour on the back of his tongue. The walls were patched with mis-aligned wallpaper. Like something trying too hard to cover the truth.

A motel for secrets. A room for silence.

And Zhao wasn't here to sleep.

He had barely slept.

Not that he needed it.

A small porcelain cup of Pu-erh tea sat untouched beside him, the steam long since faded. He wasn't here to drink. Not when everything was finally starting to fall into place.

His laptop screen flickered — an incoming video call.

Zhao didn't hesitate. He clicked accept.

And there he was.

Liu Jianhong.

A man who could buy and sell governments, who had built his empire with blood, bribes, and an unwavering belief in his own invincibility. His tailored suit was crisp, his silver hair immaculate, his expression unreadable as ever.

Zhao didn't speak first. You never spoke first with Liu.

Liu studied him through the screen, the silence stretching thin. Then, finally, he sighed.

"I expected better from you, Zhao."

Zhao's fingers tightened against the desk. He didn't blink. Didn't flinch.

Liu's voice was smooth, clipped, every syllable carrying weight. "You're wasting time."

Zhao kept his expression neutral. He had learned long ago that Liu Jianhong didn't make threats. He simply removed problems.

Liu leaned slightly forward, his shadow flickering against the darkened backdrop behind him. And that's when Zhao saw it.

Movement.

A figure, barely visible, lingering just outside the frame. Someone else was in the room with Liu.

Zhao's stomach curled.

This wasn't just a progress check.

This was a warning.

Liu's voice dropped, smooth as ice. "If you cannot handle this, I will send someone who can."

The line went dead.

Zhao sat back in his chair, tapping his fingers against the table. It was time.

He reached for his phone. Not to call Liu. Not to report back like a good little soldier.

No.

It was time to make the real call.

The real power move.

The line rang once.

Twice.

Then a voice answered. Calm. Measured. Patient. Powerful.

The man on the other end spoke first. That alone said everything about the true hierarchy Zhao operated under.

"It's time, Zhao."

Zhao closed his eyes briefly. Fifteen years. That's how long he had been playing this game. Fifteen years of pretending. Of infiltrating, working his way into Liu's inner circle, playing the role of the loyal enforcer, all while waiting for this exact moment.

Liu thought he owned me. He never understood that all I ever needed was time.

This was never about opals.

This was about revenge.

Zhao took a slow breath. "Liu is about to fall."

The voice on the other end hummed in approval. "And he still has no idea."

"No." Zhao let a smile just barely touch his lips. "Everything is in place. He still trusts me. He still believes I am his man." Only just.

A low chuckle. "And the sword?"

Zhao's grip tightened on the phone. Liu's prized Jian sword. A symbol of his power, his legacy — handed down through generations. The ultimate insult would be to strip it from him as his empire collapsed. To end the man with the prize he sought.

Zhao's voice was steel.

"When Liu falls, the sword will be mine."

There was a pause on the other end. Then —

"Good."

A heartbeat.

"Do not fail me now."

The call ended.

Zhao hadn't failed yet. His missteps so far were expected. Chaos was expected.

But he had never let the chaos consume him.

And he wouldn't now.

His burner phone buzzed.

Zhao picked up immediately. "Tell me."

Declan's voice was calm, easy, like he had all the time in the world. "They're moving."

Zhao's grip on the phone tightened. "Where?"

Declan wasn't one to rush.

"Not sure yet." A pause. "But they're stocking up. Gear, supplies. This isn't just a drive out to the bush."

Zhao stood, pacing the length of the motel room. He could almost hear Declan's smirk through the line.

"They've got an old bastard with them now, too. Ex-military. Tolliver."

Zhao froze.

The way Declan said that name meant something.

Declan continued. "Only thing I heard about their destination was one word."

Zhao waited.

Then Declan said it.

"Pilliga."

Zhao blinked. "Where?"

"The Pilliga Scrub," Declan said. "Out west. A hundred thousand hectares of dirt, ghosts, and shit that doesn't make sense."

Zhao stared at him. The name meant nothing. It could've been a province in a country he'd never visited.

Declan didn't smile. "It's not a place. It's a punishment. A fucking wasteland, full of endless twisted bush and places to die."

Zhao leaned back slowly, the word rolling around in his mind with no anchor. He didn't like it. Places he couldn't visualise made him uneasy.

"And they've gone into this… Pilliga?"

Declan gave a slow nod. "If someone wanted to bury something — really bury it — that's where they'd do it."

Zhao exhaled.

"Then let them dig."

"I'm not going into that mess," Zhao murmured. "That's your job."

Declan chuckled. "That's what I thought."

Zhao tapped a few keys on his laptop, pulling up a secure transaction window. No paper trails, no bank records — just a series of encrypted transfers bouncing through offshore accounts, disguised within layers of cryptocurrency transactions. He entered the figure, confirming the payment with a biometric scan. Within seconds, the funds were in motion, untraceable, undeniable.

"Double your usual rate," Zhao said. "And if Callahan doesn't make it out?"

Declan's voice was smooth. "Then we never had this conversation."

The call ended.

Zhao pocketed his phone, his movements precise. The tea sat untouched, long gone cold. When this was over, he would drink to Liu's fall.

The game was accelerating now.

Callahan was heading into the Pilliga, into terrain that swallowed men whole.

And Zhao?

Zhao would be waiting on the outside.

When the time came —
Declan would finish this.

243

CHAPTER 54

The road stretched long and empty ahead, headlights carving through the pre-dawn gloom.

Blake's hands clenched the wheel so hard his wrists ached, his jaw locked tight enough to splinter teeth.

The past wouldn't stay buried. Not Red. Not Parker. Not the goddamn opals.

And now Callahan was about to drag it all back into the light.

Blake rubbed his thumb against his palm, trying to steady his thoughts.

The flashback still clung to him — the memory of Parker's eyes, that moment of pure understanding before the bullet took him down.

He should have forgotten it by now.

Buried it with all the other necessary evils.

But Parker's blood was still under his nails, even after all these years.

He reached for the cigarette pack on the dashboard, pulling one free with his teeth. Flicked the lighter. Inhaled deep, holding the smoke in his lungs until the burn settled him. Focus.

He had one job now — cut off Callahan before he found the evidence. The logbook. The tape. Proof that Blake had murdered his own partner.

The glow of the cigarette pulsed in the dim cabin as he let his mind tick over the details. Gunnedah. That was his last solid lead. Callahan had been spotted heading west, and Tombs had been circling the area with his crew.

Tombs.

Blake scowled at the thought. The bikie bastard had gone quiet. Too quiet.

For years, Blake had managed men like Tombs — giving them just enough leash to run, but never enough to let them slip the collar. But now? Now Tombs was acting like he was calling his own fucking shots. That didn't sit right. And if Blake had learned anything over the years, it was that a dog who stopped barking was a dog about to bite.

He reached for his phone, thumb hovering over the call button. He could remind Tombs of his place. A quick call, a few words, and order would be restored.

But he hesitated.

No. If Tombs wasn't checking in, it was for a reason. And if Blake started rattling the cage too hard, he might not like what came snarling out.

He tossed the phone onto the passenger seat, grinding his teeth. He needed more eyes on the ground. Tombs wasn't reliable. Declan was still a wild card. And Zhao? The Chinese bastard had his own game going, and Blake still wasn't sure just how deep he was playing.

Too many moving parts. Too much slipping through his fingers.

He flicked the indicator and took the next exit. Muswellbrook. The local cops there still owed him. Some of them, anyway. Years of greasing the right wheels — covering up the right mistakes, pulling the right strings — had built a network of quiet favours. They weren't his guys, not like Tombs or Declan, but they knew better than to ignore a call from Detective Blake.

At least, they used to.

The station loomed ahead, a squat brick building with peeling paint and a handful of empty parking spaces. Blake killed the engine, stepping out into the cool morning air. The place was quiet. The overnight shift was winding down, the morning crew not in yet.

Perfect.

Inside, the air smelled of stale coffee and bad cologne. Blake walked past the front desk without a glance, heading straight for the back offices.

Sergeant Perry was hunched over a desk, flipping through paperwork. A big, tired man with too many years in the job and not enough left to give a shit. Blake rapped his knuckles on the doorframe.

"Perry."

The sergeant glanced up, his expression souring immediately. "Jesus. What the hell do you want now, Blake?"

Blake smirked, stepping inside like he owned the place. "What, no warm welcome?"

Perry leaned back in his chair, rubbing his face. "It's too fucking early for you."

Blake grabbed a chair, flipped it around, straddled it. "I need eyes. Boots on the ground."

Perry scoffed. "That right? For what?"

Blake's smile thinned. "Callahan."

Perry's expression shifted. Just slightly. "The ex-con?"

Blake nodded. "He's sniffing around places he shouldn't be. I want to know where he is."

Perry snorted. "If I had a dollar for every time some parolee went bush, I wouldn't still be working this shit job."

Blake exhaled, rolling his cigarette between his fingers. "This one's different."

Perry studied him. "How different?"

Blake met his gaze. "The kind that ends messy if we don't get ahead of it."

Perry hesitated, his fingers drumming against the desk. Then he sighed, rubbing his temple. "Look, I got enough shit on my plate already. You hear about the mess at the bikie clubhouse?"

Blake nodded, keeping his face neutral.

"House fire near Callahan's place, too," Perry added. "Neighbour swears she heard gunshots."

Blake shrugged. "Unrelated."

Perry gave him a long look. "Sure."

Blake leaned forward, his voice dropping. "Just make a few calls. Someone must've seen him. He's not exactly low-profile."

Perry sighed, rubbing his temple again. "Fine. I'll see what I can shake loose."

Blake stood, stretching. "Atta boy."

Perry shot him a glare, Blakes patronising comment cutting deep. "You pull me into some bottomless shit, Blake, and I swear to God. I won't fucking care how many favours you think I owe you"

Blake clapped him on the shoulder. "You worry too much."

He walked out, lighting another cigarette as he stepped into the early morning light. One more fire lit. Now he just had to make sure he wasn't the one getting burned.

Tombs was unreliable. Perry was slow.

But Declan got results.
And with him set in motion, Callahan was already dead.

CHAPTER 55

The pub reeked of stale beer and stubborn neglect. Low ceilings stained the colour of old smoke, tabletops blistered from years of stubbed-out cigarettes. Lighting that was barely worthy of the name. A jukebox sulked in the corner, clinging to a broken catalogue of Slim Dusty and Cold Chisel. Even the air felt used up—like it had been stuck here since the eighties, too worn-out to leave.

Tombs sat in the farthest booth, tucked in the shadows with his back to the wall, arms crossed and eyes tracking the handful of locals who hadn't made themselves scarce when his crew rolled in. The bartender, wiry and sun-dried, with a face like cracked leather, pretended not to stare. He was failing.

Good. Let the old bastard be nervous.

The beer in front of Tombs had gone warm. He hadn't touched it. He wasn't here for the taste.

He sat still, but the tension in his jaw never eased. Fingers tapped a slow, steady rhythm on the sticky tabletop — just enough motion to betray the thoughts chewing through his head. The ride back had been quiet, except for the growl of engines and the weight of what they'd lost.

Barrow was gone.

Not knifed in a fight. Not taken out up close. No chance to swing back. The bastard had gone down from a distance — clean, calculated. A sniper's shot.

And that changed everything.

Around the room, his boys lingered like shadows — some leaned heavy against the bar, others pressing knuckles to ribs or flexing swollen hands. None of them spoke. They didn't need to.

They felt it too.

Something wasn't sitting right.

Tombs ran his tongue over his teeth, the scrape of it dry, mechanical. His fingers tapped out a slow rhythm on the table — steady, deliberate, like he was keeping time with a thought he hadn't spoken yet.

Blake.

That was it. The thing gnawing at the edges.

Blake had him running in bloody circles for days. Always just enough rope to chase after Callahan, just enough clues to keep the wheels turning — scraps thrown like bones to a hungry dog. While Tombs and his boys fought in the dust and scrub, Blake was nowhere to be seen.

The hell had he been doing?

Tombs exhaled, jaw tightening as he leaned forward on his elbows. He'd gone along with it at first. The payoff had seemed worth the effort — Callahan sniffing out Red's trail, leading them to the opals. Clean win. No reason to question too hard.

But now?

Now, the game stank.

Barrow was gone, taken out with precision. Not a pub brawl. Not even a warning. A fucking sniper. And Blake hadn't even flinched. Probably didn't even know...or care. No rage. No reaction. Just more silence and shadows.

It was starting to feel like a setup.

And Tombs had survived too many setups to mistake one when it was breathing down his neck.

Across the bar, movement caught his eye. Noose ended a quiet burner call, slipping the phone back into his jacket as he crossed the room. The others didn't look up. Noose moved like a shadow, quiet and efficient. One of the few in Tombs' circle who never needed reminding to keep his mouth shut and his ears open.

Tombs raised an eyebrow as Noose slid into the booth opposite. "News?"

Noose gave the room a once-over before speaking, voice low. "One of the lads down south just checked in. Blake's been seen sniffing around Muswellbrook."

Tombs didn't move.

Noose added, "But not about Callahan."

The tapping stopped.

Tombs' voice dropped, barely above a growl. "Who, then?"

Noose hesitated — just for a breath — then said it.

"You."

Tombs sat back, slow and quiet, the booth creaking under his weight. His jaw worked side to side, like he was chewing on the words. Not tasting them. Grinding them.

So Blake was checking up on him?

That was it. That was the fucking line.

The anger didn't come fast — it never did with Tombs. It rolled in low, like thunder behind the hills, slow and building. He wasn't an idiot. He'd always known Blake played his own angles. But this wasn't strategy anymore.

This was surveillance.

This wasn't Blake making sure Tombs got the job done.

This was Blake making sure Tombs didn't become the job.

Tombs cracked his knuckles one by one, the sound sharp in the silence. His jaw worked like stone grinding stone, gaze fixed on nothing in particular as the decision settled into place.

Across the booth, Noose waited — quiet, patient. He didn't need a speech. Just a signal.

Tombs gave a single nod.

That was enough.

Noose gave a subtle tilt of his chin in reply, already understanding. Whatever patience they'd shown Blake was done. No more waiting. No more leash.

No more fucking circles.

Tombs reached into his jacket and pulled out his phone, thumb sliding across the screen as he flipped through his contacts. He found the name he wanted — buried deep — and pressed call.

One ring. Two.

Then a voice came through, smooth as polished stone and just as cold. "Yeah?"

Tombs let a smile tug at the corner of his mouth. "I need someone watched."

A pause.

"Blake?"

Tombs' smirk widened. "Now you're catching on."

Another pause, then a dry chuckle. "Alright. But it's gonna cost you."

Tombs shifted in his seat, shoulders loosening. "Don't worry about the money."

"So what should I worry about?"

He leaned back slowly, the chair creaking beneath him.

"Just be ready when I say."

The line went dead.

Tombs lowered the phone and sat still, hands braced on his knees like he was holding up the room.

Blake wasn't the only one who knew how to pull strings.

And now?

Now, he was going to teach the bastard what it felt like when those strings tightened — slow, deliberate, choking.

He reached for his beer at last, lifting it with one hand.

Time to start playing his own game.

CHAPTER 56

The 4WD sat like a predator in the dark — engine off, lights out, windows cracked just enough to hear the breath of the bush. The air was dry, still, every sound amplified. The distant call of a nightjar. The rustle of some foraging marsupial. The occasional creak of branches shifting in the breeze.

Inside, Declan sat completely still.

Only the faint blue glow of his laptop lit the cab, casting ghost-light over his face and hands. The flicker of surveillance footage moved across the screen in silence — grainy loops of bikers stepping in and out of roadhouses, of a woman locking the back gate at Redmond's property, of a porch light blinking on and off like a signal waiting to be read.

He had been following Tombs and his crew for what felt like days now. Never close enough to draw attention. Just enough to observe. To learn. They moved like men with no fear — full of piss, noise, and beer-soaked bravado.

He'd seen that before.

He'd killed that before.

Tombs was methodical, but not clever. He led with strength and threat. Noose, Wesson, and Carrick followed like iron filings to a magnet — loyal, but slow. The crew seemed to lack a second in charge. An enforcer, sharp enough to spot danger but not smart enough to plan around it. Another weakness.

They were all patterns. Predictable. Declan's kind of prey.

Until one shot went wrong.

He leaned back against the headrest, muscles coiled under the stillness. His eyes tracked the footage again, stopping on a freeze-frame.

Frank Tolliver.

The old bastard stood on a weathered farmhouse porch, arm strapped in a sling, body still like a soldier in a perimeter watch. Even wounded, he projected presence. Awareness. The kind of man who didn't blink at a fight.

The kind of man who should have been dead.

Declan stared at the image, jaw tightening.

That shot had been clean. Everything lined up — the wind, the elevation, the target profile. A perfect kill.

And Tolliver had moved.

Not panic. Not luck.

He had sensed it. Felt the pressure from the scope across his skin. The whisper of death behind him.

Declan didn't believe in luck. Not in his line of work. Men who moved like that weren't lucky — they were dangerous.

He closed the laptop, the screen fading into black. The cab darkened. Only the soft ticking of the cooling engine filled the void.

Declan exhaled slowly.

Tolliver wasn't just a factor. He was a variable. A live wire in the middle of a job that had already frayed at the edges. If it was just Tombs and the bikers, Declan could bleed them out one by one, dismantle their little crew like he had a dozen others.

But now?

Now Callahan had a ghost on his side. A man like Declan.

And that changed the game.

He drummed his fingers once against the steering wheel. Thought about the best move. Keep trailing Tombs, waiting for the opportune moment? Or shift gears and follow the ones actually making progress?

He already knew the answer.

His hand slid across to the passenger seat, grabbing his phone. He hated calls. Too many words. Too much exposure. But Zhao needed to be looped in on this.

He scrolled to the number and hit dial.

Two rings. Then the smooth, even voice on the other end.

"You have something for me?"

Declan kept his eyes on the road ahead, empty and black.

"Callahan. Redmond. Tolliver. They're preparing."

A pause.

"Preparing?"

"Supplies. Fuel. Maps. Gear."

Declan let it hang.

Zhao would connect the rest.

Another pause. A sharp breath through the line. "Destination?"

Declan tapped the steering wheel once. "Same place as before. Same fucking nightmare destination. "

He let it drop with weight.

"Pilliga."

The line went quiet.

That name meant nothing to Zhao. Declan could feel it in Zhao's questioning silence. Didn't care. What he knew was tactical.

The Pilliga was rough country. Isolated. Unpatrolled. No police presence. No backup. A place you only entered if you wanted to disappear — or if you didn't want your enemies to come out.

Zhao's voice was quieter when it returned. "Stay on them."

Declan's mouth twitched. Almost a smile. "That's the job."

The call cut off.

Declan tossed the phone back onto the seat, rolling his neck once to loosen the tension. His eyes stayed on the road. Somewhere ahead, Callahan and his crew were moving.

Tombs was still licking his wounds. Still flexing muscle and telling himself he was the top of the food chain.

But Callahan?

Callahan had made the shift.

They were going to the Pilliga.

Which meant they weren't just running anymore.

They were hunting too.

Declan opened the laptop again, switching to his alternate feed — thermal, drone-mapped, silently compiling a heat map of the area. Three dots, close together. Still at Redmond's.

For now.

He reached for the gearstick, flicked the ignition.

The 4WD rumbled to life like a panther waking. No headlights. Just the quiet hum of the engine, the dashboard's red glow lighting his fingers as he shifted into gear.

The hunt was on again.

Only this time?
He wasn't the only one with teeth.
And that made it interesting.

CHAPTER 57

Shanghai stretched beneath him like a living organism — glittering, relentless, always shifting. From the penthouse suite high above the city, it looked almost peaceful. Like a circuit board pulsing with gold and white, veined with light and power.

Wei Zheng stood in front of the glass, hands folded behind his back, his breath fogging the window just slightly with each exhale. The skyline stretched to the horizon, where a storm gathered on the edge of the world. Black clouds rolled over distant towers, thick with heat, lightning and promise.

He didn't move.

The room behind him was silent. Polished teak floors, cold and perfect. A vast desk carved from a single slab of mahogany stood in the centre, flanked by shelves that held no books — just artefacts. History curated by wealth.

On the low table to his left, a glass of whiskey sat untouched. Ice melted slowly within, the only movement in the room.

The phone in his hand buzzed once.

He answered without turning from the storm.

"Pilliga."

Zhao's voice. Distant. Precise.

Wei's mouth barely moved. "Interesting." The feigned recognition lost on Zhao.

He listened as the storm grew closer, the low rumble of thunder swallowed by triple-glazed glass.

Zhao continued, his tone clinical. "They're preparing. Stocking supplies. Fuel. Maps. They're going out there for something."

Wei turned from the window, moving with the calm of a man who had never rushed in his life. His footsteps were soundless against the floor.

"And Callahan?"

"He has help," Zhao said. "The woman — Martha Redmond. And another. Frank Tolliver."

Wei stopped.

"Tolliver." He said the name slowly, tasting it.

Zhao nodded. "Frank Tolliver. Vietnam. Covert operations. Highly decorated. Still dangerous."

Wei exhaled through his nose. Not surprise. Not fear. Just the quiet click of strategy recalibrating.

He approached the desk, ran a hand over its surface — cool and smooth like water turned to stone. Then he sat, spine straight, fingers steepled in front of him.

"I assume you are handling it."

"Declan is watching them," Zhao replied. "He knows the terrain. If they make a move, we'll know."

Wei said nothing at first. He let the silence bloom between them, knowing Zhao would feel the weight of it. A test. A pressure point.

Then:

"You've played your part well, Zhao."

He could almost hear Zhao stiffen.

The man was careful. Disciplined. But not immune to praise. Wei had spent years cultivating him — grooming him not just as an asset, but as a weapon. The first cut in a far larger kill.

What Zhao didn't know — what he would never know until it was too late — was that he was not the executioner.

He was the distraction.

The sacrificial move before checkmate.

Liu Jianhong was the target. Always had been. And Zhao's pursuit of the opals, of vengeance, of pride — that had always been the bait. The mask Wei wore to shield his real play.

Because this wasn't about opals.

It had never been about opals.

It was about the illusion of power. The hollow kingdom Liu had built on myth and fear. Wei had spent decades eroding it from the inside — buying allies, bleeding contacts, shifting loyalties grain by grain.

And now?

Now, the cracks were beginning to show.

Wei's voice remained calm. "The opals mean nothing. Their loss is the first fracture. It will spread. Liu will lose the appearance of control. The stockholders will panic. His partners will turn. And when the time is right…"

He let the words fade.

Let Zhao imagine the rest.

And, predictably, Zhao rose to the bait. His voice came low, dark, laced with satisfaction.

"He won't recover from this."

"No," Wei said softly. "He will not."

A pause.

Then, Zhao added, "And when the time comes — I will be the one to take his head."

Wei's lips twitched. A shadow of a smile. He rolled his chair slightly back, fingers brushing the edge of his desk.

Zhao's obsession made him predictable. Predictable men were useful. And they were easy to discard.

"I will leave that to you," Wei said.

Zhao acknowledged with a grunt. "I'll update you when Callahan moves."

The call ended.

Wei set the phone down. No rush. No flicker of concern.

He stood and pressed a button beneath the desk.

A moment later, the door opened.

His assistant entered. Impeccable suit. Head slightly bowed. The man crossed the room in silence and placed a small black lacquered box on the desk.

Wei dismissed him with a glance.

He opened the box.

Inside lay a sword sheath — dark, polished, elegant in its simplicity. The leather was aged, but lovingly maintained. An object with history. Purpose.

Atop it, a note written in flawless calligraphy.

"The blade comes next."

Wei traced the note with one finger.

Zhao believed he would be the one to kill Liu Jianhong.

But Wei already knew the truth.

The storm had arrived.

Outside, thunder cracked across the sky, rattling the heavens. Rain spattered against the glass in slow, steady waves.

Wei closed the box with care. No rush. No drama. Just inevitability.

The next move was already in play.

And Zhao?

He was just another piece on the board.

One more step toward the end.

CHAPTER 58

The shed smelled of old oil, dust covered canvas, and leather dried by sun and time. Dust hung in the air like breath, catching the light that streamed in through cracked tin and warped slats. Rusty tools lined the back wall, most long past their prime, each one heavy with the weight of half-finished jobs and forgotten plans. The heat inside pressed against the skin, the kind that didn't just sit on your shoulders but settled into your bones.

Dave pulled open a metal cabinet, the hinges screeching in protest. Inside — an old coil of rope, a pile of mismatched tools, a half-empty jerry can that sloshed faintly when he shook it.

"Useless," he muttered, tossing the can to the floor with a dull thud.

Martha stood by the workbench, sorting gear into piles: maps, compasses, torches, batteries. A hunting knife lay in front of her, its handle worn smooth and dark, like it had been handed down through generations. Her movements were methodical, almost surgical. No wasted energy. No hesitation.

The dogs paced near the door. Bruce, silent and broad-shouldered, watched everything. Tilly, the kelpie, moved like a shadow — restless, sharp-eyed. And Banjo, the smallest and loudest of them, circled the doorframe like it was an easy prey.

Frank stood leaning against the post beside the open door, his arm wrapped in a bandage that had long since lost its crispness. The bullet graze still had colour to it, but that wasn't the concern anymore. His breath came too fast. His colour was off. Dave saw it.

"We're not ready for this," Dave muttered, his voice low as he turned back to the bench.

Martha didn't look up. "We're never gonna be. You want perfect conditions? You're in the wrong business."

Dave gripped the edge of the table, knuckles white. "The Pilliga isn't just bush. It's a maze. A trap. You take one wrong track out there and you vanish."

"Big," Frank said from the doorway. "Bigger than you think. Bigger than anyone can measure properly."

Dave nodded. "Over five thousand square clicks of bushland. No proper roads, no phone signal, no markers. Just heat, trees, and silence. They say it swallows things. Farms, fences, people. You step off the track and you disappear."

Martha's eyes didn't waver. "I respect it."

Dave ran a hand through his hair, sweat prickling his scalp. "It's bigger than Luxembourg. Bigger than bloody Rhode Island."

Banjo let out a quiet yap, ears flicking as if the mention of it unsettled him too.

Frank pushed off the post, moving stiffly. "Used to be different. Stations out there, people running cattle, logging crews working deep into the heart of it. But the land took it all back. What's left now? Nothing but ghost trails and fire scars."

Martha crossed her arms. "Sounds like the perfect place to hide something."

Dave gave her a look. "Or to get lost forever."

"Same thing," she replied, "depending on who's doing the looking."

Frank nodded. "We'll need more fuel."

"And water," Martha added. "Food, gear, spares for the tyres. Enough to last at least a week if it all goes to hell."

Dave let out a dry laugh. "A week? You planning a camping trip?"

"I'm planning to come back."

Frank chuckled, a rasp of old laughter. But it ended in a wince. His hand moved to his ribs, subtle, but not unseen.

Dave watched him. "You alright?"

Frank waved him off. "Fine."

He wasn't.

Not ten minutes later, as they loaded gear into the back of the 4WD, Frank staggered.

It was fast. Sudden. One moment, he was handing Martha a folded tarp. The next, he went pale, knees buckling, hand slapping against the side panel of the vehicle.

Bruce barked once, sharp and low. Banjo darted in circles. Tilly growled and stood still.

"Frank —!"

"I'm fine," he grunted, but his voice was too thin. Sweat shone on his forehead. His fingers trembled against the hot metal.

Martha was there instantly, her voice a blade. "Sit down."

"I said —"

"Sit the fuck down, Frank."

There was no room to argue.

He slumped onto the step of the 4WD, breathing hard. Martha knelt beside him, fingers on his wrist, eyes scanning his face.

Dave crouched opposite her. "It's not just the bullet, is it?"

Frank didn't answer.

Martha's jaw clenched. "Pulse is slow. Too slow."

"Could be heat," Dave offered.

"Could be the years catching up."

Frank chuckled again. "Thought I had more left in the tank."

Dave ran a hand down his face. "Jesus, mate."

Frank waved him off. "You're not going in without me."

"We're not going in at all," Martha snapped, "until you look like you won't die halfway through the trip."

He tried to protest, but she stared him down.

"Five minutes. Then ten. Then twenty if we need it."

Frank grumbled but stayed put. Martha handed him a water bottle. He drank slowly, every swallow louder than it should have been.

The shed fell into a kind of hush. Not peace. Just tension stretched thin.

Outside, the breeze shifted. A dry rustle moved through the trees. The dogs lifted their heads.

Bruce growled. Tilly stood at the edge of the doorway, ears high. Banjo froze, nose twitching.

Dave followed their gaze, staring out into the scrub.

Nothing moved.

And yet —

Something was there.
Just beyond the tree line.
Just beyond sight.
Watching.
Waiting.

CHAPTER 59

The highway stretched ahead like a wound — long, empty, unhealing. Bitumen shimmered under the first bleed of dawn, the kind of soft grey light that didn't quite reach the corners of the world. Shadows still clung to the inside of the car, thick as fog.

Blake kept the windows up. The air was stale, the vents spitting dust like the whole system had given up trying to breathe.

His hands sat stiff on the wheel, fingers locked, tension buried deep in the joints.

Not fear—at least not yet. Just pressure. The kind that crept in slow. Quiet.

The dashboard clock blinked at him. Cold. Unbothered. Time was slipping through his hands, vanishing in quiet, ticking increments.

Once, he'd been ahead of time. Ahead of everyone. The one in control. The man with the maps, the phone numbers, the levers. The one who moved other people like pieces on a board — never guessing, always certain.

But now?

Now he was following. Reacting. Guessing with every step. And the bastard at the centre of it — Callahan — was still moving. Still breathing. Still digging.

The motel had smelled like damp curtains and wasted time.

Sleep was something he'd heard of, but it felt miles off.

The bed, a stale coffin of regret.

He hadn't stayed long. Couldn't stand the itch of failure in the carpet or the way the silence pressed in.

Too many players. Too many shadows. Tombs had gone quiet. Zhao — worse — was silent and unpredictable. Maybe rogue. Maybe dead. Declan was still circling, unpredictable as ever, a threat without aim. And Callahan... Christ. The bastard just kept going. Chasing ghosts like they owed him something. Still landing on his feet. Still fucking winning.

Blake ground his teeth.

He should've buried him when he had the chance. Should've shut it all down before Callahan started kicking up bones better left buried.

Now it was slipping. Coming apart at the seams.

Blake didn't like things he couldn't control.

Dust billowed behind the car as Blake swung into the Muswellbrook police station lot. The sun was fully up now, casting a pale wash across the cracked bitumen and catching on the station's faded signage like an afterthought. A couple of uniforms stood near the entrance, coffee in hand, eyes squinting toward the car.

Blake didn't acknowledge them. He moved fast — shoulders tight, jaw locked — like a man too far past tired to bother with pleasantries.

Inside, he made straight for the corner office. Knocked once. Didn't wait.

Detective Senior Sergeant Perry looked up from behind a desk cluttered with paperwork and bad coffee. His scowl landed first.

"Jesus, Blake. I got better fucking things to do than your bidding every five minutes." he said. "You look like shit."

Blake didn't bother replying. Didn't sit. He planted both hands on the desk, leaning in close enough to crowd the space.

"I need a favour."

Perry leaned back slowly, unimpressed. "Again. For fucks sake, I thought you had this shit sorted."

"Things changed."

"No kidding. You come in here looking like a kicked dog, breathing smoke like the whole state's about to burn. What's going on?"

"Callahan."

Perry blinked.

Blake didn't move. "The bloke from the ICO list. The one I asked for your help with.."

Perry stared for a beat. Then it landed. "Callahan. Right. The prison weekend handyman. Thought he was just some grunt on an ICO."

"He's not. He's heading west. Toward Gunnedah. Then who fucking knows."

Perry let out a low whistle. "Big country."

"Exactly. Once he's out there, we lose him. I need him stopped before that happens."

Perry narrowed his eyes, folding his arms. "Stopped how?"

"Doesn't matter. Roadblock, breath test, slap a defect sticker on his car. Something to slow him down."

Perry tapped a chewed pen against the desk. "No paperwork. No warrant. Just you, storming in and asking for a cowboy favour."

"You owe me."

That landed like a punch.

Perry froze, the breath caught in his throat. For a moment, neither of them spoke. Then he looked away, rubbing his jaw like the memory still itched.

"You know how deep this hole's getting?" he said finally. "Smoke coming out of half the northwest. Bikers dead or missing. Locals panicked. Now you want me to throw uniforms in front of a bloke who might not even know he's part of the story. That's how people get shot."

Blake didn't flinch. "Just slow him down."

Perry sighed, long and bitter. "Fuck. Fine. But if this blows back —"

"I know the drill."

Perry shook his head. "You always did."

Blake was already moving. He didn't say another word.

Blake was barely back in the car before his fingers were already swiping across the screen.

The line clicked.

A voice answered — calm, dry, with that same quiet smugness Blake had grown to hate.

Declan.

"Where is he?" Blake asked, not bothering with greetings.

A pause. Then that familiar low chuckle. "You're getting impatient."

"Callahan," Blake snapped. "Where the fuck is he?"

Declan let the silence stretch just long enough to make a point. "Still packing. Looks like they're heading in heavy — water, fuel, supplies. Proper gear."

Another pause.

"They keep saying one word. Pilliga." He said it as though it was the first time he had ever mouthed the word. Blake didn't need to know any different.

Blake's stomach turned. If Callahan disappeared into that goddamn scrub, it was over. They'd never find him again. Not without bodies piling up first.

"You want me to take care of it?" Declan asked, smooth as ever. Like he was offering a sandwich.

Blake didn't answer straight away. His jaw locked tight as he stared through the windscreen at nothing.

"Not yet," he said at last. "I want him boxed in first."

"You're cutting it close."

"I know."

"Clock's ticking."

Blake ended the call.

The silence that followed was worse than the voice. Heavy. Still. He loosened his collar with one hand, then adjusted the mirror.

His reflection stared back — creased, grey at the edges, a man aged a decade in a week.

He didn't look like the guy with all the angles anymore.

Didn't matter.

He wasn't done yet.

He still had time. Still had control. Just enough to tip the scales back. One more move. One more trap.

He started the engine.

Not today.

Not yet.

He still had one last shot.

And he wasn't about to miss.

CHAPTER 60

The highway stretched before them, endless and exposed, a black ribbon of bitumen cutting through a landscape that swallowed all things small and fragile. Dave kept his hands firm on the wheel, his fingers white-knuckled. Beside him, Martha shifted in her seat, her body wound tight. In the back, Frank sat still, his presence heavy, his gaze flicking from the rear window to the side mirrors, watching. Always watching.

The roadblocks had started appearing an hour ago. A pair of highway patrol cars idling at an intersection, their occupants scanning every passing vehicle. Then a breathless warning over the crackling radio waves—police checking trucks at the next service station, searching for a suspect. A name hadn't been given, but Dave didn't need to hear it. He knew damn well who they were looking for.

Up ahead, another checkpoint. The flashing lights pulsed in the distance, rhythmic and steady, like a heartbeat waiting to flatline. Two police utes, an officer with a clipboard, another walking between cars, peering in windows, looking.

Frank let out a slow breath. "Keep it steady. No sudden movements."

Martha's hands curled into fists. She had tied her hair back, hidden the worst of her bruises beneath a thick scarf. Her eyes were shadowed but sharp. "They're not gonna miss the resemblance."

"They might," Frank murmured. "If we're lucky."

Dave wasn't in the mood to rely on luck.

He eased off the accelerator, the Land Cruiser rolling towards the checkpoint like an animal being led to slaughter. Every inch of his body screamed to turn back, to take a side road, to get the hell away. But that was what a guilty man would do. That was how you got chased.

An officer lifted his hand, stepping out from the group. This is it. Then—chaos.

A burst of static over the police radio. Another officer turned, hand to his earpiece. The one holding the clipboard frowned, turning toward the parked utes. Then, suddenly, they were moving.

The radio crackled again, this time sharper, more urgent. The officer at the checkpoint touched his earpiece, his body going rigid. Then— movement. A second officer strode over, speaking fast, his face shifting from routine focus to something closer to alarm.

Then came the words that changed everything.

"Shots fired. Officers down. Need all available units—immediate response."

It was enough. Whatever manhunt they'd been running here paled in comparison. Within seconds, the checkpoint was in motion—doors slamming, engines roaring to life, dust kicking up in thick plumes as the police vehicles peeled away, lights cutting through the growing dusk.

Dave watched them go, heart hammering. They weren't lucky. They were just small fish in a pond where a much bigger predator had just surfaced.

Dave barely breathed.

"Drive," Frank said, voice level. "Now."

He didn't need to be told twice. He put his foot down, the 4wd rolling past the now-abandoned checkpoint. The police were gone. Chasing something bigger.

Whatever it was, Dave was grateful for it.

But now they sat on the verge of the Pilliga.

Frank leaned forward in his seat, arms braced against the dash, eyes locked on the tree-line ahead. He hadn't said much in the last hour — not since the last roadblock, not since the dogs were dropped off. But now, with the bush rising in front of them like a wall, something in him shifted.

"This is it," he said. Quiet. Certain.

Dave sucked in a deep breath of the dry air, holding it until it escaped in a snort.

The bitumen and graded earth had left them gradually. First gravel, then loose dirt, then nothing but wheel ruts clawed into the earth. The road didn't just end. It unravelled.

Behind them, the last thread of civilisation vanished in the dust. Ahead, the Pilliga loomed.

Martha shifted, silent, her fingers curled tight around the edge of her seat. Her jaw was locked. Eyes flat. When she breathed out, it was through her nose — sharp, like she didn't trust her voice.

Dave kept his hands firm on the wheel. Not out of fear.

Readiness.

Resignation.

The line of trees thickened, dark and tangled — like they'd been waiting.

Eucalypts and scrubby cypress pines grew too close together, their trunks twisted like old bones, bark peeling back in long curls like skin from old scars.

The undergrowth was dense — thorny scrub, fallen branches, speargrass that whipped at their shins. Everything dry. Everything sharp.

The smell shifted too.

Dust, dry sap, and something older — decay beneath the bark, as if the land had been holding its breath for a century.

The light changed.

Not just dimmer, but flatter. Paler. Like the sun didn't dare come in properly.

It felt like crossing a line.

Like the land ahead didn't belong to the same sky.

He downshifted without thinking. Slowed.

The Pilliga loomed.

Not the green postcard kind. This was bush that had its own language. Quiet. Watchful. Where nothing moved unless it wanted to be seen.

Frank glanced sideways at Dave. "You alright?"

Dave nodded once, but didn't speak.

Frank let out a breath through his nose. "I haven't been in here since I was nineteen. Never saw the point of coming back."

Martha finally spoke, her voice low and flat. "Red said the Pilliga remembers things."

Dave frowned. "Things?"

"People. Choices. Mistakes." She looked at the trees. "He always talked about it like it was a living thing. Like it watched you. Waited."

Dave didn't say anything. Just let the weight of her words settle between them.

A few metres ahead, the first shadows spilled across the track — long, strange shapes cast by crooked limbs. The kind of shadows that didn't seem to move with the sun.

They passed a fence post half-swallowed by weeds, a rusted chain swinging from one end. No gate. No welcome. Just a break in the fence like a mouth left open too long.

He pulled the car to a slow stop.

The silence inside the vehicle pressed inward.

Frank adjusted the rifle resting at his feet. "We don't have to say it, but this is the point of no return."

Martha nodded once, barely visible.

Dave looked ahead, his jaw tight.

"No turning back," he said quietly. "Not now."

Nobody moved.

Then he eased the car forward, tyres crunching over the first stretch of broken track.

The bush swallowed them.

No birdsong. No wind. Just the creak of branches and the slow, low rumble of tyres finding their way over ancient earth.

Somewhere behind them — far behind now — Tombs was still coming. A dust storm in human form, chewing up the distance.

And ahead?

Declan was waiting.

CHAPTER 61

The bush swallowed the road behind them without a sound.

No signposts. No markers. Just scrub and silence and a feeling that pressed behind the eyes.

Dave felt it hit — like stepping into water just a few degrees too cold. Not enough to panic. Just enough to know something had changed.

The Pilliga wrapped around them.

Tall ghost gums and cypress pines twisted into shapes that didn't feel entirely natural. Their trunks loomed thick and pale, bark hanging in long strips like sunburned skin. The undergrowth grew wild — wait-a-while vines, dry lantana, scattered thornbrush — and every patch of open dirt looked like something had once been dragged across it.

Frank shifted in his seat, staring out at the land.

"This place eats people."

No one laughed.

The 4wd rolled forward, tyres crunching over gravel and dry leaves. The track was barely there — just the suggestion of a path, wheel ruts left by some old farmer's ute decades ago, maybe longer. The bush had no mercy for the unprepared. A wrong turn out here wasn't just an inconvenience. It was a sentence.

Martha leaned forward, squinting through the windscreen. "We sticking to the map?"

"Best we can." Dave tightened his grip on the wheel. The paper map sat folded on the dash, the creases worn thin from years of use. The track they followed was marked in faint pencil, barely more than a ghost trail through a stretch of land so big it swallowed towns whole.

Frank grunted. "The land's changed since that map was drawn."

It wasn't a warning. Just a fact.

They drove in silence, the only sound the rumble of the engine and the rhythmic thump of the tyres over uneven ground. But the further they went, the less natural it felt.

Not the road. The land.

Dave had spent enough time in the bush to know when something wasn't right. The way the trees should sway in the wind, the rustle of branches, the distant calls of birds, the occasional skitter of a goanna across dry leaves. But here, the silence was absolute.

The bush was holding its breath.

Martha shifted in her seat. "Anyone else feel like —"

"Yes," Frank said.

Dave didn't ask. He felt it too.

The track twisted between the trees, narrowing as the vegetation thickened, the eucalypts pressing in, limbs arching overhead. The light dimmed, even though the sun hadn't fully set. Shadows moved where they shouldn't.

Something watched from the undergrowth.

Dave kept his eyes on the track, but he felt it. A weight. A presence.

Then, the smell hit.

Not rot. Not death. Something older. Like damp earth, wood smoke, and something that didn't belong. The air grew thick, the scent pressing against their lungs.

Frank stared into the scrub for a long second. "The old people say you don't walk into the Pilliga alone."

Martha gave him a sidelong look. "And yet here we are."

"They also say there are places you don't stop." His gaze swept the trees. "Places you don't look back."

Dave felt it too. The weight of history in the dirt. The sense that every footprint, every broken branch, every whisper of wind against bark had been witnessed and judged.

They weren't the first to pass through. And they weren't alone now.

Dave had heard stories. Everyone had. You didn't grow up in the bush without them. The Pilliga wasn't just a place. It was a force. It had taken people, stolen them from the world, left nothing behind but rumours and grief.

Frank sat forward, staring into the trees. "I saw him once."

Dave flicked him a glance. "Saw who?"

Frank didn't blink. "The stockman."

Martha shifted. "Oh, great. Now's the time we tell ghost stories?"

"He's not a story," Frank murmured. His voice was low, almost reverent. "Rode past me at dusk, back when I was young. Dust on his boots, hat pulled low. He never looked at me. Just rode on, into the trees. Horse didn't make a sound."

Dave felt the goosebumps rise along his arms. "Then what?"

Frank didn't take his eyes off the bush. "Then he was gone. No sound of hooves. No sign of a rider. Just the hush of the Pilliga swallowing him whole."

Martha raised an eyebrow. "Maybe you just saw a bloke on a horse."

Frank's fingers tapped the door. "If I did, he never left tracks."

The wind shifted, pushing through the trees, bringing something else. A whisper.

Low, indistinct. Like a woman's voice carried on the breeze.

Martha sat up straight. "Did you hear —"

A snap in the bush. Loud enough to cut through the roar of the engine.

Dave slammed his foot on the brake, the Land Cruiser lurching to a stop.

Silence.

Nothing moved.

He scanned the trees, breathing hard. There was something out there.

Frank's voice was quiet. "Sometimes, she calls your name."

Martha swallowed.

Dave didn't move. His knuckles were white on the wheel.

And then, somewhere in the trees — just out of sight — something moved.

The moment shattered. A figure stepped onto the track in front of them.

Dave's stomach dropped. His hands tightened on the wheel.

It wasn't a ghost.

It was a man.

Thin, dust-covered, with a ragged shirt and jeans worn to threads. His boots were caked in mud. His eyes were hollow.

Frank muttered something under his breath.

Martha tensed. "Who the hell is that?"

The man lifted a hand. Not in greeting. In warning.

Then he turned and walked away, disappearing into the trees.

Dave's pulse slammed against his ribs.

Frank exhaled. "That's not a good sign."

Dave didn't hesitate. He gunned the engine, pushing forward. Whatever that had been — ghost, warning, or trap — they weren't stopping to find out.

**

Miles behind them, Tombs was still coming.

The last stretch of road had been hell. His bike and his men were battered, their tempers frayed. They were close, but the land was working against them.

And then he saw it.

A sign, hand-painted and nailed to a tree.

TURN BACK.

A joke. Some old legend meant to scare city tourists. But it wasn't the words that stopped him.

It was what was beneath them.

A fresh set of boot prints.

Someone had stood right there. Recently. Watching.

Tombs inhaled sharply. His gut twisted, and for the first time in a long time, he felt it.

Not anger. Not frustration.

Doubt.

But he shook it off. He revved the throttle, swallowing the feeling deep.

CHAPTER 62

Dave gripped the wheel tighter.

The car crawled forward, tyres crunching through dust and loose stone. The track had been clear a few kilometres back — broad enough, straight enough. But now it was slipping, veering, softening into vague lines that barely held shape. Wheel ruts faded beneath the scrub, swallowed by earth and shadow.

Nothing looked right anymore.

No signs. No markers. Just the slow suffocation of direction.

The trees pressed closer.

Towering gums, thick and ghost-pale, their bark flaking in long curls that drifted on the still air like dead paper.

They leaned in from both sides, limbs arching overhead until the track felt less like a road and more like a throat — tightening, closing.

Even with the sun still hanging in the sky, the light was thinning.

A dull wash of grey crept over everything, like the day itself was retreating.

A shadow lay across the track now.

Not cast by anything in particular. Just there. Settling in like mist.

Dave could feel it. That pull. Not physical, but something else. Like the land was drawing them deeper with invisible hands.

Frank hadn't said a word in ten minutes. He sat rigid in the back seat, one arm braced on the window frame, his eyes flicking over the trees like he was reading them — like the bush itself might offer some kind of warning.

Martha shifted in her seat, glancing sideways at Dave. "We're going in circles."

He didn't respond right away. His jaw tightened as he adjusted his grip, knuckles pale. She was right, of course. He knew it. But saying it out loud would make it real.

Ahead, the track forked.

Left or right.

Neither looked right. Neither looked wrong. Both were swallowed by the same grey-green wall of trees.

Frank finally spoke. A quiet breath first, then words, low and steady: "We shouldn't be here."

Dave gave no reply.

He turned left.

The bush broke without warning.

One moment, they were winding through claustrophobic scrub, the next — the trees simply fell back. A clearing yawned open before them, still and oddly perfect, as if the land itself had stepped aside.

And there it was.

A shack squatted in the middle of the clearing, hunched low beneath the eucalypts like a wound that had never healed.

Dave's foot lifted from the accelerator as his heart gave a single, unexpected thud.

It was old — impossibly old — but not ruined. The tin roof sagged with rust, the edges eaten through by decades of rain and heat, yet the structure beneath it still stood firm. Too firm. The timber looked grey and sun-starved but not rotted. Not broken. It felt… wrong. As though time had skipped over it.

The door hung slightly ajar, caught on a crooked hinge. A single window stared out at them, blank and black like an empty eye socket.

Frank didn't move.

Martha leaned forward, voice low. "That's not on the map."

Dave reached for the key and killed the engine. The sudden silence was deafening.

"No," he said. "It's not."

None of them moved. The car ticked softly as the engine cooled.

The shack waited.

Maybe it was shelter. Maybe it was a warning. Either way, the Pilliga had offered it — and you didn't get many choices out here.

They stepped inside one by one, slow and cautious, like the floorboards might groan too loud or the shadows might shift if they moved too fast.

The air was thick with dust and time. It clung to their skin, caught in their throats, carried a scent that was more than just old timber — there was something else beneath it. Faint. Sharp. Almost human.

The shack was no bigger than a single room. A table stood to one side, warped and splintering, with a single chair tucked beneath it like someone had only just left. In the fireplace, a rusted kettle sat askew, black with age. Along the far wall, an iron bedframe leaned crookedly, stripped bare of mattress or blankets, just metal and silence.

Then the walls.

Scratched.

Dozens — no, hundreds — of tally marks carved deep into the timber, lines gouged with something sharp and unforgiving. Some were grouped in neat fives. Others spiralled or overlapped, desperate and uneven. There was no pattern. Just counting. Endless counting.

Martha reached out and traced them with the tips of her fingers, her voice small and hollow. "Someone lived here."

Frank stayed near the door. He hadn't stepped further than the threshold, like the shack might decide to swallow him whole if he did.

Dave turned slowly in the centre of the room, taking it all in. Empty… but not abandoned. He could feel that much. There was weight here. Like the air had soaked in too many secrets.

He looked to Frank. "Thought you didn't believe in this kind of thing."

Frank's eyes didn't move from the window. "I believe in places."

Outside, the bush stretched on — quiet, endless, unmoving.

Only it wasn't.

Something was wrong. Dave felt it in his chest. The kind of wrong that didn't make noise but pressed in from all sides, like the land itself was holding its breath. The silence had changed. It wasn't the usual hush of the bush. It was heavier. Thicker.

Dave moved toward the window, trying to shake the cold creeping down his spine. The light outside was draining away faster than it should've. Dusk was folding over the trees like a closing hand, slow and suffocating.

Then —

A sound.

Low. Drawn-out. A moaning cry that scraped across the silence like a blade. Somewhere between a growl and a scream, like a dingo imitating something human but not quite getting it right. It echoed through the trees in uneven bursts — too long, too slow.

Martha froze mid-step.

Frank didn't blink.

Dave's skin prickled, the fine hairs on his arms lifting. He'd heard dingoes before. He'd heard men scream. This was neither.

"What the fuck was that?" Martha whispered, backing away from the wall like it might answer her.

Frank's voice came steady, but darker than before. "That ain't fucking normal."

Then it came again. A second cry — from a different direction this time.

Closer.

Dave's breath caught.

It wasn't just one.

There were two. Maybe more.

Calling.

Answering.

Circling.

The bush wasn't empty anymore.

And something out there had noticed them.

**

Three hours earlier, just outside the last turnoff before the scrub thickened, Tombs had pulled over and made a call.

Not to Blake.

Someone local. Someone who owed him.

He stood in the dirt, wind tugging at his vest, phone pressed tight to his ear. "Bring the dirt bikes," he said. "All of them and any spare boys you can muster."

A grunt on the other end. "That's a long way to haul that many bikes."

Tombs didn't blink. "I'm not asking."

The reply came slow. "Be a few hours."

"Make it less."

He ended the call, then turned to his crew. "We wait here. When the bikes get here, we transfer. Hiluxes and Harleys can't go where we're headed."

He didn't explain. Didn't need to. The boys knew when a job shifted. The bush ahead was getting tighter, rougher, and Tombs wasn't about to drag his men into the Pilliga on the wrong wheels.

Three hours later, they rode.

And the bush closed behind them like a mouth.

They weren't far behind now — maybe two hours, maybe less — but the land was playing tricks. Landmarks shifted. Shadows leaned the wrong way. The scrub thickened in unnatural patterns, like the forest was trying to confuse them. Break them.

Tombs kept riding. But his men?

They were starting to fold.

The deeper they pushed, the quieter it got. The ones who'd been laughing earlier, sharing crude jokes and swigging from warm cans, had gone dead silent. Even the bikes, roaring and snarling beneath them, felt quieter somehow — like the bush was absorbing the sound. Smothering it.

The track grew mean. Potholes like sinkholes. Branches clawing at their jackets and faces. Vines that hadn't been there seconds before now curled at footpeg height.

Then the noises started.

A low cry, guttural and cracked, echoing across the trees. Not a bird. Not a dog. Something in between. Something wrong.

Carrick flinched mid-ride, his bike wobbling as he looked over his shoulder. "What the fuck was that?"

No one answered.

They didn't have to.

Another sound followed. Longer this time. Wavering like a scream dragged through water. It didn't echo properly. It just... hung there, suspended between trees, refusing to fade.

Up ahead, Wesson's head snapped around too fast. "That ain't fucking normal."

Tombs gritted his teeth and pushed forward, dust kicking beneath his tyres. "Ignore it."

But it didn't stop.

A flicker of light between the trees — brief, unnatural.

Carrick was the first to see it. He slowed, twisted his head. "The fuck was that?"

No answer.

Then a shape. Just off the track. Half-hidden between gums.

A man.

On a horse.

Motionless.

Watching.

Carrick's heart thudded against his ribs. He turned his head to call out —

Gone.

Nothing but bark and leaves.

He told himself it was just the trees. Just tricks of light and nerves. But his palms were slick on the handlebars now, breath shallow and fast.

Up ahead, Wesson's bike swerved. He yanked the brakes, skidded to a stop, and threw the thing down. His boots crunched dry leaves as he backed away, eyes wide.

"No. No. No." His voice cracked. "There's something here, man! There's — there's —"

Tombs was off his bike before the others had even stopped. He stormed over, grabbed Wesson by the jacket and hauled him close.

"Shut the fuck up."

Wesson was trembling. Not with guilt. Not with fear of punishment. This was worse.

This was a man who'd seen something his mind couldn't make sense of.

Tombs shoved him back toward the bike. "Get on."

Wesson shook his head, mouth working uselessly.

Tombs drew his pistol.

He didn't raise it. He didn't need to.

Wesson's eyes locked on the gun, then on Tombs' face — unflinching, unreadable. He turned back toward the fallen bike, hands fumbling with the grips.

Then he saw it.

A figure. Between the trees.

Too tall.

Too still.

Watching.

His breath caught in his throat. He blinked.

Gone.

His stomach lurched.

They weren't alone.

Tombs caught the shift in Wesson's face. Walked up behind him, grabbed the side of his helmet, and jerked his head forward.

"You look straight ahead," he growled. "Nothing else fucking matters."

Wesson gave a shaky nod.

The bush thickened around them.

The light fell away.

Tombs mounted his bike.

And the Pilliga, vast and breathing, swallowed them whole.

CHAPTER 63

The land had taken them in, but it wouldn't let them rest.

Frank stood just inside the doorway, arms crossed, silent. He hadn't said a word in a while.

They made camp inside the shack — not because they wanted to, but because the alternative felt worse.

Outside, the darkness pressed close, thick as smoke. The night sky should've stretched wide overhead, but the trees had swallowed it whole, their branches curling inward like ribs around a heart. The wind barely stirred. Just the occasional sigh through dry leaves, but the feeling of being watched never left.

Frank sat by the door, knife in hand. He wasn't whittling. Just holding it.

Martha shifted where she sat, restless, rubbing the back of her neck. "We're being stupid. We should've pushed on."

"Pushed where?" Dave asked. "Blind through the bush in the dark?"

She didn't answer, but the set of her jaw said she hadn't changed her mind.

Dave looked over at Frank. "This place mean something to you?"

Frank exhaled, slow. "Nah." He met Dave's gaze. "But it means something to someone."

That landed heavy, and it sure as hell wasn't comforting.

It started with the small sounds.

A branch creaking. A shift in the leaves. The kind of noises the bush made when it thought you weren't paying attention.

Then, the footsteps.

Dave tensed. So did Martha. Frank didn't move, but his grip on the knife tightened.

The steps weren't rushed. No stumbling. No animal darting through the undergrowth. Just steady. Deliberate. Someone walking.

Martha reached for her gun, slow and quiet.

The footsteps stopped just outside the shack.

Silence.

Frank shifted his grip on the knife. "That's close."

They waited, listening.

The wind slipped through a crack in the wall, soft and high-pitched, like it didn't want to be noticed. Then —

Three knocks.

Soft. Not urgent. Not angry. Just knocking.

Dave swallowed.

Martha's voice was barely a whisper. "You hearing that?"

Frank didn't blink. "Yeah."

They stayed frozen. No voice followed. No boots stepped up onto the porch. Nothing moved. Just silence.

Dave's gut twisted. He rose slowly, forcing himself toward the door. His hand met the timber, rough, dry, old, and he held it there, grounding himself.

He didn't open it.

Instead, he cleared his throat. "Who's there?"

Nothing.

Frank shifted. "Maybe you don't wanna be asking questions."

The steps started again. Not walking away. Just circling. Shifting position. Pacing the edge of the clearing.

Martha's fingers locked tighter around the grip of her gun. "If that's Declan, I'm putting a bullet in him."

Frank shook his head. "That ain't Declan."

No one corrected him.

And that said more than anything else.

Time dragged. The kind of slow that felt like a trap.

The footsteps outside had stopped, but the unease hadn't gone with them.

Martha perched on the table, tapping her boot against the floor, shoulders coiled tight. "Tell me we're not sleeping here."

Frank ran a hand down his face. "You can stay up all night if you want."

"Maybe I will."

Dave wasn't tired either. Not really. He just wanted morning to show up. To break whatever this was.

His gaze drifted to the fireplace. The ashes inside were cold, untouched for God knows how long. But the rusted kettle sitting above them. Full. Not empty. Not dry. Just waiting. Like someone had left it there recently. Ready.

He glanced at Frank, who had already clocked it. Their eyes met, but neither said a word.

Then Martha broke the silence, still staring at the wall. "Those tally marks. The ones on the door frame. Not the ones all over the wall."

Dave turned toward her. "What about them?"

She swallowed. "I counted when we came in. There were twenty-three."

He frowned. "Yeah?"

She wiped a hand across her face, like she didn't want to say it. "Now there's twenty-four."

Silence settled in.

Frank stood and stepped over to the doorframe. He ran his fingers across the carvings. Rough and shallow in places, cut deep in others. He didn't flinch. Didn't comment. Just nodded like he was logging it away. "Might've miscounted."

Martha let out a slow breath, shaking her head. "Yeah. Maybe."

But none of them believed it.

**

Miles away, Tombs was still pushing forward.

But his men were starting to crack. They had stopped to draw a breath. The dark now enveloping them.

Wesson sat hunched on the ground, a cigarette burning low between his fingers, the glow barely touching his face. He hadn't said a word in twenty minutes.

Carrick stood a few metres off, torch slicing through the trees in jittery arcs, breath heavy and uneven. "I swear to fuckin' god, I saw someone."

Tombs didn't respond. He crouched low, hands on his knees, staring at the dirt like it held answers. The map lived in his head now — but the land had its own plans. It twisted things. Shifted them. Made men doubt themselves.

Little Joey paced nearby, twitchy, barely keeping it together. "We shouldn't be out here, man."

Tombs shot him a look. "We're finding Callahan."

Joey shook his head. "Nah. This is wrong. The bush don't want us here."

Tombs snapped. He grabbed Joey by the collar, yanking him close. "Then get on your fuckin' bike and ride home."

Joey's face went pale. "And go back alone?"

Tombs let him go with a shove. "Then shut up. Put up and don't fuck up."

But the damage was done. The cracks were showing. Doubt had sunk in — and it wasn't letting go.

Then, the wind shifted.

Wesson — who hadn't spoken all night — stood abruptly.

His cigarette dropped from his fingers, the ember flaring once before dying in the dirt.

His breath caught.

Tombs frowned. "What?"

Wesson didn't answer. He just turned, slow and stiff, eyes fixed past the trees — staring into the dark like something was staring back.

Then he spoke, voice low, brittle. "Someone's out there."

Tombs narrowed his eyes. "One of ours?"

Wesson swallowed. "No."

Silence fell.

No one moved. No one breathed.

Carrick's torch wavered, its beam flickering. The light cut through the trees, catching something — a shape, half-lost in the scrub.

A man?

A shadow?

Gone.

Tombs felt it — the shift. Like the bush itself had turned its head.

Tombs didn't believe in bullshit. Didn't believe in ghost stories. But something out here was pressing in. Testing them.

And for the first time, he wondered if Callahan wasn't the one being chased…

…but the one being led.

******

Back at the shack, no one slept.

Dave sat with his eyes fixed on the door.

Frank stayed in the corner, knife still in hand.

Martha hadn't moved from the table, her stare locked somewhere deep in the dark.

None of them spoke.

They just waited — silent, still, listening for the sound that would tell them it was back.

Because something was out there.

And it wasn't done with them yet.

CHAPTER 64

Dawn came slow.

Not soft, not peaceful. Sluggish, like the sun was reluctant to lift its head.

A pale, sickly light filtered through the trees, catching on the mist that clung low to the ground. It did nothing to warm the air. If anything, the cold had deepened overnight, curling into bones and boots and breath.

Somewhere out in the scrub, a magpie warbled — low and uncertain.

A butcherbird followed, its call sharp and rising, like it was testing the silence.

Beyond that, nothing.

No rustle. No breeze. No hum of insects.

Just the bush, holding its breath as the light crept in.

Dave pushed the shack door open and stepped out into it, stretching with a grunt as stiff muscles resisted. His boots scuffed the dry ground, the sound too loud in the silence, like it didn't belong.

Because the silence was still there.

No more birdsong. No wind. No insects humming in the scrub. Just an awful, yawning stillness — like the whole bush was holding its breath.

Watching.

Behind him, the old floorboards creaked. Martha stepped out, rubbing at her eyes, hoodie zipped up against the chill. Frank followed, knife already in hand. Just holding it. His gaze was fixed ahead, sharp and unsettled.

Dave stretched his neck until it cracked, but the tension didn't ease. "We need to move."

Frank didn't answer.

He was staring at the ground near the shack door, expression unreadable.

Martha noticed. She stepped down onto the dirt and followed his eyes. "What?"

Frank crouched slowly, the knife still in one hand as his other brushed the ground. The dry crust flaked away beneath his fingers, revealing a set of prints in the thin dust.

Tracks.

He traced one with his thumb. Deep. Crisp around the edges. Recent.

Not theirs.

Dave moved closer, his frown deepening. "Could be from before. Place like this — maybe someone camped here, years ago."

Frank shook his head once. "No. These are fresh."

Martha stiffened. She glanced at the bush, then back at Frank. "You're saying someone was out here? Last night? Watching us?"

Frank stood, brushing the dirt from his fingers like he couldn't stand the feel of it. His eyes swept the trees. "Someone's always watching."

No one replied.

There was nothing to say.

**

Declan moved through the bush like he was born of it . Quiet, deliberate, invisible when he chose to be. His boots barely left a mark, each step placed with the kind of care that comes from years of knowing how to disappear.

He crouched near a dried creek bed, fingers brushing the faint indentations left in the dust. Footprints. Tyre tracks. Shallow, but fresh. Still holding their edges. The kind of prints that hadn't been kissed by sun or wind yet.

They'd come through here recently.

He let out a slow breath, eyes sweeping the ground, mapping the story in the dirt. Depth. Spacing. Direction. The way a branch was bent slightly back. A tuft of grass crushed just so. They weren't panicked. Not running.

They were searching.

Declan didn't need to chase them.

He just had to make sure they never found their way out.

His gaze drifted toward the scrub on his left, narrowing in on a rusted old fence post, half-buried in the undergrowth. A marker, if you knew what you were looking for. Not an official one. Not for tourists or trail maps. But a signpost all the same — part of a system older than GPS and better than any drawn map.

He stepped toward it, wrapped one hand around the corroded steel, and twisted.

The post gave with a groan, roots and dirt clinging to its base as he wrenched it free. Then, without ceremony, he flung it into the trees.

The silence swallowed it.

Let them wonder where the path had gone.

Let them keep walking in circles.

**

The map was useless.

Dave had it spread across the bonnet of the ute, corners pinned under rocks, creased and dust smudged. His finger traced their last known position. What should've been a clear point on the page. A grid reference. A line that connected to something.

But the bush didn't care about maps.

Frank stood beside him, arms folded across his chest, his face giving nothing away.

"We keep heading west," Dave said. "We should hit this old road."

Frank let out a breath — not sharp, but heavy. "If the road's still there."

Martha glanced up from the back of the ute, a scowl already forming. "You think the bush just swallowed it?"

Frank didn't rise to it. He simply tapped a calloused finger against the map.

"You see any signs out here?" he asked. "Any fences? Gates? Marker posts? We should've hit something by now."

Martha looked around, shoulders tight. She didn't want to admit it, but he was right.

Dave said nothing for a long moment. Then folded the map, sharp and quick, and shoved it into his jacket. "We don't have another option."

In front of them, a narrow track peeled off through the trees — rough, but just wide enough for the vehicle. The kind of path that didn't appear on any paper. The kind of path that looked like it had grown out of the dirt on a whim.

Frank squinted at it, hesitant. "Something's off."

Dave climbed into the driver's seat and started the engine. "Everything's off."

The engine rumbled to life.

And they moved out.

**

Tombs had been pushing hard. Too hard. Too fast.

And now the cracks were widening.

Wesson rode at the tail end of the pack, hunched low over the handlebars like he was trying to disappear into the machine. His fingers twitched at the grips. He hadn't spoken since the night before. Not a word. Whatever he'd seen out there in the dark had crawled inside and stayed.

Up ahead, the track opened into a thin clearing. The boys slowed. Engines idled.

Carrick swung off his bike and dropped onto a fallen log, elbows on knees, breathing like he'd just run ten k's uphill. His face was pale, eyes glassy.

"I'm done," he said.

Tombs pulled up beside him, boots hitting the dirt as he turned. "What?"

Carrick didn't lift his head. Just shook it. "I've seen enough. The bush don't want us here."

Tombs' jaw worked side to side. "We're finding Callahan."

Carrick gave a dry, broken laugh. "Then find him yourself."

Tombs moved before anyone saw it coming. Fist bunching the front of Carrick's vest, yanking him to his feet. Their faces were inches apart, close enough for Tombs to smell the sweat and fear on the younger man.

"You walk away from me," Tombs said, voice low and steady, "and you better hope the fucking bush is the only thing that finds you."

Carrick's throat bobbed. He didn't argue.

Tombs held the look a moment longer, then shoved him back hard enough to stagger.

"Get on your bike and finish what we started."

Carrick did. Shaky hands. Eyes down.

The others watched, silent.

No one made a sound.

But the fear had taken root. It was in their eyes now. In their hands. In the way they kept looking over their shoulders.

They kept riding.

But whatever power Tombs had over them. It was starting to bleed out.

And the bush was watching.

**

The track began to shrink around them.

It was subtle at first. A narrowing here, a tighter curve there, but within fifteen minutes, the change was impossible to ignore. The trees were pressing in, branches arching low and close, their bark flaking like dead skin. What had been a rough but passable trail now felt more like a corridor, the walls closing in.

Dave leaned forward, squinting through the windscreen. His hands gripped the wheel tighter than he realised.

"This isn't right," he muttered.

Martha twisted in her seat, eyes flicking from one side of the path to the other. "It looked clear before."

Frank was sitting forward now, elbows on his knees, scanning the bush ahead like it might change if he stared hard enough. "We weren't supposed to come this way."

And then —

The road ended. It felt wrong to even think of jumbled gaps between roots and grass clumps as a road.

No warning. No gradual fade. One moment, they were on a dirt track. The next — nothing.

The bush swallowed it whole.

The trail dissolved into undergrowth and twisted roots, the trees crowding together like they'd never been apart. As if the path had never existed at all.

Dave slammed the brakes. The 4wd lurched to a halt, dust curling around them.

"What the fuck?"

Martha turned to look behind them, eyes wide. "Where's the track?"

Dave stared straight ahead, jaw clenched. "It was there. We were just on it."

Frank was already climbing out. His boots crunched against the dry earth as he took a few slow steps forward. Then he stopped, turned in a slow circle. The bush around them looked the same in every direction — thick, tangled, unwelcoming.

"We've been turned around," he said quietly.

Martha's voice came out thin. "By who?"

No one answered.

Frank crouched. His eyes scanned the ground, sweeping for tyre marks, tracks — anything.

Nothing.

No fresh prints. No flattened grass. Not even their own trail.

Like they'd never been here at all.

Dave ran a hand down his face, voice low and tight. "Alright. We backtrack. Find another way."

But Frank didn't move.

He was staring at the treeline, his brow drawn low, something hard in his expression.

Then, under his breath — a muttered curse.

Dave followed his gaze.

His stomach dropped.

Not far off, pressed into a patch of dirt beneath a crooked tree — one boot print.

Deep.

Deliberate.

Pointing back the way they'd come.

Dave's mouth went dry.

Someone had been here before them.

Or worse —

Someone had led them here.

CHAPTER 65

The morning heat came early — thick, breathless, clinging to their skin like a warning. It didn't just settle over them. It pressed. The kind of heat that made your shirt stick to your back and your nerves crawl just beneath the surface.

They were being led.

Dave could feel it now, and so could Martha. The signs were too hard to ignore. But Frank? He'd felt it before either of them even realised. He'd said nothing at first. Just walked with them, quiet and sure, watching the land like a man watching a card dealer's hands, waiting for the trick.

The car was left behind. Useless to push through the twisted scrub any further in it, but that just brought Frank closer to the bush.

He noticed things. Small things.

A branch snapped at the wrong angle.

A stone sitting too clean in the dirt, like it had been placed, not dropped.

The way the track kept subtly curving back on itself, never quite taking them as far forward as it should've.

This wasn't a pursuit anymore.

Declan wasn't tracking them.

He was guiding them.

They paused near the edge of a dry creek bed, the air heavy with stillness. Dave pulled the map from his jacket and unfolded it across his thigh, tracing the line he thought they'd followed.

Before he could speak, Frank reached over and shut it with a firm hand.

Dave looked up. "We need to —"

"No."

Frank's voice was flat, anchored in something unshakable. His gaze locked on Dave's, calm but unyielding. There was no argument in it, only certainty.

"The map's bullshit now," Frank said. "The land ain't lying to us. He is."

Martha frowned, shifting her weight. "What?"

Frank lifted his chin toward the trail ahead. "Look at it. Open. Easy. A neat little funnel leading right through those trees."

Then he turned and pointed behind them.

The trail back was thick with undergrowth. Twisted. Half-blocked. Smothered by scrub.

Martha's breath caught. "Jesus."

Frank gave a slow nod. "This is a pen. We've been herded. Clean trail forward, nowhere else to go."

Dave swore under his breath. He'd known something was off. Every step had felt heavier. The air too still. The bush too quiet. But now Frank had made it plain.

They were being played.

Martha took a step back, eyes scanning the tree line, one hand tightening on the strap of her rifle. "So, what's the move?"

Frank didn't answer right away.

He stood still, just breathing, eyes scanning the bush like it was a board and he was waiting for all the pieces to settle.

Then, the faintest smile.

"We lead him in."

**

Declan crouched low beside a termite mound, rifle resting across his lap, its weight balanced like a second spine.

The heat didn't bother him. Neither did the silence.

He was used to both.

He'd seen all kinds of men lose their nerve in places like this. Big talkers. Ex-soldiers. Wannabe bushmen with boots too clean. The Pilliga would strip them bare. But Callahan? He was lasting longer than expected. Slower to unravel.

Didn't matter.

A fresh trail ran through the clearing ahead — tracks cut sharp into the dust, spaced just right, heel-to-toe, the rhythm of movement unmistakable.

Declan's lips curled.

Perfect.

He moved like breath. Quiet and quick. Just two steps forward.

Then stopped.

His eyes narrowed.

The tracks were… wrong.

Too neat.

Too placed.

They weren't the marks of a man moving through the bush — they were an invitation.

His gut twisted, a cold knot winding tight just beneath the ribs.

Then —

A shot.

Crack.

It ripped through the stillness like lightning across a dead sky. Declan threw himself sideways instinctively. A split-second later, a bullet slammed into the tree he'd just left, exploding bark in a vicious burst. Splinters bit into his arm and neck as he hit the ground hard, shoulder-first, rolling.

The rifle was already in his hands.

Finger on the trigger.

But —

Nothing.

No sound. No movement. Just trees and dust and that awful quiet, louder now than any gunfire.

Declan stayed low, heart steady despite the adrenaline burning under his skin.

He scanned the tree line.

Still nothing.

But it was clear now.

He wasn't the one pulling strings anymore.

Callahan and his crew had flipped the board.

**

Blake had crossed every line there was.

Some slow. Some sharp.

It started with a quiet favour. Then a call to an old mate in air branch, trading stories and promises he couldn't keep. Now he sat in the back of a black government chopper, strapped in tight while the rotors pounded through the heavy air above the Pilliga.

The headset buzzed against his skull. His collar was soaked. Sweat ran down the back of his neck, trapped between body armour and panic.

He wiped a hand across his forehead. "Christ."

The search had collapsed.

The roadblocks. The breath tests. The half-baked patrols. All of it. Nothing but noise. Callahan had slipped through. Tombs was off the leash. Declan had seemingly gone rogue. And now Blake was stuck in the sky, hovering over a sea of trees that stretched forever in every direction.

The last card in his hand, and it was burning.

The pilot's voice crackled in his ear. "You see anything, sir?"

Blake leaned forward, peering out the side window. The landscape below was endless. Tight canopies of grey-green scrub, shifting like scales. They could be anywhere down there.

But they weren't invisible.

He narrowed his eyes. "We'll find them."

He didn't say what came next.

He didn't have to.

Because if he didn't get Callahan now, if he didn't bring back something that looked like control — he was done.

This was the last move.

And he knew it.

**

Back on the ground, Frank didn't stop moving.

He veered off-track without a word, pushing through the undergrowth with a pace that was fast but deliberate. No wasted steps. Every break in the brush chosen. Every heel drag intentional. He didn't just want to lose Declan.

He wanted to confuse him.

Behind him, Martha kept low, her rifle snug against her shoulder, eyes flicking between shadows. "We get him?"

Frank didn't look back. Just moved between two tight eucalypts and exhaled, low and even. "No. But we made him duck."

Dave caught up beside them, breath sharp. His eyes scanned the canopy, the scrub, the world shifting around them like it had a mind of its own. "If we can shake him, we cut west. Get ahead of whoever else is out there. If he's on us. Fuck we could have Blake and Tombs out there too."

Frank gave a quick nod. "Exactly."

They reached a dense tangle of brush — thick enough to stop a quad, quiet enough to hide footprints. Frank dropped low and grabbed a handful of dirt. He tossed it over his shoulder in a wide arc, letting it scatter across the faint path they'd left behind.

Dave raised an eyebrow. "That's not gonna do much."

Frank didn't answer. Instead, he reached into his jacket pocket and pulled out a thin coil of wire.

A snare. Small. Simple. Silent.

Martha blinked. "You always carry that?"

Frank grinned, not breaking stride. "Bush gives you tools. You just gotta use 'em. Sometimes you got to bring your own."

He bent low, hands working fast and sure, threading the snare into a narrow pinch point between roots — easy to miss, hard to avoid.

Dave shook his head, but a ghost of a smile curled at the edge of his mouth.

This wasn't just survival anymore.

They were fighting back.

**

Declan moved through the trees with a hunter's grace, each footfall silent, every sense tuned to the land. His rifle hung loose across his chest, but his eyes were doing most of the work now.

Callahan had turned the game.

That much was clear.

And it meant one thing. He wasn't dealing with an amateur anymore.

Declan wasn't angry. That wasn't his nature. Not when things got interesting.

He was… intrigued.

His lips twitched, not quite a smile. He dropped to a crouch beside a disturbed patch of earth, the dirt faintly brushed with motion — almost too deliberate. His fingers swept through it, slow and methodical.

A thin glint of wire caught the light.

A snare.

A trap.

For him.

He let out a low, humourless chuckle. "Clever bastards."

It wasn't mockery. It was approval.

Then he heard it. Distant at first, but rising quick.

The rhythmic thump of helicopter blades cutting through hot air.

Declan's head tilted back. Through the treetops, he spotted it — a black shape skimming low across the canopy, dipping, scanning.

A police chopper. Feds.

His jaw tightened.

Blake.

He stood slowly, brushing dirt from his palms onto his jeans, rifle still slung. Whatever Blake was doing up there, it wasn't for show. That kind of bird meant desperation. And desperation made people sloppy.

Everything had just changed.

Callahan could wait.

He had a new problem to deal with.

CHAPTER 66

The heat pressed down like a weight, thick and unmoving, leeching moisture from the air and patience from the body. The light filtering through the eucalypts was sharp and uneven, dancing across the scrub in flickers that played tricks on the eyes. Dust clung to skin, to clothes, to thought. Even the wind, when it came, brought no relief — just a dry hiss through brittle leaves and distant rustles that never quite resolved themselves.

Dave pushed a branch aside, its bark rough against his palm. Sweat trickled down his temple. The land was changing again — less dry clay now, more loose grit underfoot, the ground shifting with a subtle menace beneath every step.

A goanna scurried through the undergrowth off to the left, claws clicking against stone, tail dragging a crooked line through the dust.

Somewhere behind it, a crow called — long and harsh, like it was laughing at something unseen.

Dave stole a glance at Frank up ahead. The old man moved slowly but with purpose, reading the signs the land gave, though they were growing harder to see.

The bush was closing in now.

Drawing tighter with each passing hour, as if it knew they didn't belong.

Then, without warning, Frank vanished.

It was sudden. Too sudden for a cry, too fast for anyone to react. One step, and he was gone, the earth beneath him collapsing in a dull, echoing crack.

The ground gave way like paper soaked through with rot.

"Frank!" Dave surged forward, stumbling as the soil shifted beneath his boots. He dropped to his knees at the edge of a freshly exposed hole. A hidden creek bed, long dried and hollowed out by erosion. Jagged roots jutted from the walls, and ten feet below, Frank lay on his back, groaning, his hat lost, one hand clutched to his side. The red smear down his forearm was already mixing with dust.

Martha was beside him in an instant. Somehow navigating the broken gully with ease. She knelt, peering down, voice sharp. "Shit. Frank. Talk to me!"

"I'm alive," Frank muttered, breath wheezing. "Bit winded. Might've left half my arse on a rock, but I'll live."

Dave dropped down carefully onto the old creek bed, extending a hand. It took both of them to haul Frank up, every muscle burning, the effort hampered by the loose soil that shifted with every movement. They dragged him over the edge just as the bank gave another groan, crumbling further into the void.

They lay there for a moment, panting, the three of them sprawled across the brittle edge of a land that no longer wanted them.

Then Dave felt it. That sense again. That weight between the trees. Watching.

He turned, scanning the bush. Nothing moved.

But someone was out there.

**

Declan crouched low among the scrub, tucked into the shadow of a weathered termite mound, his rifle balanced across his thighs. From this vantage, he'd watched the whole thing unfold. The collapse, the panic, the narrow escape. It had been a gift. A golden opportunity.

He could have ended it then.

The rifle's scope aligned with Callahan's chest as he helped Frank up. One breath, one squeeze of the trigger. A clean shot. The kind he'd taken dozens of times before.

But he hadn't taken it.

His finger had hovered, trembling slightly. The edge wasn't there. The clarity. The cold detachment.

He breathed in through his nose, forcing the air slow, measured.

"You're slipping," he whispered to himself. "Too long out here. Should've finished this already."

He adjusted the scope again, but the moment was gone. They were moving, dragging Frank clear. He'd missed it.

Declan cursed under his breath and slid back behind cover. This wasn't like him. He didn't hesitate. He didn't miss.

Something about this place… about them… it was starting to get under his skin.

He needed to fix it. Fast.

**

High above the trees, the helicopter disappeared into the distance, its echo swallowed by the bush. Blake stood alone now, boots sinking slightly into the soft earth as he adjusted the sling of his rifle. The silence left in the chopper's wake was immense. Not peaceful — oppressive.

He wiped sweat from his brow. The sun was already high and unforgiving, turning his shirt into a damp second skin. He took one step forward and almost crushed a coiled brown snake nestled beneath a patch of dry leaves.

"Jesus —" He recoiled, heart hammering.

The snake slipped away, smooth and silent. Indifferent.

Blake stood still for a moment, breath short, then pushed on. He parted a branch — and walked face-first into a spider web as thick as netting. He shouted, flailing, yanking at the sticky threads now clinging to his arms and face. He tore free, tripping backwards, landing hard.

Breathing heavy, he slapped something crawling on his neck. A crushed spider dropped into the dirt beside him.

He stood, shaking with fury, brushing himself off with fast, angry swipes. The bush was laughing at him. Mocking his every step.

But he would not be humiliated. Not by some bastard trees and bugs.

He gritted his teeth and started walking again, handgun raised.

He wasn't here to be tested.

He was here to end this.

**

Tombs stood on a mound of loose scrub and ochre dust, his boots sinking into the dry red dirt. Behind him, his men gathered in silence. The ones left, anyway. He didn't ask where the others were. One had fled in the night. One was limping too hard to ride. One had simply… disappeared.

He spat.

The bush was a bastard, twisting things, swallowing time and men. But he wasn't done.

He looked at the men who remained. Noose, Carrick, Wesson and the rest. The last of the hard ones. Too dumb to be scared, too mean to stop. And then the rest of the dumb as shit followers.

"No more tracking," Tombs growled. "No more waiting."

He turned toward the scrub.

"Find Callahan. I don't give a shit how. We burn this place down if we have to."

His voice echoed flatly across the ridge, swallowed by the trees.

They kicked the bikes into gear.

**

The day deepened.

The sun rose higher.

Somewhere ahead, Dave, Martha, and Frank picked their way through the thickening scrub, every footstep slower than the last. The land had turned against them, and they knew it. Every sound was suspect. Every movement deliberate.

Declan followed.

Blake pushed blindly.

Tombs hunted like a wounded animal.

And the Pilliga?

The Pilliga waited.

Not with patience.

With purpose.

CHAPTER 67

The silence was changing.

Not gone — just different. No birdcalls. No distant engines. Just the sound of boots on cracked dirt and the occasional whip of a branch dragged too close.

Dave wiped a line of sweat from his brow. The air was still thick, wet with heat, but it was more than that now. The bush was shifting. Growing mean. Like it had decided, finally and fully, that they didn't belong here.

They moved fast. Low. Weaving through dry grass and dense scrub. Branches clawed at their clothes. Dust stuck to sweat-slicked arms. The ground grew soft beneath their boots, the kind of soft that whispered sinkhole, or worse.

Frank was ahead, moving on instinct. But Dave saw it in the set of his shoulders, the way his right foot dragged slightly more than the left.

"You alright?" Dave asked, just loud enough to cut through the drone of insects.

Frank didn't look back. "Been worse."

That was all he gave. All he needed to give.

The trees thickened again. Eucalypts warped and towering, their limbs leaning in like curious giants. The dirt turned to powder beneath their feet. Then, suddenly, the bush parted — a rare opening — and revealed a wide scar cutting through the land.

A creek bed.

Martha stepped ahead, letting out a breath she'd been holding since sunrise. Her hand wrapped around a low-hanging branch for balance as she surveyed the path. "We might actually catch a break."

Frank didn't wait. He scrambled down the embankment with more speed than grace.

Dave followed — and stopped cold.

The bed was empty. Bone dry. Not a puddle, not a patch of damp earth. Just cracked clay and dust.

Martha hissed out a curse. She kicked a loose rock. It bounced once, then clattered to a stop. The land gave back nothing.

Frank knelt, pressing two fingers to the dirt. He shook his head slowly. "Been dry for months. Bush does this. Gives you a path, just to take it away."

Dave rubbed at the back of his neck, eyes scanning the distant treeline. Their water supply was holding, but not for long. And they'd just burned a full hour on a dry hole.

"So now what?" Martha asked, voice brittle.

Dave looked upstream. "We follow it. Might lead to something that hasn't run dry."

Frank climbed to his feet, brushing grit from his knees. "Yeah. Might."

They climbed out of the bed and kept moving. The trees swallowed them again. The land pulling them deeper.

******

Declan crouched low beside a burnt-out log, sweat dripping from his temple, pooling at his jaw. The bush pulsed around him. No breeze. No birds. Just the whisper of his own breath and the sting of grit in the cuts along his legs.

He'd moved too fast. Focused too long. And now the land had teeth.

His boot slid. A patch of shale gave way underfoot. He dropped hard. His knee slammed into a jagged rock, and pain bloomed like a firecracker behind his eyes.

"Shit," he muttered.

He sat there, teeth clenched, blood already darkening the fabric above his kneecap. He touched it once, checked for breaks. None. Just torn skin. Another weakness.

He leaned back against the trunk behind him and closed his eyes for a moment.

This wasn't how he worked. He didn't stumble. He didn't bleed. He didn't fuck up.

But Callahan was still ahead. Still breathing.

Declan opened his eyes, grabbed his rifle, and pushed back to his feet.

Time to end it.

**

Blake was losing.

Not to Callahan. Not yet.

To the bush.

His shirt clung to him, soaked through. His hat was gone. He'd thrown it somewhere back in frustration, and now the sun drilled into his scalp like a hot nail. Sweat pooled under his collar. His map was useless. His GPS flickered like it was trying to lie to him.

He hadn't seen a landmark in an hour.

The trees blurred together. Gums with bone-white trunks, bark peeling like old flesh. The sound of cicadas was a screech now, a banshee wail that drilled into his ears.

Something moved.

He spun, gun raised.

Nothing.

Branches. Shadows. The shimmer of heat.

He turned again. Another noise.

A twig cracked.

Blake fired.

The shot echoed off the trees—a violent, unnatural bark that tore through the bush.

Then silence.

Except for the endless, skull-ringing whine of the cicadas.

Nothing moved.

Until a voice cut through the quiet.

"Scared of the bush, mate?"

Blake froze. His heart thudded in his chest.

Declan.

His grip tightened on the pistol. He scanned the bush. No one there. Just a voice, drifting like smoke.

He turned in a slow circle. Hands shaking.

Nothing. Just more questions.

The bush gave no answers.

**

Tombs was done.

He stood on a low ridge, watching the landscape burn in the late afternoon sun. His boots were caked with dust. His knuckles split from riding too hard, too far. Around him, the last of his crew looked barely human — hollow eyes, cracked lips, sweat-streaked faces.

He didn't care.

He wasn't here to care.

He heard the echo of Blake's shot. West of their position.

He grinned. A sick, twisted grin.

"There's our direction."

The men behind him didn't cheer. They just moved. Because Tombs wasn't a man anymore. He was a promise.

A promise of violence.

Callahan had made it this far.

But the bush didn't care who you were.

And neither did Tombs.

He was going to finish this. Even if it meant burning everything down.

Above them all, the bush kept breathing. Watching. And waiting.

The storm was almost ready.

CHAPTER 68

The land ahead offered no welcome — just heat, dust, and silence. Wide and dry, stretched flat like an open dare. It was the kind of country that didn't care who you were or how far you'd come.

The past few days had been survival, nothing more. Outpacing Tombs, sidestepping Declan, slipping past the traps Blake had hidden behind his polished badge and broken promises. But that was behind them now. Running wasn't the point anymore.

Now, they had a destination.

Dave adjusted the straps of his pack, feeling the pull settle across his shoulders like a familiar weight. He glanced at the old map in Martha's hands, smudged with dirt and sweat, the ink just barely holding on.

Martha squinted into the tree-line. "We don't even know what the hell we're walking into."

Dave gave a tight nod. "Yeah. That's why we're going."

Frank wiped the sweat from his brow, eyes fixed on the scrub ahead. His voice was dry, like gravel in his throat. "It's gonna be a bastard of a walk."

Dave adjusted his grip on the gear, fingers tightening. "Then we'd better get on with it."

They moved on, boots crunching over the brittle crust of leaf litter and sunbaked soil. Every step stirred up dust, each breath tasting like scorched bark and old ash.

At first, the scrub closed in around them. Tight, clawing. Branches dragged at their sleeves, dry leaves rasping together like teeth on stone. The bush whispered and watched, always just out of reach.

But the land began to open.

The trees thinned. Bark peeled back in long, curling strips, as if the bush was shedding skin. The ground grew harder beneath their feet — flattened, compacted, stamped down years ago by wheels that hadn't turned in a long time.

Up ahead, Dave spotted the outline of a fence post — sun-bleached and half-collapsed, leaning like a drunk too stubborn to fall.

Then, something broke the line of trees.

A shape. Squat. Angular. Black against the bright sky.

It didn't belong.

Dave slowed, the air catching in his throat. His eyes narrowed, locked onto the silhouette. It was too straight, too deliberate. Something manmade where there shouldn't be anything at all.

They were close now.

Too close for comfort.

**

Declan crouched at the edge of a dry creek bed, fingers curled into the dirt like he was trying to read it. His knee throbbed. Sharp and stiff from that fall earlier, but he pushed the pain aside.

He was slipping. He could feel it in his gut. In the silence. The bush had turned on him. And worse, the rhythm was gone. That internal beat he used to trust like gospel had gone quiet.

He'd hesitated once. Wouldn't happen again.

His boot caught on something buried.

A metallic rasp. He looked down.

A saw blade. Rusted. Half-choked by earth. But those teeth still gleamed like they hadn't forgotten what they were made for.

He stared at it, unmoving.

They weren't just wandering.

They were stepping into something old. Something that had been left behind for a reason. Something that should've stayed buried.

Declan's smile came slow and tight. No humour. No warmth. Just a hard flicker of recognition.

No more running.

**

The trees finally broke.

Dave stepped through first, blinking as the canopy gave way to light and ruin.

It wasn't just a clearing. It was a graveyard.

The bush peeled back to reveal rusted tin sheeting, collapsed timber frames, coils of iron chain eaten through by decades. Not a homestead. Not a house. This place had been built for labour, for sweat and sawdust and men who didn't ask for comfort.

Frank moved slow, eyes sweeping the space. He stepped over what remained of a fence post, crouched beside a rusted gear half-swallowed by dirt. "Old sawmill," he muttered. "Or what's left of it."

Dave looked around, brow furrowed. "What the hell was a sawmill doing all the way out here?"

Frank ran a hand across the edge of the gear, his voice low, almost respectful. "Red cedar, mostly. Used to be plenty through here, before they cut it all to shit. Prized timber. Straight grain. Good for furniture, cabinets, anything that needed to look expensive."

He stood, nodding toward one of the darker, harder-looking beams in the wreckage. "And Ironbark. Toughest bloody stuff you could find. Splits saws, snaps nails. But it lasts. They used it for railway sleepers. Wharf pylons. Ship hulls. Stuff meant to take a beating and keep standing."

Dave let his eyes drift across the ruin, lips pressed tight. "Ironbark again."

Frank glanced over, puzzled. "What about it?"

"It keeps coming back," Dave said. "The prison. The trees. This place. Red. Even me, maybe. Always battered, never breaks."

Martha kicked aside a strip of roofing iron, her lip curling. "Figures Red would bury his secrets somewhere like this. Looks like hell chewed it up and spat it out."

Dave didn't answer.

He was already walking toward the heart of the ruins, eyes scanning the wreckage like it might speak if he looked hard enough.

The coordinates had led them here.

To ruin. To rust. To memory buried beneath the dust.

Whatever Red had hidden. Whatever truth still clung to this place. It was waiting in the bones of the sawmill.

And if they weren't too late, they'd dig it out before someone else did.

CHAPTER 69

The sawmill rose out of the earth like a half-buried skeleton, a forgotten ruin stitched together with rust and rot. The roof sagged at awkward angles, corrugated iron sheets curling like burnt paper. The timber walls had greyed into brittle bone, cracked and peeling from decades of sun and silence. What machinery remained was slumped in decay. Old belts torn loose from their wheels, rusted chains dangling like vines, logging carts tilted on broken axles, long since robbed of purpose.

Dave stepped through the clearing first, boots sinking into mulch-thick sawdust baked hard by the heat. His eyes moved slow, careful. There was no telling what might be waiting in the shadows of a place like this. Martha followed, her rifle low but ready, eyes scanning the structure with a soldier's caution. Frank brought up the rear, slower than usual, his face unreadable as he swept the ruins with a veteran's eye.

The air was thick with the smell of iron, dust, and old eucalyptus. Heat shimmered in the clearing, turning every shadow into a threat.

Dave dragged a hand through his hair, breathing shallow. "Alright… where the hell did he leave it?"

It wasn't obvious. Of course it wasn't. Red never made things obvious. There were no crates marked with crosses, no glint of treasure waiting to be scooped up. If Red had hidden something here, it would only make sense to those who'd known him. Really known him.

Frank broke away from the others and moved toward the skeletal remains of the old cutting bay. His hand ran along a scorched steel support, fingertips catching on the rough flakes of rust. "He left something," Frank murmured. "Just a matter of seeing it."

They split up, searching. Dave combed the edge of the structure, eyes drawn to broken floorboards and rusted pulleys. Martha paced between the derelict carts, kicking aside collapsed planks and splintered beams.

Then Frank stopped.

Not because of anything on the ground — but something above.

A eucalypt stood on the far edge of the mill site, tall and warped, its thick arms stretched high above the clearing. At first glance, it was just another old tree. But then something caught the sun — a flicker of light from up in the fork, sharp and sudden, like glass.

Frank narrowed his eyes.

There, half-swallowed by decades of growth, a toy plane lay wedged in the crook of the branches. Metal. Weathered. The fuselage glinted faintly — a shard of old cockpit plastic or mirror still clinging inside, just enough to shine.

He tilted his head, then called out. "Look."

Martha came up beside him. Her brow furrowed. "A plane?"

Dave squinted toward the tree. And something clicked.

Of course. Red wouldn't bury anything outright. He'd mark the spot in his own way — something personal, something hidden in plain sight for anyone who understood the chase.

Dave's eyes dropped to the base of the tree.

A patch of dirt. Different from the rest. No grass, no weeds. Just fallen bark and dried leaves, the ground loose, disturbed. The kind of patch a man might stand on and feel a whisper of something below.

Martha crouched, brushing aside the top layer. The thin layer of soil crumbled easily under her hand.

She looked up. "This is it."

Frank didn't say anything. Just nodded.

Then they heard it.

A noise at the edge of the trees.

Something stumbling.

Dragging.

Dave turned, already reaching for his sidearm.

Blake emerged from the bush like a man clawed from the grave.

His shirt was shredded, soaked in blood and dirt. One side of his face was swollen, raw and pulsing from a bite or a sting, the skin stretched taut and angry. His lips were split, nose scabbed, arms scored with scratches so deep they looked like war paint.

He staggered into the clearing like he didn't see them — like the only thing in the world was that patch of dirt beneath the tree.

Martha's grip tightened on her rifle. Frank straightened.

Blake's cracked lips moved, breath hitching. He knew.

His hand twitched, and the gun appeared in his grasp like a trick. He didn't raise it high. Just enough to make it count.

"Step away," he rasped.

His voice was dry, shredded by dehydration, but his intent was sharp as glass.

Dave didn't move. "Blake, you're cooked. You need water. Sit down."

Blake's trigger finger twitched. "Give it to me."

Dave's eyes stayed locked on his. "We didn't dig."

Blake's hands were shaking. The barrel of the gun wavered, but didn't drop. His breath came hard and fast, his whole body vibrating with a tension that looked ready to snap.

"No one else takes it," he whispered. "That's the rule."

Then the sound changed.

Not from Blake.

From the bush.

Low at first. Then louder. Rising like a storm.

Engines.

The unmistakable roar of bush bikes chewing through the trees.

Martha turned, eyes wide. "Shit."

Blake flinched at the noise, his fried nerves not catching up in time. His eyes darted toward the treeline, but his gun didn't lower.

Frank's jaw set hard. "Tombs."

Dave nodded, his voice low. "We're out of time."

Frank stepped forward. "What's the play?"

Martha flicked the safety off her rifle, her stance shifting into readiness. "We hold them off. We hold the ground."

Blake's gun still hovered.

The engines screamed closer.

Dave took a breath. The sawmill had given up its secret. But now, the bush was about to take it back by force.

The ruins held their breath, waiting to see who would bleed for what lay buried beneath the dirt.

CHAPTER 70

The earth trembled beneath their boots. It felt like an approaching army. That low, savage growl of bush bikes rolled through the trees like a warning. Closer, faster, tearing through scrub and shadows. Dave stiffened, jaw tight. Martha shifted beside him, rifle low but ready. Frank didn't move. His eyes were on the treeline, reading the rhythm of the engines like a coming storm.

They had no cover. Just the skeletal remains of the old sawmill, the warped tree where Red had left his last clue, and the half-dug patch of dirt that could change everything.

Blake stood apart, swaying on his feet. He looked cooked. Sunburnt, hollow-eyed, skin flaking, sweat caked into the filth on his face. But his hand hadn't dropped. That pistol was still up, pointed straight at the spot where Dave had started to dig. He didn't blink. Didn't breathe. Just stared like the ground itself had betrayed him.

Then the bikes hit the clearing.

The first to arrive slid in fast. Front tyre carving a line through the dirt, boots hitting hard. Tombs. The bastard stood tall as he cut the engine, eyes already sweeping the scene. More riders peeled in behind him, fanning out, the snarl of their engines tapering off one by one until all that remained was silence and the sharp tang of exhaust clinging to sawdust and rust.

Tombs saw it all. Blake, cracked and twitching. Dave, crouched and tense. Frank, already calculating. The tree. The dirt.

That grin spread across his face, slow and dangerous.

"Well, well," he said, voice thick with dust and triumph. "Looks like we got here just in time."

The first shot cracked across the clearing like a whip.

High. Wide. A warning or a message.

The second wasn't.

It punched through the air, closer. Too close. Dave dropped, shoulder hitting dirt as bullets sliced overhead. Martha was already returning fire, the crack of her rifle snapping through the wreckage. The old sawmill echoed like a drum, every shot bouncing off rusted steel and dry timber.

Tombs' men didn't charge. They fanned out, smart enough to corner, dumb enough to think it'd be easy. Boots hit the ground in different directions. Bikes revved, some still idling, others peeled off into the bush to cut them off.

Frank didn't run. He moved low, fast, dropping behind the old timber cart. Dust plumed around him. His gun was steady, breath slower than it should've been.

Blake was gone. Slipped into the chaos like a ghost, vanished into the bones of the sawmill. One second there, next second nothing. The bastard moved like he'd done this before. He probably had.

Tombs strode forward through the mess, bold as hell, laughing like the devil had just told him a joke. His pistol hung easy in one hand, eyes locked on Dave.

"You boys find something, Callahan?"

Dave didn't answer. His jaw clenched, hands slick on the grip of his weapon.

No words.

Just another shot. This one aimed to kill, or distract.

It happened fast.

Too fast.

Martha was mid-step, shifting position, rifle raised. Then hands closed around her from behind.

She twisted hard, let out a sharp yell, and threw an elbow back. Solid hit. The grunt behind her said it landed, but the bastard didn't let go.

A hand clamped over her mouth. Another around her waist. She kicked, thrashed, teeth bared, but he was bigger, wired tight with adrenaline and desperation.

Dave turned just in time to see her boots leave the ground.

"Martha —!"

The bike roared. Dust spat up in clouds. She was hauled onto the bike like a dead weight but still fighting, her eyes locked on Dave for a half second, wide, furious, unbroken.

Then they were gone.

Swallowed by the trees.

Dave's shot rang out a heartbeat too late. Just sound and smoke and the hollow ache of too slow.

Dave was already charging forward, gun up, heart thundering in his chest, when Frank's arm shot out and yanked him back.

"Mate," Frank snapped, voice sharp. "Look."

Dave turned — just in time to see it happen.

One of Tombs' grunts was crouched by the tree, right where they'd been about to dig. But he wasn't pulling up a canvas sack or a buried bundle.

He was dragging out something heavy. Solid. Metal.

A bloody case.

He staggered as he lifted it. Two hands, shaky from the weight or the adrenaline, maybe both. The lock was rusted, edges dented but still sealed tight.

He didn't even glance inside.

"Move!" someone shouted. It could've been Tombs, could've been anyone.

The case was hurled onto the back of a bike. Tyres bit into the dirt. Engines screamed.

And just like that, they were gone, splitting off, scattering like rats. Dust churned where they'd been, already starting to settle.

Dave's chest rose and fell in sharp, shallow breaths.

Martha was gone.

So was the prize.

Frank's hand gripped his arm again — hard this time.

"We need a bike. Now."

The engines were already screaming, tearing through the trees, chewing up dirt and scrub like the land had pissed them off personally.

Dust twisted in the air, thick and choking. Bikes shot off in every direction. Tombs' crew peeling away from the ruins, scattered but focused. The case was gone, clutched tight by some bastard who didn't even pause to check if it was real. Just slung it over his back like it belonged to him and gunned the throttle.

Dave's brain hadn't caught up yet.

Martha. Gone.

The prize. Gone.

Everything they'd bled for. Ripped away in a matter of seconds.

Frank grabbed his sleeve. "Mate. Now or never."

A low groan cut through the chaos.

One of the bikers lay sprawled nearby, blood seeping from a gut wound, his hand twitching near the throttle of a still-running bike. His helmet was cracked. His face wasn't much better.

Dave didn't hesitate.

He lunged.

Frank was already moving with him, grabbing the bloke by the collar and yanking him off the bike like he weighed nothing. The biker hit the dirt hard, moaning once before going still.

Dave threw a leg over the seat, fingers closing around the throttle. Frank jumped on behind him, one arm hooking around Dave, the other gripping his sidearm tight.

Dave revved once.

Twice.

The back wheel spat up dust as they tore out of the clearing, chasing the sound of engines and the trail of everything slipping through their fingers.

The chase was on.

The bush blurred into streaks of green and brown as Dave leaned into the throttle, the engine howling beneath him. Every bump in the track jolted through his spine, the bike fishtailing on loose dirt, tyres spitting grit into the trees behind them.

Up ahead, shadows moved, fast and low. Two riders veered left, cutting hard through the scrub. Martha's captor. No mistaking the second figure slumped behind the driver, limbs fighting to break free.

To the right. Three more. One of them had the case.

Frank's voice was tight in his ear. "We split 'em. Case goes right."

Before Dave could answer, the crack of gunfire ripped through the trees.

Behind them.

Blake.

The psycho was still breathing. Still armed. Still dangerous. Distant and on foot, but possessed by something wild.

Bullets snapped past Dave's head, slicing branches and bark, chewing into tree trunks.

He ducked low, gunning the throttle harder, weaving through the tight lines of eucalypts. A branch whipped across his arm, slicing skin, but he didn't flinch.

Frank twisted around, firing over Dave's shoulder — two clean shots. Controlled. Measured.

Ahead, one of the riders made a mistake.

Too fast into the bend.

His back tyre skidded, caught a root, and the whole bike snapped sideways. The rider went airborne, hit the dirt hard and rolled. The case tumbled loose, landing with a dull thud, half-buried in red dust.

Dave braked hard, tyres skidding, gravel spraying. The bike bucked as he swung off, eyes on the dented metal case.

He reached for it — fingers just brushing the edge —

And the roar of another bike blasted through the trees.

Frank's eyes snapped up. "Incoming!"

Tombs' man came straight at them, full throttle. No hesitation. No attempt to stop. Just raw speed and murder in his eyes.

Dave swore and dived back onto the bike, jamming the throttle as Frank hauled himself up behind.

The other rider grabbed the case mid-roll, muscles straining, bike wobbling under the weight — but he recovered.

And then he was gone.

Dust swallowed him.

"Son of a —" Dave growled, cutting the corner and tearing after him.

The case was gone again.

And the Pilliga was far from finished.

The Pilliga was a living thing now. Part of the chase and it was enjoying every damn second.

Engines howled through the trees like bloodhounds off the leash. Tyres tore up the earth, flinging dust into the sky, choking the air with red grit and panic. Riders zigzagged through the scrub, lines broken, formation gone. This wasn't a chase anymore.

It was a free-for-all.

No sides. No orders. Just chaos.

And hunger.

And noise.

And Martha was gone.

She'd fought. Christ, she'd fought. Elbows, fists, headbutts — anything she could throw. But the bastard who had her was solid, experienced, and didn't give a shit about pain. His grip was like iron. One arm clamped around her middle, the other on the throttle, forcing the bike over terrain that jarred every bone in her body.

The bike kicked under them, jarring over roots and ruts, bouncing hard enough to lift her off the seat. She almost got a leg loose, almost, but he read it, adjusted, yanked her closer.

Bastard.

Branches slapped her face, tore at her clothes. Her vision blurred, but her anger sharpened. She tasted blood. Didn't care whose.

She wasn't going quietly.

Not now. Not to them.

Not ever.

The case was still in play.

Too heavy to carry easy, too valuable to leave behind.

It flew from one set of hands to the next like a live grenade. One rider had it. Then another. No one got far.

A gunshot cracked through the trees. A scream followed. Someone hit the dirt hard.

The case tumbled, bounced, skidded across the dry ground, then vanished in a cloud of dust.

Seconds later, a new hand scooped it up, not even stopping to see who'd just fallen or worse.

No one checked inside. No one had the time.

Didn't matter.

They all knew what it was worth, maybe not the full truth, not the sword, not the bloodline or the legacy. But they knew enough.

If they lost it, they lost everything.

And in the Pilliga, nothing stayed in your hands for long.

Dave's jaw was set hard, teeth grinding, eyes locked on the bastard up ahead.

The rider was fast, reckless, maybe — but not fast enough.

He weaved through the trees like he knew them, bike tilting dangerously with every shift. But Dave was closing the gap, throttle pinned, branches whipping past his face.

Frank leaned into him from behind, rifle up, bracing against Dave's shoulder.

He fired.

The shot cracked like thunder, punching into a tree just inches from the rider's head.

The bastard flinched, ducked low, but he didn't drop the case.

Didn't even slow down.

"Close," Frank muttered, cold and focused as he worked the bolt. "Next one's better."

Dave didn't say a word.

He just twisted the throttle harder and chased the bastard into the trees.

Blake moved through the ruins like a broken animal. Staggering, bleeding, half-blind from dust and dehydration.

His shirt was stuck to his skin, blood crusted along one side. His left eye was nearly swollen shut, the welt beneath it pulsing like it had a heartbeat of its own.

But the gun in his hand never wavered.

It hung low but steady, like a part of him. Like it knew what came next.

His breath dragged in and out, ragged, catching on the edges of ribs he hadn't remembered cracking. Every step was pain. Every step was fire in his lungs.

But his mind? Sharp. Focused. Diamond-edged.

One thought cut through the haze, louder than the gunfire, louder than the bikes, louder than the screaming inside his skull.

No one else gets it.

Not Callahan. Not Tombs. Not the bastards chasing dust through the trees.

It was his.

And he'd kill every last one of them to make sure of it.

Tombs' crew was coming apart at the seams.

What had started as a pack — tight, ruthless, moving with purpose — was now a mess of scattered bodies and splintered loyalty.

Some were chasing the case, engines howling through the bush like wild dogs on scent.

Others were peeling away, riding blind through the scrub, instincts screaming louder than orders.

One rider broke formation, veering toward the sound of Martha's bike. Whether he meant to help or claim her for himself — no one could say. Not even him.

Another had ditched his bike completely, smoke curling from the wreck. He staggered through the bush, gun up, eyes wide, firing at anything that moved. Maybe he thought he saw Callahan. Maybe he was just shooting ghosts.

This wasn't a hunt anymore.

It was a collapse.

Men weren't following commands. They were following fear.

And fear didn't give a damn who you were riding for.

The chase had torn itself apart.

The Pilliga didn't care who was chasing who. It had taken them all. Swallowed them in dust and noise and blood. What started as a pursuit had twisted into something primal. Something feral.

Engines howled through the trees. Gunfire cracked like dry bones. The air stank of fuel, sweat, and desperation.

Visibility was gone. Just flashes of movement through the haze, men blurring between trunks, vanishing into smoke and shadows.

The trees leaned closer, bending inward like they were watching. Waiting. Old and knowing. Like they'd seen this all before.

No one was calling orders. No one was thinking straight. The lines were gone.

The prize. The case, kept changing hands, a battered thing too valuable to let go. Too dangerous to hold for long.

Someone would fall. Then someone else.

And when the bush was done chewing through them —

Only one bastard would crawl out, bloodied and breathing, with the case in hand.

This wasn't a chase anymore. It was a cull.

CHAPTER 71

The bastard thought he had her locked down.

He rode like a man who didn't expect to lose, one hand clenched tight around Martha's wrist, the other gripping the throttle like it owed him something. She'd fought. Elbowed, kicked, twisted like a wild thing. But he was big, and the bike was faster than her fists.

The scrub clawed at them as he tore through the Pilliga, weaving down old logging tracks barely wide enough for a goat. Trees whipped past. Branches slapped at her face. Dust clogged her throat.

But he didn't slow down.

Too sure of himself.

Too stupid to read the land.

The track curved. Dropped. Bent back in on itself.

And just like that — he was lost.

The bush spat them out again.

Straight into the clearing they'd left behind.

The sawmill.

The bastard blinked, confused. Martha felt it in his grip — a hesitation, a flicker of panic. She twisted to look.

The ruins loomed up ahead like a ghost. Rusted carts. Broken timbers. Empty windows staring like eyes.

And then — movement.

A figure stepped from the wreckage.

Blake.

He looked like death with a sunburn. Clothes in tatters. One eye swollen half-shut. Blood dried to crust along one side of his neck. But his stance was solid. Balanced. Like all the pain had burned away and left only focus.

In his hands, something simple. A thick branch, heavy as a crowbar.

Martha's captor tensed.

Too late.

Blake moved first.

The branch came down in a brutal arc, full force, no warning. It smashed across the rider's head with a crack like a door being kicked in.

The bastard went flying. The bike twisted out beneath him, wheels bucking. Martha was ripped loose — she hit the dirt hard, rolled twice, came up gasping.

The bike toppled. The rider hit harder. Metal screamed as it tore through the gravel.

And then — stillness.

Dust curling in the hot air.

The only sound was Blake's ragged breath.

He dropped the branch. Let it fall like it meant nothing.

Then he looked down at Martha, a crooked grin splitting his battered face.

"You can thank me later."

Martha's lungs burned as she pulled herself upright, dirt and blood smearing her palms. Her limbs ached from the fall, but she was on her feet, every nerve wired. She locked eyes with Blake.

He leaned casual against a timber post, grinning like he'd just saved the goddamn day. Like he expected applause.

Her stomach twisted.

Blake. Her so-called saviour.

He raised an eyebrow, smug. "Always figured you'd end up like him, you know."

She wiped blood from her lip. "What?"

His voice dropped to a slow, slick drawl. "Your brother. Red."

Her muscles went still.

Blake took a step closer, hands loose, tone cold and oily. "Same brand of idiot. Reckon you both thought you were the centre of something. But nah. Just noise. Just shadows pretending to mean something."

Martha didn't move.

Blake kept going, digging in.

"Red was a cockroach. Always in the wrong place, thinking he mattered. He didn't." He smirked. "And neither do you."

Martha moved.

No hesitation.

Her fist cut through the air and connected with his jaw — bone on bone, sharp and clean. The sound rang out like a rifle crack, echoing through the wreckage.

Blake's head snapped sideways. His legs buckled. And then he dropped.

Folded up, right there in the dust.

Didn't even groan.

Martha stood over him, fists still clenched, chest heaving. For a second, just a second, the silence stretched.

She thought it would feel good.

It didn't.

There wasn't time.

She spun and ran.

Her boots pounded the ground, cutting through the wreckage and into the bush beyond —

And straight into something solid.

A shape.

A shadow.

A man.

A hand clamped around her arm.

Not a grab. Not a stumble. A grip. Tight, deliberate, cold.

Martha gasped, instinct kicking in, trying to twist free, but the hold didn't shift. Didn't flinch. Like it was welded to her skin.

She turned —

And saw him. Not a biker. And despite having never laid eyes on this man before. She knew him.

Declan.

Standing in the gloom like he'd been there the whole time. Not panting. Not sweaty. Calm as a breeze through dead grass.

His eyes met hers, pale and unreadable. Amused.

Like she was right on schedule.

"Easy," he said, voice low. Almost gentle.

But the grip on her arm stayed iron.

Her chest tightened. This wasn't like the biker — clumsy, aggressive, all fists and noise. Or Blake, drunk on ego and sweat.

Declan was something else.

He wasn't in a hurry. And that was worse.

Because it meant he could afford to wait.

Every instinct screamed at her. Fight, claw, bite, run. Do something. Anything.

But his hand didn't shift. His stance didn't change. He had her, and she knew, deep down, he wouldn't let go until he wanted to.

Behind them, the forest erupted.

Gunfire barked in the distance. Engines screamed. Metal slammed into earth. The chaos they'd left behind was catching up.

Declan's gaze flicked upward, scanning the treeline. He didn't tense. Just watched, head tilting slightly.

Then that small, crooked smile.

"Hell of a mess you lot made."

Martha didn't speak.

Didn't blink.

Because she knew. Tombs' men were dangerous, sure. Blake was unhinged. The others were brutes.

But Declan?

Declan was a different breed.

He didn't chase. He didn't shout.

He just waited. And took what he wanted.

And right now, what he wanted was her.

**

The forest shook with violence.

Engines snarled through the undergrowth, tyres chewing through dry bark and brittle scrub. Gunfire cracked sharp against the air. Short, savage bursts that echoed between the trees. Every shot a scream. Every scream a warning.

And still, the bastard case was moving.

Dave hunched low over the handlebars, the stolen bike rattling beneath him like it was held together with spit and rust. Frank clung tight behind, rifle pressed to his shoulder, scanning ahead as the bush ripped past in a blur of dust and blood.

Up ahead, the rider clutching the case was starting to lose it. His back wheel fishtailed over loose rock. The weight of the case threw him off balance, every bump a fight to stay upright.

Frank didn't waste time.

He lined the shot.

Pulled the trigger.

The back tyre exploded in a puff of dust and shredded rubber. The bike bucked like it'd been shot in the spine. The rider screamed. One raw, useless sound, and went down hard, the case flinging from his grip, somersaulting through the dirt.

Dave skidded, ready to dive for it —

But another bike screamed past from the left, close enough to smell the bastard's sweat.

The second rider snatched the case mid-slide, snatching it like it was made of gold.

Then he was gone. Swallowed by the trees.

Dave swore, voice ragged. "Fuck!"

Frank was already reloading. "Stay on him!"

The chase twisted through narrowing bush, branches clawing at their arms, the earth fighting every move. Behind them, chaos reigned.

Another rider hit a tree and didn't get up.

One flipped over a fallen log, his bike cartwheeling, limbs scattering.

Another dropped his weapon and ran.

No sides anymore. No ranks. No plan. Just panic.

Tombs' crew were cracking.

Splintering.

Losing.

But Dave knew better than to think it was over.

Tombs didn't quit. Tombs didn't retreat.

Tombs burned.

And if he had to torch the whole goddamn Pilliga to take them down with him?

He would.

This wasn't a chase anymore.

This was the last roll of the dice.

The final turn.

No more plans. No more hiding.

Whoever held the case at the end of this?

They'd win.

Everyone else would die trying.

**

The bush closed in like a vice, branches clawing, shadows twitching. The air was thick. Clogged with dust, gunpowder, the reek of sweat, grease, and fresh blood. The kind of air that stuck in your throat and told you flat-out this was the end of the line.

Every man still standing had been dragged beyond the edge. Bones aching. Hearts hammering. Vision blurred from heat and adrenaline. But no one backed off.

Not yet.

Not with the case still out there.

Not until someone had it in their hands and everyone else was down.

Or dead.

Martha was in Declan's hands.

She felt it. Heat through her sleeve, the pressure of his fingers firm, measured. Not crushing. Not yet.

He wasn't shaking. Wasn't sweating. Just calm. Too calm.

His face gave her nothing. No smirk, no threat. Just eyes that didn't blink enough.

"Not gonna hurt you," he said, low.

Like he believed it.

Martha's gut twisted. Bullshit.

She jerked back hard, but his grip held. Steady, unbothered. Like she was testing a fence post, not a man.

He wasn't wrestling her. Wasn't trying to drag her anywhere.

He was waiting.

Watching.

And somehow, that was worse.

There was something behind his patience. Something that hadn't shown its teeth yet.

She felt it crawl down her spine.

What the hell was he waiting for?

**

Blake lay twisted in the dirt like a wreck left behind — forgotten but not finished.

Dust coated every inch of him, clinging to the sweat-stained fabric of his shirt, turning the blood streaks on his arms to muddy smears. His lips were cracked, caked with grit. His face was slack, mouth slightly open, breath rattling slow and shallow through his teeth. A fly landed on his cheek and wandered, undisturbed.

But the worst of it was the welt. Dark and rising, already swollen on the side of his jaw where Martha had put him down. It stood out against his skin like a badge of failure. Of weakness.

And Blake didn't wear failure well.

For now, he was still. Eyes closed, limbs heavy. A man pulled into the dark by pain, heat, and exhaustion.

But beneath the surface, the engine was still running. Slow. Burning.

Because Blake didn't stay down. Not for long. He was the kind of bastard who crawled back when no one expected him. Who took a beating and came up swinging. The kind who remembered every slight, every hit, every word.

And when he opened his eyes again, when the fog in his head cleared, he wouldn't care who was in the way.

He'd make someone pay.

**

Gunfire split the air — sharp, jagged, echoing off bark and bone.

The engines were thinning, but the bush was still alive with motion. Some men were fleeing, crashing through the trees without looking back. Others were still firing, desperate to hit something. Anything. A few just lay sprawled in the dirt, not moving. Not breathing.

Dave leaned hard into a bend, the bike fishtailing through loose dirt as Frank braced behind him, rifle raised.

Another burst of gunfire.

Frank's shot cracked like thunder. One of Tombs' men went down screaming, clutching his leg as his bike peeled sideways and slammed into a gum tree. The crunch of impact echoed through the trees. Metal and bark and bone.

One less bastard.

But it wasn't enough.

They were still outnumbered. Still hunted.

The gang was breaking. You could see it in the way they rode — sloppy, scattered, no discipline left. Fear had crept in, clawing up from their guts. The lines were gone now. It was just chaos.

But Tombs?

Tombs was still coming.

Dave could feel it. That low, steady pressure pushing in from behind. A presence that didn't buckle. Didn't bleed like the others. Tombs didn't crack. He just tightened the grip.

That final push was coming.

And when it hit, it'd come like a storm.

Tombs didn't know how to quit.

He only knew how to finish.

The Case Was Still in Play.

It had changed hands too many times already.

Passed from one bloodied rider to the next, dropped, grabbed, ripped away in the blur of dirt and gunfire. It didn't stay with anyone for long. Couldn't. Not in this chaos.

The bastard ahead of them had it now — clutching the case tight against his side, hunched over his bike like he could will himself to the finish line.

But Dave could see it.

The way his elbows jerked on every bump. The way his rear wheel kept sliding wide. He was riding sloppy. Tired. Running on fumes and panic.

The bastard was losing control.

Dave leaned into the throttle, engine snarling beneath him. The wind tore past his ears. His jaw was locked tight, eyes locked on the bastard's back.

That case was theirs.

He wasn't letting it slip away again.

Not after everything they'd crawled through to get this far.

Not after Martha.

Not after Red.

Not after the bodies left behind.

This ended now.

The trees pressed in tighter now, gnarled limbs arching overhead like a ribcage, casting long, twisted shadows across the churned-up earth. The sun had started its slow bleed toward the horizon, painting everything in rust and ash.

The ground beneath the tyres had turned soft and treacherous. It shifted like it was breathing, like the bush itself had taken notice and decided to join the fight.

Dave could feel it in his gut.

The Pilliga wasn't just watching anymore.

It was closing in.

Every man left in this mess was running ragged, cut, bruised, bleeding through shirts and boots, lungs burning. No plans left. No tactics. Just raw instinct and the need to finish what had started.

But none of them slowed.

Not for the blood. Not for the heat. Not for the land trying to swallow them whole.

Because this wasn't just a chase anymore.

It was a reckoning.

And no one was walking away empty-handed.

The next move would decide it all

One trigger pull.

One wrong breath.

One heartbeat too slow.

That was all it would take.

The next move wasn't just about the case anymore — it was about who came out breathing. Who got to crawl away with something to show for all the blood, all the dirt, all the damage.

Someone was going to win.

Someone else was going to bleed out in the dust.

And maybe — just maybe — nobody was getting what they came for.

Not unless they took it.

It wasn't about who won. It was about who survived.

CHAPTER 72

He was coming undone.

Dave saw it in the way the bike wobbled, the rider's shoulders twitching with each turn. Jerky, panicked, off-kilter. The case slung across his back was doing more harm than good now. Too heavy. Too awkward. Slamming his balance every time the terrain dipped or bucked.

They'd been running flat-out too long. Burning too hot. And now the cracks were showing.

The ground ahead was hell. Dry, broken-up dirt, deep ruts, scrub clawing at the trail like it wanted them all dead. If the bastard didn't crash on his own, Frank was ready to help him along.

Frank raised the rifle, tucked it into his shoulder, and exhaled slow.

One clean shot.

The bullet punched through the chain mid-spin — metal snapped with a sound like a whipcrack.

The bike seized instantly.

The rider barely had time to scream. The back tyre kicked up, the whole machine lurching sideways before flipping end over end, spitting him into the dirt like garbage from a skip.

The case flew, spinning through the air, then slammed into the ground and tumbled to a stop.

The biker didn't.

His body crunched into a tree trunk and stayed there, twisted and unmoving.

Dave was off the bike before it stopped moving, boots skidding in the dust. He hit the ground running, scooped up the case, and held it tight.

It was finally in his hands.

And it felt heavier than it should've.

Like everything that had led them here was packed inside it.

Waiting.

The second his hands hit the case, Dave knew something wasn't right.

This thing was solid. Hard-edged. Military-grade. The kind of case you didn't stumble across in a bushland treasure hunt.

He adjusted his grip. The weight was strange, uneven. Like something long and rigid ran the length of it, tucked beneath whatever else was inside.

Dave's gut twisted.

This wasn't just opals.

Frank skidded up beside him, breathing hard. His eyes locked on the case.

"That's a lot of hardware for a few rocks."

Dave slung it over his shoulder and tightened the strap.

"Whatever it is, we're not hanging around to unwrap it. I don't know how many blokes Tombs brought with him, but it's like we knock one down and two more rise up. We need to get out of here now."

They moved.

Fast.

Because someone was going to come looking.

And whatever was inside that case?

It was worth killing for.

They tore through the scrub like the devil was chasing them.

The bike snarled beneath them, tyres clawing at the dirt, flinging gravel and bark behind in long, angry arcs.

Branches slapped at their arms. Dust choked their lungs. The wind stung their eyes. But they didn't slow.

Dave leaned forward, throttle wide open. The case slammed against his back with every rut and jolt, a dead weight that refused to settle. It threw off his balance, made his shoulders burn, but he kept going.

Frank didn't speak. Just gripped tight and scanned the bush like he expected it to shoot back.

The trees blurred past. The Pilliga gave no relief, just more scrub, more dust, more heat curling up off the ground like breath from something half-asleep and angry.

The light changed slowly, gold slipping into a blood-red haze. Shadows stretched long and sharp across the dirt, the kind that made you feel watched even when no one was there.

And then, through the trees — a shape.

Metal. Still. Waiting.

Their vehicle.

Right where they'd left it.

Finally.

The old 4wd sat just where they'd left it. Dust-caked, dented, half-camouflaged under the branches they'd dragged over it like a makeshift shroud. It looked like part of the bush now. Forgotten. Unimportant.

Until now.

Dave throttled back, bringing the bike to a rough stop. The engine sputtered once and died. Silence dropped around them — heavy, loaded.

Then it came. Low and distant. A sound more felt than heard.

The rumble of engines.

Still a way off, but closing.

Dave swung off the bike, the case thumping against his back as he landed. His shoulders ached from the weight of it. From the hours. From the week. From the goddamn chase.

He listened, eyes on the treeline. The sound was clearer now. Multiple bikes. No order. Just a mob of men chasing the same ghost.

Frank pulled the branches away from the vehicle's bonnet, sweat running down his face, mixing with the dirt. "How long you reckon we've got?"

Dave didn't look at him. He was still listening.

The growl was growing teeth.

"Not long enough," he muttered.

And they moved.

The bikes were coming.

The case was theirs.

But Martha wasn't.

Frank leaned back against the car, chest heaving, one hand still on his sidearm, the other wiping grime from his face. He watched Dave like a man watching a fuse burn low.

"Alright," he said, voice rough. "What now?"

Dave set the case down beside the front tyre. His fingers peeled off it slow, stiff from the grip. Cramping. Shaking just a little.

He didn't answer right away.

He just stared at the dirt.

Then finally, "We find Martha."

Frank let out a dry laugh that didn't sound like a laugh. "Yeah? And how the hell do we do that?"

The bush said nothing.

The engines in the distance kept coming.

And Dave had no answer.

For the first time since all this kicked off, he was standing still. No plan. No thread to pull.

Just a name.

And a direction he didn't know.

Dave's phone buzzed. He had no idea how a signal had found him out here.

A sharp, unnatural sound in the silence. Both men froze.

Frank pushed off the Patrol, eyes narrowing. "That them?"

Dave didn't answer. Just fished the phone from his pocket with stiff fingers, his skin tacky with dried sweat.

One message.

Short. Cold. Clinical.

Meet me in two hours at the turnoff from the main road. I'll exchange the woman for the case.

That was it.

No name.

Didn't need one.

Dave read it once. Then again. The words didn't change.

His thumb hovered over the screen, then dropped to his side.

He looked at Frank.

Frank looked back.

Neither spoke.

Then, together, same breath, same weight behind it —

"Fuck."

**

Somewhere behind them, buried in dust and wreckage, Blake stirred.

Pain anchored him. Sharp in the jaw, dull in the ribs, ringing behind his eyes like church bells after a bender.

The punch hit him again, a ghost of impact that cracked through his skull and settled in his teeth.

Martha.

He spat blood into the dirt. Wiped his mouth. Tasted iron and fury.

The world spun once, then steadied.

There was a bike nearby. The one he'd knocked the bastard off earlier. It lay half on its side, engine cold, still waiting.

Blake got to his knees. Then to his feet.

Everything hurt.

Didn't matter.

He swung a leg over the seat, hands clamping down on the grips. His body screamed, but he didn't listen.

In the distance, the bush still echoed with the low, hungry growl of engines.

They were out there.

The chase hadn't stopped.

And neither had he.

He twisted the throttle.

The bike snarled back to life.

And Blake disappeared into the trees, chasing the scent of blood and dust like it was the only thing keeping him breathing.

The pain didn't matter. The blood didn't matter. Only payback.

342

CHAPTER 73

Dave's hands clenched the wheel hard enough to make his knuckles pale and the steering column creak. The old Patrol hummed beneath them, every vibration running straight up his arms. The road stretched ahead in a line of pale dust and dry heat, broken only by the occasional shimmer off the bitumen where it hadn't yet crumbled into gravel.

Frank rode quiet in the passenger seat, one arm resting on the door, the other near his lap where his sidearm sat holstered but ready. His eyes kept drifting back to the rear seat. The case hadn't shifted. Not since they'd dumped it there, but it seemed to grow heavier with every passing kilometre. Like it was filling the car with something more than weight.

They hadn't said much since they left.

The bush outside was all gum trees and silence, nothing but the rustle of leaves and the faint thrum of engines far behind or maybe ahead — it was hard to tell anymore.

Frank finally broke the quiet. "This doesn't feel right."

Dave didn't answer straight away. Just kept his eyes on the road, fingers tight around the wheel.

He nodded once. "It's not."

The turnoff wasn't much. Just a junction where the sealed road bled into a strip of baked dirt, rough and rutted, like the land itself had tried to erase it.

A battered metal sign leaned at an angle, half-swallowed by saltbush. The name, Baradine, was just about legible through the rust and bullet holes. The distance beneath had been blasted clean off, nothing left but a warped smear of grey.

And right there, at the edge where the bush began to close in, Declan.

He stood like he'd been carved from the scrub itself. Still. Quiet. Not hiding, not armed, at least not visibly, but completely in control. He could've been waiting ten minutes or ten hours. It didn't matter. The land bent around him like it knew he didn't answer to time.

Beside him, Martha.

She wasn't bound. Wasn't bruised.

But she wasn't safe either.

Her arms were folded. Her jaw was clenched. That fire behind her eyes hadn't dimmed.

Dave eased the car to a stop. Dust swirled around the vehicle like smoke off a fire that hadn't finished burning.

He didn't shut off the engine.

Frank leaned forward slightly, eyes flicking from Martha to Declan. His hand hovered near the door. "You seeing what I'm seeing?"

Dave nodded once, jaw tight. "Yeah."

This wasn't about leverage.

It was about power.

And Declan? Declan had all of it — for now.

Dave stepped out of the Patrol slow, deliberate. No sudden moves. No heat in his hands, not yet. Just dust on his boots and too much weight in his chest.

Declan didn't move. He just watched, head tilted slightly like he was studying a stray dog to see if it would bite or run.

"Thought you'd take longer," he said, voice quiet, almost conversational. Like they were old mates meeting for a beer.

Dave didn't answer.

Martha stood beside him, her arms crossed, back straight, every part of her screaming she didn't belong next to a bloke like Declan. Her eyes locked on Dave.

"You good?" he asked, low.

She gave the barest nod. "Just make the trade so I don't have to keep listening to him."

Declan's smirk twitched. "You wound me, love. I've been nothing but charming."

She didn't even glance his way. Didn't dignify it with a response.

Dave stepped in closer. He could feel Frank behind him, still in the car, still watching, gun likely in his lap. Just in case.

"Alright," Dave said, voice flat. "Let's get this done."

Declan's expression barely shifted.

"You sure about that?"

Dave's brow furrowed. "What the hell does that mean?"

Declan's gaze slid past him, toward the scrub and the broken horizon behind it. "Means you've got bigger problems, mate."

He didn't raise his voice. Didn't reach for a weapon.

But Dave felt it.

The shift.

The trap tightening.

Engines.

At first, just a murmur. Low, distant, buried under the dry hush of the trees.

Then louder.

The sound thickened, rising through the dust like thunder underfoot.

Headlights cut through the gloom. Sharp beams slicing the air.

One.

Two.

Five.

More.

Bikes.

Dave's pulse jumped.

Tombs. His boys, whoever was still standing, back again, fuelled by either fresh rage or a second wind of stupidity.

How many did the bastard have? It was like he'd tapped into some endless supply of arseholes.

Frank was already moving, rifle up, pivoting toward the noise.

"Shit," he muttered, the word clipped, tight between his teeth.

The bikes came in hard. Fast. Snarling like animals set loose, tyres chewing through gravel and bush, the roar of their engines swallowing everything else.

And Declan?

He didn't blink.

Didn't flinch.

Just stood there. Watching it all roll in like it was part of the plan.

Dave felt it drop, low, cold in his gut.

This wasn't a trade.

This was a goddamn ambush.

The bikes tore through the dust, snarling toward them like wolves let off the chain.

Tombs' men didn't come in a line. They spread out, rough and unpredictable, engines growling, tyres skidding as they carved wide arcs through the clearing. Cutting off exits, boxing them in.

Declan didn't so much as blink.

He tilted his head toward Martha, voice low and amused. "Guess we'll find out who wants it bad enough."

Martha didn't even glance at him.

Her eyes were locked on Dave.

The air split.

A gunshot cracked like lightning. Sharp, sudden, brutal.

No one knew who fired first. Maybe one of Tombs' boys. Maybe Frank. Maybe some twitchy bastard who couldn't keep his finger off the trigger.

Didn't matter.

That first shot shattered the moment.

And everything went to hell.

The bikes came in hard. Tyres screaming, gravel and dust ripping through the air like shrapnel.

Frank fired. A tight shot, clean and fast. It whistled past a rider's helmet, made the bastard jolt sideways, engine snarling as he fought to stay upright.

Dave yanked his gun free, boots crunching over the dirt as he moved for the car, where the case still sat in the back, heavy and waiting.

Martha didn't hesitate. She broke from Declan in a sprint, feet pounding across the gravel, heading straight for cover.

And Declan?

He didn't move.

Didn't twitch.

Just stood there, arms loose, expression unreadable, like the whole thing was unfolding exactly how he'd pictured it.

Dave didn't stop to figure it out.

Because Tombs' men were on them now.

And there was no slowing down.

The clearing exploded.

Gunfire ripped through the night, sharp and savage. Engines screamed. Bikes weaved through dust-thick air, headlights carving wild arcs through the chaos.

Frank dropped a rider with a clean shot to the shoulder. The impact spun the bastard off his bike, body tumbling into the dirt with a hard, crunching thud.

Another came in low. Too close.

Martha didn't flinch. She grabbed a splintered chunk of timber from the ground and swung hard, catching him square across the face as he roared past. Blood flew. His bike skidded, crashed, engine still howling.

Dave made another break for the car.

He didn't get far.

A biker lunged, cutting him off. A fist swung wild. Dave ducked, slammed his shoulder into the bastard's ribs, drove him to the ground. They rolled in the dirt, fists and knees and elbows, each one fighting like the other didn't deserve to breathe.

Tombs' men were everywhere. Coming in fast, scattered, unpredictable.

The fight fractured into pieces. A dozen brawls in motion. Guns, fists, boots. No one holding back.

There was no plan now.

Just blood, grit, and fury.

**

Blake had dumped the bike just short of the treeline. Left it half-toppled in the dirt, engine ticking as it cooled. He wasn't up for riding anymore. Not after what his body had been through.

Now he was on foot, moving slow. Careful.

Each step sent a jolt through his battered frame. His jaw throbbed where Martha had smashed him. His ribs ached. His legs barely felt like they were his.

But his mind?

Sharp. Cold. Locked on.

He stuck to the edges, creeping through the low scrub, keeping to the shadows while the fight exploded ahead of him.

Gunfire. Screams. Chaos.

Let them tear each other to pieces.

Let them burn it all down.

All he had to do was wait.

And when the dust settled?

He'd be the one left standing.

The case was still in the back of Callahan's car. He'd seen the way Tolliver looked back at it. The way Callahan had darted toward it.

Still locked. Still theirs.

But getting to it?

That was going to cost.

**

Dave spat blood into the dirt, wiped his mouth with the back of his hand. A biker groaned nearby, twitching, but not getting up again.

He looked at Martha — eyes sharp, jaw tight.

"Get to the car." Screaming through the chaos.

Frank was already slinging his rifle back over his shoulder, chest heaving from the last sprint. He didn't speak. Just nodded.

Martha didn't flinch. Didn't argue.

They moved as one.

Straight into the thick of it. Straight into the teeth.

Because that case wasn't anybody's elses yet.

And if they didn't claim it now, someone else would.

Easy. Right.

Too much blood had hit the dirt for this to end easy.

Frank ducked low, blood in his teeth, rifle slung and useless now. The chaos behind him was deafening. Engines screaming, gunfire snapping through the trees, bodies moving like shadows in dust. It was like Tombs men had turned on themselves. Shooting at anything that moved.

Frank didn't wait.

Martha was at his side, jaw clenched, hands shaking from adrenaline, eyes locked on the somewhere just beyond the clearing.

"That's our way out," she hissed.

They sprinted.

A biker lunged from the smoke — Frank shoulder-checked him hard, sending the bastard sprawling into the dirt. Martha leapt over him, not even looking back.

Another shot cracked past her head. She flinched but didn't stop.

They hit the 4wd just as a second biker closed in.

Martha reached for the door — Frank spun, rifle raised.

Click.

Empty.

He didn't hesitate, grabbed a chunk of timber from the ground and drove it into the biker's face. The man dropped.

Martha flung the driver's door open and Dave was already there, bleeding, panting, stumbling from the wreckage like a ghost.

"You good?" she barked.

"No," Dave rasped. "Get in."

They piled in.

Frank slammed the door shut, climbed into the back, rifle across his knees.

Dave twisted the key, engine caught with a cough, then roared to life.

He floored it.

The car tore through the clearing, smashing through scrub and dust, branches clawing at the windows like the bush itself didn't want to let them go. Dave spun the wheel, and the car found the main road again.

Behind them — noise.

Bikes? Voices? Gunfire?

It didn't matter.

They were moving.

But so was everyone else.

Bikes peeled away, chasing after Dave and his group.

Declan, who had stood back watching the chaos, quietly climbed into his vehicle and followed. The smirk on his face never shifted.

The junction quickly became a swirling mass of dust, devoid of people.

Except Blake.

He stumbled through the dust toward the bike he'd dumped earlier, his body a wreck. Every step was a curse. Every breath, a fight.

Then — headlights.

One lone highway patrol car.

Routine patrol. Wrong place. Wrong time.

Blake didn't hesitate. He waved his arms, flagging it down.

The officer stepped out, hand on his radio, one foot still in the door.

Blake flashed his badge, an old reflex, but changed his mind.

He'd been pushed to the edge.

Over the edge.

Dragged across it, leaving ragged strips of himself behind.

"Fuck it."

He pulled his weapon.

The shot was quick.

The cop dropped like a sack of meat.

A second later, Blake was behind the wheel.

He wiped the blood from his lip, coughed, and flicked on the sirens.

Flashing blue lit the trees.

He grinned.

"Let's see who outruns me now."

The first turn was too sharp. The front bumper clipped a burnt-out fencepost, tearing part of it loose.

He hit the highway like a mad dog, swerving wide, kicking up gravel, one headlight crunching into a low-hanging branch before he even righted the wheel.

The sirens wailed. The lights pulsed blue through the cracked windscreen.

Blake didn't care.

He just kept driving.

CHAPTER 74

The 4wd tore through the backroads, dust slicing through the edge of dawn.

Dave gritted his teeth, hands locked on the wheel, the case in the back rattling with every brutal turn. The engine growled like it knew what was chasing them, tyres skimming the edge of grip as they hammered across cracked bitumen and gravel washouts.

Beside him, Martha reloaded her rifle, eyes sharp, scanning the mirrors like she expected ghosts.

Frank sat in the back, pistol resting in his lap, fingers twitching, breath coming fast.

The chase wasn't over.

Not yet.

Not until the last bastard was down.

And not until they got the hell out of this nightmare.

The dust behind them lit up with the sick yellow glare of headlights. Shadows surged through the haze. Tombs' remaining men, still chasing, still clawing at their heels.

But the pack was fraying at the edges.

One rider took a bend too hard, too fast. His back tyre caught loose gravel, and the bike snapped sideways like a kicked dog. He flipped, body cartwheeling through the air, landing with a sound no one should survive.

Another roared closer, gun out, teeth bared. Frank didn't hesitate. One shot. Clean. The front tyre burst, and the bike went sideways. The rider hit the road chest-first, skidding across the bitumen in a spray of sparks and blood.

A third came screaming up on the left — close. Too close.

Martha leaned out the window, calm as ice, and pulled the trigger.

One shot.

The rider jerked, arms slackening. His bike veered hard, spiralled, then dropped into a ditch with a crunch of metal and bone.

The road behind them was chewing through bodies.

But not fast enough.

Only two bikes still clung to their tail.

Tombs was one of them.

The other, his last loyal shadow. A thickset bastard with a snake curling up his forearm, jaw clenched like it was bolted shut. His face was all fury now. Not fear. Not desperation. Just hate.

They weren't charging in. Not yet.

They hovered in the rearview, holding back, engines growling just outside the edge of range. Patient. Calculating. Waiting for something to crack.

Waiting for the 4wd to give out.

And it nearly did.

The engine coughed, temperature gauge climbing, dashboard flickering like a dying torch. Dave cursed under his breath, eyes flicking to the warning lights. The old four-wheel drive had taken a beating — and it wasn't built for a war.

Frank shifted in the back, just starting to speak —

Then —

Another glow in the mirrors.

Different headlights. Sleek. Low. A blue glow.

Then a sound.

One quick, sharp chirp of a siren and the blue strobe.

It sliced through the dust like a blade.

At first, Dave thought it was the real cops.

A single highway patrol car, closing in fast, lights flashing through the dust.

But then Martha leaned forward, eyes narrowing.

"That's not a cop."

And Dave knew.

A stolen patrol car.

Blake.

He was back in it. Siren still flashing. Headlights uneven. The bumper dragging sparks across the bitumen.

There was nothing clean about the way he drove.

He wasn't chasing.

He was hunting.

And he was coming for everything.

The road twisted ahead, narrow and cracked, chewing up the last light of day.

They weren't heading to anywhere. Just away — from the wreckage behind, from the bastards chasing, from the deal that had gone to hell in a heartbeat.

The 4wd shuddered with every turn. Engine too hot. Tyres worn down to nerves. Dave could feel it straining beneath his hands, like the car itself was trying to outrun the inevitable.

Behind them, the sound never stopped.

Tombs and his last man, still clinging on, revving hard through the dust. Not chasing anymore. Hunting.

And now, Blake.

The stolen highway patrol car tore up the road behind them, sirens flashing blue through the dusk. It swerved like a drunk, one headlight shattered, bumper dragging sparks, but it was gaining.

Dave glanced at the mirror. His stomach tightened.

Blake was coming in fast. Too fast.

The tension hit like a hammer. No more second chances. No more standoffs. No more rules.

Just four vehicles, one stretch of broken road, and nothing left to lose.

And Declan...he was out there somewhere. Of that much, he was sure.

The chase erupted, metal, rubber, gunfire, gravel —

And it all came down to who cracked first.

Snake-Tattoo made his move.

Gunned the bike forward, gripping his pistol in one hand, trying to pull up alongside the car. He was close.

Martha spotted him in the mirror.

She didn't wait.

One shot.

It caught him high in the shoulder. Not a kill shot, but enough to tear his balance apart.

The bike wobbled, skidded.

And that's when Blake arrived.

The stolen cop car came screaming up behind him, sirens flashing, bumper dragging.

Snake-Tattoo looked back, just in time to see death bearing down on him.

He tried to swerve.

Too late.

Blake didn't flinch. Didn't slow. Didn't blink.

The car hit the bike dead-on.

The impact tore the bike apart. Shrapnel and sparks exploding across the road. Snake-Tattoo was launched into the air like a broken doll.

He hit the tarmac hard. Rolled. Twisted. Didn't get up.

And Blake?

Blake just kept going.

Didn't even lift his foot off the accelerator.

The road stretched long and empty ahead of them.

No more bikers. No more screaming engines behind them. Just three vehicles clawing through the dark.

Tombs.

Blake.

And Dave.

The last men standing.

Baradine rose out of the horizon like a ghost town, still asleep, streetlights flickering, shopfronts closed tight against the early morning chill. A town that hadn't yet opened its eyes, unaware of the storm screaming its way in.

Dave's tyres hit the bitumen, headlights spearing through the gloom. He didn't slow down.

Behind him, Tombs was still coming. Silent now, determined, eyes locked on the Dave's car, like a predator sizing up his final kill.

But it was Blake who tore into town like a demon unchained.

The rear of the stolen patrol car was on fire, flames licking from the boot, trailing black smoke down the highway like a fuse. Something inside had caught. Fuel line, wiring, didn't matter.

Blake didn't stop to check. He didn't care.

He liked the fire.

The siren still wailed. Warped, broken, the speaker half-melted.

He clipped a parked ute outside the servo. Sent it spinning into the glass doors with a sound like the sky splitting. Debris exploded across the pavement. A fuel sign wobbled, then fell, slamming down behind him in a shower of sparks.

Dave caught the flicker in the rear-view. Blake's rear bumper on fire, sparks spraying. Just a second's distraction. Enough. The Patrol clipped the gutter, bounced up onto the footpath, tyres thudding over the concrete, before Dave yanked it back onto the road.

Frank held on, white-knuckled. "Jesus Christ, he's gonna burn the whole town down!"

"No," Dave muttered, jaw tight. "He's gonna take us with it."

Blake roared past a bakery, smashed into a sandwich board and a bin, both launching into the air and vanishing into the front window of a newsagent.

The street lit up like a warzone. Fire in the mirror. Smoke in their lungs.

And still — no slowing.

They tore straight through the heart of Baradine. Past the butcher's, the pub, the post office. Dogs barking from near dark yards, porch lights flickering on as the world woke up to hell on wheels.

Three left.

No rules.

No brakes.

And no turning back.

The 4wd was coughing smoke now. Every gear shift felt like a gamble.

Tombs was still close, riding the edge, waiting for a mistake.

Blake was behind. Unhinged, bleeding, smiling like this was the best day of his life.

And Dave?

He wasn't sure why he hadn't turned off. Why he hadn't ditched the road and vanished into the bush.

He just kept heading south.

Not for safety. Not even for the girls. Not yet.

It felt like something was pulling him. Like all the weight, all the blood, all the bad choices,

They were dragging him back to where it started.

Ironbark.

He didn't say it out loud.

Didn't need to.

But deep down, he knew.

That's where it would end.
One way or another.

CHAPTER 75

The 4wd was done.

Dave felt it in the rattle of the steering column, the whine of the engine, the smell of something burning under the hood. It had taken them as far as it could. Longer than it should've, but its lungs were failing. One more climb, one more hard turn, and the whole thing would seize.

Behind them, Blake's stolen patrol car was worse off. The rear was well on fire now, flames licking along the bumper, trailing smoke down the bitumen. He was still pushing it, sirens flashing like some kind of dying warning, but the car wouldn't last another kilometre.

Tombs was further back, but gaining. His bike was coughing on the last of its fuel, sputtering on every twist of the throttle. His face was a storm cloud, eyes fixed dead ahead. He knew the smell of failure, but he wasn't ready to give in.

And then it all gave out.

Dave's Patrol coughed, jerked, and rolled to a wheezing stop on the edge of Coonabarabran, just as the first houses crept into view, framed by dusty trees and the faint flicker of the growing early morning light. The three of them tumbled out — Martha gripping the case, Frank stretching his legs, Dave staring down the road like he was trying to see the future.

Somewhere behind them, a dull whump echoed through the trees — Blake's car finally giving up, burning bright at the limit of their vision, a few kilometres back.

A couple of minutes later, Tombs coasted past the patrol car wreck, flipped Blake the finger as he passed, and rolled to his own stop in a petrol-dry crawl. He kicked the stand down, swore once, and stood there — breathing like a man deciding who to kill next.

Dave didn't wait.

They left the 4wd right where it died and cut through a back street, moving fast. They needed wheels. Something fast, something discreet. Anything that could keep them in front.

That's when they saw it.

A tiny white car, clean and polished, parked outside a brick home with a flapping "Open House" banner. The logo on the door was bright and cheery — "Dunlop Property Group." The keys were still in the ignition, a clipboard on the dash, a few stray flyers in the footwell.

Martha raised her eyebrows. "Bit early for a fucking open house."

Dave didn't hesitate. "Get in."

Frank blinked. "Mate. That thing's a shoebox."

"It's got wheels," Martha snapped, already climbing into the front passenger seat with the case jammed against her knees.

Frank climbed in last, knees up around his ears, shoved against the back of Martha's seat, muttering, "This is bloody criminal."

Dave turned the key. The engine purred like it had no idea what was coming.

They rolled out fast, tyres barely gripping the street as they took the first corner on a squeal.

**

Behind them, the wreckage still smoked. Blake, already on foot, staggered toward a delivery van idling by the edge of a depot. Keys in the ignition. Engine running. The driver hadn't put up a fight — just froze when Blake flashed a badge, then a blade.

It was an old Hiace, dented to hell, rust curling around the doors, grease-stained paperwork scattered across the dash. The back was crammed with parcels, stacked tight and rattling with every step.

Blake climbed in, slammed the door, and dropped the van into gear.

The engine howled as he tore away, leaving smoke and silence behind.

**

Tombs? He didn't need to chase. Not right away. A dusty 4WD camper pulled up alongside him — two grey nomads with matching sun hats and a half-eaten meat pie between them. He smiled. Flagged them down. Lied through his teeth. Something about a flat tyre, an urgent call to make, a mate down the road. He climbed in, nodded thanks, and leaned back as the couple drove him toward town.

**

In the Mini, Frank shifted again. "We gonna open that thing or what?"

"No time," Dave said, eyes on the mirror.

"Who knows how close they are," Martha added. "We open it when we stop."

Frank leaned back with a groan. "Bloody hell. I feel like a hostage in a clown car."

Dave smirked. The road opened ahead, empty for now.

They were still in front.

But just barely.

CHAPTER 76

The Mini Cooper rattled over the patched-up bitumen, its tiny engine whining under the weight of three grown adults and a case that didn't belong in anything smaller than a coffin. Dave gripped the wheel tight, jaw set, his eyes locked on the road that twisted southward like it had answers waiting at the end.

Ironbark was hours away.

The deadline was worse than that.

In the passenger seat, Martha adjusted the rifle between her knees, eyes scanning the road ahead like it might jump up and bite them. She'd said little since they'd jacked the car outside that open house. Keys in the ignition, real estate flyers stacked on the back seat. No one stopped them. No one even looked.

Frank had crammed himself into the back like a circus act, the case now wedged against his knees, crushing his shins every time Dave hit a bump. He didn't complain. Not aloud, anyway.

The silence stretched. It carried weight.

Then Dave cleared his throat. "You two don't have to keep going."

Martha didn't answer at first. She turned slightly, looked at him. "What?"

"You've done enough," Dave said, not looking at her. "You want to pull out, I'll drop you. Nearest town. You can lay low, wait for this to blow over."

Frank snorted in the back. "Blow over? Mate, the only thing blowing over is this bloody car if we take a corner too hard."

Martha leaned back in her seat, her eyes narrowed. "You serious?"

"Yeah," Dave said. "I am."

Martha shook her head, not in disbelief, but like she was warding off something. "You think after all this I'm gonna tap out now? You think I'm walking away while that case is still in play. While those bastards are still breathing?"

"I had to offer," Dave muttered.

"Well, don't."

Frank chuckled low. "If either of you think I'm crawling out of this shoebox and letting you have all the fun, you're more bent than I thought."

Dave nodded once. That was that.

Behind them, somewhere well behind, the game was still crawling forward.

Blake was limping his way through the outskirts of Coonabarabran in a battered parcel delivery van he'd ripped off from a depot worker with a pocket knife and a thousand-yard stare. The thing bucked and wheezed like it was made from stitched-up rust and spite, held together by sheer bloody-mindedness. It sagged in the rear, overloaded with parcels that thumped and shifted with every jolt. Blake hadn't looked back at them once. Didn't care. He just needed forward motion.

He'd torn out of town without looking back, tyres spitting gravel, chasing nothing but the trail of dust ahead, like if he drove fast enough, he could catch what he'd already lost.

Tombs had made a call.

A mate. Old contact. One of those blokes who never asked why. Just checked the tank, grabbed the keys, and drove.

Now he waited.

Stood by the edge of a rural servo, a barely covered pistol tucked under one arm, a cigarette burning low between his teeth. The light was dim and dirty, that thin stretch of grey that comes just before the sun rises high.

The world was waking up.

Birds starting up in the trees. A distant truck groaning over a hill. Wind sliding through the dry grass like it didn't want to be noticed.

Tombs stood still, watching the highway like it owed him something. Breathing deep.

He wasn't out of the game.

Not yet.

But for now, Dave was still ahead.

The sun hadn't yet fully cracked the horizon when the Mini rolled through the edge of a new town. Its engine coughed and stuttered, running hot, every vibration rattling through the tiny chassis. Dave didn't stop. Didn't ease up. Just kept one foot down, the needle edging toward the red.

The streets were empty. Dark shopfronts, shuttered windows, silence broken only by the distant creak of a weathered flag on a café awning. A wide paddock opened beside the road, a skin of early mist clinging to it like lungs holding their breath.

In the back, Frank shifted.

Grunted.

Swore under his breath as his knees jammed against the seat in front of him. "Fuckin' clown car…"

Dave glanced at the mirror. "Don't."

Frank looked up. "Just a look."

"We don't have time," Martha snapped, eyes fixed forward. "You know that."

But Frank was already moving. He dragged the case onto his lap, careful but eager, brushing dirt from the latches. The thing was heavier than it looked. Solid. Cold. Industrial. The kind of box meant to carry more than just a payday.

He thumbed the catch.

Nothing.

Stuck. Grit or rust, maybe both.

He fiddled with it, fingers digging in, and finally, with a soft scrape and a click, it gave.

He opened it just a crack.

Just enough.

Silence.

Then a breath, long and low.

"Fuck me," he muttered. "I thought this was opals, mate. And yeah — there's opals in here by the looks…"

His eyes didn't move. His voice dropped.

"But mate…" He looked up at Dave and Martha, his face pale. "This is way more.

Frank stared down into the case like it might bite. "No wonder they're all coming for us."

CHAPTER 77

Declan sat on the bonnet of his dusty Hilux, engine still warm, eyes fixed on the pale strip of highway winding southward. The air was sharp with burnt fuel and eucalyptus, the last tendrils of chaos still drifting in the rearview of the world. But he wasn't rattled. He never was.

He'd set the table. Let them all take their seats. And now they were eating each other alive.

He lit a cigarette with steady fingers. The flick of the lighter was the only sound.

The deal had been bullshit from the start. He knew that. So had Dave, probably. But Declan hadn't needed it to go smooth. He'd needed it loud. Messy. Distracting. Let Tombs burn what was left of his gang. Let Blake spin himself out. Let Callahan and his crew run.

That was the point.

In the chaos, nobody looked at Declan. Not properly. Nobody questioned why he'd shown up without backup, why he hadn't brought a weapon into the trade. Why he hadn't stopped Martha when she ran.

Because he hadn't needed to.

He already had what he wanted.

He reached into the glovebox and pulled out a slim black device. The screen glowed faintly. A red dot blinked on the map, moving slow, steady, southbound.

He smiled.

"You should've checked your jacket, love."

When he'd grabbed Martha, back in the bush, just for a heartbeat, he hadn't manhandled her. Just a firm grip and a hand quick enough to slip the tracker into the lining of her coat. Tiny. Weightless. Completely forgettable.

Except it wasn't just a tracker.

He turned the volume knob on the device. A quiet hiss of static. Then, voices.

"…how far to Ironbark?"

Declan's smile widened.

It wasn't just about knowing where they were anymore.

It was knowing what they were saying. What they were planning. What they were afraid of.

He closed the glovebox, took one last drag of his smoke, and flicked the butt into the dirt.

They could run to the ends of the earth if they wanted.

But Ironbark would do.

He'd be there before them.

And this time, he wouldn't be watching. He'd be writing the ending.

The call came through as the dim morning light crept across the world.

Zhao was already awake, standing by the wide glass windows of his motel room. He didn't pace. He didn't fidget. He simply waited, one hand tucked behind his back, the other holding a short glass of something expensive and unnecessary.

When his phone buzzed, he answered without looking.

"Talk."

Declan's voice crackled through, raw and dry from dust and distance. "They've got the case. Headed south. Ironbark, if I had to guess."

Zhao didn't speak.

"They've lost half their tail. Tombs is hanging on, Blake's still kicking, but the rest. Gone. They're bleeding."

Still, silence.

Declan hesitated, then pressed on. "I want more. You said this would be clean. It's not. You want me to see it through, I need more."

Zhao took a sip of his drink.

"You'll be paid," he said, finally. Calm. Absolute. "It's not my money anyway. And now I need you to bring my last chess piece. Forget Ironbark. He will come to me."

"The pieces are already there. Been waiting since last night."

He ended the call without waiting for a reply.

Zhao set the glass down on the edge of the windowsill. Watched the reflection of his own face in the shaded glass.

Declan thought he understood the game. Thought he was making moves.

Let him think that.

Zhao's real plan hadn't even started yet.

And nobody, not Declan, not Dave Callahan, not anyone — was ready for what was coming.

CHAPTER 78

The Mini skidded to a halt in a cloud of gravel and dust, its tiny frame rattling like it was about to fall apart for good. Dave's hands stayed tight on the wheel, white-knuckled. Ahead, Ironbark Prison rose like a scar on the land — cold, grey, and unforgiving. A slab of concrete and history, hemmed in by razor wire and rusted fences.

They'd made it.

Or maybe… they'd just brought the fight home.

The car park wasn't empty. A few staff cars, a battered ute, someone's sun-faded green Torana. The early shift was already inside. The machine of the prison system ticking over like it did every morning — unaware of the firestorm about to crash through its gates.

Dave checked the clock on the dash.

8:57 a.m.

He kicked open the door, boots crunching on gravel. Martha was right behind him, the case tight in her grip. Frank dragged himself out slower, one hand on the door, the other hovering near his chest like he was daring it to give out again.

Dave stormed up to the entry, pushed through the doors.

The front officer barely looked up.

"Callahan. Signing in."

The guard gave a nod, checked the time.

"On time as usual."

Dave gave a tight nod. One minute to spare.

Then — outside.

The roar of an engine.

A violent crunch. Metal on concrete, something caving in under speed and fury.

Frank burst through the front doors, breath ragged, eyes wild. "Blake's here!" he shouted. "He's fucking mad — not angry. Mad. Proper gone."

Martha stormed in behind him, dragging the case like it was part of her. Her face was set in stone. "And another car. I'd bet my life it's Tombs."

A split second later, the outer doors slammed open.

Blake.

He stalked into the foyer like a revenant — shirt torn, blood smeared down one side of his face, pupils wide and black. His gun was already up.

The officer behind the desk stood frozen. "Sir, you can't —"

The crack of the shot shattered the air, punching a hole in the plaster just inches from the guard's head.

From the hallway, the warden appeared — mid-stride, mid-sentence. "What the hell is —?"

Another shot sliced past, close enough to part his hair.

He flinched, ducked low. "Call the cops! Get them here! All of them! Get this place on lockdown."

Blake lurched forward like a drunk marionette, arms loose but eyes locked, wild and unblinking.

Dave saw it in an instant . This wasn't a man anymore. This was a loaded gun wrapped in skin and rage.

"Move!" he barked, grabbing Martha's arm.

He hauled open the secured staff door just as the warden swiped his card, hands shaking. The lock buzzed. Dave shoved through, dragging Martha with him. He took the case from her, and they both stopped to breathe. Just for a second. Frank followed, one hand on the wall to steady himself, the other gripping his chest like it was ready to cave in.

The alarms kicked up — shrill and urgent. Radios crackled to life behind them.

The front desk officer hadn't moved. Still frozen, mouth slightly open, gunfire still ringing in his ears.

The warden ran after them, voice cracking. "You can't go down there! That's restricted!"

Dave didn't even look back. "Then stop us."

They plunged down the stairs and into the tunnels. Concrete halls running under the prison like veins. Service corridors. Old maintenance shafts. Routes for guards to move unseen. Dave had painted down here. Repaired lights. Fixed broken locks and patched old water damage. He knew every sharp turn and echo.

The air changed, cooler, damp, heavy with the sweat of history.

Behind them, the warden stumbled, stopping short, one hand braced against the wall. His face had gone pale.

"He knows these passages…" he muttered, breath shivering. "Blake. He's been here."

But Dave was already moving, faster now, every step dragging them deeper into the old bones of Ironbark.

They passed storerooms, old offices, metal lockers dented from decades of use. Paint peeled in long, curling strips. The air was stale, thick with the smell of time.

Dave slowed. He was thinking. Working something through. The others could see it in the creased brow and the wordless movement of his lips.

He stopped outside one door.

A storeroom.

He said nothing. Just opened it and stepped inside, closing the door behind him.

Twenty seconds. Maybe thirty.

When he came out again, he wasn't empty-handed.

He carried an old canvas mail bag, something he had seen in there before — faded green, stamped with a flaking correctional services logo, the kind used decades ago to haul documents and inmate gear.

He tossed it to Frank without a word.

"Careful," was all he said.

Frank caught it, eyebrows knitting, but he didn't ask. Just slung it over his shoulder and kept moving.

They rounded the next corner, climbed a set of stairs, crashed through a door and stepped into the edge of the high-security wing.

The lights flickered once, humming like they weren't sure they wanted to stay on.

Everything was still.

Too still.

But Dave felt it in his bones.

They were in the right place.

Red's old cell stood at the end of the corridor like a scar in the concrete. The door hung open, dark inside, the metal rusted and scabbed with age.

Dave moved first, stepping into the hallway. The shadows stretched long, distorted by the flickering lights above. Each footfall echoed off the concrete like a countdown.

Behind them, on the stairs — footsteps.

Heavy. Dragging. Off-kilter.

Blake.

He lurched into view like something broken that wouldn't die. His shirt was soaked with sweat, one sleeve half torn. Blood down the side of his face. And in his hand — a gun, raised and trembling.

Dave didn't flinch.

He lifted the silver case, holding it out like bait.

"This what you want?"

Blake blinked, slow, like his brain was buffering. His jaw ticked, finger twitching on the trigger.

Dave started walking. Deliberate. Calm.

He dragged the case down the hall beside him, the metal edge scraping across the floor, sharp, grating, final.

Stopped outside Red's cell.

Then, with a grunt, he swung and hurled it through the open door.

It hit the concrete with a hollow, empty thud.

Echoes rippled.

"Take it!" Dave shouted, voice sharp as broken glass. "It's all yours, ya fucker!"

Blake didn't hesitate.

Blake moved without thought.

He stepped into the cell, drawn like an addict to a fix, eyes locked on the case sitting in the middle of the floor like a holy relic. He didn't even glance back.

And behind him — the door moved.

No hands. No push. No mechanism triggered.

It just swung shut.

A slow, final groan of old hinges and iron weight.

Clunk.

Locked.

Like Red himself had reached from beyond the grave and finished what he'd started.

Blake spun, eyes wide, confusion collapsing into rage. He slammed a fist against the inside of the door.

"NO!"

He turned, snarled, raised his gun and fired. The report of the shot cracked through the high-security wing like a whip.

Then another.

And another.

Rounds ripped into concrete. Screamed off steel. Sparks lit the cell like dying fireworks.

Somewhere in the madness, Blake turned—eyes locking on the case.

He stumbled to it, yanked it open.

Empty.

Just dust and foam and betrayal.

He let out a sound no human should make. Deep and broken, like a dying cow strangled mid-bellow.

It bounced off the walls, ragged and wide-eyed, before curdling into a growl.

He howled, pulled the trigger again and again, teeth clenched like a rabid dog.

Until the gun clicked dry.

Nothing left but the echo of madness and the slow, shuddering rasp of his breath.

Outside the cell, Dave had already gone. The second Blake had stepped into the cell, he had turned and bolted back down the corridor, away from the storm.

Back to Martha. Back to Frank.

Back to whatever came next.

**

The front doors of the prison slammed open.

Tombs stormed in like he owned the place — blood on his knuckles, boots scuffing over the foyer tiles, handgun clenched in his fist. Behind him, sirens screamed through the air, growing louder by the second. Backup was coming.

But he'd arrived first.

And he wasn't alone.

Four prison guards stood in a line — vests strapped tight, shotguns raised, faces blank as concrete.

Tombs slowed. Eyed them.

"Well," he muttered, lips curling into something close to a grin. "Didn't think the welcome party would be so formal."

The guards didn't blink.

One took a step forward, barrel rising an inch.

Tombs raised his hands, still smirking. "Alright, alright…"

His eyes flicked toward the hallway behind them.

Then he gave a half-shrug. "Just here to visit my uncle… or brother… or…"

A beat.

"Ahh, shit."

He exhaled, long and low.

"…guess I'm fucked."

CHAPTER 79

The sirens cut through the morning like blades.

Blue and red light danced across the prison walls as the convoy rolled in. Three police cars, one unmarked, and a van with its back doors flung open. Perry had arrived.

Doors slammed. Boots hit gravel. Officers spilled out, weapons holstered but hands twitchy. The storm might've passed, but the air still buzzed like it hadn't finished with them yet.

Perry was already barking. "Secure the perimeter. I want eyes on every bloody door. Nobody leaves. Nobody speaks unless it's to me."

Inside, the corridors were a war zone of noise and blood. A guard with a shattered arm sat slumped against the wall. Another was being loaded onto a stretcher, head wrapped in gauze, mumbling about gunfire and a ghost with a badge.

Paramedics swarmed the foyer. Someone vomited behind the front desk. The air reeked of sweat, cordite, and panic.

Perry stepped inside and didn't slow. "Who's in charge here?"

A junior officer tried to speak. Perry didn't wait for the answer.

The prison had survived — but only just.

And the reckoning was here.

**

Red's old cell pulsed with tension.

Blake paced inside like a dog that knew the leash had snapped too late. His clothes hung off him in tatters, his eyes two hollow rings of rage and exhaustion. Every few seconds, he'd test the door, rattle the handle, throw his shoulder against it. Nothing. The thing had jammed shut like it had been waiting all these years for someone just like him.

Footsteps echoed.

Then a voice, sharp and cutting, bounced off the concrete.

"Blake!"

Detective Perry came into view, jaw tight, coat still dusted with the chaos of the car park. He stopped dead in front of the cell, fury radiating off him like heat from a flame.

"Senior Detective Sergeant Adrian Blake," Perry snapped. "The hell have you done?"

Blake turned, grinned. Blood on his teeth. "Morning, Perry."

Perry didn't flinch. "You've just set fire to half the goddamn state. You started a war in the Pilliga. You've got bodies stacked from here to the border — gunfights, stolen vehicles, explosions, attempted murder. And for what? A fucking box of rocks?"

Blake spread his arms, mocking. "You forgot the part where I walked in here without even getting shot."

Perry's eyes narrowed. "Not yet."

Then, his radio came to life.

"Unit Four, urgent update — officer shot. Critical. Bodycam confirms shooter ID. It's Adrian Blake. Over."

The corridor went still.

Blake froze for just a breath. Just long enough to register that the hole he'd dug had finally hit bottom.

Perry stepped closer to the bars, voice like a blade sliding through grit. "You're done."

******

The lunchroom was fluorescent and stale. Old pies in the fridge. A microwave that hadn't worked properly since 2009. The kind of room where nothing ever happened — until now.

Dave sat stiff in the corner, one boot jiggling under the table, eyes locked on a crack in the far wall. He hadn't blinked in minutes.

At his feet, the old prison mail bag sat quietly on the lino. No one had asked about it. No one had touched it. It looked like it belonged there. Just another piece of forgotten prison clutter.

Martha held a paper cup of tea. Still full. Hands wrapped tight around it like it might anchor her to the room. She didn't sip. Just stared.

Frank shifted in his seat, massaging his chest like the ache was crawling deeper. His shirt was streaked with sweat and dust, and one sleeve was ripped at the elbow.

The warden paced, muttering. One of the guards was slumped on a plastic chair, face pale, holding a wet cloth to a gash on his scalp. Another leaned against the wall near the exit, trying and failing not to stare at them.

They weren't in cuffs.

But they weren't free either.

They were stuck in limbo. Waiting for Perry. Waiting for whatever came next.

And outside those thin concrete walls?

It felt like the world was still burning.

The buzz of a phone cut through the silence.

Not Dave's phone.

McBride's. Still in his pocket after everything. Forgotten until now.

Dave pulled it out slowly, screen glowing with a number that meant nothing — but felt like everything.

No one stopped him. No one said a word.

He answered.

Zhao's voice came through like silk over a knife.

"You did well, Mr Callahan. But I'm afraid I need one last thing from you."

Dave didn't speak.

Didn't need to.

Zhao continued, cool and precise:

"I have them. Your wife. Your daughter. They're safe… For now."

Dave's jaw clenched. But still, nothing. He didn't move.

Zhao paused. Then:

Thump. Thump.

The sound of movement. A door opening.

Then, faint, shaky —

"Daddy…?"

Dave's chest stopped rising. Stopped falling.
Just silence. Stone.
Zhao's voice again:
"You know what I want. And you know what happens if I don't get it."
The line went dead.
Dave stared at the phone.
Didn't move. Didn't blink.
Martha leaned forward, voice low. Careful.
"What is it?"
Dave looked up.
His face was hollowed out, carved from something hard and ancient.
"They've got my girls."

CHAPTER 80

Martha didn't say anything straight away.

She just stood. Pulled her phone from her pocket. Walked toward the back of the lunchroom, away from the warden and the guards and the flickering light.

Dave didn't move. Didn't speak.

He just watched her.

Her fingers flew across the screen. A number she knew by heart.

The phone pressed to her ear.

One ring.

Two.

She turned her back to the room.

Murmured something low, too quiet to catch.

Then her whole body shifted. Just a little. Like her bones had slumped beneath the skin.

She hung up. Turned back around.

Her face was pale. Set like stone.

"There was an incident," she said quietly. "People hurt."

A pause.

Her voice cracked. Not from emotion. From disbelief.

"The girls are gone."

Silence dropped like a hammer.

No one moved.

Dave's phone buzzed again, the vibration dull against the table. He didn't rush to check it. Just turned the screen toward him, already expecting what he'd see.

No name. No number. Just a string of coordinates, followed by a single line of text:

Bring the contents. Come alone. You know what's at stake.

There were no threats, no demands dressed up in bravado. Just quiet certainty, like the words had already decided the outcome.

Dave didn't speak. Didn't lift his head. He didn't need to.

He knew exactly what it meant.

Dave shifted in his chair, shoulders tight, fingers curling around the strap of the mail bag beneath the table. Every second that passed chipped away at his focus, his breath shallow in his chest.

They weren't in cuffs, but they might as well have been. Two guards lingered by the door, and the warden hadn't stopped pacing.

Then Frank groaned.

Loud. Wet. Real enough to make everyone turn.

He clutched his chest, gasping, eyes rolling like he was about to go down hard.

One of the guards leapt to his feet. "Shit — he's having a turn!"

The warden spun, shouting, "Get medical! Now!"

In the scramble, no one noticed Martha lean forward. She didn't speak. Just mouthed one word across the table.

Go.

Dave didn't wait.

He stood fast, mail bag tight in his grip, and slipped through the door while everyone was watching Frank sink to the floor.

By the time someone turned to shout his name, he was gone.

Dave moved like a shadow through the staff corridor, the familiar hum of the fluorescent lights overhead barely registering. He kept low, hugging the walls, muscle memory guiding him.

He knew this route. Knew it from the old painting gigs, the maintenance jobs. Knew every blind corner and every shortcut through Ironbark's guts.

A side exit loomed ahead. He shouldered through it.

Outside, the sting of sunlight, the raw slap of open air.

He stayed low, boots crunching across gravel, heart pounding in rhythm with every step. Past the loading dock. Past the fence line. Toward the outer car park. He didn't know what he was looking for, just anything with an engine and keys.

Then he saw it.

A dusty ute, big and idling, nose pointed at the road.

The guy leaning against the back bumper looked half-asleep, halfway through a cigarette, high-vis vest hanging open like he owned the place.

Dave didn't hesitate.

He didn't know it had been Tombs' ride. And he didn't care.

Dave moved in fast. Quiet, efficient. Just behind the smoker now. No warning. No hesitation.

He brought the elbow around hard. Caught the guy in the temple. The sound was soft and wet. The man dropped like a sack of grain, half-spun, hitting the dirt with a grunt and a twitch.

Dave didn't stop. He hauled the bastard out of the way, dumped him behind a stack of bins. Grabbed the mail bag, slung it on to the seat, slid in behind the wheel.

The engine was already idling. Warm. Ready.

He dropped it into gear.

Gravel spat behind him as he yanked the wheel and peeled out.

Didn't look back.

Didn't breathe.

Ironbark vanished in the mirror, shrinking to nothing behind him.

Cassie's voice still echoed in his skull.

"Daddy?"

And now he was moving.

IRONBARK

CHAPTER 81

The wind slipped through the cracks in the tin like breath through broken teeth. The abandoned dairy sat hunched against the outskirts of Singleton, its walls buckled, its roof rust-stained and rattling with every shift of the breeze.

Inside, Zhao sat calmly on an upturned crate. No slouch in his shoulders. No twitch in his hands. Just stillness.

A steaming cup rested between his fingers, the scent of black tea curling faintly into the air. A small camp stove flickered at his feet, blue flame ticking quietly beneath the dented kettle. Near it, atop a cluttered bench, an old oil burning lamp cast a dull glow across the room.

He sipped once. Let it settle.

This wasn't panic. This wasn't scrambling. This was something else.

Control.

Around him, the space was staged. Gear in neat piles, a go-bag against the far wall, another phone charging off a portable battery. A black duffel zipped and ready by the exit. Two routes out, both checked twice. One led through the dry paddocks and onto an old fire trail. The other, straight onto the bitumen.

Zhao checked his watch.

Time moved like it always did.

Steady. Unforgiving.

And now, it was almost time.

The door groaned as Zhao tested the padlock. Heavy metal, scabbed with rust, looped through a thick chain drawn tight across the cool room's latch. It clinked softly as it settled back into place.

Inside, the dark was absolute.

A stifled sound. Something between a cry and a thump, muffled by thick insulated walls.

Zhao didn't flinch. He didn't speak.

He just listened for a moment. Long enough to hear movement. Breath. Life.

Then he turned and walked away, his footsteps echoing down the concrete floor like nothing about it mattered.

The chain didn't rattle again.

Zhao stepped outside into the light, the breeze dragging through broken rafters and rusted beams. He lit a cigarette with steady fingers, the flame sharp against the wind.

The phone rang once. Twice.

He answered.

"Declan."

The voice on the other end was tight, almost distracted. "Everything seems complete."

Zhao exhaled smoke. "No complications?"

"Nah., I did it quiet. Neighbour said she hadn't seen Sally in days, but no one thought much of it. The girl. Cassie, screamed a bit. They were shaken up but breathing. They're yours now…and" Declan paused, as if for just one moment he questioned his own actions.

"… there's a fuckload of heat. That stunt in the Pilliga — Tombs went feral. Blake too. Place lit up like a war zone. But Ironbark seems to have brought them both undone."

Zhao didn't respond.

Declan kept going. "That's the last job, yeah? You've got what you want. I've earned every cent."

There was a pause.

"I don't like what this turned into," Declan said, his voice lower now. "Remember. You said they wouldn't get hurt."

Zhao flicked ash into the dust. "And have they?"

"I'm just saying —" Declan stopped himself. "Look. Just don't forget what you promised. The girls are bait. That's all. They get out of this. That was the deal."

Zhao didn't answer.

He ended the call.

Declan stared at the dead screen for a long moment, the silence louder than anything Zhao had said. Silence that seemed to carry something more. Something final.

"What the fuck have I done?"

**

The burner buzzed in Zhao's pocket.

No ID. Just a number.

He answered without hesitation. "Zhao."

The voice on the other end was sharp. Measured. But beneath it — disappointment.

"I'm an hour away."

Zhao went still.

 Liu.

"I thought you were in Hong Kong," he said, calmly.

"I was. Then I started asking questions."

Zhao walked to the far side of the dairy where the roof had half-caved in, letting in a hard strip of early light.

"You've been busy," Zhao said.

"So have you," Liu replied. "I want the sword. I want answers. And I want to look you in the eye when I get them."

Zhao paused. Then nodded, though the other man couldn't see it.

"Come," he said. "Everything you're chasing… is already here."

He hung up.

No smile. No satisfaction.

Just the weight of inevitability settling over everything.

Zhao stood at the edge of the ruined dairy, the phone still in his hand, the line long dead.

The sky was beginning to shift. Slate grey clouds giving way to bruised light. A wind moved through the bones of the building, whistling low through shattered rafters and corrugated iron.

He finally smiled.

Not the smug twist of a man who'd won.

Something deeper.

Expectation.

Anticipation.

Destiny.

He turned slowly, eyes scanning the scene. The rusting sheds. The chained cool room. The long gravel drive winding back to the road.

Every piece in place.

Declan, paid and discarded.

Liu, charging toward him — blood in his voice.

The Jian, so close now he could almost feel the weight of it.

And the Callahan women, locked away like a fuse waiting for fire.

Zhao's fingers flexed at his sides. Everything had moved. Every trap had sprung. There was no more chaos. Only conclusion.

He stepped back inside, letting the shadows take him.

Let them come.

All of them.

This ends where it began.

With me.

CHAPTER 82

The Bentley moved like a shadow across the land, sleek, silent, indifferent to the dirt-smeared utes and battered four-doors that dotted the rural highway. Its polished black frame shimmered in the early light, low and smooth as it cut through the rolling hills of the Lower Hunter Valley.

Inside, Liu sat composed in the back seat, a thin line of tension in his shoulders the only betrayal of thought. He watched the landscape drift past his window. The jagged silhouettes of gum trees, dry grass waving like brittle flags, rusted tractors left to die in overgrown paddocks. A windmill turned lazily in the distance, forgotten but not yet fallen. Here and there, old sheds leaned sideways, their corrugated roofs slumping like collapsed hats.

It was all so... careless.

This land didn't plan. It didn't arrange or contain. It just was. Raw. Sprawling. Brutal.

Liu's fingers tapped idly on the armrest.

How strange, he thought, that something as sacred as the Jian — his family's sword, his birthright — was now tangled in this wild place. How strange that destiny, which should have followed bloodlines and honour, had instead come to rest in the dust of this half-forgotten continent.

He let the thought hang as they crested a rise. The road ahead narrowed. Trees thickened.

They were getting close.

The Bentley glided over the bitumen, its engine a low whisper beneath the hum of rural quiet. Fences blurred past. Lone cows stood in empty paddocks. A roadhouse sign leaned crooked at a fork they didn't take.

Liu sat back, one leg crossed, a hand resting lightly against his chin. His gaze was fixed on the middle distance, but his thoughts were elsewhere — sharper. Focused.

Zhao.

Reliable. Loyal. Once, those words had been enough. But lately, the loyalty felt thinner. The reports messier. Too much noise. Too much blood. The pursuit of the Jian had become something theatrical.

Zhao had always done what he was told. But now?

Now he acted as though the blade might answer to him.

Liu's lip curled faintly.

A dog that forgets its leash isn't dangerous. Just confused.

"He forgets his place," Liu murmured aloud. "But I will remind him."

He turned his head as the driver signalled, slowing for a narrow turnoff ahead, just visible between two gnarled gums.

Almost there.

And Zhao's moment of clarity was coming with it.

Inside the Bentley, the luxury was discreet — custom leather, soft lighting, the hum of climate control barely audible over the tyres rolling clean across the road.

A small screen glowed in the centre console. Liu's hand moved to it without looking. Another call. Another update.

"Mr Liu," came the voice of one of his senior advisors, translated smoothly through the earpiece. "There's been a shift in shareholder structure within the Jiangtai Consortium. Minor, but unexpected."

Liu didn't blink. "Consolidate. Delay filings if you must."

Another screen lit up — text scrolling fast in Mandarin.

"Foreign partner in Riyadh has changed position. No formal notification."

Liu waved it away. "Then remind them who they're partnered with."

There was a pause.

"Sir, one more thing. A whisper — unverified — of movement in your Shanghai logistics interests. Something subtle. Anomalous trades."

Liu's brow lifted slightly. "Who?"

"No names. Not yet."

"Then find one. And deal with it."

The screen dimmed again. Silence returned.

Just the road. The hum. The narrowing space between him and destiny.

Liu didn't see it — not yet.

But Wei's hand had already begun to close.

The next call came through faster than the others — voice tight, urgent. One of his senior analysts. Trusted. Persistent.

"Mr Liu, you need to see this. I believe someone is actively positioning against —"

Liu tapped the console.

The voice cut out mid-sentence.

The screen went black.

His eyes didn't move from the road ahead.

Later, he thought. The sword comes first. Then everything else.

Outside the tinted windows, the rural sprawl gave way to narrow scrub-lined roads, the air thick with dust and rising heat.

Liu didn't know it yet — but he had just silenced the first alarm bell.

And Wei, his upstart rival was already inside the walls.

The Bentley turned off the bitumen, tyres crunching onto gravel, the road narrowing as scrub closed in from either side. Dust rose behind them in long, curling ribbons. The trees grew tighter here — bone-grey gums and wiry wattles crowding the path, their shadows flickering like ghosts across the bonnet.

Ahead, half-swallowed by overgrowth and time, sat the husk of the old dairy.

Rusted roofing. Concrete stained by years of sun and neglect. A place long forgotten by most.

But not by Zhao.

And not by Liu.

He sat straighter in his seat, adjusted his jacket with the care of a man preparing for a meeting that mattered. His fingers brushed the cufflinks once — ceremonial, not sentimental. Then he nodded to the driver.

"Stop here. I'll walk the rest."

The Bentley rolled to a halt. The door opened with a soft click.

Dust kissed his polished shoes as he stepped out.

The air was dry. Still.

He looked toward the decaying building, toward the place where legacy waited.

"Time to restore what was stolen," he murmured.

And with that, he started walking.

He believed the storm had passed.

He didn't realise he was walking straight into its heart.

CHAPTER 83

Dave drove like the road owed him answers.

The car rattled over rough bitumen, engine straining with every gear change. Trees blurred past in streaks of green and shadow. Dust curled in the rearview, a dirty tail chasing him south.

Beside him, the mailbag sat heavy on the passenger seat. Too heavy. Not just the weight of what was inside, but what it meant. The opals. The sword. His family.

Everything had started with a map. A hunt. A maybe. Turned into a bag of opals and whatever else.

Now it was leverage.

Now it was everything.

He gripped the wheel tighter, jaw clenched. Tried to push Cassie's voice from his head. The small, frightened 'Daddy?' that had slipped through the phone like a knife between his ribs. It played again. And again. Like she was still speaking. Like he could still answer.

He couldn't.

Not yet.

A battered road sign flew past the window —

Singleton 14km

Dave didn't lift his foot. He put it down harder.

Thoughts flashed through his mind. Just a flicker, barely a memory, but enough.

Sally laughing in the kitchen, sleeves rolled, dancing with Cassie to some tinny radio song. The old kettle whistling. Bills stacked on the fridge, but none of it mattered right then.

That life was small. Broke. Real. Something he longed for now more than any coloured stones.

Dave gripped the wheel tighter, knuckles bone-white.

"Hold on," he muttered. "I'm coming."

Dave spotted the old building through a break in the trees. Its roof partially collapsed, weatherboards bleached grey, metal siding peeled like skin.

He pulled the car off the road, hidden behind a stretch of thick scrub. Turned the engine off. Silence wrapped around him like a shroud.

He didn't get out right away.

Instead, he sat there, hands on the wheel, eyes fixed ahead but not seeing.

After a beat, he reached for the mailbag in the passenger seat. Unzipped it slow.

Inside: padded canvas rolls of opals, rough, polished, every kind. The colours shifted like oil on water, alive in the early morning light. Velvet pouches nestled deeper in the bag, spilling uncut stones — diamonds, rubies, emeralds. Chaos and beauty. A king's ransom.

Beneath it all, wrapped tight in old linen, something longer, heavier. Dave pulled back the fabric.

A sword.

The Jian.

Its surface was ancient steel, etched with marks he didn't understand. But he felt them. This thing had a presence. Not just weight. History.

And tucked beneath it all, almost forgotten, was something smaller. A leather-bound notebook, water-warped. A police logbook.

Taped to the front, sealed tight in a plastic pouch: a cassette tape.

Dave stared at the name printed across the cover.

"Constable Parker," he muttered. The man Red had supposedly murdered.

He slid the logbook and tape back into the bag, then hesitated.

No. Not now.

He pulled them out again and tucked them under the driver's seat, out of sight.

Then he slung the mailbag over his shoulder.

No weapon.

Just him now.

He stepped out. Boots crunched dry grass. The breeze caught the trees and whispered through the ruin ahead.

He stood still, breathing.

Then walked toward the dairy.

"Time to end this."

CHAPTER 84

The air inside the dairy was stale. Thick with dust, old rot, and the ghost of milk long soured. Light filtered in through rusted tin slats in broken walls, casting thin gold lines across the concrete floor.

Dave stepped through the entrance, cautious, the mail bag slung over his shoulder. His boots echoed slightly in the hollow space, but he didn't call out. He didn't need to. Zhao was already waiting.

He emerged from the shadows near the centre of the room, sharp suit somehow uncreased despite the ruin around him. Calm. Controlled.

"Put it there," Zhao said, nodding toward a rusted workbench.

Dave did. No words. Just unclipped the mail bag and laid it flat.

Zhao approached, movements deliberate. He patted Dave down, checked the bag again, and gave a small nod.

"Empty it."

Dave unzipped it, slow. He reached in and began placing the contents on the workbench, one item at a time.

Soft, padded pouches of opals. Velvet bags with uncut stones — rubies, emeralds, flashes of colour that defied the gloom.

And then — wrapped tight in aged linen — the Jian.

Zhao's eyes lingered there.

"That's it?" he asked, not looking up.

Dave gave a short nod.

Zhao pulled a plastic tie from his pocket. "Turn around."

Dave hesitated for the briefest second, then turned. The plastic zip bit tight around his wrists.

Zhao gestured to a battered milk crate near the wall. "Sit."

Dave sat. Quiet. Watching.

Across the workbench, the sword waited.

And so did the storm.

Footsteps approached from the far end of the dairy.

Not hurried. Not cautious. Just measured. Expensive shoes crunching across dirt and broken glass.

Liu stepped through the doorway like a man entering a boardroom, not a battlefield. Dark suit immaculate. Tie straight. A thin sheen of dust clinging to his cuffs, but otherwise untouched by the ruin around him.

He didn't flinch at the sight of Dave, hands bound, seated like an afterthought, or the clutter of gemstones and the linen-wrapped relic on the bench.

His gaze found Zhao.

"You have it?"

Zhao inclined his head. Nothing more.

Liu advanced with a kind of quiet gravity, the kind of presence that made rooms fall silent. His eyes swept the workbench, ignoring the glittering stones. Rubies, opals, diamonds — meaningless distractions. Until they reached the object wrapped in linen.

The Jian.

That's when he stopped.

Something in his posture shifted — barely perceptible, but real. His shoulders lifted. Chin raised. For a moment, the composure cracked just enough to reveal the hunger beneath.

He looked at Zhao again. "Unwrap it."

Zhao didn't move. Not right away.

Liu stepped closer, voice soft with reverence. "All this chaos. The blood. The money. The mess." He gestured slightly toward Dave. "All of it… worth it. To have it returned."

He reached for the sword.

Zhao's hand shot out.

Not to strike. Not yet.

Just to block.

Liu blinked, not in fear — more in disbelief.

Zhao's voice was low. "Let me present it properly."

Liu allowed it. With a nod, he stepped back.

He still believed this was his moment.

He didn't realise it was Zhao's.

Dave shifted slightly on the crate, hands bound tight behind his back. Something in the air had changed. Not just tension. Something colder. He could feel it in Zhao's posture, the way his fingers lingered too long on the linen wrap.

Zhao peeled back the final layer, revealing the Jian in full. The blade was beautiful. Ancient. Alive in a way that made the rest of the room dull by comparison. Etched steel, darkened with age. Symbols carved with impossible precision. The Jian wasn't just old — it was imperial. Its hilt was wrapped in worn black silk, the threads unravelled in places, but beneath the grime, the craftsmanship was unmistakable. The bronze guard bore intricate carvings of dragons curling around clouds, and just above the tang, etched into the steel, was a fading imperial seal. The mark of Kangxi himself. It was a gift once, centuries ago. Not ceremonial but earned. A blade meant to be used and remembered. The steel shimmered faintly, wave-patterned and cold, with edges honed to a ghostly thinness. This wasn't treasure. It was history with a sharp edge.

He held it with reverence, kneeling slightly as if presenting it in supplication.

Liu stepped forward, chin high. Ready to accept the offering he believed was rightfully his.

Zhao bowed his head.

Then moved.

The motion was sudden. Brutal.

He rose and drove his shoulder into Liu's chest, knocking the older man backward. Liu stumbled, tripped over debris, and fell to his knees with a grunt of pain.

Dave flinched. "Jesus."

Zhao didn't even look at him.

He stood tall now, the Jian resting across his palms like a blade of judgment.

His voice was calm. Too calm.

"And now," he said, eyes on Liu, "it is time for you to pay for what you've done."

Liu stared up, stunned. Humiliated. Dust smeared across his tailored slacks. One hand pressed to his ribs. No longer the master of anything.

Dave sat frozen on the crate, helpless.

The sword hung in the air between them like a question.

Zhao now held every answer.

Liu blinked up at Zhao, blood smeared across his cheek, disbelief flickering into something colder. Fear, maybe. Or realisation. This wasn't a ceremonial return. This wasn't honour. This was something older. Dirtier.

Zhao stood above him, the Jian balanced loosely in his hands. Not offering it anymore. Measuring it. Weighing the distance between past and punishment.

Dave sat motionless on the crate, jaw clenched, wrists aching in the ties. His eyes flicked to the cool room door. Locked. That's where they had to be. No movement. No sound. His family. But at the moment he had nothing.

Liu straightened slowly, trying to speak, trying to summon whatever authority he still believed he had.

Then he felt it.

A tingle at the base of his neck. Cold. Prickling.

Like the future had just pressed a knife to his spine.

Zhao said nothing.

He didn't need to.

This wasn't about returning the sword.

This was about drawing blood with it.

CHAPTER 85

The Jian caught what little light there was — silver edge, flawless spine. It looked older than the walls around them. It was, but it gave the sense that it was older than the land itself.

Liu knelt in the centre of the room, spine straight despite the blow that had dropped him. Blood trickled from his mouth. His hands hung loose at his sides. Defiant.

Zhao circled him slowly.

Measured steps. Blade in one hand, the other behind his back, like this was a lesson. A ritual. Something rehearsed a thousand times in silence.

Dave sat on the milk crate, wrists bound, watching. The air in the dairy had thickened, gone hot and stale, like the place itself was holding its breath.

Zhao stopped behind Liu.

"This Jian," he said softly. "This sword was never the goal. Not really."

Liu didn't answer. Didn't move.

"I served you for twelve years," Zhao went on. "Twelve years. Loyalty. Silence. Violence, when needed. All for what?" He stepped closer. "To stand beside a man who called the deaths of children collateral damage."

His voice didn't rise. It didn't need to.

"My wife died from poisoned groundwater. My son lasted six weeks after her. Six. You remember the name of the village?" Zhao leaned in. "Of course you don't."

Liu's jaw flexed.

"I knew what you were the moment I met you. But I still bowed. I still served. Because revenge…" Zhao inhaled slowly. "Revenge requires patience."

He stepped forward, the Jian blade now at his side.

"This sword," he said, almost reverent, "was just the key to get close enough to your throat."

Dave felt something shift. Not in the air — in Zhao. Like everything that had held him together up until now had done its job. And now… it was gone.

Zhao looked down at Liu.

"Everything led here."

Liu's silence said everything. He wasn't afraid. He just didn't care.

And that made it worse.

Zhao shifted the Jian in his grip, the blade whispering as it moved through air.

"You still think you're untouchable," he said. "Even now. Here on your knees."

Liu looked up, blood on his lips, a flicker of interest in his eyes.

Zhao gave a humourless smile. "While you were chasing old myths and trinkets, Wei was pulling apart your empire. Piece by piece. Quietly. Efficiently."

He circled again, slower this time. Like a shark narrowing its loops.

"Shareholder shifts. Offloaded assets. Shell takeovers. Your own people — bought and turned. I watched it. I helped it." He knelt briefly beside Liu, voice low. "Your fall is already underway. You just haven't hit the ground yet."

Liu's lip twitched.

Then he laughed.

Not loud. Not manic. Just a dry, sandpaper chuckle that rattled in the bones of the dairy.

"You think I didn't see Wei coming?" he said, voice steady now. "I've had eyes on that little bastard since before he could spell treachery."

Zhao's eyes narrowed.

Liu raised his chin. "I let him try. That was his test." He coughed, spat blood to the side. "By now his accounts are frozen. His allies are cutting deals to save themselves. He was dead before he moved."

Zhao stood still.

And for the first time, something cracked in him.

Just a little.

A shift in his shoulders. A tremble at the corner of his mouth.

Because Liu wasn't broken.

Not yet.

Not even close.

Zhao's grip tightened on the hilt. His breath hitched — not from effort, but from rage barely contained.

"You still think this is a negotiation," he said, voice cracking like dry ice. "You still think you're the architect."

He stepped closer. The Jian lifted, its weight steady, its edge catching the faint morning light that spilled through broken rafters.

Liu didn't flinch. His mouth pulled into something almost like pity.

Zhao's composure faltered. His words came fast now, teeth bared.

"You think I wanted the sword? The stones? I wanted you. On your knees. Stripped of your lies. And I wanted the world to see what men like you leave behind. Burned fields. Poisoned water. Dead sons."

Liu met his gaze.

Unblinking.

Unbroken.

Zhao's hands shook as he raised the Jian higher. "This isn't justice."

The tip hovered over Liu's neck.

His voice dropped to a whisper, almost reverent.

"It's correction."

Dave's hands were slick with blood, the plastic ties biting deeper every time he moved. His wrists burned, nerves flaring with every shift.

The milk crate beneath him groaned as he inched it sideways — closer to the wall, to the rusted edge of a steel shelf jutting out like a broken tooth.

He twisted. Pulled. Pressed the ties against it.

Nothing.

Tried again. Harder. Slower. Teeth clenched. A grunt buried in his throat.

Across the room, Zhao loomed above Liu, the Jian poised, ready to fall.

Dave's eyes flicked to the cool room.

Silent.

Still.

The door was shut. No cries. No sound. Just cold metal and his family locked inside.

A pressure built behind his eyes — rage, fear, helplessness all tangled in a knot so tight it threatened to choke him.

He looked back at Zhao.

The sword rose higher.

And Dave knew — he was out of time.

Every part of him screamed: Do something. Anything.

He pressed harder.

The ties held.

But they wouldn't for long.

Not if he pushed just once more…

Liu straightened, even on his knees. His spine like iron, blood on his chin, but his eyes… calm.

Unshaken.

"You want revenge?" he said, voice steady. "Then do it. Spill my blood. Swing my sword."

Zhao took one step closer, the Jian gleaming in his grip.

Liu tilted his head. "But know this — your moment ends the second the blade touches my skin. You'll never leave this country alive. The people I command… they'll burn you down to ash."

Zhao didn't blink.

Didn't flinch.

He just breathed, deep and slow, his expression unreadable.

Then he raised the sword again.

Steel whispered upward through the air, tracing a glittering arc above Liu's neck.

Dave froze on the crate, breath locked in his throat.

Liu didn't move.

Didn't bow.

He only stared into Zhao's eyes and said, "Do it."

Zhao stepped forward.

Dave braced, ankles planted, wrists screaming against plastic.

Liu didn't flinch. Didn't breathe. Just stared straight ahead.

Zhao exhaled.

The Jian rose higher still, gleaming like it remembered the wars it once knew.

"Do it," Liu said, voice louder, steady, absolute.

Zhao stepped in —

The sword paused at its peak, glinting in the half-light —

A single breath from blood.

Dave launched forward like a man with nothing left but a gamblers last throw of the dice.

CHAPTER 86

Dave didn't think.

He launched.

A blind, desperate lunge. Hands still zip-tied, wrists raw and bleeding, but his whole body moving like it had one shot left and nothing else.

He hit Zhao centre-mass, the impact heavy and full of old muscle memory. Like those footy tackles from a lifetime ago, back when pain didn't come with stakes this high.

Zhao grunted, thrown sideways, arms flailing. He smashed into the cluttered bench behind him. A rusted tin can clattered to the floor.

Then the lantern tipped.

The old glass oil lamp — half-full, burning low — rattled off the edge and exploded on the concrete.

Glass. Fire. A thin trail of flame licking across spilt fuel.

No one noticed it.

Not yet.

Dave hit the floor hard, breath torn from his chest, wrists still pinned behind him, plastic biting into raw skin. He twisted, rolled, trying to get his feet under him — but the zip tie still held, tight as a noose.

Zhao groaned, still on his side, sucking air like a man trying to stay conscious. But his hand found his pistol.

Steel scraped leather.

He turned, eyes wild, lips pulled back in a snarl.

The barrel rose.

Right at Dave's head.

And behind them, on the floor, near the bench, the fire had taken hold.

A snake of flame hissed across an old oil stain. Licked up a torn rag. Caught a pile of shattered wooden crates.

The heat was building. The smoke hadn't reached them yet — but it would.

Zhao's finger tightened on the trigger.

Dave didn't flinch. There was nowhere to go. Nothing he could do. Just the sound of his own heartbeat in his ears and the cool breath of death hovering close.

Then —

A shadow moved.

Liu.

Blood streaked his cheek. Dust clung to his once-pristine suit. But his spine was straight. His hands steady. And in them, raised with quiet finality, was the Jian.

He didn't shout. Didn't warn.

Just took one step forward —

And swung.

The blade carved the air like silk through water. One clean, silent arc.

Zhao didn't even register it. Not until his head was already leaving his shoulders.

A spray of red. A thud.

His body folded like wet canvas, gun clattering useless to the floor.

Then, crack.

The Jian struck the rusted steel column behind Zhao. A flash of metal meeting metal. The blade vibrated —

Then fractured.

It shattered in Liu's grip. Splinters of centuries-old steel raining onto the blood-slick floor.

Liu stared at the broken hilt in his hands.

The sword had fulfilled its purpose.

And now, it was gone.

The sword had waited centuries. It chose its moment. Then it broke.

For a moment, the room held still.

Zhao's body at Liu's feet. The shattered remains of the Jian scattered across the floor. Smoke curling upward like breath held too long.

Then came the sound.

Not a scream. Not a shot.

Crackling.

The fire had grown. Swept along dry timber, licking the walls, feeding on history and dust. Flames bloomed across the far side of the dairy, hungrily climbing toward the rafters.

Heat pressed in. The air changed, thicker, sharper. Choking.

Dave's chest heaved. He turned his head —

The cool room door.

Still locked. Still sealed tight.

Still holding Sally and Cassie.

He forced his body to move, legs scraping, wrists useless, eyes burning from smoke.

"Shit," he whispered. "No, no, no —"

Behind that door. His family.

Behind that door. Everything.

And behind the door, his world was about to burn.

CHAPTER 87

The fire had taken hold fast.

Flames licked across the timber walls, clawing higher, devouring everything with dry, crackling hunger. Smoke pumped through the space, thick and bitter, stinging Dave's eyes and throat.

Zhao's head lay in the spreading fire, jaw slack, eyes gone glassy. Nothing left now but bone and vengeance turning slowly to ash.

Liu stood over Dave, chest rising and falling in short, controlled breaths. The hilt of the shattered Jian blade hung limply in one hand, its edge still slick with blood, its tip blackened from the strike.

Dave shifted on the floor, wrists raw, the plastic ties biting deeper with every movement. He'd torn at them. Teeth, steel, anything he could find, but they wouldn't give.

Liu knelt, expression unreadable. "You saved me."

Dave didn't look at him. He was staring past, toward the cool room. Toward the door. Toward what was behind it.

"They're in there," he rasped. "My wife. My daughter."

A beat passed. The fire cracked louder.

Liu's voice was quieter this time. "I owe you my life."

Dave turned to him, eyes wild. "Then help me save mine."

Dave pushed himself up, ran and crashed into the cool room door shoulder-first, the metal biting back. A thick padlock stared him down, unmoving, unbreakable.

"Cassie!" he shouted. "Sally!"

Muffled banging answered him. A cry. Faint. Desperate.

The door throbbed with heat, but the seals hadn't failed yet. Inside, the cool room was holding like a dying lung. Trapping breath, not letting the fire in. But not for long.

He kicked the door, rammed it again, the plastic ties on his wrists digging deeper, holding fast. He couldn't get leverage. Couldn't get force. The heat was a second skin now. Sweat, smoke, and panic.

Liu appeared at his side, breathing hard, soot clinging to his face. He tried the lock, tried smashing it with a broken plank, then grabbed a rusted shard of steel and sawed at the plastic around Dave's wrists. It slipped. Cut skin, deep. And then the ties snapped.

Inside the cool room, another thump. A sob.

Dave pressed his forehead against the metal. The heat bit into his skin instantly. "No… no, no, no…"

Liu froze.

The flames had reached the ceiling, roaring above them now, chewing toward the door. The heat was unbearable. The room was choking.

Liu looked at Dave.

"I'm sorry," he said. Quiet, broken.

And then he turned, vanishing into the smoke, the hilt of the shattered sword still gripped in his hand.

Dave didn't move.

Couldn't.

He just stared at the door. His life was behind it.

And he was about to burn with it.

Dave was raw now. Lungs burning, arms numb, eyes streaming with smoke and desperation.

He slammed his shoulder into the door again and again. It didn't budge. His breath came in ragged gasps, each one a knife.

From inside — Cassie's voice, high and terrified.

"Daddy!"

It shattered him.

His knees gave out. He collapsed at the base of the door, coughing, broken, forehead pressed to the burning steel like it was a gravestone. Smoke rolled in around him, thick as grief.

"I'm sorry," he whispered. "I'm so sorry."

Then —

A crack of thunder.

A single gunshot.

The padlock exploded, clanging to the floor in twisted pieces.

Dave blinked through the smoke.

Didn't question it.

Didn't stop to wonder.

He surged to his feet, shouldered the door, and it flew open.

Light spilled in.

And so did he.

Dave didn't hesitate.

Didn't question the miracle.

He lunged through the shattered door, the heat biting at his skin, smoke swirling like a living thing trying to claw him back.

Inside, cold walls, acrid air, the hum of old silence broken by coughing, gasps, the sound of his daughter's sobbing.

Sally was slumped in the corner, coughing, eyes wide.

Cassie was curled beside her, face streaked with soot, hands still zip tied, whispering through cracked lips.

"Daddy…"

Dave dropped to his knees, heart pounding harder than it ever had.

He tore at the ties with his hands, wrestling like an animal. His raw and bloody wrists screamed. It didn't matter. He grabbed the shard of metal Liu had used, from the floor and sawed.

Fast. Rough. No finesse.

He wasn't thinking. Just cutting.

He freed them.

Pulled them both close.

Then staggered back, out into the corridor, through smoke and fire, dragging them with him.

The heat chased them.

They stumbled out into the pale morning air.

Cool. Clean. Real.

Dave fell to his knees on the dirt.

Clutching his family.

Alive.

**

The shot had rung out clean. No panic. No rush. Just breath, scope, pressure, and steel.

Now, the rifle lay across Declan Holt's lap, the barrel still warm.

He sat on a scrubby ridge overlooking the smoking ruin of the dairy, the wind tugging gently at his jacket.

Below, through heat shimmer and smoke, he watched Dave stagger into the open. Two figures clutched in his arms, all three silhouetted against the growing fire and smoke.

Declan took a drag on his cigarette. Held the smoke in. Let it curl out slow.

No fanfare. No fist-pumping glory.

Just that one moment. That one choice.

He muttered to himself, voice barely more than gravel on wind:

"I might be an arsehole…"

A pause.

"…but I'm not a complete arsehole."

He flicked the ash. Let the silence settle.

Then reached beneath his shirt.

Pulled out a thin chain, dull silver, old. Two rings slid free: one thick, plain gold. A wedding band. The other finer, delicate.

They caught the sun for a moment. Then turned dark in his palm.

He stared at them. Long enough to forget the fire, forget the wind.

His thumb moved over the smaller band. A child's ring.

"I'm sorry," he said, voice barely there. "I should've gone with you."

Just seven words. But they cracked something open.

The rage had filled the hole they left. Kept him alive. Kept him sharp.

But this morning… this almost…

He ran his thumb over the ring again.

Not that man. Not anymore.

He tucked the chain back in, stood up slow, and turned away from the ruin.

The fire would burn itself out.

He wouldn't.

CHAPTER 88

The fire behind them crackled and spat, its glow licking the pale morning sky. Smoke rose in lazy tendrils, not frantic anymore, just the slow, exhausted breath of something that had burned too long. The shell of the dairy sagged inward, charred and skeletal.

Dave stood with his arms around Sally and Cassie, one on each side, drawing them in as close as he could. Cassie's face was buried in his chest, her hands fisted into the fabric of his shirt. Sally leaned her head against his shoulder, silent tears streaking soot down her face. They weren't crying anymore, but they trembled with the kind of relief that doesn't make sense right away. The kind that crashes in after the fear has passed but before the mind can make sense of it.

No one spoke. The fire did the talking behind them. The wind picked up a little and carried the smoke sideways across the paddock, brushing ash into the grass.

Dave closed his eyes. His lips moved more than his voice did.

"We're okay," he whispered, more to himself than to them.

And for the first time in a long while, he believed it.

Sally clutched him tighter, her arms wrapped around his middle like she was afraid he'd vanish again if she let go. Her breath hitched against his chest, soft and shaky. Dave could feel her heartbeat thudding in time with his, both of them wired and broken in the same rhythm.

Cassie made a sound, half sob, half laugh and wiped at her face with the back of her hand, leaving a black streak across her cheek. Her eyes were wide and red, but alive. She looked up at him like she wasn't sure he was real.

Dave dropped to his knees in the dirt.

Cassie fell into him without hesitation, wrapping her arms around his neck, burying her face in his shoulder. She was crying again, properly this time, but it didn't sound like pain. It sounded like release.

He held her like he'd never let her go again. Sally dropped down beside them, her hand on Cassie's back, the three of them tangled in a tight, trembling knot on the scorched grass. Smoke clung to their clothes, dust lined their skin, and Dave felt every bruise, every ache, but none of it mattered.

They were together.

They were whole.

Kilometres away, the fire was just a dull orange smear in the mirror.

Liu sat in the back of a sleek black car as it tore down the highway, tyres humming against the bitumen. His driver said nothing — knew better than to speak. Liu stared out the window, jaw clenched, one hand gripping the armrest hard enough to blanch his knuckles.

He wanted out. Out of this country. Out of this mess. Out of the dust and the blood and the shame.

He had dishonoured himself.

He had walked away from that shed knowing Dave might die. That the girl, Cassie might die. And for what? The sword? Revenge?

A shiver crept down his spine. Not from the cold, but from something deeper. Guilt, maybe. Or fear. His hands, normally so precise, so steady, trembled in his lap.

He glanced at his reflection in the tinted glass.

Pale. Drawn.

A man who had almost lost everything he pretended not to care about.

He adjusted his collar. Composed his features.

By the time they reached the turnoff, the moment had passed.

He was Liu again. Sharp, unreadable, untouchable.

But the tremble in his hands… that would take longer to forget.

******

Dave led them across the paddock to the car he'd stashed beneath the trees. A dusty four-wheel drive with faded rego stickers and a cracked taillight. The one Tombs had arrived in, before the world caught fire.

Sally looked at it, then at him, but didn't ask. She just climbed in, still shaky, still silent. Cassie followed, curling up in the back seat, arms wrapped around her knees.

Dave started the engine. The sound was rough, but steady. It would get them where they needed to go.

They pulled onto the narrow road, the old dairy shrinking behind them in the rear-view mirror, smoke trailing into the sky like a dying signal flare. No sirens. No tyres screaming through the bush. Just the hollow hum of worn rubber on bitumen.

Sally rested her head against the window and spoke without turning. "What now?"

Dave gripped the wheel a little tighter.

"I'll take you somewhere safe," he said. "Then I have to go back."

She turned her head slightly. "Back where?"

"Ironbark," he said. "I have to face what's waiting for me."

The words were calm, settled. He wasn't bracing for impact anymore. In his mind, he ticked the boxes.

The logbook. The cassette. Perry. My ICO. Every decision, every body left behind. This doesn't get to stay unfinished. It ends where it started.

The car rolled on, heat haze dancing over the road ahead. He didn't know if the prison would take him back or lock him up for good. But it didn't matter.

He had a name to clear. And debts to settle.

They pulled into a quiet roadside stop. A little gravel bay beside an old timber picnic table, the kind of place no one ever really stopped unless they had to. The fire was long behind them now, and the heat had eased. A breeze rustled through dry grass, carrying the scent of eucalyptus and ash.

Dave killed the engine. For a moment, they all just sat there, the silence almost strange after everything.

Cassie opened her door and slid out. She stretched her legs, wincing a little, then looked down at her feet. She frowned.

"Guess I'll need new school shoes again."

Sally blinked, then followed her gaze.

Dave stepped out and joined them, and all three looked down together.

Cassie's black leather school shoes, scuffed, battered, and now completely caked in cow shit, were barely hanging on. One sole had started to peel. The laces were stiff with mud and whatever else she'd walked through back at the dairy.

For a second, no one spoke.

Then Cassie snorted.

Sally burst out laughing.

Dave grinned, let it build, and felt the tightness in his chest crack open.

They stood there in the dust, laughing so hard it hurt. Not because it was funny, though it was, but because it was the first time in days they'd been able to laugh at all.

Dave leaned down and kissed the top of Cassie's head.

"We'll get you new ones," he said. "Proper good ones."

The sun lifted a little higher. The road stretched ahead.

But for now, they stayed a moment longer. Together, laughing, alive.

CHAPTER 89

The borrowed four-wheel drive rolled up the back road toward Ironbark, its tyres crunching over gravel as the prison loomed into view. Dave turned into the staff entrance without slowing, the battered vehicle groaning as it pulled up unevenly against the edge of the car park.

He sat for a moment, hands resting on the wheel, eyes on the building ahead. The engine ticked quietly in the silence.

This was where it started. Where it all circled back to.

He climbed out and shut the door gently behind him, the dust of the road still clinging to his boots and cuffs. The sun was higher now, casting long shadows across the yard. Ironbark's perimeter fence shimmered faintly with heat, but the place felt still, like it hadn't even noticed he was gone.

He walked up to the staff gate and hit the buzzer.

The intercom crackled. "State your name."

"Callahan," he said. "I need to speak to the warden."

A pause.

Then: "Wait there."

The gate buzzed open. Dave stepped through.

Detective Senior Sergeant Perry was waiting inside, starched shirt neatly buttoned, badge clipped to his belt, eyes hard behind his glasses. He stood straight, arms folded, every inch the no-nonsense cop, even if the faint lines around his eyes looked deeper than they had a week ago.

He didn't offer a greeting. Just stared.

"David Callahan? I understand you're neck deep in all this shit. You've got some explaining to do," he said flatly.

"I know," Dave replied.

"Come with me."

Perry turned and started down the hall. Dave followed, the echo of their footsteps bouncing off cold concrete walls.

Perry led him to the warden's office without a word. The corridors were quiet, just the distant echo of footsteps and the low murmur of radios behind locked doors. The office smelled faintly of old coffee and vinyl polish.

They sat. Perry behind the desk, arms folded. Dave across from him, hands resting on his knees.

Then he talked.

He laid it all out. The map scratched into the cell wall, the coordinates, the plane. The opals. McBride. Zhao. The bikers. The buried case. Every step, every deal, every betrayal. Names, places, bodies. He held nothing back.

By the time he got to the fire at the dairy, he felt hollowed out.

Like the weight he'd been carrying, Red's legacy, Parker's secrets, all that blood, had finally been set down.

Perry didn't interrupt. Didn't write anything down. He just listened, expression unreadable, the occasional muscle twitch in his jaw the only sign he was taking it in.

When Dave finished, the silence lingered.

Dave slid the logbook and cassette across the desk.

Perry hesitated for half a second, then opened the cover. The pages were yellowed, brittle in places, but the handwriting was clear. Tight, methodical. A cop's handwriting.

He skimmed the first few pages, flipping slowly, eyes narrowing as he read.

Flip.

Another pause. Perry's fingers curled slightly against the edge of the page.

"'If anyone finds this — I didn't run. I didn't quit. I just couldn't carry it anymore.'"

Perry looked up, the colour drained from his face.

"Holy shit," he muttered. "It was Blake. Not Red. Blake murdered Parker."

He closed the book slowly, like he was sealing something away.

"The bastard's been hiding in plain sight this whole time," he said, mostly to himself. "And we locked up the wrong man."

Dave didn't speak. He didn't need to.

Perry picked up the cassette and frowned. "We've got nothing that'll play this."

He stood, pulled open the office door, and called out to a passing officer. "Hey — anyone here drive a dinosaur? I need a cassette deck."

A minute later, a younger guard appeared, holding up a dusty boom box with cracked buttons and a faded logo across the front.

"Got this." the guard said. "Still works — just don't turn it up past halfway or it screams, and fast-forward eats the tape."

Perry took it, gave Dave a last glance, then disappeared down the hallway. Dave stayed seated, the buzz of fluorescent lights humming above him.

Through the thin office walls, he heard a faint click, then a low, warbling hiss.

Then a voice.

Parker.

"Jesus Christ." Parker's voice was barely a breath. "You set this whole thing up. The opals. The smuggling gig. Liu Jianhong. You —"

Then Blake's voice. "It didn't have to come to this. For fucks sake."

A silence followed. Long and ugly.

Then a gunshot.

Dave closed his eyes.

The truth was finally speaking, and it was loud enough to echo through the walls.

Perry returned ten minutes later, boom box still in hand, jaw tight. His eyes flicked to Dave, then away again. He didn't speak. He didn't need to.

Whatever doubts he'd had, were gone now.

They walked in silence through the corridors, boots echoing off concrete and steel. As they neared the far wing, the sharp whine of an angle grinder cut through the air, high-pitched and angry, bouncing off the walls.

Outside Red's old cell, two officers were crouched by the door, sparks spraying as the grinder chewed through the thick metal. The lock was warped, jammed solid. The cell hadn't been meant to hold anyone eternally. No one remembered that until the door shut behind Blake and refused to open.

From inside came the familiar, rasping bark of a man who'd lost patience hours ago.

"Get me the fuck out of here! It smells like shit!"

Perry didn't break stride. He barely glanced at the door.

"No, Blake," he muttered. "That's just you."

The grinder screeched louder, drowning out Blake's next string of abuse. Perry kept walking.

He didn't tell them to hurry. Didn't tell them to stop.

He just walked away. Calm, steady, the truth finally in his hands.

They made it back to the main corridor before Perry stopped.

He turned to face Dave, his expression unreadable, but the sharp edge was gone.

"You're good to go at five," he said. "Same as always."

Dave gave a small nod. No thank you, no smile. Just understanding. It was enough.

Perry looked at him for a moment longer, then added, almost like an afterthought, "Three more Sundays, mate. Then you're free."

He gave a dry, tired exhale.

"Might be the only part of this shitshow that ends clean."

Then Perry turned and walked away, shoulders squared, already bracing for the paperwork storm he knew was coming.

Dave watched him go, the corridor quiet now behind him.

Three more Sundays.

And then, for the first time in a long time, freedom.

The front gate buzzed and clunked open.

Dave stepped out into the afternoon light, squinting against the sun as it dropped lower in the sky. The warmth hit him like something unfamiliar. Clean. Untouched by smoke or blood or noise.

Frank stood by the same beaten-up four-wheel drive Dave had arrived in, hands in his pockets, one boot resting against the tyre. He gave a small nod, nothing more, but his eyes said it all.

Martha was leaning against the bonnet, arms crossed, chin slightly lifted. She looked like she'd been there a while, like she'd already decided they weren't leaving without him. There was dust on her jeans, a fresh scratch across one cheek, and the kind of calm you only get after surviving something that nearly ate you whole.

No one said anything.

They didn't need to.

Dave crossed the yard toward them. Frank pushed off the tyre. Martha shifted just enough to make room between them.

He stopped beside them, and for the first time in days, maybe longer, he let himself breathe.

The past was still close. The wreckage of it still smoking in the distance.

But the road ahead?

It was open.

CHAPTER 90

Frank leaned against the bonnet of his ute, the late afternoon sun sinking low behind him. His phone was pressed to his ear, the call quiet in his hand, the air still. Out here, everything felt slower. Calmer.

Martha's voice crackled through the line, soft and dry with that familiar edge.

"I'm home," she said. "Dogs are fed. Garden's still alive — just. I had to rip out that bloody rosemary bush though. Thing was half dead."

In the background, he could hear the dogs barking, some distant clang of a screen door swinging shut.

Frank smiled. "Back to normal, huh?"

"Close enough," she said. "Still haven't had time to fix the front gate."

"Want me to take a look when I'm over?"

"Only if you bring the good wine this time. None of that rubbish in the green bottle."

Frank chuckled, running a hand over his face. "No promises."

There was a pause, comfortable, like neither of them needed to fill the silence too quickly.

Martha spoke first. "You alright?"

"Getting there," Frank said. "Just got one last bit of business to sort."

"Oh?"

"Declan Holt."

Another pause, but this one heavier.

"Careful," she said.

"I'm always careful."

"Bullshit," she replied, but there was a smile in it.

He didn't answer. Just looked toward the door of the run-down house behind him.

"I'll call you later," he said. "Tell the dogs I said g'day."

"You tell Holt he owes us. Redemption shouldn't come with a paycheque."

He hung up, slipped the phone into his pocket, and turned toward the house.

Time to settle accounts.

**

The door creaked as Frank stepped inside, letting it fall shut behind him with a heavy click.

The place was typical Declan, clean but impersonal. Rented cottage, barely lived in. One suitcase in the corner, a half-packed duffel beside it. On the small kitchen table, a sleek laptop glowed in the dim afternoon light, its screen filled with rows of numbers and open transfer tabs.

Declan sat behind it, relaxed in a button-up shirt with the sleeves rolled, a glass of scotch resting loosely in one hand. He didn't look up straight away. Just tapped something on the keyboard, brows flicking in mild interest.

"Frank," he said eventually, like they'd scheduled a catch-up. "Nice of you to drop by."

Frank didn't answer. He stepped further in, boots thudding against the wood floor, and let his eyes sweep the room.

"Looks like you've done alright," he said. "For someone who barely lifted a finger."

Declan smiled without showing teeth. "Takes a certain kind of effort to stay out of the blood, mate. You'd know that better than most."

He sipped his drink, then motioned lazily to the screen. "Zhao paid in full. Blake paid more. None of them asked for receipts."

Frank folded his arms. "You get a frequent flyer card with that conscience, or is it just cash-back these days?"

Declan chuckled. "Still sharp."

There was an edge beneath it though. A flicker of something behind the eyes. He wasn't stupid. He knew why Frank was here.

Frank stepped closer, closing the space between them.

"You knew where they were. Dave's girls. You gave them to Zhao."

Declan shrugged. "Didn't take much digging. You lot were loud."

Frank's voice dropped, quiet but cold. "But you also saved them. Shot the lock."

Declan said nothing. Just took another sip of his drink and stared at the screen.

Frank nodded slowly.

"That's why I'm not dragging you out by the collar."

Declan said nothing.

The laptop screen blinked to standby. The room felt smaller.

He finally looked up. No bravado. No smirk.

Just a quiet, almost reluctant nod.

Frank tilted his head.

"So which is it?" he asked. "Rat or saviour?"

Declan leaned back in his chair, the scotch glass still in his hand.

"Depends who's asking," he said.

But the joke didn't land. Frank didn't smile.

Frank let the silence hang just long enough to bite, then spoke, calm, firm.

"You're going to donate it."

Declan blinked. "Sorry?"

"All of it. Every dollar you made off this mess — Zhao, Blake, the lot. It goes to the Bush Widows Organisation."

Declan snorted, leaning back in his chair. "Come on, Frank. I didn't pull the trigger on anyone. I kept my hands clean. I earned this."

"You profited off every body that hit the dirt," Frank said. "That's not clean. That's clever."

Declan raised his glass like a toast. "Cheers to clever."

Frank didn't move. Just stared.

"You can be better than this," he said quietly. "Or you can stay what you are."

A long pause.

Declan's jaw twitched. He looked down at the laptop, then back up at Frank. No eye-rolls now. No smug grin. Just a man weighing up whether he still had a soul left to answer to.

Without another word, he turned the laptop back on, opened a new browser tab, and typed.

Bush Widows Organisation.

He clicked through the donation page. Entered the numbers manually. Big ones.

Frank didn't say a thing. Just stood there, arms folded and watched every click.

Declan hit "Confirm."

A quiet chime sounded. The page refreshed. It was done.

Click.

Declan sat back and closed the laptop with a soft thud, eyes lingering on the screen a second longer than necessary.

Frank didn't speak. He hadn't needed to push hard, and that alone surprised him.

Declan reached up, rubbing his jaw, then let his hand drop to the chain beneath his shirt. He pulled it out slowly, just far enough for the two rings to catch the light.

"Happy now?" he muttered. Not to Frank. Not really.

Maybe this was what she'd wanted. Not absolution. Just movement. Something that didn't end in blood or fire.

He let the chain slide back beneath the fabric and sat still.

Frank broke the silence.

"You've got talent," he said quietly. "But you're a bloody mess."

Declan arched an eyebrow, unimpressed.

Frank kept going. "I reckon with some guidance, you could actually make a difference."

That earned a scoff. "You want to team up now?"

"No," Frank said, deadpan. "I want to keep you out of prison."

He paused, let the words land.

"Teaming up might just be a side effect."

Declan leaned back in his chair, head tilted, appraising Frank like he hadn't really seen him until now.

After a moment, he nodded once.

"Alright," he said. "But I drive."

Frank smirked. "You still got a car."

Declan shrugged, grabbed his jacket off the chair. "I've got three, but those are just details."

They walked out together, the last of the sun bleeding across the sky. Not friends. Not enemies.

Just two men with unfinished business.
And maybe, just maybe, something worth chasing.

CHAPTER 91

The clock on the wall ticked over to five.

Dave peeled off his work gloves, hung them on the same hook he'd used every Sunday for the last few months, and gave the room one last look. Quiet shift. No drama. Nothing worth remembering.

And yet, everything felt different.

He signed out at the desk, nodding to the guard behind the glass. The man gave a small nod back. Nothing over the top, but not the usual indifference either.

As he stepped through the internal gate, two more guards looked up. One offered a simple, "Take care, Callahan." The other just tipped his chin, like you would to a mate after a long day's work.

That wouldn't have happened a month ago.

Dave didn't say anything. Just nodded in return, calm, steady.

The automatic doors clicked open, and he stepped out into the late afternoon sun.

Same light. Same dust hanging low over the trees.

But this time, the weight wasn't there.

This time, he wasn't walking out with something chasing him.

The visitor's car park was nearly empty.

All except for one vehicle.

A brand-new twin cab ute — metallic grey, spotless, not a speck of dust on it despite the wind kicking up around the yard. It idled quietly, like it had been waiting for him.

Dave slowed, eyes narrowing. He didn't recognise it, but something about the presentation was too neat, too deliberate to be random.

A man stepped out from the driver's side. Well-dressed, slim, hair neatly parted. He wore polished shoes that didn't belong anywhere near red dirt and a pressed shirt that hadn't seen a wrinkle all day. There was a calmness about him, and a subtle accent Dave couldn't place.

"Mr Callahan?" the man asked.

Dave stopped in front of the ute, arms relaxed at his sides. "Yeah."

The man reached into his jacket and produced a sealed envelope and a single car key.

He handed them over carefully, like he was passing on something more than just paper and metal.

"This is from Mr Liu," he said. "He said you'd understand."

Then, without another word, he turned and walked away. No small talk, no smile. Just purpose, precision, and distance.

Dave looked down at the envelope in one hand, the key in the other.

Yeah.

He understood.

Dave leaned against the side of the ute, the warmth of the metal steady against his back. The engine had cut off, leaving only the hum of distant cicadas and the crunch of gravel as the suited man disappeared down the road.

He tore the envelope open along the fold and pulled out the contents.

The letter was handwritten — precise strokes, each word placed with care. Liu's handwriting. Clean. Controlled.

Just one line.

A life for a life. Use it well.

No signature. No flourish.

Dave folded the letter back and looked at what came next.

A property deed. Rural land, modest house, three-bedroom, good shed, a stretch of bushland out back.

Attached beneath it, business paperwork in his name. Something simple and solid. A salvage yard and small mechanic's workshop registered under Callahan Services Pty Ltd.

At the bottom of the stack: a bank deposit slip. Not millions. Not even close. But enough.

Enough to clear debts. To start fresh. To breathe.

He held it all for a moment, feeling the weight settle in his chest. Not like a burden. Like something that had finally landed after drifting for too long.

The turnoff was barely marked. Just a rusted post and a hand-painted number half-swallowed by grass. Dave eased the ute off the bitumen and onto the gravel, tyres crunching over the dry track.

The road wound through a narrow stretch of bush, opening onto a clearing where a humble weatherboard house sat beneath the limbs of a wide old gum tree. Fresh coat of paint. New gutters. Solid.

He pulled up beside the front steps and shut off the engine.

The place was quiet. Still. Like it had been waiting for him.

Dave stepped out and stood for a moment, soaking in the silence.

Then he pulled out his phone and dialled.

Sally answered on the second ring.

"What is it?" she asked, her voice soft but curious.

Dave looked at the house. Its windows catching the last of the light, the gum leaves whispering above.

"Let me come get you and Cassie," he said. "You need to see this for yourself."

An hour later, the ute rolled back up the gravel track, this time with Sally in the passenger seat and Cassie dozing in the back.

They climbed out slowly, looking around, unsure.

Dave walked them up the steps and unlocked the door. No big speech. Just a quiet gesture.

Inside, the house was warm with late light, wood floors glowing, kitchen tiles still smelling of grout and fresh paint.

Sally turned in the entryway, eyes wide.

"Dave…" she whispered.

He handed her the deed, the paperwork folded neatly in the envelope.

"It's ours," he said. "All of it."

Cassie drifted through the hallway, bare feet on polished timber, then reappeared.

"Does this mean we're staying?"

Dave looked around, at Sally, at the house, at the space that finally felt like enough.

"Yeah," he said. "I reckon we are."

CHAPTER 92

The morning air was crisp, sharp enough to see each breath as they stepped out onto the back veranda. Smoke drifted from the chimney, curling above the tin roof in lazy spirals before vanishing into the cloudless blue. The dogs lay curled near the steps, sunning themselves in matching patches of light.

It was Easter Sunday.

Dave, Sally, and Cassie had been staying with Martha since Friday, soaking up the stillness like a kind of medicine. The house was full but comfortable. Laughter came easy. The shadows that had followed them for months had thinned, even if they hadn't disappeared.

Frank was there too. Already chopping wood when they arrived that first afternoon. Martha hadn't said anything. She didn't need to. The way he moved around the kitchen. The way she passed him a mug without asking how he took it. The way they sat together without filling the silence.

It was obvious.

No one said a word. No one needed to.

Lunch was a spread that looked like it would feed twenty. Roasted lamb, hot bread, potatoes baked in their skins. Bowls of roasted vegetables and warm apple crumble cooling on the windowsill. They sat outside, wrapped in jumpers and flannel, the table crowded and the conversation easy.

Cassie buzzed around the yard with a basket of foil-wrapped eggs, sugar high already kicking in. She darted between the trees and the shed, holding up every new find like treasure.

Dave watched her for a moment, barefoot, laughing — and let out a long breath he hadn't realised he'd been holding.

Maybe they were finally getting somewhere.

Later, as the sun dipped below the tree line and the chill crept in, they moved onto the veranda. Blankets across laps, mugs of tea or wine in hand. The dogs were asleep again, twitching occasionally at dreams only they understood.

Above them, the stars came out slow and clear. Bright pinpricks in the black, as if the sky had finally decided to share their beauty.

No one rushed to speak. The kind of silence that came not from awkwardness, but peace.

Then Frank cleared his throat.

"Cops finally cleaned up the dairy," he said, voice low. "Zhao's body's been recovered. Scene of crime unit went over the place top to bottom."

Martha nodded, eyes on the stars.

"They found the opals too," he added. "Officially taken into evidence now."

No one said much after that.

Even Cassie, curled up in a blanket at Sally's feet, had gone quiet. Just the wind through the trees and the gentle crack of the firepit in the yard below.

That place, the blackened shell of the dairy, lingered in all their minds. Not the stones. Not even the blood.

Just the weight of it.

The things they'd carried out with them.

The things they'd left behind.

**

The scream cut through the house like a blade.

Dave was out of bed before he'd fully opened his eyes. Sally was already halfway down the hallway. Martha and Frank emerged from the main bedroom across the hall, startled but calm.

They found Cassie sitting upright in the bed, blankets tangled around her legs, her tiny fists balled into her eyes as she sobbed. Her breath came in shallow, panicked bursts.

Sally climbed in beside her without a word, gathering her up, whispering quiet things. Nothing specific, just sound and comfort. Cassie clung to her, shaking.

Dave stood in the doorway, jaw clenched, helpless.

Martha stepped up beside him, her voice low.

"Does she have them often?"

Dave didn't look at her. "Every few nights."

Martha watched the bed for a moment, Sally gently rocking their daughter back and forth.

"What about Sally?"

Dave swallowed. "She doesn't say so. But I know."

Martha glanced sideways at him. "And you?"

He hesitated.

Then: "Middle of the day. Hit me like a brick sometimes."

She nodded, like that made perfect sense.

They stood there a while longer, listening to the sounds of Cassie's breathing slow, her sobs fading.

Then Martha said, quietly, like it had only just occurred to her, "You need to go back."

Dave finally turned to look at her.

"To the dairy," she said. "Not to dig anything up. Not for answers. Just to see it. Stand in it. Let it shrink. Make it small again."

They left Martha's late Monday morning, the dogs barking from the veranda as the ute pulled out onto the road. The sky was pale with early autumn haze, gum trees waving gently in the rear-view mirror.

Dave drove in silence for a while, Sally resting her arm on the open window, Cassie dozing in the back with a half-eaten Easter egg still in her lap.

About thirty kilometres from home, Sally broke the quiet.

"She was right, wasn't she?"

Dave didn't need to ask who she meant.

He nodded. "Yeah."

They didn't say anything else, just watched the signs roll past until Dave flicked the indicator and turned off the highway.

The old road to the dairy was rougher than he remembered. The bush had crept back in since the fire, narrow branches clawing at the sides of the ute as they bumped along the track.

The clearing opened slowly, the scorched remains of the shed rising from the earth like a memory made solid.

The dairy was quiet now.

The blackened frame still stood, though most of the roof had collapsed. Charred walls stretched toward the sky like broken ribs. No tape, no cones. Just ruin and regrowth.

But there was no menace anymore. No echo of screams or gunfire. Just the wind.

They stepped out together.

Dave didn't say a word. Neither did Sally. Cassie held both their hands as they walked slowly through the grass, their footsteps crunching over blackened wood and dried leaves.

The inside of the shed was mostly hollow now. Open to the sky, scattered with ash and dirt and pieces of burnt tin. But through a crack in the concrete floor, something green had pushed through. Delicate stems, purple wildflowers blooming against the ruin.

Cassie knelt beside them.

"Can I pick some?" she asked.

Sally crouched beside her and brushed a hand gently through her hair.

"Of course, sweetheart."

Cassie gathered the flowers carefully, fingers brushing away dust, eyes full of wonder.

They stayed there a while, soaking in the silence. No ghosts. No fear.

Just a place.

The road home was smooth and quiet, late sunlight flickering through the trees as the ute rolled on. Dave drove with one hand resting loose on the wheel, the other holding Sally's fingers where they curled around his leg.

Cassie hummed quietly in the back seat, swinging her legs and staring out the window like they hadn't just stood in the ashes of something that nearly broke them.

Dave caught a glimpse of her in the rear-view mirror, something small cupped in her hands.

"What you got there, baby girl?"

Cassie grinned and held them up. A little collection of stones, dusty and dull.

Most were nothing. Just old rubble.

But a few caught the fading light just right. Glinting faintly, smooth and pale with a whisper of colour beneath the surface.

"Just some shiny rocks I found."

She turned her attention back to the window, content.

Dave didn't say anything. Just glanced at Sally. She was already watching him.

They held each other's gaze for a moment. Long and quiet.

Then she smiled.

And Dave turned back to the road, the wheel steady in his hand, the last of the day slipping over the horizon.

The End.

Afterword

Before we go any further, let me make one thing absolutely clear: **the treasure in this story is not real.** Don't go out bush with a shovel, don't go hunting down maps, and don't go thinking you'll stumble across a fortune. It isn't there. It never was.

If you want black opals, there's only one place you should head— Lightning Ridge. It's a town built on dust, heat, and hope. The miners there spend their lives chasing colour underground, pulling stone from narrow shafts in ground so unforgiving it has broken more men than it has made rich. Black opal is the rarest and most valuable of all opals, with a dark body tone that makes the flashes of red, blue, and green blaze even brighter. Some of the finest stones ever found have fetched hundreds of thousands of dollars, snapped up by collectors in Asia, Europe, and America. But for every fortune made, there are countless busted shafts and busted dreams. That's the Ridge. If you want to see it for yourself, you can buy a permit, take a chance on a patch of earth, and try your luck. Or, if you don't feel like digging holes under the summer sun, you can wander into one of the local shops and spend a fortune instead. Either way, the miners who call Lightning Ridge home will appreciate the business.

The Jian sword carries a very different kind of weight. Known in China as the "gentleman of weapons," the Jian has been around for over two thousand years. Unlike heavier battlefield blades, it was designed for precision, grace, and balance. Wielded by scholars and warriors alike, it became as much a symbol of intellect and philosophy as of war. In martial arts, the Jian represents control and discipline, every movement an extension of thought and spirit. In legend, it has often been tied to justice, loyalty, and betrayal—themes as old as humanity itself. That made it the perfect weapon to slip into this tale, its history echoing against the dust and danger of the Australian outback.

As for Ironbark Prison—don't waste your time searching for it. It doesn't exist. What you've read here is a construct, a mishmash of country prisons across New South Wales. A place imagined from sandstone walls, steel doors, and a lifetime of stories stitched together. A prison of the mind as much as the map.

The Pilliga, though—that's very real. Sprawling across more than half a million hectares, it's one of the largest surviving forests in New South Wales. Thick with ironbark, cypress pine, and scrub, it's a place that swallows sound and bends direction. For thousands of years, it was home to Aboriginal people, rich with sacred sites and Dreaming stories. Later it became the hunting ground of timber cutters, graziers, and soldiers who trained beneath its canopy. It's a land full of myths—yowies in the night, ghost lights drifting between the trees, shadows that move where they shouldn't. The Pilliga is not gentle country. It's a place that tests you, and if you enter unprepared, it will break you.

And then there's the giant sandstone arrow. You can only see it from above—an almost perfect arrow formed by a massive sandstone escarpment, pointing straight into the wilderness. I first spotted it while wandering Google Earth. If you want to see it yourself, type in these coordinates: 32°46'04"S 150°10'20"E. It's one of those features that makes you wonder: is it chance, or something older, something carved by time with uncanny precision?

A warning while we're here: the Australian bush is not forgiving. It's not a backdrop, not a theme park—it's a living force. Out here, the heat kills, the cold kills, and water doesn't flow where you expect it. The distances are vast and merciless. If you want to explore the landscapes that shaped this story, go with respect, and go prepared. Otherwise, you may not come back.

As for what comes next… well, the story isn't over. Frank, Declan, and Martha aren't done yet. They're about to be dragged into another relentless, high-stakes adventure in the wilderness—different land, same truth. Out here, the country doesn't care whether you live or die.

And that's where I'll leave you—until the next time.

Soundtrack to Ironbark

Every chase has its soundtrack. These are just some of the songs that echo the heart of Ironbark — raw, restless, and heavy with reckoning. Turn the sound up, wind the window down, breathe in the dust. Feel the speaker vibrating the door trim as the road runs out ahead.

1. The Poor – More Wine Waiter Please
2. Paul Kelly – Careless
3. Weddings Parties Anything – Father's Day
4. The Cruel Sea – Better Get a Lawyer
5. James Reyne & James Blundell – Way Out West
6. Spy vs Spy – Snowblind
7. The Saints – Stranded
8. Johnny Cash – The Man Comes Around
9. Paul Kelly – Down on My Speedway
10. Black Sorrows – Hold On to Me

Bonus Track (Writer's Anthem):

11. Def Leppard – Action

Spotify Link.

Acknowledgments

First and foremost, to my wife and daughter—thank you for always having my back, and for putting up with me when I get that faraway look in my eyes. You've endured more than a few half-finished conversations while I've been lost in thought, wondering how Dave might survive the next obstacle, or whether it's even possible to drive a burning police car through the dawn of a country town. I couldn't have done this without your patience and support.

To my dad, my brother Jason, and my stepson Travis—your belief in me, in one way or another, has left its mark on these pages. Jason especially, for being someone I can always talk absolute bullshit with—those conversations have been as important as any research.

Thanks also to the members of the Lake Macquarie Fellowship of Australian Writers, whose knowledge, encouragement, and good humour have been invaluable along the way. A special mention to Jan, who caught the fact that I'd accidentally deleted an entire crucial chapter. That kind of sharp eye saved me more than once.

And finally, thank you to the readers—for taking a chance on a new author, for opening the first page, and for staying with me to the last. I hope you enjoyed the ride, and that you'll be back for the next one.

Coming Soon: Thunderhead

A storm doesn't just bring rain. Sometimes it brings reckoning.

High in the Barrington Tops, a light plane goes down in the teeth of a thunderhead. Among the wreckage lies more than twisted metal—something built in secrecy, something never meant to be found.

Survivors stagger from the crash, hunted through the wilderness. In the valleys below, Frank Tolliver is drawn back into a fight he thought he'd left behind. Alongside him: Declan Holt and Martha, bound once again to the kind of trouble you don't walk away from.

But the storm hides more than broken bodies. Shadow teams are moving through the bush. Old secrets are waking. And out there in the freezing rain, something new has been born—an intelligence that doesn't sleep, doesn't feel, and doesn't forgive.

The wilderness doesn't care if you live or die. Neither does what's coming.

About the Author

Wayne Russell was born and bred in the Hunter Valley and Newcastle's suburbs. He spent more than three decades working with Australia Post, but stories were always running in the background, waiting their turn.

He writes thrillers rooted in the Australian landscape—dust, ironbark, backroads, and scrub. His characters are ordinary people thrown into extraordinary situations, where the bush itself becomes an adversary as much as any villain.

Wayne lives in Newcastle with his family. When he's not writing, he's usually buried in research, chasing down old maps, forgotten history, or the strange details that eventually find their way into his work.

He writes the kind of books he wants to read—fast, fierce, and unapologetically Australian.

Find out more at **www.waynerussellbooks.com**